THE VAMPIRES
By Étienne Csok; Salon, 1907

PLATE I

Vampires and Vampirism

Montague Summers

Dover Publications, Inc.
Mineola, New York

Bibliographical Note

This Dover edition, first published in 2005, is an unabridged republication of *The Vampire: His Kith and Kin*, originally published in 1929 by E. P. Dutton & Company, New York. "The Quest for Montague Summers" by Felix Morrow, reprinted in this edition, first appeared in the 1960 edition of the original work, published by University Books, New Hyde Park, New York.

Library of Congress Cataloging-in-Publication Data

Summers, Montague, 1880–1948.
　　[Vampire]
　　Vampires and vampirism / Montague Summers.
　　　　p. cm.
　　Originally published: The vampire. New York, E.P. Dutton, 1929.
　　Includes bibliographical references and index.
　　ISBN 0-486-43996-8 (pbk.)
　　　1. Vampires. I. Title.

GR830.V388 2005
398'.45—dc22

2004061803

Manufactured in the United States of America
Dover Publications, Inc., 31 East 2nd Street, Mineola, N.Y. 11501

CONTENTS

v

LIST OF ILLUSTRATIONS

INTRODUCTION

In all the darkest pages of the malign supernatural there is no more terrible tradition than that of the Vampire, a pariah even among demons. Foul are his ravages ; gruesome and seemingly barbaric are the ancient and approved methods by which folk must rid themselves of this hideous pest. Even to-day in certain quarters of the world, in remoter districts of Europe itself, Transylvania, Slavonia, the isles and mountains of Greece, the peasant will take the law into his own hands and utterly destroy the carrion who—as it is yet firmly believed —at night will issue from his unhallowed grave to spread the infection of vampirism throughout the countryside. Assyria knew the vampire long ago, and he lurked amid the primaeval forests of Mexico before Cortes came. He is feared by the Chinese, by the Indian, and the Malay alike ; whilst Arabian story tells us again and again of the ghouls who haunt ill-omened sepulchres and lonely cross-ways to attack and devour the unhappy traveller.

The tradition is world wide and of dateless antiquity. Travellers and various writers upon several countries have dealt with these dark and perplexing problems, sometimes cursorily, less frequently with scholarship and perception, but in every case the discussion of the vampire has occupied a few paragraphs, a page or two, or at most a chapter of an extensive and divaricating study, where other circumstances and other legends claimed at least an equal if not a more important and considerable place in the narrative. It may be argued, indeed, that the writers upon Greece have paid especial attention to this tradition, and that the vampire figures prominently in their works. This is true, but on the other hand the treatise of Leone Allacci, *De Graecorum hodie quorundam opinationibus*, 1645, is of considerable rarity, nor are even such volumes as Father François Richard's *Relation de ce qui s'est passé de plus remarquable a Sant-Erini*, 1657, the *Voyage au Levant* (1705) of Paul Lucas, and Tournefort's *Relation d'un Voyage du Levant* (1717), although perhaps not altogether uncommon and certainly fairly well known by repute, generally to be met with in every library. The study of the Modern Greek Vampire in Mr. J. G. Lawson's *Modern Greek Folklore and Ancient Greek Religion* has, of course, taken its place as a classic, but save incidentally and in passing Mr. Lawson does not touch upon the tradition in other countries and at other times, for this lies outside his purview.

Towards the end of the seventeenth century, and even more particularly during the first half of the eighteenth century when in Hungary, Moravia, and Galicia, there seemed to be a veritable epidemic of vampirism the report of which was bruited far and wide engaging the attention of curia and university, ecclesiastic and philosopher, scholar and man of letters, journalist and virtuoso in all lands, there appeared a large number of academic theses and tractates, the majority of which had been prelected at Leipzig, and these formally discussed and debated the question in well-nigh all its aspects, dividing, sub-dividing, inquiring, ratiocinating upon the most approved scholastic lines. Thus we have the monographs of such professors as Philip Rohr, whose "Dissertatio Historico-Philosophica" *De Masticatione Mortuorum* was delivered at Leipzig on 16 August, 1679, and issued the same year from the press of Michael Vogt ; the *Dissertatio de Uampyris Seruiensibus* of Zopfius and van Dalen, printed at Duisburg in 1733 ; and the *De absolutione mortuorum excommunicatorum* of Heineccius, published at Helmstad in 1709. Of especial value are Michael Ranft's *De Masticatione Mortuorum in Tumulis Liber*, Leipzig, 1728, and the *Dissertatio de Cadaueribus Sanguisugis*, Jena, 1732, of John Christian Stock. These dissertations, however, are extremely scarce and hardly to be found, whilst even so encyclopaedic a bibliography as Caillet does not include either Philip Rohr, Michael Ranft, or Stock, all of whom should therein assuredly have found a place. In this connexion must not be omitted the *De Miraculis Mortuorum*, Leipzig, Kirchner, 1670, and second edition, Weidmann, 1687, a treatise by Christian Frederic Garmann, a noted physician, who was born at Mersebourg about 1640 and who practised with great repute at Chemnitz. Garmann discusses many curious details and continued to amass so vast a collection of notes that after his death there was published in 1709 at Dresden by Zimmerman a very much enlarged edition of his work, " exornatum, diu desideratum et expetitum, beato autoris obitu interueniente." During the eighteenth century the tradition of the Vampire was dealt with by two famous authors, of whom both concentrated upon this as their main theme, that is to say by Dom Augustin Calmet, O.S.B., in his *Dissertations sur les Apparitions des Anges, des Démons et des Esprits et sur les revenants et vampires de Hongrie, de Bohême, de Moravie, e de Silésie,* Paris, 1740, and by Gioseppe Davanzati, Archbishop of Trani and Patriarch of Alexandria, in his *Dissertazione sopra I Vampire,* Naples, 1774. As I have very fully considered both these important works they require no more than a bare mention here.

Of a later date we find in French a few books such as the *Histoire des Vampires* (1820) of the enormously prolific Collin de Plancy, the *Spectriana* (1817) and *Les ombres sanglantes* (1820) of J. P. R. Cuisin, and Gabrielle de Paban's *Histoire des Fantômes et des Demons* (1819) and *Démoniana* (1820), but these with many more of that class and epoch, although they are sometimes written not without elegance and industry and one may here and there meet with a curious anecdote or local legend, will not, I think, long engage the consideration and regard of the more serious student.

In English there is a little book entitled *Vampires and Vampirism* by Mr. Dudley Wright, which was first published in 1914 ; second edition (with additional matter), 1924. It may, of course, be said that this is not intended to be more than a popular and trifling collection and that one must not look for accuracy and research from the author of *Roman Catholicism and Freemasonry.* However that may be, it were not an easy task to find a more insipid olio than *Vampires and Vampirism,* of which the ingredients, so far as I am able to judge, are most palpably derived at second, and even at third hand. Dom Calmet, sometimes with and sometimes without acknowledgement, is frequently quoted and continually misunderstood. In what the " additional matter " of the second edition consists I cannot pretend to say but I have noticed that the same anecdotes are repeated, *e.g.* on p. 9 we are told the story of a shepherd of " Blow, near Kadam, in Bohemia," and the relation is said to be taken (*via* Calmet, it is plain,) from " De Schartz [rather Charles Ferdinand de Schertz], in his *Magia Postuma*, published at Olmutz in 1706." On p. 166 this story, as given by " E. P. Evans, in his interesting work on the *Criminal Prosecution and Capital Punishment of Animals*," is told of " a herdsman near the town of Cadan," and dated 1337. Pages 60-62 are occupied with an Oriental legend related by " Fornari, in his *History of Sorcerers*," by which is presumably intended the *Histoire curieuse et pittoresque des sorciers* . . . *Revue et augmentée par Fornari*, Paris, 1846, and other editions, a book usually catalogued under Giraldo, as by Caillet and Yve-Plessis, although the latter certainly has a cross-reference to Fornari. In greater detail Mr. Dudley Wright narrates this legend which he has already told (pp. 60-62), on pp. 131-137. Such repetition seems superfluous. In the Bibliography we have such entries as " Leo Allatius," " *Encyclopaedia Britannica* " ; " Frazer's *Golden Bough*," " Nider's *Formicarius*," " Phlegon's *Fragments*," " William of Newbury," all of which are not merely unscholarly and slovenly, but entirely useless from the point of view of reference. I also remark blunders such as " Philip Rehrius," " Nicolas Ramy's *Demonolatrie*," " Rymer's *Varney the Vampire*." Who Rymer might be I cannot tell. *Varney the Vampire* was written by Thomas Preskett Prest.

It may, I think, not unfairly be claimed that the present work is the first serious study in English of the Vampire, and kindred traditions from a general, as well as from a theological and philosophical point of view. I have already pointed out that it were impossible to better such a chapter as Mr. J. C. Lawson has given us in his *Modern Greek Folklore and Ancient Greek Religion*, a book to which as also to Bernhard Schmidt's *Das Volksleben der Neugriechen und das Hellenische Alterthum*, I am greatly indebted. But any wider survey of the vampire tradition will soon be found to demand an examination of legend, customs, and history which extend far beyond Greece, although in such an inquiry the beliefs and practice of modern Greece must necessarily assume a prominent and most material significance.

In the present work I have endeavoured to set forth what might be termed " the philosophy of vampirism," and however ghastly and macabre they may appear I have felt that here one must not tamely shrink from a careful and detailed consideration of the many cognate passions and congruous circumstances which—there can be no reasonable doubt—have throughout the ages played no impertinent and no trivial but a very vital and very memorable part in consolidating the vampire legend, and in perpetuating the vampire tradition among the darker and more secret mysteries of belief that prevail in the heart of man.

In many countries there is thought to be a close connexion between the vampire and the werewolf, and I would remark that I have touched upon this but lightly as I am devoting a separate study to the werewolf and lycanthropy.

The Vampire, his Kith and Kin will be shortly followed by *The Vampire in Europe*, in which work I have collected and treat of numerous instances of vampirism old and new, concretely illustrating the prevalence and phases of the tradition in England and Ireland, in ancient Greece and Rome as well as in modern Greece, in Hungary and Bohemia, in Jugo-Slavia, Russia, and many other lands. In this volume will be found related in detail such famous cases as that of Arnold Paul, Stanoska Sovitzo, Millo the Hungarian, the vampires of Temeswar, Kisilova, Buckingham, Berwick, Melrose Abbey, Croglin Grange, and many more.

A survey of " The Vampire in Literature " which I attempt in Chapter V of the present volume has not, to the best of my belief, been usefully essayed by any English writer. I cannot hope that my purview is complete, for I feel confident that several pieces must inevitably have escaped me. Here too one is faced with the question what to notice and what to exclude. Vampirism is so wide a term that in some senses it might arguably be held to cover no small range of ghost stories and witch sagas where the victims peak and pine and waste away until they fall into an early grave. The choice is bound to be somewhat arbitrary, and so open to censure and objections, both on account of inclusions and omissions, and, superficially at least, these criticisms will hardly seem a little rigid and unfair. There is one vampire story, an excellent fiction and admirably discoursed, which I heard very many years ago, and which I believe is in print, but it has till now completely baffled all my recent explorations. I have no doubt that some of my readers will know the tale.

The Bibliography has offered its own difficulties with

reference to the choice of books for inclusion, and a certain amount of selection seemed inevitable. I have, I hope, duly listed the majority of those works which deal with the Vampire and the vampire tradition at any length, or which even if they devote but a few pages to the Vampire have given the subject serious and scholarly consideration. The denizens of Grub Street, ever busily agog, have from time to time attempted to scribble something on sorcery, on the invisible world, on occult crafts, and of late they seem to have been especially pretentious and prolific. I am well aware that in a number of trivial and catch-penny compositions it may be found that actually more space has been devoted to the vampire than is afforded in several of the volumes I mention, important studies which cover a fairly wide range in travel, in folk-lore, in demonology. Whilst, obviously enough, all the titles I include have by no means the same value even the least remarkable owns a particular reason to justify its presence. Under fiction it seemed to me that one should cast the net a little wider, and accordingly—on account of its very rarity if for no other reason—I have found a place for so poor a book as Smyth Upton's *The Last of the Vampires*, and what is more a rampant tract such as *The Vampyre* (1858) is not excluded. It will be remarked that many of the books to which I refer in my chapters and whence I quote are not to be found in this Bibliography as they lie something outside its scope. Moreover to rehearse books of reference and the standard authors seemed entirely superfluous.

During the course of a long and arduous task I have been much helped by the kindly and valuable suggestions of many friends amongst whom I must particularly mention Mrs. Agnes Murgoçi, the late Chevalier W. H. Grattan Flood, Dr. Havelock Ellis, Dr. Rouse, Mr. Edward Hutton, Mr. W. J. Lawrence, and Mr. N. M. Penzer. I am especially grateful to Dr. R. Campbell Thompson for generous permission to quote at length the exorcisms from his classic works upon Babylonian demonology and Semitic magic. Both Mr. G. Willoughby-Meade and his publishers have put me under great obligations by allowing me so extensively to use his work *Chinese Ghouls and Goblins*, Constable and Co., 1928.

I cordially thank my friend Mr. Laurence Housman for giving me leave to reproduce his drawing " Cauchemar," as also

Messrs. Macmillan for a similar permission with regard to the illustration of Malay vampires, which originally appeared in Dr. W. W. Skeat's *Malay Magic*.

The little cylinder delineated upon the cover of the book* is a reproduction from the *Revue d'Assyriologie*, vol. VII, and represents a Babylonian vampire. The original is in the Louvre collections.

In festo B.M.V. del Divino Aiuto.
1928.

---

*Omitted from this edition

THE QUEST FOR MONTAGUE SUMMERS
by Felix Morrow

You who open this book because you wish to read about vampires may very well wish to hurry past an introduction written by someone other than the author and so I must tell you in this very first sentence, before I lose you, that what you will read further on will be puzzling and startling to you unless you first listen to me. Just what will you make of the author's earnest advice concerning how to dispose of the body of a vampire? Or of his description of what the usual vampire looks like? Is he pulling your leg or does he really believe it? Nor is it a question merely of personal belief on his part. With vast erudition he summons up Holy Writ, early, medieval and later church fathers and theologians; and it becomes clear that he feels confident that he speaks for all true Roman Catholics and, indeed, for all true Christians. Side by side with this, however, he takes the most enormous delight in freezing our blood and standing our few hairs on end with the most dreadful but fascinating stories of endless evil done through the centuries. Just what is going on? We may well wonder.

So, willy nilly, you must tarry as long as need be to learn what we have managed to find out about the author.

In 1956 I arranged for the first proper publication in the United States of the author's *The History of Witchcraft and Demonology*. Although I found the book fascinating, I found it necessary to write a foreword dissociating myself from the views of the author and contrasting them with another, more tenable theory of the nature of witchcraft. I found Summers' views valuable "precisely because they provide us in modern English with what is actually the best account of the Roman Catholic version of the history of witchcraft and the church's fight against it. It was his contention, and we are inclined to agree with him, that his account is not only the true story as it appeared to the Catholic church in the seventeenth and eighteenth centuries, but that this remains, in spite of what Catholic apologists may say in encyclopaedias and other public forums, the true position of the Roman Catholic Church today." In 1958, I also arranged for the publication of the author's *The Geography of Witchcraft.* In this book, much more than in the first, the author was careful to distinguish between genuine instances of demoniacal possession and those outbreaks of contagious hysteria that led to the sacrifice of many harmless lives. Thus when he writes of the Salem witch trials he puts the blame where it belongs, on the malicious adolescent girls who first denounced mumbling old women, and on the neurotic adults who encouraged them. Summers does name some few among the many tried and condemned to death in witchcraft trials who, he believes, actually were members of covens of witches. But he does acknowledge often enough the tragedy of the implication of innocent people. So it seemed safe enough to me to publish that second book without any introduction.

In the course of publishing those books and preparing for the publication of the present work, we consulted the usual authorities and, from their leads, went on to whatever else could be found. The picture that emerged follows.

Montague Summers was born April 10, 1880 and died August 8, 1948 at the age of 68. He graduated Clifton College and Trinity College, Oxford. Then, in his own words, as reported in the excellent and authoritative tool of our trade *Twentieth Century Authors,* "I gave concentrated study to theology, and after ordination [as a Roman Catholic priest] I worked for some time in the slums of London, and also on more than one country mission. For health's sake, I resided abroad during considerable periods, mainly in Italy and southern France." For some years he then lived in Sussex and, finally, "I moved to Oxford in order to work at the Bodleian Library where I am engaged in daily research."

This pleasant picture naturally leads on to a long and impressive list of the books to which this English priest gave birth.

The books divide into two main groups. One includes those already mentioned, plus a sequel to the present work entitled *The Vampire in Europe,* another *The Werewolf,* and a number of similar works.

The other group, for which the author is indeed far more famous, includes his masterly editing of the plays of Elizabethan and Restoration dramatists (Jonson, Wycherley, Congreve, Vanbrugh) and *The Gothic Quest,* which has become the standard history of the Gothic novel. In one of the literary works, *Essays in Petto* (1928), we come for the first time upon a photograph of the author. He smiles benignly at us out of the frontispiece, presumably then 48 years old but looking, rosy and plump, much younger. It is a picture of a merry soul steeped in literature, including some of the wittiest and raciest of our language. That round face underlines for us the fact that this is the outstanding editor of the coarse satires written by Wycherley under the patronage of the mistress of Charles II; Congreve's cynical and witty *Love for Love* and *The Way of the World; Volpone, 'Tis a Pity She's a Whore,* and so on. We are delighted to have this picture rounded out for us by *A Reminiscence* written by Allan Wade, founder of the Stage Society and the Phoenix Society, who gratefully records how helpful he found the collaboration of Montague Summers during the 1920's in producing the Restoration comedies. Wade adds this delightful vignette:

"The audiences must often have been amused by the sight of Montague Summers in full clerical costume, prominent in his box and pointedly enjoying the more highly spiced passages in Restoration plays."

In this friendly reminiscence, written just after Summers' death, Wade nevertheless feels it necessary to tell us other things which recall the later witch-hunter. A group broke off from the Phoenix Society and Summers left with them. Everything Wade and the Phoenix did thereafter he found it necessary to disapprove while still praising the productions from his own time. He spoke, too, of himself as the actual director of the earlier plays; Wade gently denies the possibility. Rancorously Summers stared through Wade and his associates in public as though they were sworn enemies.

In the same spirit Summers attacked Margaret Murray, the author of the remarkable article on witchcraft in recent editions of the Encyclopaedia Brittanica. It is not enough for him to say that she is wrong, he must speak of her "ignoble fatuities." And her "monstrous extravagances." Nor does he stop with unbelievers. Even in a passing reference to Father

Herbert Thurston, the Jesuit author of the article on witch-craft in the Catholic Encyclopaedia, Summers cannot resist saying: "Even the ultracautious—I had almost said skepti-cal—Father Thurston acknowledges."

From all this, to sum up, the reader is prepared to find an author vast in erudition, but unfair to his opponents, doing his Godly work with such gusto that we shiver with delight as he shivers with horror. In reality, of course, the old boy is having a great time raising his hands in holy horror. All this is now clear enough.

Now, however, comes a great mystification. After *The History of Witchcraft and Demonology* (1926), *The Geography of Witchcraft* (1927), *The Vampire* (1928), *The Vampire in Europe* (1929), if memory serves it was at this point that the Jesuit author of the article on witchcraft in the Catholic Encyclopaedia found it necessary to challenge publicly the author of this multivolumed Roman Catholic view of occult phenomena. In England *The History of Witchcraft* had been a best seller, and the volumes that followed were only less pop-ular. Father Thurston asked his opponent, politely enough, by what authority he wore the priest's biretta? Where had he been ordained and by what ecclesiastical authority? We look again at the smiling frontispiece of the English priest and wait for him to answer. In vain.

We find it impossible to believe that Montague Summers has been masquerading as a priest. How can it be, this author of a score of distinguished books? The priest we saw, year after year, in his favorite chair in the Bodleian Library in Oxford? The priest we saw in his box at the Stage Society? The Roman Catholic authority whose new books, year after year, are so respectfully reviewed everywhere?

Look a little more closely at the reception accorded his books. The *Times Literary Supplement* is admiring and respectful enough. But now we notice that its reviews never speak of him as a priest, while its reviews of his opponent always speak of Father Thurston. He is always referred to by both names as Montague Summers. Now, retracing our steps, we come upon this astonishing paragraph in 1927 in the *Times Literary Supplement* review of *The Geography of Witchcraft:* "The more Mr. Summers gives proof of general ability, of schol-arship and of wide reading, the more the suspicion deepens that a mystification is in progress and that he is amusing us at our expense." Before we knew of Father Thurston's unanswered questions, it had seemed to us that the *Times* writer had not grasped the seriousness with which Summers says of himself that his view is "an absolute and complete belief in the supernatural, and hence in witchcraft." But now it becomes clear that the *Times* writer had been thinking of the same things as Father Thurston.

Look above at the quotation from *Twentieth Century Authors* with which we began. You will note that Summers had written "after ordination" and the editors had added in brackets [as a Roman Catholic priest]. This is immediately after Summers came down from Oxford to London. However, upon examination, it is clear that Summers could have meant only his ordination as a minister in the *Church of England*. For that is where he began! The editors of *Twentieth Century* had assumed that he meant his ordination as a Roman Catholic priest and he—to whom proof was submitted and, further, the work went through several editions in his own lifetime—let their error stand without correction.

He came down from Oxford sometime early in the century. He leaves the Church of England sometime around 1910 and ceases to have a public existence until nearly fifteen years later when he collaborates with the Stage Society and appears in his box at the Restoration dramas. In 1926, at the age of 46, he publishes his first book on the subject in question, *The History of Witchcraft*.

These dates lend credence to the unfriendly story told of him. That when he left the Church of England he spent the ensuing years in France and Italy in occult circles, became an adept in black magic, and it was then, like the abbé in *La Bas,* that he assumed clerical garb. The story is scarcely refuted by the only autobiographical details he ever volunteered, those few vague words in *Twentieth Century Authors* quoted above: "For health's sake, I resided abroad during considerable periods, mainly in Italy and southern France."

The most that can be said for Montague Summers is the considered opinion of a distinguished scholar and Carmelite father, the literary executor of Montague Summers, whose *Memoir* is as yet not completed but which we would be honored to publish when it is. He does not doubt that Montague

Summers became a sincere Roman Catholic and died in the faith. But when? I think he would like to say that it happened shortly after Summers left the Church of England, but he cannot be sure. He cannot close the door to the serious possibility of a period in which Montague Summers frequented occult circles on the basis of comradeship. He tends to believe that Montague Summers was actually ordained a priest somewhere on the continent. But by whom and under what circumstances he does not know, although he hopes that a large quantity of Montague Summers' papers which disappeared after his death will shortly be found and throw new light on the question. He hazards the guess that ordination could well have been at the hands of an Old Catholic bishop, for those were the years of a number of expulsions and schisms in which some splendid elements were driven from the church. The bishop in question may even have been in proper communication with the Holy See. Even in this case, however, the ordination was irregular and subject to ecclesiastical censure. The priest is first of all a priest assigned to a parish (if he is not a member of a monastic order), and this Summers never claimed. Nor had Summers properly put himself in communication with the ecclesiastical authorities in England when he returned from the continent. But that, at whatever point, Summers did become a Catholic and a true one, by the time he began to write his studies in the occult, the Carmelite father is altogether certain.

Here we must take leave of our reader, except to suggest to him that he will understand all this better if he knows a little more about the prevalence of occult circles on the continent at the turn of the century. It was a time when it was possible for William Butler Yeats and Lord Dunsany, among others, to belong to the occult Order of the Golden Dawn. Perhaps the most complete yet very short atmospheric picture is provided in the excellent historical introduction recently written by an Oxonian for a new edition of Huysmans' *Down There.** It is summed up there in the incredible but nevertheless true story of the priest who provided the materials for Huysmans' evil story. These things seem novel but real to us when we read

---

Down There (La Bas) A Study in Satanism by J. K. Huysmans, Translated by Keene Wallis, Introduction by Robert Baldick, University Books, 1958.

them in Montague Summers' own books, when he is telling us with deep indignation about monsters like Gilles de Rais or those who sat for their portraits to De Sade. It seems much harder to believe that the same things were happening at the end of the nineteenth century. Perhaps it is very curious that one can find no personal reference by Summers to what he must have seen with his own eyes in these circles during his years on the continent. That the fascination of the occult never left him the reader will find in the following pages.

VAMPIRES AND VAMPIRISM

CHAPTER I

The Origins of the Vampire

THROUGHOUT the whole vast shadowy world of ghosts and demons there is no figure so terrible, no figure so dreaded and abhorred, yet dight with such fearful fascination, as the vampire, who is himself neither ghost nor demon, but yet who partakes the dark natures and possesses the mysterious and terrible qualities of both. Around the vampire have clustered the most sombre superstitions, for he is a thing which belongs to no world at all ; he is not a demon, for the devils have a purely spiritual nature, they are beings without any body, angels, as is said in *S. Matthew* xxv. 41, " the devil and his angels."[1] And although S. Gregory writes of the word *Angel*, " nomen est officii, non naturae,"—the designation is that of an office not of a nature, it is clear that all angels were in the beginning created good in order to act as the divine messengers (ἄγγελοι), and that afterwards the fallen angels lapsed from their original state. The authoritative teaching of the Fourth Lateran Council under Innocent III in 1215, dogmatically lays down : " Diabolus enim et alii daemones a Deo quidem natura creati sunt boni, sed ipsi per se facti sunt mali." And it is also said, *Job* iv. 18 : " Ecce qui seruiunt ei, non sunt stabiles, et in Angelis suis reperit prauitatem." (Behold they that serve him are not steadfast, and in his angels he found wickedness.)

John Heinrich Zopfius in his *Dissertatio de Uampiris Seruiensibus*, Halle, 1733, says : " Vampires issue forth from their graves in the night, attack people sleeping quietly in their beds, suck out all their blood from their bodies and destroy them. They beset men, women and children alike, sparing neither age nor sex. Those who are under the fatal malignity of their influence complain of suffocation and a total deficiency of spirits, after which they soon expire. Some who, when at the point of death, have been asked if they can tell what is causing their decease, reply that such and such persons, lately dead, have arisen from the tomb to torment and torture them." Scoffern in his *Stray Leaves of Science and Folk Lore* writes : " The best definition I can give of a vampire is a living, mischievous and murderous dead body. A living dead body! The words are idle, contradictory, incomprehensible, but so are Vampires." Horst, *Schriften und Hypothesen über die Vampyren*, (Zauberbibliothek, III) defines a Vampire as " a dead body which continues to live in the grave ; which it leaves, however, by night, for the purpose of sucking the blood of the living, whereby it is nourished and preserved in good condition, instead of becoming decomposed like other dead bodies."

A demon has no body, although for purposes of his own he may energize, assume, or seem to assume a body, but it is not his real and proper body.[2] So the vampire is not strictly a demon, although his foul lust and horrid propensities be truly demoniacal and of hell.

Neither may the vampire be called a ghost or phantom, strictly speaking, for an apparition is intangible, as the Latin poet tells us :

Par leuibus uentis uolucrique simillima somno.[3]

And upon that first Easter night when Jesus stood in the midst of His disciples and they were troubled and frightened, supposing they had seen a spirit, He said : " Uidete manus meas, et pedes, quia ego ipse sum : palpate, et uidete : quia spiritus carnem, et ossa non habet, sicut ne uidetis habere." (See my hands and feet, that it is I myself ; handle and see : for a spirit hath not flesh and bone, as you see me to have.)[4]

There are, it is true, upon record some few instances when persons have been able to grasp, or have been grasped by and felt the touch of, a ghost, but these phenomena must be admitted as exceptions altogether, if indeed, they are not to be explained in some other way, as for example, owing to the information of a body by some spirit or familiar under very rare and abnormal conditions.

In the case of the very extraordinary and horrible hauntings of the old Darlington and Stockton Station, Mr. James Durham, the night-watchman, when one winter evening in the porter's cellar was surprised by the entry of a stranger followed by a large black retriever. This visitor without uttering a word dealt him a blow and he had the impression of a violent concussion. Naturally he struck back with his fist which seemed however to pass through the figure and his knuckles were grazed against the wall beyond. None the less the man uttered an unearthly squeak at which the dog gripped Mr. Durham in the calf of the leg causing considerable pain. In a moment the stranger had called off the retriever by a curious click of the tongue, and both man and animal hurried into the coal-house whence there was no outlet. A moment later upon examination neither was to be seen. It was afterwards discovered that many years before an official who was invariably accompanied by a large black dog had committed suicide upon the premises, if not in the very cellar, where at least his dead body had been laid. The full account with the formal attestation dated 9th December, 1890, may be read in W. T. Stead's *Real Ghost Stories*, reprint, Grant Richards, 1897, Chapter XI, pp. 210-214.

Major C. G. MacGregor of Donaghadee, County Down, Ireland, gives an account of a house in the north of Scotland which was haunted by an old lady, who resided there for very many years and died shortly after the beginning of the nineteenth century. Several persons who slept in the room were sensibly pushed and even smartly slapped upon the face. He himself on feeling a blow upon the left shoulder in the middle of the night turned quickly and reaching out grasped a human hand, warm, soft, and plump. Holding it tight he felt the wrist and arm which appeared clothed in a sleeve and lace cuff. At the elbow all trace ceased, and in his astonishment he released the hand. When a light was struck nobody could be seen in the room.

In a case which occurred at a cottage in Girvan, South Ayrshire, a young woman lost her brother, a fisher, owing to the swamping of his boat in a storm. When the body was recovered it was found that the right hand was missing. This occasioned the poor girl extraordinary sorrow, but some few nights later when she was undressing, preparatory to bed, she suddenly uttered a piercing shriek which immediately brought the other inmates of the house to her room. She declared that she had felt a violent blow dealt with an open hand upon her shoulder. The place was examined, and distinctly marked in livid bruises there was seen the impression of a man's right hand.

Andrew Lang in his *Dreams and Ghosts* (new edition, 1897), relates the story of "The Ghost that Bit," which might seem to have been a vampire, but which actually cannot be so classed since vampires have a body and their craving for blood is to obtain sustenance for their body. The narrative is originally to be found in *Notes and Queries*, 3rd September 1864, and the correspondent asserts that he took it "almost *verbatim* from the lips of the lady" concerned, a person of tried veracity. Emma S—— was asleep one morning in her room at a large house near Cannock Chase. It was a fine August day in 1840, but although she had bidden her maid call her at an early hour she was surprised to hear a sharp knocking upon her door about 3.30. In spite of her answer the taps continued, and suddenly the curtains of her bed were slightly drawn, when to her amaze she saw the face of an aunt by marriage looking through upon her. Half unconsciously she threw out her hand, and immediately one of her thumbs was sensibly pressed by the teeth of the apparition. Forthwith she arose, dressed, and went downstairs, where not a creature was stirring. Her father upon coming down rallied her a little upon being about at cockcrow and inquired the cause. When she informed him he determined that later in the day he would pay a visit to his sister-in-law who dwelt at no great distance. This he did, only to discover that she had unexpectedly died at about 3.30 that morning. She had not been in any way ailing, and the shock was fearfully sudden. On one of the thumbs of the corpse was found a mark as if it had been bitten in the last agony.

The disturbances at the Lamb hostelry, Lawford's Gate, Bristol, which aroused something more than local interest in the years 1761-62, were not improbably due to witchcraft and caused by the persecutions of a woman who trafficked in occultism of the lowest order, although on the other hand they may have been poltergeist manifestations. The two little girls, Molly and Dobby Giles, who were the subjects of these phenomena, were often severely bitten and pinched. The impressions of eighteen or twenty teeth were seen upon their arms, the marks being clammy with saliva and warm spittle, " and the children were roaring out for the pain of the pinches and bites." On one occasion whilst an observer was talking to Dobby Giles she cried out that she was bitten in the neck when there suddenly appeared "the mark of teeth, about eighteen, and wet with spittle." That the child should have nipped herself was wholly impossible, and nobody was near her save Mr. Henry Durbin who recorded these events, and whose account was first printed in 1800, the year after his death, since he did not wish his notes to be given to the public during his lifetime. On 2nd January, 1762, Mr. Durbin notes : "Dobby cried the hand was about her sister's throat, and I saw the flesh at the side of her throat pushed in, whitish as if done with fingers, though I saw none. Her face grew red and blackish presently, as if she was strangled, but without any convulsion or contraction of the muscles." Thursday, 7th January, 1762, we have : "Dobby was bitten most and with deeper impressions than Molly. The impression of the teeth on their arms formed an oval, which measured two inches in length." All this certainly looks as if sorcery were at work. It may be remembered that in Salem during the epidemic of witchcraft the afflicted persons were tormented "by *Biting, Pinching, Strangling, etc.*" When Goodwife Corey was on trial, "it was observed several times, that if she did but bite her under lip in time of examination, the Persons afflicted were bitten on their arms and Wrists, and produced the *Marks* before the Magistrates, Minister, and others."

In *The Proceedings of the National Laboratory of Psychical Research*, Vol. I., 1927, will be found an account of the phenomena connected with Eleonore Zügun, a young Rumanian peasant girl, who in the autumn of 1926, when only thirteen years old was brought to London by the Countess Wassilko-Serecki, in order that the manifestations might be investigated at "The National Laboratory of Psychical Research," Queensberry Place, South Kensington. The child was said to be persecuted by some invisible force or agent, which she knew as *Dracu, Anglice* the Devil. There were many extraordinary happenings and she was continually being scratched and bitten by this unseen intelligence. It must suffice to give but two or three instances of the very many "biting phenomena." On the afternoon of Monday, 4th October, 1926, Captain Neil Gow an investigator in his report, notes :

" 3.20. Eleonore cried out. Showed marks on back of left hand like teeth-marks which afterwards developed into deep weals. . . . 4.12. Eleonore was just raising a cup of tea to her lips, but suddently gave a cry and put the cup down hastily : there was a mark on her right hand similar to that caused by a bite. Both rows of teeth were indicated." Of the same incident, Mr. Clapham Palmer, an investigator who was also present writes : " Eleonore was in the act of raising the cup to her lips when she suddenly gave a little cry of pain, put down her cup and rolled up her sleeve. On her forearm I then saw what appeared to be the marks of teeth indented deeply in the flesh, as if she or someone had fiercely bitten her arm. The marks turned from red to white and finally took the form of white raised weals. They gradually faded but were still noticeable after an hour or so." Such bitings not infrequent occurred, and photographs have been taken of the marks.

It were an interesting question to discuss the cause of these indentations and no doubt it is sufficiently remarkable, but however that may be such inquiry were impertinent here, for it is clearly not vampirism, nor indeed cognate thereto. The object of the Vampire is to suck blood, and in these cases if blood was ever drawn it was more in the nature of a scratch or slight dental puncture, there was no effusion. Again the agent who inflicted these bites was not sufficiently material to be visible, at any rate he was able to remain unseen. The true vampire is corporeal.

The vampire has a body, and it is his own body. He is neither dead nor alive ; but living in death. He is an abnormality ; the androgyne in the phantom world ; a pariah among the fiends.

Even the Pagan poet taught his hearers and his readers that death was a sweet guerdon of repose, a blessed oblivion after the toil and struggle of life. There are few things more beautiful and there are few things more sad than the songs of our modern Pagans who console their aching hearts with the wistful vision of eternal sleep. Although perhaps they themselves know it not, their delicate but despairing melancholy is an heritage from the weary yet tuneful singers of the last days of Hellas, souls for whom there was no dawn of hope in the sky. But we have a certain knowledge and a fairer surety for " now Christ is risen from the dead, the first-fruits of them that sleep." Yet Gray, half Greek, seems to promise to his rustics and his hinds as their richest reward after life of swink and toil dear forgetfulness and eternal sleep. Swinburne was glad :

> That no life lives for ever ;
> That dead men rise up never ;
> That even the weariest river
>   Winds somewhere safe to sea.

.   .   .   .   .

> Only the eternal sleep
> In an eternal night.

Emily Brontë lusted for mere oblivion :

> Oh, for the time when I shall sleep
> Without identity.
> And never care how rain may steep,
> Or snow may cover me !

Flecker in utter despair wails out :

> I know dead men are deaf, and cannot hear
> The singing of a thousand nightingales   .   .   .
> I know dead men are blind and cannot see
> The friend that shuts in horror their big eyes,
> And they are witless—

Even more beautifully than the poets have sung, a weaver of exquisite prose has written : " Death must be so beautiful. To lie in the soft brown earth, with the grasses waving above one's head, and listen to silence. To have no yesterday, and no to-morrow. To forget time." Poor sorry souls ! How arid, how empty are such aspirations when we think of the ardent glowing phrase of the Little Flower : " Je veux passer mon ciel à faire du bien sur la terre ! " And "Even in the bosom of the Beatific Vision the Angels watch over us. No, I shall never be able to take any rest until the end of the world. But when the Angel shall have said ' Time is no more,' then I shall rest, then I shall be able to rejoice, since the number of the elect will be complete."

So we see that even for those who take the most pagan, the most despairing, the most erroneous views, the ideal is oblivion and rest. How fearful a destiny then is that of the vampire who has no rest in the grave, but whose doom it is to come forth and prey upon the living. In the first place it may briefly be inquired how the belief in vampirism originated, and here it is not impertinent to remark that the careful investigations in connexion with psychic phenomena which have been so fruitful of recent years, and even modern scientific discovery, have proved the essential truth of many an ancient record and old superstition, which were until yesterday dismissed by the level-headed as the wildest sensationalism of melodramatic romance. The origins of a belief in vampirism, although, of course, very shadowy, unformed and unrelated, may probably be said to go back to the earliest times when primitive man observed the mysterious relations between soul and body. The division of an individual into these two parts must have been suggested to man by his observation, however crude and rough, of the phenomenon of unconsciousness, as exhibited in sleep and more particularly in death. He cannot but have speculated concerning that something, the loss of which withdraws man for ever from the living and waking world. He was bound to ask himself if there was any continuance in any circumstances at present veiled from, and unknown to, him of that life and that personality which had obviously passed elsewhere. The question was an eternal one, and it was, moreover, a personal one which concerned him most intimately, since it related to an experience he could not expect to escape. It was clear to him before long that the process called death was merely a passage to another world, and naturally enough he pictured that world as being very like the one he knew, only man would there enjoy extended powers over the forces with which he waged such ceaseless war for the mastery during his period on earth. It might be that the world was not so very far away, and it was not to be supposed that persons who had passed over would lose their interest in and affection for those who for a little while had been left behind. Relations must not be forgotten just because they did not happen to be visibly present, any more than to-day we forget one of the family who has gone on a voyage for a week or a month or a year. Naturally those whose age and position during their lifetime had entitled them to deference and respect must be treated with the same consideration, nay, with even more ample honours since their authority had become mysteriously greater and they would be more active to punish any disrespect or neglect. Hence as a family venerated the father of the house both in life and after death, which was the germ of ancestral worship, so the tribe would venerate the great men, the chieftains and the heroes, whose exploits had won so much not only for their own particular houses, but for the whole clan. The Shilluk, a tribe who dwell upon the western bank of the White Nile, and who are governed by a single king, still maintain the worship of Nyakang, the hero who founded the dynasty and settled this people in their present territory. Nyakang is conceived as having been a man, although he did not actually die but vanished from sight. Yet he is not altogether divine, for the great god of the Shilluk, the creator of mankind and the world, Juok, is without form, invisible and omnipresent. He is far greater than and far above Nyakang, and he reigns in those highest heavens where neither the prayers of man can reach his ears, nor can he smell the sweet savour of sacrifice.

Not only Nyakang, but each of the Shilluk kings after death is worshipped, and the grave of the monarch becomes a sanctuary, so that throughout the villages there are many shrines tended by certain old men and old women, where a ritual which is practically identical in each separate place is elaborately conducted. Indeed, the principal element in the religion of the Shilluk may be said to be the veneration of their dead kings.[5]

Other African tribes also worship their dead kings. The Baganda, whose country Uganda lies at the actual source of the Nile, think of their dead kings as being equal to the gods, and the temples of the deceased monarchs are built and maintained with the utmost care. Formerly when a king died hundreds of men were killed so that their spirits might attend upon the spirit of their master, and what is very significant as showing that these people believe the king and his ghostly followers could return in forms sufficiently corporeal to perform the very material function of eating is that on certain solemn days at earliest dawn the sacred tomtom is beaten at the temple gates and crowds of worshippers bring baskets of food for the dead king and his followers lest being hungry he should become angered and punish the whole tribe.[6]

In Kiziba, which lies on the western side of the Lake Victoria Nyanza, the religion of the natives consists of the worship of their dead kings, although there is a supreme god Rugada, who created the world, man and beasts, but even their hierarchs know little about him and he receives no sacrifice, the business of the priests being to act as intermediaries between the people and the dead monarchs.[7]

So the Bantu tribes of Northern Rhodesia acknowledge a supreme deity, Leza, whose power is manifested in the storm, in the torrential rain clouds, in the roar of thunder and the flash of lightning, but to whom there is no direct access by prayer or by sacrifice. The gods, then, whom these tribes worship are sharply divided into two classes, the spirits of departed chiefs, who are publicly venerated by the whole tribe, and the spirits of relations who are privately honoured by a family, whose head performs the sacerdotal functions upon these occasions. " Among the Awemba there is no special shrine for these purely family spirits, who are worshipped inside the hut, and to whom family sacrifices of a sheep, a goat, or a fowl is made, the spirit receiving the blood spilt upon the ground, while all the members of the family partake of the flesh together. For a religious Wemba man the cult of the spirit of his nearest relations (of his grandparents, or of his deceased father, mother, elder brother or maternal uncle) is considered quite sufficient. Out of these spirit relatives a man will worship one whom he considers as a special familiar, for various reasons. For instance, the diviner may have told him that his last illness was caused because he had not respected the spirit of his uncle ; accordingly he will be careful in the future to adopt his uncle as his tutelary spirit. As a mark of such respect he may devote a cow or a goat to one of the spirits of his ancestors."[8] This custom is very significant, and two points should be especially noted. The first is that the deceased, or the spirit of the deceased, is not merely propitiated by, but partakes of, blood, which is spilt for his benefit. Secondly, the deceased, if not duly honoured, can cause illness, and therefore is capable of exercising a certain vengeful or malevolent power. The essential conception that underlies these customs is not so very far removed from the tradition of a vampire who craves to suck blood and causes sickness through his malignancy.

Very similar ideas prevail among the Herero, a Bantu tribe of German South-West Africa, who believe that Ndjambi

Karunga, the great good god who dwells in heaven above is
far too remote to be accessible, wherefore he neither receives
nor requires worship and offerings. "It is their ancestors
(*Ovakuru*) whom they must fear ; it is they who are angry
and can bring danger and misfortune on a man . . . it
is in order to win and keep their favour, to avert their dis-
pleasure and wrath, in short to propitiate them, that the
Herero bring their many offerings ; they do so not out of
gratitude, but out of fear, not out of love, but out of terror."[9]
The Rev. G. Viehe, a missionary among the tribe writes :
"The religious customs and ceremonies of the Ovaherero
are all rooted in the presumption that the deceased continue
to live, and that they have a great influence on earth, and
exercise power over the life and death of man."[10]

The religion of the Ovambo, another Bantu tribe of German
South-West Africa, runs on practically the same lines. The
supreme being, Kalunga, the creator, desires neither adoration
nor fear. The whole religion is the worship, or rather the
propitiation, of the spirits of the dead. Every man at death
leaves behind him a phantom form which continues a certain
kind of life (not very clearly defined) upon earth, and this
spirit has power over the living. Especially may it cause
various kinds of sickness. The spirits of private persons can
only exert their influence over the members of their own
families ; the souls of chiefs and great warriors have a much
wider scope, they can influence the whole clan for weal or woe ;
they can even to some extent control the powers of nature
and ensure a bountiful corn-crop by their careful provision of
rain, since under their kindly direction there shall be neither
too little nor too great an abundance. Moreover, they can
ward off disease, but if on the other hand they be offended
they can visit the tribe with pestilence and famine. It may be
particularly noted that among the Ovambo the phantoms of
dead magicians are dreaded and feared in no ordinary manner.
The only way to prevent the increase of these dangerous
spirit folk is by depriving the body of its limbs, a precaution
which must be taken immediately after death. So it is
customary to sever the arms and legs from the trunk and to
cut the tongue out of the mouth, in order that the spirit may
have no power either of movement or of speech, since the
mutilation of the corpse has rendered a ghost, who would

assuredly be both powerful and truculent, inoperative and incapable.[11] It will later be seen that the mutilation, the cutting off of the head, and especially the driving of a stake through the body with other dismemberments, were resorted to as the most effective means, short of complete cremation, of dealing with a vampire, whilst according to Theosophists only those become vampires who have during their lifetime been adepts in black magic, and Miss Jessie Adelaide Middleton says that the people who become vampires are witches, wizards and suicides.[12]

Canon Callaway has recorded some very interesting details of Amatongo or Ancestor Worship among the Zulus.[13] A native account runs as follows: " The black people do not worship all Amatongo indifferently, that is, all the dead of their tribes. Speaking generally, the head of each house is worshipped by the children of that house ; for they do not know the ancients who are dead, nor their laud-giving names, nor their names. But their father whom they knew is the head by whom they begin and end in their prayer, for they know him best, and his love for his children ; they remember his kindness to them whilst he was living, they compare his treatment of them whilst he was living, support themselves by it and say, ' He will still treat us in the same way now he is dead. We do not know why he should regard others besides us ; he will regard us only.' So it is then although they worship the many Amatongo of their tribe, making a great fence around them for their protection ; yet their father is far before all others when they worship the Amatongo. Their father is a great treasure to them even when he is dead." It would appear that among the Zulus the spirits of those who are recently deceased, especially the fathers and mothers of families, are most generally venerated and revered. As is natural, the spirits of the remoter dead are forgotten, for time passes and their memory perishes when those who knew them and sang their praises follow them into the world beyond. As we have remarked, in nearly every case we find recognized the existence of a supreme being, who is certainly a high spiritual power that had never been a man, and the homage paid to whom (in those very rare instances[14] where such worship is conceived of as desirable or even possible) differs entirely from the cult of the dead, be they family ancestors or some line of ancient kings. There are, of course, many other gods in the African pantheon, and although the natives will not allow that these were ever men, and indeed sharply differentiate in ritual practice their worship from the cult of the spirits and phantoms, yet in nearly all cases it is to be suspected, and in many cases it is certain, that these gods were heroes of old whose legend instead of becoming faint with years and dying away grew more and more splendid until the monarch or the warrior passed into pure deity. A similar process holds forth in heathen religions the wide world over, and with regard to the Baganda polytheism the Rev. J. Roscoe remarks " The principal gods appear to have been at one time human beings, noted for their skill and bravery, who were afterwards deified by the people and invested with supernatural powers."[15]

It is said that the Caffres believe that men of evil life after death may return during the night in coporeal form and attack the living, often wounding and killing them. It seems that these revenants are much attracted by blood which enables them more easily to effect their purpose, and even a few red drops will help to vitalize their bodies. So a Caffre has the greatest horror of blood, and will never allow even a spot fallen from a bleeding nose or a cut to lie uncovered, but should it stain the ground it must be instantly hidden with earth, and if it splotch upon their bodies they must purify themselves from the pollution with elaborate lustral ceremonies.[16] Throughout the whole of West Africa indeed the natives are careful to stamp out any blood of theirs which happens to have fallen to the ground, and if a cloth or a piece of wood should be marked thereby these articles are most carefully burned.[17] They openly admit that the reason for this is lest a drop of blood might come into the hands of a magician who would make evil use of it, or else it might be caught up by a bad spirit and would then enable him to form a tangible body. The same fear of sorcery prevails in New Guinea, where the natives if they have been wounded will most carefully collect the bandages and destroy them by burning or casting them far into the sea, a circumstance which has not infrequently been recorded by missionaries and travellers.[18]

There are, indeed, few if any peoples who have not realized the mysterious significance attached to blood, and examples of this belief are to be found in the history of every clime. It is expressed by the Chinese writers on medicine[19]; it was held by the Arabs[20]; and it is prominent among the traditions of the Romans.[21] Even with regard to animals the soul or life of the animal was in the blood, or rather actually was the blood. So we have the divine command, *Leviticus* xvii. 10-14 : " Homo quilibet de domo Israel, et de aduenis qui peregrinantur inter eos, si comederit sanguinem, obfirmabo faciem meam contra animam illius, et dispertam eam de populo suo. Quia anima carnis in sanguine est : et ego dedi illum uobis, ut super altare in eo expietis pro animabus uestris, et sanguis pro animae piaculo sit. Idcirco dixi filiis Israel : Omnis anima ex uobis non comedet sanguinem, nec ex aduenis, qui peregrinantur apud uos. Homo quicumque ex filiis Israel, et de aduenis, qui peregrinantur apud uos, si uenatione atque aucupio ceperit feram uel auem, quibus esci licitum est, fundat sanguinem eius, et operiat illum terra. Anima enim omnis carnis in sanguine est : unde dixi filiis Israel : Sanguinem uniuersae carnis non comedetis, quia anima carnis in sanguine est : et quicumque comederit illum, interibit." (If any man whosoever of the house of Israel, and of the strangers that sojourn among them, eat blood I will set my face against his soul, and will cut him off from among his people : Because the life of the flesh is in the blood : and I have given it to you, that you may make atonement with it upon the altar for your souls, and the blood may be for an expiation for the soul. Therefore I have said to the children of Israel : No soul of you, nor of the strangers that sojourn among you, shall eat blood. Any man whatsoever of the children of Israel, and of the strangers that sojourn among you, if by hunting or by fowling, he take a wild beast or a bird, which is lawful to eat, let him pour out its blood, and cover it with earth. For the life of all flesh is in the blood : therefore I said to the children of Israel : You shall not eat the blood of any flesh at all, because the life of the flesh is in the blood, and whosoever eateth it, shall be cut off.)[22] The Hebrew word which is translated " life "[23] in this passage and particularly in the phrase " Because the life of the flesh is in the blood," also signifies " Soul," and the *Revised Version* has a marginal note : " Heb. *soul*." Since then the very essence of life, and even more, the spirit or the soul in some mysterious way lies in the blood we have a complete explanation why the vampire should seek to vitalize and rejuvenate his own dead body by draining the blood from the veins of his victims.

It will be remembered that in a famous necromantic passage in the *Odyssey*,[24] when Ulysses calls up the ghosts from the underworld, in order that they may recover the power of speech, he has to dig deep a trench and therein pour the blood of sacrifice, black rams, and it is only after they have quaffed their fill of this precious liquor that the phantoms may converse with him and enjoy something of their human powers and mortal faculties.

Among the many references to funereal customs and the rites of mourning in Holy Writ there is one which has a very distinct bearing upon this belief that blood might benefit the deceased. The prophet Jeremias in fortelling the utter ruin of the Jews and the complete desolation of their land says : " Et morientur grandes, et parui in terra ista : non sepelientur neque plangentur, et non se incident, neque caluitium fiet pro eis."[25]   (Both the great and little shall die in this land ; they shall not be buried nor lamented, and men shall not cut themselves, nor make themselves bald for them.)   And again the same prophet tells us that after the Jews had been carried away in captivity of Babylon : " Uenerunt uiri de Sichem et de Silo, et de Samaria octoginta uiri : rasi barba, et scissis uestibus et squallentes : et munera, et thus habebant in manu, ut offerrent in domo Domini."[26] The word " squallentes " which the *Douai Version* renders " mourning " is translated by the *Authorised Version* as " having cut themselves " and the same rendering is given in the *Revised Version*. These customs of shaving part of the head and the beard which is referred to in the words " nor make themselves bald for them " and more particularly the practice of cutting or wounding the body in token of mourning were strictly forbidden as savouring of heathenish abuse. Thus in *Leviticus* xix. 28, we read : " Et super mortuo non incidetis carnem uestrum, neque figuras aliquas, aut stigmata facietis uobis. Ego Dominus." (You shall not make any cuttings in your flesh, for the dead, neither shall you make in yourselves any figures or marks : I am the Lord.) And again (xxi. 5) the same command with regard to mourning is enforced : " Non radent caput, nec barbam, neque in carnibus suis facient incisuras." (Neither shall they shave their head, nor their beard, nor make incisions in their flesh.) S. Jerome, however, tells us that the custom persisted. For he says in his *Commentary on Jeremias*, xvi. 6, which may be dated 415-420 :[27] " Mos hic fuit apud ueteres, et usque hodie in quibusdam permanet Iudaeorum, ut in luctibus incidant lacertos, et caluitium faciant, quod Iob fecisse legimus."[28] And yet these observances had been, as we saw, most sternly forbidden, nay, and that most emphatically and more than once. Thus in Deuteronomy they are sternly reprobated as smacking of the grossest superstition : " Non comedetis cum sanguine. Non augurabimini, nec obseruabitis somnia. Neque in rotundum attondebitis comam : nec radetis barbam. Et super mortuo non incidetis carnem uestram, neque figuras aliquas, aut stigmata facietis uobis. Ego Dominus." (You shall not eat with blood. You shall not divine nor observe dreams. Nor shall you cut your hair round-wise : nor shave your beard. You shall not make any cuttings in your flesh, for the dead, neither shall you make in yourselves any figures or marks : I am the Lord.) "Filii estote Domini Dei uestri : non uos incidetis, nec facietis caluitium super mortuo. Quoniam populus sanctus es Domino Deo tuo : et te elegit ut sis ei in populum peculiarem de cunctis gentibus, quae sunt super terram." (Be ye children of the Lord your God : you shall not cut yourselves, nor make any baldness for the dead ; because thou art a holy people to the Lord thy God : and he chose thee to be his peculiar people of all nations that are upon the earth.)

Presumably these two customs were thus sternly prohibited as largely borrowed by the Jews from the Pagan people around them, who might indeed as having no hope make such extravagant and even indecent exhibition of their mourning for the departed, but which practices would at the least be highly unbecoming in the chosen people of Jehovah. Assuredly, even if they go no deeper, these observances are tainted with such savagery and seem so degrading that it is not surprising to find ordinances among other peoples, for instance the code of Solon at Athens, forbidding mourners to wound and scratch their faces and persons. The laws of the Ten Tables also which were largely based on this earlier legislation do not permit women to tear and disfigure their faces during the funeral rites. These two customs, shaving the head and lacerating the face, are found the whole world over at all times and among all races. The former hardly concerns us here, but it is interesting to inquire into the idea which lay at the root of this "cuttings in the flesh for the dead." This practice existed in antiquity among the Assyrians, the Arabs, the Scythians and such peoples as the Moabites, the Philistines, and the Phœnicians.[29] Jordanes tells us that Attila was lamented, "not with womanly wailing, empty coronach and tears, but with the blood of warriors and strong men."[30] Among many African tribes, among the Polynesians of Tahiti, the Sandwich Islands and the whole Pacific Archipelago; among the Aborigines of Australia, New Zealand and Tasmania; among the Patagonians; among the Indians of California and North America; as among very many other races, mourning for the dead is always accompanied by the laceration of the body until blood freely flows, and it is even not unknown for relatives of the deceased to inflict terrible mutilations upon themselves, and he who is most pitiless and most barbarous is esteemed to show the greater honour and respect to the departed. The important point lies in the fact that blood must be shed, and this appears to constitute some covenant with the dead, so that by freely bestowing what he requires they prevent him from returning to deprive them of it forcibly and in the most terrifying circumstances. If they are not willing to feed him with their blood he will come back and take it from them, so naturally it is believed to be far better to give without demur and gain the protection of the ghost, rather than to refuse what the phantom will inevitably seize upon in vengeance and in wrath.

Many Australian tribes considered blood to be the best remedy for a sick and weakly person, and there is, of course, no small modicum of truth in the idea when we consider the scientific transfusion of blood as is practised in certain cases by doctors at the present time, a remedy of which there are many examples in the middle ages and in later medicine.[31]   Bonney, the Australian traveller, tells us that among certain tribes on the Darling River in New South Wales, " a very sick or weak person is fed upon blood which the male friends provide, taken from their bodies in the way already described,"[32] that is to say by opening a vein of the forearm and allowing the blood to run into a wooden bowl or some similar vessel. " It is generally taken in a raw state by the invalid, who lifts it to his mouth like jelly between his fingers and thumb." It must be remembered that the Aborigines firmly believe in the existence of the soul after death, and since blood during the life proves the most helpful and sustaining nourishment it will communicate the same vitalizing qualities if bestowed upon one who has passed beyond, for they do not entertain the idea that death is any great severance and separation.

This certainly gives us a clue to the belief underlying the practice of scratching the body and shedding blood upon the occasion of a death, and there can be no doubt that, although possibly the meaning was obscured and these lacerations came to evince nothing more than a proof of sorrow at the bereavment, yet fundamentally the blood was offered by mourners for the refreshment of the departed to supply him with strength and vigour under his new conditions.[33] These practices, then, involved a propitiation of the dead ; further, a certain intimate communication with the dead, and assuredly bear a necromantic character, and have more than a touch of vampirism, the essence of which consists in the belief that the dead man is able to sustain a semi-life by preying upon the vitality, that is to say, by drinking the blood of the living. Accordingly we are fully able to understand why these customs, heathenish and worse, were so uncompromisingly denounced and forbidden in the Mosaic legislation. It was no mere prohibition of indecorous lamentations tinged with Paganism, but it went something deeper, for such observances are not free from the horrid superstition of black magic and the feeding of the vampire till he suck his full of hot salt blood and be gorged and replete like some demon leech.

The word Vampire (also vampyre) is from the Magyar *vampir*, a word of Slavonic origin occuring in the same form in Russian, Polish, Czech, Serbian, and Bulgarian with such variants as Bulgarian, *vapir, vepir* ; Ruthenian *vepyr, vopyr, opyr* ; Russian *upir, upyr* ; South Russian *upuir* ; Polish *upier*. Miklosich[34] suggests the Turkish *uber*, witch, as a possible source. Another derivation, which is less probable is from the root *Pi*—to drink, with the prefix *va*, or *av*. From the root Pi—come the Greek πίνω I drink, some tenses of which are formed from the root *Po*—, such as a perfect πέπωκα[35] ; a future passive ποθήσομαι[36] ; to which must be added the perfect infinitive πεπόσθαι[36] which occurs in Theognis.[37] Hence we have the Aeolic πώνω, and also probably ποταμός, properly perhaps of fresh, drinkable water πότιμον ὕδωρ.[38]

The Sanskrit is pâ, pî, pi-bâmi (bibo) ; pâ-nam (potus) pâ-tra (poculum) ; Latin po-tus, po-to, po-culum, etc., with which are connected bibo and its many forms and compounds (root-bi-) ; Slavonic, pi-tî (bibere) ; Lithuanian, po-ta (ebriositas), and a vast number of other variants.

Ralston must certainly be quoted in this connexion, although it should be borne in mind that he is a little out of date in some details. *The Songs of the Russian People* from which (p. 410) I cite the following passage was published early in 1872. Of Vampires he writes : " The name itself has never been satis-factorily explained. In its form of *vampir* [South Russian *upuir*, anciently *upir*], it has been compared with the Lithu-anian *wempti* = to drink, and *wempti*, *wampiti* = to growl, to mutter, and it has been derived from a root *pi* [to drink] with the prefix *u* = *av*, *va*. If this derivation is correct, the character-istic of the vampire is a kind of blood-drunkenness. In accordance with this idea the Croatians called the vampire *pijauica* ; the Servians say of a man whose face is coloured by constant drinking, that he is ' blood-red as a vampire ' ; and both the Servians and the Slovaks term a hard drinker a *Vlkodlak*. The Slovenes and Kashubes call the vampire *vieszey*, a name akin to that borne by the *witch* in our own language as well as in Russian. The Poles name him *upior* or *upir*, the latter being his designation among the Czekhs also." The Istrian vampire is *strigon*, and among the Wallachians there is a vampire called *murony*. In Greece there are some local names for the vampire, (Cyprus), σαρκωμένος, "the one who has put on flesh " ; (Tenos), ἀναικαθούμενος, " he who sits up in his grave " ; in Cythnos, ἄλυτος " incorrupt " ; in Cythera, ἀνάρραχο, λάμπασμα, and λάμπαστρο, three words of which I can suggest no satisfactory explanation and which ever so great an authority on Greece as Mr. J. C. Lawson finds unintelligible. Newton, *Travels and Discoveries in the Levant* (I, p. 212) and more particularly Pashley, *Travels in Crete* (II, p. 207), mention a term used in Rhodes and generally in Crete, καταχανας, the derivation of which is uncertain. Pashley thinks it may have meant a " destroyer," but Mr. Lawson connects it with κατὰ and the root χαν—, I gape or yawn, in allusion to the gaping mouth of the vampire, *os hians, dentes candidi*, says Leone Allacci.

St. Clair and Brophy in their *Twelve Years' Study of the Eastern Question in Bulgaria*, 1877, have a note (p. 29, n. 1) : " The pure Bulgarians call this being [the Vampire] by the genuine Slavonic name of *Upior*, the Gagaous (or Bulgarians of mixed race) by that of *Obour*, which is Turkish ; in Dalmatia it is known as *Wrikodlaki*, which appears to be merely a corruption of the Romaic βρυκόλαξ."

The word *vampir, vampyr*, is apparently unknown in Greece proper and the general modern term is βρυκόλακας, which may be transliterated as *vrykolakas* (plural *vrykolakes*). Tozer gives the Turkish name as *vurkolak*, and Hahn records that amongst some of the Albanians βουρβολάκ-ου is used of the restless dead. It is true that in parts of Macedonia where the Greek population is in constant touch with Slavonic neighbours, especially in Melenik in the North-East, a form βάμπυρας or βόμπυρας has been adopted,[39] and is there used as a synonym of *vrykolakas* in its ordinary Greek sense, but strangely enough with this one exception throughout the whole of Greece and the Greek islands the form " Vampire " does not appear. Coraes denies the Slavonic origin of the word *vrykolakas*, and he seeks to connect a local variant βορβόλακας with a hypothetical ancient word μορμόλυξ alleged to be the equivalent of μορμολύκη[40] which is used by the geographer Strabo, and μορμολυκεία used by Arrianus of Nicomedia in his Διατριβαὶ Ἐπικτήτου[41] and the more usual μορμολυκεῖον[42] found in Aristophanes, *Thesmophoriazuasae* (417) :

εἶτα διὰ τοῦτον ταῖς γυναικωνίτισιν
σφραγῖδας ἐπιβάλλουσιν ἤδη καὶ μοχλούς,
τηροῦντες ἡμᾶς, καὶ προσέτι Μολοττικοὺς
τρέφουσι, μορμολυκεῖα τοῖς μοιχοῖς, κύνας.

The word occurs again in Plato, *Phaedo*[43] : " τοῦτον οὖν πειρώμεθα πείθειν μὴ δεδιέναι τὸν θάνατον ὥσπερ τὰ μορμολύκεια." It is, of course, a derivation and diminutive of Mormo (Μορμώ), a hobgoblin, or worse, a ghoul of hideous appearance. The theory is patriotic and ingenious, but Bernard Schmidt and all other authorities agree that it is entirely erroneous and the modern Greek word *vrykolakas* must undoubtedly be identified with a word which is common to the whole Slavonic group of languages. This word Slovenian *volkodlak, vukodlak, vulkodlak,* is a compound form of which the first half means "wolf," whilst the second half has been identified, although the actual relation is not quite demonstrable, with *blaka,* which in Old Slavonic, New Slavonic, and Serbian signifies the "hair" of a cow or a horse or a horse's mane.[44] Yet whatsoever the analytical signification of the compound may precisely be, the synthesis in the actual employment of all Slavonic tongues, save one, is the equivalent of the English "werewolf"; Scotch "warwulf"; German "Werwolf" and French "loup-garou." The one language in which this word does not bear this interpretation is the Serbian, for here it signifies "a vampire."[45] But it should be remarked in this connexion that the Slavonic peoples, and especially the Serbians believe that a man who has been a werewolf in his life will become a vampire after death, and so the two are very closely related.[46] It was even thought in some districts, especially Elis,[47] that those who had eaten the flesh of a sheep killed by a wolf might become vampires after death.[48] However, it must be remembered that although the superstitions of the werewolf and the vampire in many respects agree, and in more than one point are indeed precisely similar, there is, especially in Slavonic tradition, a very great distinction, for the Slavonic vampire is precisely defined and it is the incorrupt and re-animated dead body which returns from its grave, otherwise it cannot be said strictly to be a vampire. As we shall have occasion to observe it were, perhaps, no exaggeration to say that the conception of the vampire proper is peculiar to Slavonic peoples, and especially found in the Balkan countries, in Greece, in Russia, in Hungary, Bohemia, Moravia, and Silesia. There are, of course, many variants, both Western and Oriental ; and other countries have tales of vampires which exactly fit the Slavonic norm, but outside the districts we have specified the appearances of the vampire are rare, whilst in his own domain even now he holds horrid sway, and people fear not so much the ghost as the return of the dead body floridly turgescent and foully swollen with blood, endued with some abominable and devilish life.

In Danish and Swedish we have *vampyr*; the Dutch is *vampir*; the French *le vampire*; Italian, Spanish, Portuguese, *vampiro ;* modern Latin, *vampyrus.*[49] The *Oxford English Dictionary* thus defines vampire : " A preternatural being of a malignant nature (in the original unusual form of the belief an animated Corpse), supposed to seek nourishment and do harm by sucking the blood of sleeping persons ; a man or woman abnormally endowed with similar habits." The first example which has been traced of the use of the word in literature seems to be that which occurs in *The Travels of Three English Gentlemen,* written about 1734, which was printed in Vol. IV. of the *Harleian Miscellany,* 1745, where the following passage occurs : " We must not omit Observing here, that our Landlord [at Laubach] seems to pay some regard to what Baron *Valvasor* has related of the *Vampyres,* said to infest some Parts of this Country. These *Vampyres* are supposed to be the Bodies of deceased Persons, animated by evil Spirits, which come out of the Graves, in the Night-time, suck the Blood of many of the Living, and thereby destroy them." The word and the idea soon became quite familiar, and in his *Citizen of the World* (1760-2) Oliver Goldsmith writes in every-day phrase : " From a meal he advances to a surfeit, and at last sucks blood like a vampire."

Johnson, edited by Latham, 1870, has : " Vampire. Pretended demon, said to delight in sucking human blood, and to animate the bodies of dead persons, which, when dug up, are said to be found florid and full of blood." A quotation is given from Forman's *Observations on the Revolution in* 1688, 1741, which shows that so early the word had acquired its metaphorical sense : " These are the vampires of the publick and riflers of the kingdom." David Mallet in his *Zephyr, or the Stratagem,* has :

> Can Russia, can the Hungarian vampire
> With whom call in the hordes and empire,
> Can four such powers, who one assail
> Deserve our praise should they prevail ?

A few travellers and learned authors had written of vampires in the seventeenth century. Thus we have the famous *De Graecorum hodie quorundam opinationibus* of Leone Allacci,[50] published at Cologne in 1645 ; there are some detailed accounts in the *Relation de ce qui s'est passé a Sant-Erini Isle de l'Archipel*[51] by Father François Richard, a Jesuit priest of the island of Santorini (Thera), whose work was published at Paris in 1657 ; Paul Ricaut, sometime English Consul at Smyrna in his *The Present State of the Greek and Armenian Churches Anno Christi*, 1678, 8vo, London, 1679,[52] mentions the tradition with a very striking example, but he does not actually use the word vampire.   In 1679 Philip[53] Rohr published at Leipzig his thesis *De Masticatione Mortuorum*, which in the eighteenth century was followed by a number of academic treatises, such as the *Dissertatio de Hominibus post mortem Sanguisugis, uulgo dictis Vampyren*, by John Christopher Rohl and John Hertel, Leipzig, 1732 ; the *Dissertatio de cadaueribus sanguisugis* of John Christian Stock, published at Jena in the same year ; the *Dissertatio de Uampyris Seruiensibus* of John Heinrich Zopfius and Charles Francis van Dalen which appeared in the following year ; all of which in some sense paved the way for John Christian Harenberg's *Von Vampyren*.[54]

In 1744 was published at Naples " *presso i fratelli Raimondi* " the famous *Dissertazione sopra I Vampiri* of Gioseppe Davanzati, Archbishop of Trani. This book had already widely circulated in manuscript—"la sua Dissertazione sopra i Vampiri s'era sparsa per tutta l'Italia benchè mano-scritta," says the anonymous biographer—and a copy had even been presented to the Holy Father, the learned Benedict XIV, who in a letter of 12th January, 1743, graciously thanked the author with generous compliment upon his work.   " L'abbiamo subito letta con piacere, e nel medesimo Tempo ammirata si per la dottrina, che per la vasta erudizione, di cui ella è fornita " ; wrote the Pope.   It will not then be unfitting here to supply some brief notice—of the *Dissertazione sopra I Vampiri*, which although it ran into a second edition, " Napoli. M.DCC.LXXXIX. Presso Filippo Raimondi," in England seems almost entirely unknown since strangely enough even the British Museum Library lacks a copy.   We would premise that as the good Archbishop's arguments and conclusions are philosophical it is quite allowable for us, whilst fully recognizing his scholarship and skill in handling his points, not to accept these but rather to maintain the contrary.

Gioseppe Davanzati was born at Bari on 29th August, 1665. After having commenced his studies at the Jesuit

College in his native town, he passed at the age of fifteen to the University of Naples. Already had he resolved to seek the priesthood, and after a course of three years, his parents being now dead, he entered the University of Bologna, when he greatly distinguished himself in Science and Mathematics. Some few years were next spent in travelling, during which period he made his headquarters at Paris, " essendo molto innamorato delle maniere, e de'costumi de' Francesi." Spain, Portugal, the Low Countries, Germany, Switzerland were visited in turn, and we are told that he repeatedly expressed his wish to cross over to England, " nobil sede dell 'Arti e delle Scienze " but that by some accident his desire was again and again frustrated. Early in the reign of Clement XI, (1700-1721) he was recalled to Italy, and having been raised to the priesthood by the Bishop of Montemartino (Salerno) he was appointed Treasurer of the famous Sanctuary of S. Nicholas at Bari. His genius speedily attracted attention, and before long he was sent by the Pope as Legate Extraordinary to the Emperor Charles VI, to Vienna, a difficult and important mission which he discharged so admirably well that upon his return he was rewarded with the Archbishopric of Trani and other honours. This noble prelate remained high in favour with the successors of Clement XI, Innocent XIII (1721-1724), Benedict XIII (1724-1730), and Clement XII (1730-1740), and when on the death of this latter Pontiff Cardinal Prospero Lorenzo Lambertini was elected and took the title of Benedict XIV an old and intimate friend of his own was sitting in the chair of S. Peter. Although five and seventy years of age, Archbishop Davanzati journeyed to Rome to kiss the feet of the new Pope by whom he was welcomed with the utmost kindness and every mark of distinction. Upon the death of Monsignor Crispi, Archbishop of Ferrara, the Supreme Pontiff on 2nd August, 1746, preconized Gioseppe Davanzati as Patriarch of Alexandria, a dignity vacant by the aforesaid prelate's decease. Early in February, 1755, Archbishop Davanzati contracted a severe chill which turned to inflammation of the lungs. Upon the night of the sixteenth of that month, having been fortified with the Sacraments of the Church he slept peacefully away, being aged 89 years, 5 months, and 16 days.

The *Dissertazione sopra I Vampiri* owed its first suggestion

to the various discussions which were held at Rome during
the years 1738-39 in the apartments of Cardinal Schrattem-
bach, Bishop of Olmütz, and which arose from the official
reports of vampirism submitted to him by the chapter of
his diocese. The cardinal sought the advice and co-operation
of various learned members of the Sacred College and other
prelates of high repute for experience and sagacity. Amongst
these was Davanzati who frankly confesses that until the
Cardinal consulted him and explained the whole business
at length he had no idea at all what a vampire might be.
Davanzati commences his work by relating various well-
known and authenticated cases of vampires, especially those
which had recently occurred in Germany during the years
1720-1739. He shows a good knowledge of the literature of
the subject, and decides that the phenomena cannot enter
into the category of apparitions and ghosts but must be
explained in a very different way, He finds that with but
few exceptions both ancient and modern philosophers seem
ignorant of vampirism, which he justly argues with pertinent
references to the *Malleus Maleficarum* and to Delrio must
be diabolical in origin be it an illusion or no. He next considers at some length in several chapters of great interest the
extent of the demon's power. Chapter XIII discusses
" Della forza della Fantasia," and in Chapter XIV he argues
" Che le apparizioni de'fantasmi, e dell' ombre de' Morti,
di cui fanno menzione gli Storici, non siano altro che effetto
di fantasia." Here we take leave to join issue with him, and
to-day it will very generally be agreed that his line of argument is at least perilous. Nor can we accept " Che l'appar-
izione de' Vampiri non sia altro che paro effetto di Fantasia."
The truth lies something deeper than that as Leone Allacci
so well knew. Yet with all its faults and limitations the
Dissertazione sopra I Vampiri is deserving of careful consideration for there is much that is well presented, much that
is of value, although in the light of fuller investigations and
clearer knowledge the author's conclusion cannot be securely
maintained.

Even better known than the volume of Davanzati
is the *Dissertations sur les Apparitions des Anges, des Démons
et des Esprits, et sur les Revenants et Vampires de Hongrie,
de Bohême, de Moravie, et de Silésie*, published at Paris,

chez Debure l'aîné, 2 vols., 12mo, 1746.[55] The work
was frequently reprinted, and translated into English
1759 ; into German 1752 ; second edition 1757-8. In
its day it exercised a very great influence, and as it is still
constantly referred to, it may not be impertinent to give a
brief account of the eminent authority, its author.

Dom Augustin Calmet, who is so famous as a biblical exe-
getist, was born at Ménil-la-Horgne, near Commercy, Lorraine, on 26th February, 1672 ; and died at the Abbey of
Senones, near Saint-Dié, 25th October, 1757. He was educated by the monks of the Benedictine Priory of Breuil, and
in 1688 he joined this learned order in the abbey of St. Mansuy
at Toul, being professed in the following year, and ordained
17th March, 1696. At the Abbey of Moyen-Moutier, where he
taught philosophy and theology, he soon engaged the help
of the whole community to gather the material for his vast
work on the Bible. The first volume of this huge commentary
appeared at Paris in 1707, *Commentaire littéral sur tous les livres
de l'Ancien et du Nouveau Testament*; and the last of the twenty-
three quarto volumes was published only in 1716. Several
most important reprints were issued throughout the eighteenth
century, including two Latin versions, the one by F. Vecelli
which came from houses at Venice and Frankfort, six volumes
folio, 1730 ; the other by Mansi, Lucca, 9 vols., folio, 1730-1738,
of which version there are at least two subsequent editions.
It is impossible that in some small points so encyclopædic
a work should not be open to criticism, but its merits are
permanent and the erudition truly amazing. Yet this was
only one of many learned treatises which Dom Calmet published on Biblical subjects, and so greatly was their value
esteemed that his dissertations were rapidly translated into
Latin and the principal modern European languages. When
we add to these his historical and philosophical writings the
output of this great scholar is well-nigh incredible. So remarkable a man could not fail to hold high honours in his own
Congregation, and it was only at his earnest prayer that Pope
Benedict XIII refrained from compelling him to accept a
mitre, since this Pontiff on more than one occasion expressed
himself anxious to reward the merits and the learning of the
Abbot of Senones.

To-day, perhaps the best known of Dom Calmet's works

in his *Traité sur les Apparitions des Esprits, et sur les Vampires*, and in his preface he tells us the reasons which induced him to undertake this examination. One point which he emphasizes must carefully be borne in mind and merits detailed consideration. Vampires, as we have seen, particularly infest Slavonic countries, and it does not appear that this species of apparition was well known in western Europe until towards the end of the seventeenth century. There undoubtedly were cases of vampirism, as will be recorded in their due order, and certain aspects of witchcraft have much in common with the vampire tradition, especially the exercise of that malign power whereby the witch caused her enemies to dwindle, peak and pine, draining them dry as hay. But this is not vampirism proper. The fuller knowledge of these horrors reached western Europe in detail during the eighteenth century, and it at once threw very considerable light upon unrelated cases that had been recorded from time to time, but which appeared isolated and belonging to no particular category. Writing in 1746, Dom Calmet, who had long studied the subject, remarks that certain events, certain movements, certain fanaticisms, certain phenomena, it may be in the physical or in the supernatural order, distinguish and characterise certain several centuries. He continues : " In this present age and for about sixty years past, we have been the hearers and the witnesses of a new series of extraordinary incidents and occurrences. Hungary, Moravia, Silesia, Poland, are the principal theatre of these happenings. For here we are told that dead men, men who have been dead for several months, I say, return from the tomb, are heard to speak, walk about, infest hamlets and villages, injure both men and animals, whose blood they drain thereby making them sick and ill, and at length actually causing death. Nor can men deliver themselves from these terrible visitations, nor secure themselves from these horrid attacks, unless they dig the corpses up from the graves, drive a sharp stake through these bodies, cut off the heads, tear out the hearts ; or else they burn the bodies to ashes. The name given to these ghosts is Oupires, or Vampires, that is to say, blood-suckers, and the particulars which are related of them are so singular, so detailed, accompanied with circumstances so probable and so likely, as well as with the most weighty and well-attested legal deposition that it seems impossible not to subscribe to the belief which prevails in these countries that these Apparitions do actually come forth from their graves and that they are able to produce the terrible effects which are so widely and so positively attributed to them. . . . The Brucolaques (*vrykolakes*) of Greece and the Archipelago are Apparitions of quite a new kind." The author then says that he has solid reasons for treating the subject of Vampires, and especially for dealing with those who infest Hungary, Moravia, Silesia and Poland, although he well knows that he is laying himself open to damaging criticism on both sides. Many persons will accuse him of temerity and presumption for having dared to cast doubts upon certain details in these well-authenticated accounts, whilst others will attack him for having wasted his time in writing seriously on a subject which appears to them frivolous and inept. " Howbeit," he continues, " whatever line anyone may choose to adopt, it is to my mind useful and indeed necessary to investigate a question which seems to have an important bearing upon Religion. For if it be a truth that Vampires may actually thus return from their graves, then it becomes necessary to write in defence of, and to prove, this truth ; if it be an error and an illusion, it follows in the interests of religion that those who credit it must be undeceived and that we should expose a groundless superstition, a fallacy, which may easily have very serious and very dangerous consequences."

In the first chapter of his Second Volume, which section directly discusses Vampires,—the first volume being preliminary and generally concerned with apparitions of various kinds,—Don Calmet again defines a Vampire, and at the risk of a certain amount of repetition his words must once again be quoted[56] : " The Apparitions (Revenans) of Hungary, or Vampires . . . are men who have been dead for some considerable time, it may be for a long period or it may be for a shorter period, and these issue forth from their graves and come to disturb the living, whose blood they suck and drain. These vampires visibly appear to men, they knock loudly at their doors and cause the sound to re-echo throughout the whole house, and once they have gained a foothold death generally follows. To this sort of Apparition is given the name Vampire or Oupire, which in the Slavonic tongues means a blood-sucker. The only way to obtain deliverance from their molestations is by disinterring the dead body, by cutting off the head, by driving a stake through the breast, by transfixing the heart, or by burning the corpse to ashes."

It may be remarked here that although in the course of this book there will be occasion to deal with many ghosts of the vampire family and to treat of cognate superstitions and traditions the essential feature of the Vampire proper lies in the fact that he is a dead body re-animated with an awful life, who issues from his tomb to prey upon the living by sucking their blood which lends him new vitality and fresh energies. Since he is particularly found in Greece it is to a Greek writer we may go for a description of this pest. One of the earliest —if indeed he were not actually the first—of the writers of the seventeenth century who deals with vampires is Leone Allacci, (Alacci), more commonly known as Leo Allatius.[57] This learned scholar and theologian was born on the island of Chios in 1586, and died at Rome 19th January, 1669. At the age of fourteen he entered the Greek College in Rome, and when he had finished his academic course with most honourable distinction, returned to Chios where he proved of the greatest assistance to the Latin Bishop Marco Giustiniani. In 1616 Allacci received the degree Doctor of Medicine from the Sapienza, and a little later, after having been attached to the Vatican library, he professed rhetoric at the Greek College. In 1622 Pope Gregory XV sent him to Germany to superintend the transportation to Rome of the Palatinate library of Heidelberg, which Maximillian I had presented to the Pope in return for large subsidies that enabled the war to be carried on against the federation of Protestant Princes. This important task, which owing to a disturbed state of the country was one of immense difficulty, Allacci accomplished most successfully, and during the reigns of Urban VIII and Innocent X he continued his work in the Vatican library, especially concentrating upon the Palatinate manuscripts. In 1661 Alexander VI, as a recognition of his vast researches and eminent scholarship, appointed him custodian of the Library. He was an earnest labourer for reunion, in which cause he wrote his great work *De Ecclesiae Occidentalis atque Orientalis perpetua consensione*, published at Cologne in 1648, a dissertation wherein all points of agreement are emphasized, whilst the differences are treated as lightly as possible.

Allacci, in his treatise *De Graecorum hodie quorundam opinationibus*, Cologne, 1645, discusses many traditions, and amongst others he deals at some length with the vampire, concerning whom he says : "The *vrykolakas* is the body of a man of wicked and debauched life, very often of one who has been excommunicated by his bishop. Such bodies do not like other corpses suffer decomposition after burial nor fall to dust, but having, so it seems, a skin of extreme toughness become swollen and distended all over, so that the joints can scarcely be bent ; the skin becomes stretched like the parchment of a drum, and when struck gives out the same sound, from which circumstance the *vrykolakas* has received the name τυμπανιαῖος ('drum-like')." According to this author a demon takes possession of such a body, which issues from the tomb, and, generally at night, goes about the streets of a village, knocking sharply upon doors, and summoning one of the household by name. But if the person called unwittingly answers he is sure to die on the following day. Yet a *vrykolakas* never cries out a name twice, and so the people of Chios, at all events, always wait to hear the summons repeated before they reply to anyone who raps at their door of a night. "This monster is said to be so fearfully destructive to men, that it actually makes its appearance in the daytime, even at high noon,[58] nor does it then confine its visits to houses, but even in fields and in hedged vineyards and upon the open highway it will suddenly advance upon persons who are labouring or travellers as they walk along, and by the horror of its hideous aspect it will slay them without laying hold on them or even speaking a word." Accordingly a sudden death from no obvious cause is to be regarded with the gravest suspicion, and should there be any kind of molestation, or should any story of an apparition be bruited abroad they hasten to exhume the corpse which is often found in the state that has been described. Thereupon without any delay "it is taken up out of the grave, the priests recite the appointed prayers, and it is thrown on to a fiercely blazing pyre. Before the orisons are finished skin will desquamate and the members fall apart, when the whole body is utterly consumed to ashes." Allacci proceeds to point out that this tradition in Greece is by no means new nor of any recent growth, for he tells us "in ancient and modern times alike holy men and men of great piety who have received the confessions of Christians have tried to disabuse them of such superstitions and to root this belief out of the popular imagination." Indeed a *nomocanon* or authoritative ordinance[59] of the Greek church is cited to the following effect : " Concerning a dead man, if he be found whole, the which they call *vrykolakas*.

"It is impossible that a dead man should become a *vrykolakas*, unless it be by the power of the Devil who, wishing to mock and delude some that they may incur the wrath of Heaven, causeth these dark wonders, and so very often at night he casteth a glamour whereby men imagine that the dead man whom they knew formerly, appears and holds converse with them, and in their dreams too they see strange visions. At other times they may behold him in the road, yea, even in the highway walking to and fro or standing still, and what is more than this he is even said to have strangled men and to have slain them.

"Immediately there is sad trouble, and the whole village is in a riot and a racket, so that they hasten to the grave and they unbury the body of the man . . .   and the dead man—one who has long been dead and buried—appears to them to have flesh and blood . . .   so they collect together a mighty pile of dry wood and set fire to this and lay the body upon it so that they burn it and they destroy it altogether."

What is exceedingly curious is that after so emphatically declaring these phenomena to be a superstition and an idle fantasy, the *nomocanon* continueth as follows : " Be it known unto you, however, that when such an incorrupt body shall be discovered, the which, as we have said is the work of the Devil, ye must without delay summon the priests to chant an invocation to the All Holy Mother of God . . .   and solemnly to perform memorial services for the dead with funeral-meats."[60] This provision is at any rate pretty clear evidence that the author or authors of this ordinance must have had some belief in the *vrykolakas*, and it appears to me that they would not have added so significant a cautel unless they had deemed it absolutely necessary, and having salved their consciences by speaking with rigid officialism, they felt it incumbent upon them to suggest precautions in case of the expected happening, and the consequence of difficulties and mistrust. In fact, they were most obviously safeguarding themselves.

Allacci, at any rate, had no hesitation about declaring his own views, and he thoroughly believed in the vampire. He says, and says with perfect truth : " It is the height of folly to attempt to deny that such bodies are not infrequently found in their graves incorrupt and that by use of them the Devil, if God permit him, devises most horrible complots and schemes to the hurt and harm of mankind." Father François Richard, reference to whose important work has been made above, distinctly lays down that particularly in Greece the devil may operate by means of dead bodies as well as by sorcerers, all this being allowed by some inscrutable design of providence. And there can be no doubt that the vampire does act under satanic influence and by satanic direction. For the wise words of S. Gregory the Great, although on another occasion,[61] may most assuredly be applied here: "Qui tamen non esse incredibilia ista cognoscimus, si in illo et alia facta pensamus. Certe iniquorum omnium caput diabolus est : et huius capitis membra sunt omnes iniqui." All this, of course, under divine permission. The authors of the *Malleus Maleficarum* in the First Part teach us how there are " Three Necessary Concomitants of Witchcraft, which are the Devil, a Witch, and the Permission of God." So are these three necessary concomitants of Vampirism, to wit, the Devil, the Dead Body, and the Permission of God." Father Richard writes : " The Devil revitalizes and energizes these dead bodies which he preserves for a long time in their entirety ; he appears with the actual face and in the likeness of the dead, stalking abroad up and down the streets, and presently he will parade the country roads and the fields ; he bursts his way into men's houses, filling many with awful fear, leaving others dumb with horror, whilst others are even killed ; he proceeds to acts of violence and blood, and strikes terror into every heart." The good Father proceeds to say that at first he believed these appearances to be merely ghosts from Purgatory returning to ask for help, masses and pious prayers[62] ; but on learning the details of the case he soon found that he had to deal with something very other, for such ghosts never commit excesses, violent assaults, wreaking the destruction of cattle and goods, and even causing death. These appearances then are clearly diabolical, and the matter is taken in hand by the priests who assemble on a Saturday, that being the only day of the week on which a *vrykolakas* rests in his grave and cannot walk abroad.

It may be remembered that Saturday was the one day of the week which was particularly avoided by witches for their assemblies, and that no Sabbat was held on this day. for Saturday is sacred to the Immaculate Mother of God.[63] " It is well known," says that great Doctor S. Alphonsus,[64] " that Saturday is dedicated by Holy Church to Mary, because, as S. Bernard tells us, on that day, the day after the death of Her Son, She remained constant in faith." (Per illud triste Sabbatum stetit in fide, et saluata fuit Ecclesia in ipsa sola; propter quod, aptissime tota Ecclesia, in laudem et gloriam eiusdem Uirginis, diem Sabbati per totius anni circulum celebrare consueuit.)[65] In England this excellent practice of devotion was known as early as Anglo-Saxon times, since in the Leofric Missal a special mass is assigned to Saturdays in honour of Our Lady.

Mr. G. F. Abbott, in his *Macedonian Folklore*,[66] relates that in Northern Greece " People born on a Saturday (hence called Σαββατιανοὶ or Sabbatarians) are believed to enjoy the doubtful privilege of seeing ghosts and phantasms, and of possessing great influence over vampires. A native of Socho assured the writer that such a one was known to have lured a *vrykolakas* into a barn and to have set him to count the grains of a heap of millet.[67]   While the demon was thus engaged, the Sabbatarian attacked him and succeeded in nailing him to the wall . . . At Liakkovikia it is held that the Sabbatarian owes his power to a little dog, which follows him every evening and drives away the *vrykolakas*. It is further said that the Sabbatarian on these occasions is invisible to all but the little dog."

The priests then on a Saturday go in procession to the grave where lies the body which is suspect. It is solemnly disinterred, " and when they find it whole, they take it for certain that it was serving as an instrument of the Devil."

This abnormal condition of the dead is held to be a sure mark of the vampire, and is essential to vampirism proper. In the Greek Church it is often believed to be the result of excommunication, and this is indeed an accepted and definite doctrine of the Orthodox Church, which must be considered in turn a little later.

It is not impossible, I think, that cases of catalepsy, or suspended animation which resulted in premature burial may have helped to reinforce the tradition of the vampire and the phenomenon of vampirism. Some authorities consider catalepsy as almost entirely, if not wholly, psychic, and certainly not a disease in any correct sense of the word, although it may be a symptom of obscure diseases arising from nervous disorders. A celebrated medical authority has pronounced that "in itself catalepsy is never fatal." It belongs to the domain of hypnotism, and is said to be refreshing to the subject, especially when he is exhausted by long mental exertion or physical toil. Very often it arises from conscious or sub-conscious auto-suggestion, and it has been described as "the supreme effort of nature to give the tired nerves their needed repose." No doubt the fatal mistake so often made in the past was that of endeavouring by drastic measures to hasten restoration to consciousness, instead of allowing nature to recuperate at will. If the attempt is successful it comes as a fearful shock to the nerves which are craving for rest ; if the effort is seemingly without result the patient is in imminent danger of an autopsy or of being buried alive, a tragedy which, it is to be feared, has happened to very many. It is clear that as yet serious attention has not been adequately given to this terrible accident. A quarter of a century ago it was computed that in the United States an average of not less than one case a week of premature burial was discovered and reported. This means that the possibility of such danger is appalling. In past centuries when knowledge was less common, when adequate precautions were seldom, if ever, employed, the cases of premature burial, especially at such times as the visitation of the plague and other pestilences must have been far from uncommon. Two or three examples of recent date, that is to say occuring at the end of the last century, may profitably be quoted as proving extremely significant in this connexion.

A young lady, who resided near Indianopolis, came to life after fourteen days of suspended animation. No less than six doctors had applied the usual tests, and all unhesitatingly signed certificates to witness that she was dead. Her little brother against this consensus of opinion clung to her and declared that she had not died. The parents were in bitter

THE RESUSCITATED CORPSE

(From the Musée Wiertz)

[see p. 34

PLATE II

PLATE III

CHILD DEVOURED BY A WILD MAN

By Luke Cranach

[see p. 60

agony, but at length it was necessary to remove the body. The boy endeavoured to prevent this, and in the excitement the bandage which tied up the jaw was loosened and pushed out of place, when it appeared that her lips were quivering and the tongue gently moving. "What do you want, what do you want ? " cried the child. "Water," distinctly, if faintly, came the answer from the supposed corpse. Water was administered, the patient revived, and lived her full span of years, healthy and normal until she was an old woman.

A lady who is now the head matron of one of the largest orphan asylums in the United States has been given over as dead no less than twice by the physicians in attendance ; her body has twice been shrouded in the decent cerements of the grave ; and twice has she been resuscitated by her friends. On the second occasion, in view of the former experience, extraordinary precautions were taken. All known tests were applied by the physicians, and humanly speaking all possible doubt was set at rest. The doctors had actually left the house, and the undertaker was at his sad business. It chanced that the body was pierced by a pin, and to the joy of her friends it was noted that a small drop of blood shortly afterwards oozed from the puncture. The family insisted upon the preparations being stayed ; vigorous treatment was unremittingly applied, and the patient returned to life. To-day she is an exceptionally active and energetic administratrix. It should be remarked that the lady declared that she had never for a moment lost consciousness, that she was fully cognizant of all that went on around her, that she perfectly understood the meaning of all the tests which were so assiduously employed, but that all the while she felt the utmost indifference with regard to the result. The verdict of the physicians that she was dead did not cause her either the slightest surprise or the smallest alarm. A very similar accident occurred to a gentleman of good estate, one of the most prominent citizens of Harrisburg, in Pennsylvania. After a long illness he apparently died from inflamatory rheumatism, which was complicated with heart trouble. All preparations were made for the funeral, but his wife determined that this should not take place for at least a week, so great was her fear of premature burial. In the course of two or three days it was noticed that the body had moved ; the eyes were wide open, and one of the arms had altered the position in which it had been carefully placed. His wife shrieked out his name, upon which he slowly arose, and with assistance was supported to a chair. Even before the arrival of the physicians, who were instantly summoned, he had regained a marked degree of strength, together with an ability of movement which had not been possible throughout the whole course of his illness. He was soon in excellent health, and what is very remarkable, he stated that during the time of suspended animation he was perfectly aware of everything that was going on all around, that the grief of his family filled him with terrible agony, and he dreaded the preparations for interment, but that he was unable to move a muscle or utter a word.

The death of Washington Irving Bishop, the well-known thought-reader, caused a great sensation at the time. On many occasions he had been in a cataleptic state for several hours, and once, at least, his trance was so long that two physicians pronounced him to be dead. There is little doubt that eventually the autopsy was performed with irregular haste, and that the unfortunate subject was not dead before the surgeon's knife had actually penetrated his brain.

Although through the ages few cases have been actually recorded the incidents of premature burial and of autopsy performed on the living must be numberless. One such accident nearly occurred to the great humanist Marc-Antoine Muret,[68] who, falling ill upon a journey, was conveyed to the local hospital as a sick stranger, name unknown. Whilst he lay, not even unconscious, upon the rough pallet, the physicians, who had been lecturing upon anatomy and were anxious to find a subject to illustrate their theories, gathered round in full force. They eagerly discussed the points to be argued, and deeming the patient dead, the senior physician gravely pronounced, pointing to the patient: " Faciamus experimentum in anima uili." The eyes of the supposed corpse opened widely, and a low, but distinct voice answered : " Uilem animam appellas pro qua Christus non dedignatus est mori."

As was customary in the case of prelates, when Cardinal Diego de Espinosa, Bishop of Sigeunza and Grand Inquisitor of Spain under Philip II died after a short illness, the body was embalmed before it lay in state. Accordingly in the presence of several physicians the surgeon proceeded to operate

for that purpose. He had made a deep incision, and it is
said that the heart had actually been brought into view and
was observed to beat. The Cardinal recovered consciousness
at the fatal moment, and even then had sufficient strength
to grasp with his hand the scalpel of the anatomist. In the
earlier years of the nineteenth century both Cardinal Spinola
and the octogenarian Cardinal della Somaglia were prepared
for embalmment before life was extinct.

In the Seventh Book of the *Historia Naturalis*, (*liii*, 52,
ed. Brotier, Barbou, 1779), Pliny relates many instances of
persons who, being deemed dead, revived. " Auiola consularis
in rogo reuixit : et quoniam subueniri non potuerat præ
ualente flamma, uiuus crematus est. Similis causa in L.
Lamia prætorio uiro traditur. Nam C. Ælium Tuberonem
prætura functum a rogo relatum, Messala Rufus, et plerique
tradunt. Hæc est conditio mortalium : ad has, et eiusmodi
occasiones fortunæ gignimur, uti de homine ne morti quidem
debeat credi. Reperimus inter exempla, Hermotini Clazo-
menii animam relicto corpore errare solitam, uagamque e
longinquo multa annunitiare, quæ nisi a præsente nosci non
possent, corpore interim semianimi : donec cremato eo inimici
(qui Cantharidæ uocabantur) remeanti animæ uelut uaginam
ademerint. Aristeæ etiam uisam euolantem ex ore in Pro-
conneso, corui effigie, magna quæ sequitur fabulositate.
Quam equidem et in Gnossio Epimenide simili modo accipio :
Puerum æstu et itinere fessum in specu septem et quinquaginta
dormisse annis : rerum faciem mutationemque mirantem
uelut postero experrectum die : hinc pari numero dierum
senio ingruente, ut tamen in septimum et quinquagesimum
atque centesimum uitæ duraret annum. Feminarum sexus
huic malo uidetur maxime opportunus, conuersione uuluæ :
quæ si corrigatur, spiritus restituitur. Huc pertinet nobile
apud Græcos uolumen Heraclidis, septem diebus feminæ
exanimis ad uitam reuocatæ.

Uarro quoque auctor est, xx. uiro se agros diuidente Capuæ,
quemdam qui efferretur, foro domum remaasse pedibus. Hoc
idem Aquini accidisse. Romæ quoque Corsidium materteræ
suæ maritum sumere locato reuixisse, et locatorem funeris ab
eo elatum. Adiicit miracula, quæ tota indicasse conueniat.
E duobus fratribus equestris ordinis, Corsidio maiori accidisse,
ut uideretur exspirasse, apertoque testamento recitatum

heredem minorem funeri institisse ; interim eum, qui uidebatur extinctus, plaudendo conciuisse ministeria, et narrasse " a fratre se uenisse, commendatum sibi filiam ab eo. Demonstratum præterea, quo in loco defodisset aurum nullo conscio, et rogasse ut iis funebribus, quæ comparasset, efferretur." Hoc eo narrante, fratris domestici propere annuntiauere exanimatum illum : et aurum, ubi dixerat, repertum est. Plena præterea uita est his uaticiniis, sed non conferenda, cum sæpius falsa sint, sicut ingenti exemplo docebimus. Bello Siculo Gabienus Cæsaris classiarus fortissimus captus a Sex. Pompeio, iussu eius incisa ceruice, et uix cohærente, iacuit in litore toto die. Deinde cum aduesperauisset, cum gemitu precibusque congregata multitudine petiit, uti Pompeius ad se ueniret, aut aliquem ex arcanis mitteret : se enim ab inferis remissum, habere quæ nuntiaret. Misit plures Pompeius ex amicis, quibus Gabienus dixit : " Inferis diis placere Pompeii causas et partes pias : proinde euentum futurum, quem optaret : hoc se nuntiare iussum : argumentum fore ueritatis, quod peractis mandatis, protinus exspiraturus esset " : idque ita euenit. Post sepulturam quoque uisorum exempla sunt : nisi quod naturæ opera, non prodigia consectamur.

It was truly said by Pliny that " Such is the condition of humanity, and so uncertain is men's judgement that they cannot determine even death itself." The words of the wise old Roman have been re-echoed by many a modern authority. Sabetti in his Tractatus XVI, " De Extrema Unctione," *Compendium Theologiæ Moralis*, (ed. recognita T. Barrett ; Pustet ; 1916 ; p. 776) asks : " *Quid sacerdoti agendum sit, si ad ægrotum accedat, eumque modo mortuum, ut uulgo dicitur, inueniat ?* In the course of resolving this, he lays down : " Iam age ex sententia plurimorum medicorum doctissimorum probabile est homines in omnibus ferme casibus post instans mortis, ut uulgo dicitur, seu post ultimam respirationem, intus aliquamdiu uiucre, breuius uel diutius, iuxta naturam causae quae mortem induxit. In casibus mortis ex morbis lenti progressus probabile est uitam interne perdurare aliquot momenta, sex circiter, uel, iuxta quosdam peritos, unam dimidiam horam : in casibus uero mortis repentinae uita interna perdurat longius, forte non improbabiliter, usque ad putrefactionem." Professor Huxley wrote : " The evidence of ordinary observers on such a point as this (that a person is really dead) is absolutely worthless. And, even medical evidence, unless the physician is a person of unusual knowledge and skill, may have little more value." *The British Medical Journal*[70] remarks : " It is true that hardly any one sign of death, short of putrefaction, can be relied upon as infallible." Sir Henry Thompson wrote : " It should never be forgotten that there is but one really trustworthy proof that death has occurred in any given instance, *viz., the presence of a manifest sign of commencing decomposition.*" And Professor P. Brouardel emphatically declares : " We are obliged to acknowledge that we have no sign or group of signs sufficient to determine the moment of death with scientific certainty in all cases." Colonel E. P. Vollum, M.D., Medical Inspector of the United States Army, and Corresponding Member of the New York Academy of Sciences, who himself was upon one occasion almost buried alive, most emphatically declared that " even stoppage of the beating of the heart, and breathing, for a considerable time, with all other appearances of death, excepting decomposition, do not make it certain that a person is dead," and he also added the terrible warning that " the suspended activity of life may return after the body has been interred." It is unnecessary to enter into these painful cases of premature burial, but there is overwhelming evidence that such accidents were far from uncommon. Dr. Thouret, who was present at the destruction of the famous vaults of Les Innocens, told Mons. Desgenettes that there could be no doubt many of the persons must have been interred alive, since the skeletons were found in positions which showed the dead must have turned in their coffins. Kempner supplies similar particulars when describing disinterments which have taken place in New York and other districts of the United States, also in Holland and elsewhere.

The celebrated investigator, Dr. Franz Hartmann, collected particulars of more than seven hundred cases of premature burial and of narrow escapes from it, some of which occurred in his own neighbourhood. In his great work *Premature Burial*[71] he tells us of the terrible incident which happened to the famous French tragedienne, Mlle. Rachel, who on 3rd January, 1858, " died " near Cannes, and who was to be embalmed, but after the proceedings had commenced she suddenly returned to life, only to expire in reality some ten hours later from the shock and from the injuries which had been inflicted upon her. Another case which is of particular interest as having occurred in Moravia, where the belief in vampires is particularly strong, is that of the postmaster in a small town who, as it was thought, died in a fit of epilepsy. About a year afterwards it became necessary to disinter some of the bodies from the graveyard in order to enlarge one of the transepts of the parish church, and the dreadful fact was revealed that the unfortunate postmaster must have been buried whilst still alive, a discovery which so horrified the physician who had signed the death certificate that he lost his reason.

In the chancel of S. Giles, Cripplegate, there is still to be seen a monument sacred to the memory of Constance Whitney, whose many virtues are described in somewhat rhetorical fashion upon a marble tablet. A figure above this scroll represents the lady in the act of rising from her coffin. This might be taken to be a beautiful symbolism, but such is not the case, for it represents an actual circumstance. The unfortunate lady had been buried while in a condition of suspended animation, and consciousness returned to her when the sexton opened the coffin and desecrated the body in order to steal a valuable ring which had been left upon one of her fingers.[72] In former years when the rifling of tombs and body-snatching were by no means an infrequent practice, many similar cases came to light, and there can be no doubt that no inconsiderable proportion of persons were buried in a state of trance or catalepsy.

The story of Gabrielle de Launay, a lady whose cause was tried before the High Court of Paris, about 1760, caused a profound sensation throughout the whole of France. When eighteen years of age Gabrielle, the daughter of M. de Launay, the President of the Civil Tribunal of Toulouse, was betrothed to Captain Maurice de Serres. Unhappily the latter was suddenly ordered abroad to the Indies on active service. The President, fearing that his child might die in a foreign land, refused to allow the marriage to be celebrated immediately so that she might accompany her husband under his protection. The lovers parted heart-broken, and in about two years' time news reached France of the gallant young soldier's death.

This, however, proved to be false, although his safety was not known until, after an absence of well-nigh five years, he presented himself once more in Paris. Here he happened to pass the church of S. Roch, the entire façade of which was heavily draped with black and shrouded for the funeral of some person of distinction. Upon enquiry, he learned that the mourning was on account of a young and beautiful lady who had died suddenly after two days' illness, the wife of the President du Bourg, who before her marriage had been Mlle. Gabrielle de Launay. It appeared that, owing to the report of the death of Maurice de Serres, M. de Launay had compelled his daughter to marry this gentleman, who although nearly thirty years her senior was a figure of great wealth and importance. As may be imagined, the young captain was distracted with grief, but that night, taking a considerable sum in gold, he visited the sexton of the cemetery of S. Roch and with great difficulty bribed him to exhume the corpse of Madame du Bourg in order that he might once more look upon the features of the woman whom he had so passionately loved. With every precaution, under the pale light of a waning moon, the terrible task was completed, the coffin was silently unscrewed, and the unhappy lover threw himself upon his knees in an agony of grief. At last the grave-digger suggested that everything must be replaced in order, when with a terrible cry the young officer suddenly seized the cold, clay body and, before the bewildered sexton could prevent him, threading his rapid course among the tombs, with lightning speed he disappeared into the darkness. Pursuit was useless, and nothing remained but for the poor man to replace the empty shell in the grave, to shovel back the earth and arrange the spot so that there might be no trace of any disturbance. He felt sure, at least, that his accomplice in so terrible a crime, a sacrilege which would inevitably bring the severest punishment upon those concerned in it, must maintain silence, if only for his own sake.

Nearly five years had passed when M. du Bourg, who upon the anniversary of his wife's death each June attended a solemn requiem, as he was passing through a somewhat unfrequented street in the suburbs of Paris came face to face with a lady in whom he recognised none other than the wife whose death he had mourned so tenderly and so long.

As he attempted to speak, she with averted looks swept past him as swiftly as the wind and, leaping into a carriage with emblazoned panels, was driven quickly away before he could reach the spot. However, M. du Bourg had noticed the arms of the noble house of de Serres, and he determined that inquiry should at once be made. It was no difficult task for a man of his position to obtain an order that the grave of his wife might be examined, and when this was done the empty broken coffin turned suspicion into certainty. The fact that the sexton had resigned his post and had gone no one knew where, but seemingly in comfortable circumstances shortly after the funeral of Madame du Bourg lent its weight to the investigations which were now taken in hand. Experienced lawyer that he was, M. du Bourg accumulated evidence of the first importance. He found that it was said that Captain Maurice de Serres had married his young and lovely wife, Madame Julie de Serres, some five years previously and, as it was supposed, then brought her back with him from some foreign country, to Paris.

The whole city was astounded when the President du Bourg demanded from the High Court the dissolution of the illegal marriage between Captain Maurice de Serres and the pretended Julie de Serres, who, as the plaintiff steadfastly declared, was Gabrielle du Bourg, his lawful wife. The novelty of the circumstances caused the profoundest sensation, and vast numbers of pamphlets were exchanged by the faculty, many of whom maintained that a prolonged trance had given rise to the apparent death of Madame du Bourg, and it was stated that although she had continued to exist for a great number of hours in her grave, cases of similar lethargies had been recorded, and even if such fits were of the rarest, yet the circumstance was possible. Madame Julie de Serres was summoned to appear in Court and answer the questions of the Judges. She stated that she was an orphan born in South America, and had never left her native country until her marriage. Certificates were produced, and on every side lengthy arguments were heard, which it is unnecessary to detail. Many romantic incidents ensued, but these, however interesting, must be passed over, for it shall suffice to say that eventually, mainly through the sudden introduction of her little daughter, amid a pathetic scene, the identity of Julie de Serres with Gabrielle du Bourg, *née* Launay, was established and acknowledged. In vain did her advocate plead that her marriage to M. du Bourg had been dissolved by death, although this fact most certainly ought to have been accepted as consonant with sound theology.[73] None the less the result was that, in spite of her prayer to be allowed to enter a cloister, she was ordered to return to her first husband. Two days after, the President du Bourg awaited her arrival in the great hall of his mansion. She appeared, but could scarcely totter through the gates, for she had but a few moments previously drained a swift poison. Crying " I restore to you what you have lost," she fell a corpse at his feet. At the same moment Captain de Serres died by his own hands.

It cannot escape notice that these events very closely resemble that novella of Bandello (II, 9), which relates the true history of Elena and Gerardo, adventures nearly resembling the tragic tale of *Romeo and Juliet*. Elena and Gerardo are the children of two nobles of Venice, Messer Pictro and Messer Paolo, whose palaces fronted each other on the Grand Canal. Gerardo chances to see Elena at her window, and from that hour he knows neither happiness nor sleep until he has declared his consuming passion. A kindly nurse brings them together, and in her presence they exchange rings and vows of tenderest love before the statue of Madonna the Virgin, spending long nights in amorous ecstasy and bliss. For these unions were fast binding, although not a sacrament, indeed, until then had received the benison of Holy Church. It is a common saying to apply to any man : " Si, è ammogliato ; ma il matrimonio non è stato benedetto." Wherefore the spousals of the lovers remained a secret.

In a little while Messer Paolo, thinking great things of his son's career in the world, dispatches the young man to Beirut, and Gerardo needs must go. But when he had been absent some six months Messer Pictro informs his daughter that he has appointed a day for her marriage with a young man of ancient house and fair estate, and not daring to tell her father what had passed, she sunk under her silent grief, and upon the evening before her new nuptials she fell into a swoon across her bed, so that in the morning she was found cold and stark as a stiffening corpse. The physicians assembled in numbers and talked learnedly ; remedies of every sort were applied without avail; and no one doubted she was dead. So they carried her to church for burial and not for marriage. That night they bore in sombre and silent procession upon a black gondola to the Campo which is hard by San Pietro in Castello, where lies the Sacred Body of Venice's great patriarch, San Lorenzo Guistiniani. They left her there in a marble sarcophagus outside the church, with torches blazing around.

Now it happened that Gerardo's galley had returned from Syria, and was newly anchored at the port of Lido. Many friends came to greet him, and as they talked, marking the funeral cortège, he idly asked who was gone. When he learned it was Elena, grief fell upon him like a cloud of night. But he dissembled until all had departed, when, calling his friend the captain of the galley, he told him the whole story of his love, and swore he would once again kiss his wife, even if he had to break open her monument. The captain tried in vain to dissuade him, but seeing it was of no avail the two men took a boat and rowed together to San Pietro. It was long after midnight when they landed and made their way to the place of sepulture. Pushing back the massive lid, Gerardo flung himself upon the body of his Elena. At length the good captain, who feared the Signors of the Night would visit the spot and put them under arrest, compelled the hapless lover to return to the boat, but he could no whit persuade him to leave Elena's body, and this Gerardo bore in his arms and reverently laid it in the boat, himself clasping it in his arms with many a sad kiss and bitter sigh. The captain, much alarmed, scarce dared to make for the galley, but rowed up and down and out to the open lagoon, the dying husband yet laid by his dead wife. However, the sea-breezes freshened with their salt tang, and far over the waters the horizon lightened towards dawn. It was then that the spark of life awoke in Elena's face; she moved gently, and Gerardo, starting from his grief, began to chafe her hands and feet. They carried her secretly to the house of the captain's mother; here she was put in a warm bed, possets and food were administered; presently she opened her eyes, and lived. A gracious and lordly feast was made by Messer Paolo for his son's return, and when all the company were assembled Gerardo entered, leading Elena in bridal array, and kneeling at his father's feet he said : " Lo, my father, I bring you my wedded wife whom I have this day saved from death." Great were the rejoicings, and Messer Pictro was summoned from his house of mourning to a home of gladness. So when the whole truth had been told him and he welcomed back not only his dead daughter but her husband also with a joyful heart and with thanksgiving, he blessed the young couple, and on the morrow morn Holy Church with solemn rite hallowed the bond of matrimony whose joys had already been sweetly consummated.

The parallels between the two adventures are very striking. Our main interest in the sad story of de Serres and his love, which assuredly might have ended far otherwise, lies in the fact that the unfortunate Gabrielle du Bourg was actually buried as dead in her coffin, and only restored to life after several days had passed. Occasionally epitaphs may be seen both abroad and in England, which record some premature burial. Such a one was placed over the tomb of a Mrs. Blunden in the cemetery of Basingstoke, Hampshire, and this tells how the unfortunate lady was prematurely interred, but the original inscription is to a large extent obliterated.[74] Unfortunately overwhelming evidence proves that such terrible accidents are far from rare, for Mr. William Tebb, in his authoritative work *Premature Burial*[75] had collected of recent years from medical sources alone two hundred and nineteen narrow escapes from being buried alive ; one hundred and forty-nine premature interments that actually took place ; ten cases of bodies being dissected before life was extinct ; three cases in which this shocking error was very nearly made ; and two cases where the work of embalmment had already begun when consciousness returned.

There is no greater mistake than to suppose that most cases of premature burial, and of escape from premature burial, happened long ago, and that even then the majority of these took place under exceptional conditions, and for the most part in small towns or remoter villages on the continent. Amazing as it may appear in these days of enlightenment, the number of instances of narrowest escapes from premature burial, and also of this terrible fate itself, has not decreased of recent years, but it has, on the contrary, increased. In a letter on page 1,104 of the *Lancet*, 14th June, 1884, the witness describes in detail the appearance presented by two bodies which he saw in the crypt of the cathedral of Bordeaux, when part of the cemetery there had been dug up and many graves disinterred. In *La Presse Médicale*, Paris, 17th August, 1904, there is an article, " The Danger of Apparent Death," by Doctor Icard of Marseilles, whose study *La Mort réelle et la Mort apparente* when published in 1897 attracted great attention. The writer, an eminent figure in the medical world, describes in detail some twelve cases of the revival of persons who had been certified as dead by their doctors, the body in one instance recovering consciousness when several physicians were present and the funeral ceremonies had actually commenced. It should be remarked that Dr. M. K. Boussakis, Professor of Physiology at the Faculty of Medicine of Athens, was one of the eye-witnesses upon that occasion, and a similar case is mentioned on the authority of Dr. Zacutus Lusitanus, who was also present. It should be remembered that Greece is the country where belief in the vampire still most strongly survives.

A terrible case of actual interment whilst still alive is described in a letter published in the *Sunday Times*, 6th September, 1896. Some years ago the Paris *Figaro*, in an article of some length considered the terrible possibilities of being buried alive, and within fifteen days the editor received over four hundred letters from different parts of France, and all these were from persons who had either themselves been buried alive, or been on the point of being so interred, or who had escaped a premature grave through some fortunate accident.

In September, 1895, a boy named Ernest Wicks was found lying on the grass in Regent's Park, apparently dead, and after being laid out in the S. Marylebone mortuary was brought back to life by the keeper, Mr. Ellis. When the doctor arrived the lad was breathing freely though still insensible, and a little later he was removed to the Middlesex Hospital. Here the surgeon pronounced him to be " recovering from a fit." At an inquest held at Wigan, 21st December, 1902, Mr. Brighouse, one of the County Coroners for Lancashire, remarked with great emphasis upon the extraordinary circumstances, for he informed the jury that the child upon whom they sat had " died " four times, and the mother had obtained no less than three medical certificates of death, any one of which would have been sufficient for the subject to have been buried. In 1905, a Mrs. Holden, aged twenty-eight, living at Hapton, near Accrington, " died," and the doctor did not hesitate to give a certificate of death, when all the arrangements for the funeral were made. Fortunately, the undertaker noticed a slight twitch of the eyelids, and eventually the woman's life was saved, and she lived well and strong under perfectly normal conditions. On 7th January, 1907, the *Midland Daily Telegraph* reported the case of a child who "to all intents and purposes died" whilst an operation was being performed upon it. However, the patient who had been certified dead more than half-an-hour before recovered. On 14th September, 1908, the papers published the details of an extraordinary trance of a Mrs. Rees, Nora Street, Cardiff, who appeared to have had a very narrow escape from premature burial. To go back some forty years, there may be found fully reported in the *British Medical Journal*, 31st October, 1885, the famous case of a child at Stamford Hill who fell into convulsions and passing into a trance was supposed to have died, recovering consciousness only after five days. Hufeland, dealing with these instances of trance, remarks that "Six or seven days are often required to restore such cases. Dr. Charles Londe[76] says that fits of this kind "last for days and days together," and that "it seems not improbable that people may have been buried in this state in mistake for death." A case of exceptional interest is described as occurring in 1883 by the Professor of Medicine in the University of Glasgow, Dr. W. T. Gairdner.[77] The person whom he was treating remained in a trance which lasted twenty-three consecutive weeks, and so remarkable a circumstance attracted very considerable attention at the time, giving rise to a lengthy controversy.

It should be more widely known that the ordinary simulacra of death are utterly deceptive and Dr. John Oswald remarks in his profound work *Suspended Animal Life*,[78] "in consequence of an ignorant confidence placed in them [the signs of death] persons who might have been restored to life . . . have been consigned to the grave." In September, 1903, Dr. Forbes Winslow emphasized the fact that "all the appearances of death may be so strikingly displayed in a person in a cataleptic condition that it is quite possible for burial to take place while life is not extinct," and he added "I do not consider that the ordinary tests employed to ascertain that life is extinct are sufficient; I maintain that the only satisfactory proof of death is decomposition."

Even from this very hasty review, and examples might be multiplied, indeed are multiplying in every direction almost daily, terrible truth though it may be, it is obvious that premature burial is by no means an uncommon thing, whilst recovery from catalepsy or deep trances, sometimes lasting very many days, is even more frequent, and such cases have been recorded in all ages, times without number. It is, I think, exceedingly probable that extraordinary accidents of this kind, which would have been gossiped and trattled throughout large districts, and, passing from old to young, whispered round many a winter's fireside, were bound soon to have assumed the proportions of a legend which must, consciously or unconsciously, have continually gathered fresh accretions of horror and wonder in its train. It is possible, I say, that hence may have been evolved some few details which notably helped to swell the vampire tradition. I do not for a moment wish to imply that these circumstances, which we have just considered at some length, however striking and ghastly, were in any way the foundation of the belief in vampires. I would rather emphasize that the tradition goes far deeper and contains far more dark and scathful reality than this. I would not even suggest that premature burial and resuscitation from apparent death added anything essentially material to the vampire legend, but I do conceive it probable that these macabre happenings, ill-understood and unexplained, did serve to fix the vampire tradition more firmly in the minds of those who had been actual witnesses of, or who by reliable report knew of similar occurrences, and were fearful and amazed.

There are to be read examples of persons who, after death, have given evident signs of life by their movements. One such case is related by Tertullian,[79] who tells us that he himself witnessed it, " de meo didici." A young woman, who had once been in slavery, a Christian, after she had been married but a few months died suddenly in the very flower of her age and happiness. The body was carried to the church, and before it was entrusted to the earth, a service was held. When the priest, who was saying the requiem " praesente cadauere," raised his hands in prayer, to the astonishment of all the young girl who was lying upon her bier with her hands laid in repose at her side, also lifted her hands and gently clasped them as if she too were taking part in the supplication of the Mass, and then toward the end she refolded them in the original position.

Tertullian also says that on one occasion, when a body was about to be interred, a body which was already in the grave seemed to draw to one side as though to make place for the newcomer.

In the life of S. John the Almsgiver, Patriarch of Alexandria, written by Leontius Archbishop of Cyprus, we are told that when the saint who was aged sixty-four, died at Amanthus in Cyprus, 11th November, 616,[80] his body was brought with great veneration and holy observance to the principal church of that place. Here was opened a magnificent tomb in which two bishops had already been buried. It is said that out of respect the two bodies drew one to the right and one to the left, and that this took place in the sight of all who were present, " non unus, neque decem, neque centum uiderunt, sed omnis turba, quae conuenit ad eius sepulturam." It must be remembered that Archbishop Leontius had his facts from those who had actually been present at the interment, and the same account may be found in the *Menology* of Symeon Metaphrastes.

Evagrius Ponticus relates[81] the legend of a certain Anchorite named Thomas, who died in the Nosokomeion at Daphne, a suburb of Antioch, where was the shrine of the martyr S. Babylas.[82] The hermit, a stranger, was buried in that part of the cemetery used for beggars and the very poor. In the morning, however, the body was found to be lying by a rich Mausoleum in the most honourable part of the grounds. It was again interred, but when on the following day it was found by the sexton that the same thing had happened a second time, the people hastened to the patriarch Ephraim[83] and told him of the marvel. Thereupon the body was borne with great rejoicing with an attendance of wax flambeaux and fuming frankincense into the town, and honourably enshrined with worship meet in one of the churches, and for many years the city annually observed the festival of the Translation of S. Thomas Eremita. The same story is related by the ascetical writer, the monk Johannes Moschus, in his very beautiful treatise Λειμών *Pratum spirituale*, " The Spiritual Meadow,"[84] but Moschus says that the remains of the hermit rested in his grave whilst in veneration for his sanctity the bodies of those who were buried near had been found to have issued forth and modestly lay at some considerable distance.

In Hagiology there are many instances of the dead hearing, speaking and moving. Thus in the life of S. Donatus, the patron of Arezzo, who succeeded the first bishop S. Satyrus towards the end of the third century, we are told that Eustasius, receiver-general of the revenues of Tuscany, being called away on a journey, for safety sake left the public funds in the hands of his wife, Euphrosina. This lady, being afraid that her house might be robbed, secretly buried the chests in the earth. She told the matter to no one, but unhappily before her husband's return she expired suddenly in the night, and it was quite unknown where she had concealed her charge. Eustasius was beside himself with grief and fear, for it seemed inevitable that he should be accused of peculation by his enemies, and condemned to death. In his despair he betook himself to S. Donatus, and the holy man asked him that they might visit the grave of Euphrosina. A great company gathered in the church, when the saint, going up to the grave, said in a loud voice that might be heard by all : " Euphrosina, tell us we pray thee, where thou didst put the public funds." The woman answered from her tomb, and certainly her accents were heard revealing the hiding-place. S. Donatus went with the receiver-general to the spot indicated, and there they found the money carefully secured.[85]

It is related in the life of the famous Anchorite, S. Macarius of Egypt, who died A.D. 394,[86] that one of the monks of his laura was accused of murder, and as those who lay the charge spoke with great gravity and sureness, S. Macarius bade them all resort to the grave of the deceased, where, striking his staff upon the ground, he adjured the dead man in these words : " The Lord by me bids you tell us whether this man, who is now accused of your murder, in truth committed the crime, or was in any way consenting thereto ? " Immediately a hollow voice issuing from the tomb declared : " Of a truth he is wholly innocent, and had no hand at all in my death." " Who then," inquired the saint, " is the guilty one ? " The dead man replied : " It is not for me, my father, to bear witness ; let it suffice to know that he who has been accused is innocent. Leave the guilty in the hands of God. Who can say whether the all-holy and compassionate God may not have mercy upon him and bring him to repentance."[87]

In the history of S. Rheticus, as related by C. Vettius Aquilinus Juvencus, the Latin poet of the fourth century, who was so popular in the Middle Ages,[88] we are told that when the saint had expired,[89] his body was carried in solemn procession to the grave of his deceased wife, and suddenly, to the amazement of all present, the dead man arose on his bier and said : " Dost thou remember well, my dear wife, that which thou didst ask me upon thy death-bed ? Lo, here am I come to fulfil the promise made so long syne. Receive me then whom you have sweetly expected all this while." At these words it appeared as if the deceased wife, who had been dead for many years, revived again, and breaking the linen bands which enswathed her, she stretched forth her hands to her husband. (Deprensa est laeuam protendens femina palmam, inuitans socium gestu uiuentis amoris.) The corpse was lowered into the tomb, and there the twain lie in peace, awaiting the resurrection of the just.[90]

Not unsimilar is the legend of S. Injurieux, whose dead body moved out of its own grave to repose in that of his wife Scholastica. Injurieux was a noble senator of Clermont in Auvergne, who married in virgin wedlock a lady of rank, Scholastica. S. Gregory of Tours, in his *Historia Francorum*,[91] tells us that Scholastica died first, and Injurieux, standing by the coffin in which her body was laid, as she was about to be carried forth to burial said in the presence of all : " I thank Thee, O, God, for having bestowed upon me this maiden treasure, which I return into Thy hands unspotted, even as I received it." The dead wife smiled at these words, and her voice was heard to reply : " Why dost thou speak, O my husband, of these things which concern no one but ourselves ? " Hardly had the lady been buried in a magnificent tomb, when the husband died also, and for some reason was temporarily interred in a separate grave, at a distance from the monument of his wife. On the next morning it was found that Injurieux had left the place where he had been laid, and his dead body reposed by the side of that of Scholastica. No man dared disturb the two corpses, and to the present day the senator and his wife are popularly called " The Two Lovers."[92]

In his *Vies des Saints*[93] Monsignor Guérin relates the following story of S. Patrick[94] : "St. Patrice commande à la mort de rendre ses *victimes* afin que leur propre bouche proclame devant le peuple la vérité des doctrines qu'il leur annonce ; ou bien il s'assure si son ordre de planter une croix sur la tombe des chrétiens, et non des infidèles, a été fidélement exécuté, en interrogeant les morts eux-mêmes, et en apprenant de leur bouche s'ils ont mérité ce consolant hommage."

In this connexion—the tradition of a dead person who speaks—the story of S. Melor may be not impertinent. About the year 400 A.D., there was a certain Duke of Cornwall named Melian, whose brother, Rivold, conspired against him and put him to death. The duke had left a young son, Melor, whom the usurper feared to slay, but sent to be brought up under the strictest rule in one of the Cornish monasteries, where the novice continually edified the community by his holy life, having (so it is said) the gift of miracles. After a few years Rivold, being afraid lest the boy should depose him, bribed a soldier named Cerialtan to murder Melor secretly. This was accordingly done. The assassin cut off the head of Melor, and carried it to the duke. He had murdered the boy in the depths of the forest, whither he had enticed him, and as he was making his way through the thicket he chanced to look back his eyes being attracted by a great light. And lo, all around the body stood a company of angels, robed in white albs, and holding in their hands tapers which glistered as golden stars. When he had gone a little further, the wretched murderer was overcome by parching thirst, and almost fainting on his path he cried out in an agony: "Wretched man that I am ! I die for a draught of cool water." Then the head of the murdered boy spoke to him, saying : " Cerialtan, strike upon the grass of this lawn with thy stick, and a fountain shall spring forth for thy need." The man did so, and having quenched his thirst at the miraculous well, he went swiftly on his way. Now when the head was brought into the presence of Duke Rivold this evil tyrant smote it with his hand, but he instantly sickened, and three days afterwards he died. The head was then taken back to the body and was honourably buried with it. And not many years afterwards the relics were translated with great worship to the town of Amesbury, which is in Wiltshire.[95]

In his *Histoire hagiologique du diocèse de Valence*,[96] l'abbé

Nadal tells us that when S. Paulus[97] succeeded S. Torquatus
as bishop of St-Paul-Trois-Châteaux, shortly after his con-
secration a certain Jew, a common usurer, came up to him
in the streets of the city and loudly demanded a large sum of
money which, as he said, had been lent to Bishop Torquatus,
the predecessor of Paulus. In order to ascertain whether
this claim was equitable or not, S. Paulus, robed in full ponti-
ficals, visited the tomb of S. Torquatus in the cathedral,
and touching the place of sepulture with his crozier requested
Torquatus to declare whether the money had been repaid
or no. The voice of the dead bishop immediately answered
from the grave : "Verily hath the Jew received his money,
returned unto him at the appointed time, with interest, ay, and
double interest." The chronicles tell us that this undoubtedly
took place, for many were present and bear witness that they
both saw and heard these things.

Eugippius, who succeeded the martyr S. Vigilius in the see
of Trent, has left us a life of S. Severinus, who was one of the
last Christian bishops among the Roman inhabitants of the
district of the Danube, immediately before the withdrawal
to Italy. On one occasion S. Severinus having watched all
night by the bier of a priest named Silvanus bade him at dawn
once more speak to his brethren who longed to hear his voice,
for he had been an eloquent and fervent preacher. Silvanus
opened his eyes and the saint asked him if he wished to return
to life. But the dead man answered : "My father, detain
me no longer here I pray thee, nor delay for me that hour of
everlasting rest which those who sleep in Jesus most sweetly
enjoy." And then, closing his eyes, in this world he woke
no more.

This happening must at once bring to mind the famous
miracle of S. Philip Neri, who was the spiritual director of
the Massimo family. In 1583 the son and heir of Prince
Fabrizio Massimo died of a fever at the age of fourteen, and
when, amid the lamentations of the bereaved parents and the
weeping relatives, S. Philip entered the room, he laid his hand
upon the brow of the youth, and called him by name. Upon
this the dead boy returned to life, opened his eyes, and sat up
in the bed. "Art thou unwilling to die ? " asked the saint.
"No," sighed the youth gently. "Art thou resigned to yield
they soul ? " "I am." "Then go," said S. Philip. " Va,

che sii benedetto, e prega Dio per noi ! " The boy sank back on his pillow with a heavenly smile, and a second time expired. On 16th March every year a *festa* is held in the family chapel within Palazzo Massimo in memory of this miracle.[98]

It is related in the life of S. Theodosius the Cenobite, written by Bishop Theodore of Petra[99] (536), that a large sepulchre having been made near the monastery, S. Theodosius said : " The tomb is now finished indeed, but who will be the first among us to occupy it ? " Whereupon a certain monk named Basil, falling upon his knees, prayed that this honour might be his, and within the space of about a month, without pain or disease, he passed away as a man who takes his rest in sleep. Yet for full forty days afterwards S. Theodosius, at matins and at the other hours, saw the dead monk still occupying his place in the choir. It was he alone who saw the monk, but others, especially one Aetius, heard his voice. Whereupon Theodosius prayed that all might see the apparition of Basil, and assuredly the eyes of all were opened so that they beheld him in his wonted place in their midst. When Aetius would joyfully have embraced the figure it vanished from his touch, saying the words : " Hold, Aetius. God be with you, my father and my brethren. But me shall ye see and hear no more."

It was the custom of S. Gregory, Bishop of Langres,[100] to rise from his bed at night, when everyone else was fast in repose, and going quietly into the church to spend several hours at his devotions. This was long unobserved, but it so happened that one night one of the brethren lay awake, and he observed the bishop on his way down the corridors. From curiosity he stole softly after him, and presently saw him enter the Baptistry, the door of which seemed to open to him of its own accord. For some time there was silence ; and then the voice of the bishop was heard chanting aloud the antiphon, when immediately afterwards many voices took up the psalm, and the singing, decani and cantori, continued for the space of three hours. " I, for my part," says S. Gregory of Tours, " think that the Saints, whose Relics were there venerated and preserved, revealed themselves to the blessed man, and hymned praises to God in company with him."

Examples of later date when under exceptional conditions dead persons have returned to life, are not infrequently to be found. S. Stanislaus the Martyr, Bishop of Cracow,[101] had bought for church purposes very ample estates from one Peter. This man died some few years afterwards, whereupon his heirs claimed the property. They had discovered that the bishop had taken no acquittance, and accordingly as he had no document to show in proof of his right, the courts ordered him to return the land to the plaintiffs. But the saint went to the tomb of the deceased, and having touched the body he bade it to arise and follow him. Peter instantly obeyed the summons, and this pale and ghastly figure accompanied the bishop into the King's Court. Whilst all trembled and were sore amazed Stanislaus said to the Judge : " Behold, my lord, here is Peter himself who sold me the estate. He has come even from the grave to vindicate the truth." In hollow accents the phantom or corpse confirmed the statement of the bishop in every particular, and fearful as they sat the judges reversed their former decision. When this had been done the figure seemed to fade away from their sight. The body had returned to the tomb, and here it lay decently composed, having yielded up his breath a second time.[102]

A not dissimilar incident is said to have occurred in the life of S. Antony of Padua, whose father was accused at Lisbon of having been privy to the death of a certain nobleman, even if he had not actually slain him, as was implied. The saint, having requested that the body of the murdered man should be brought into court, solemnly adjured him saying : " Is it true that my father in any way consented unto or contrived thy assassination ? " With a deep groan the body made reply : " In no wise is the accusation true. It is altogether false and framed of malice." Whereupon the magistrates convinced by this positive declaration set free the prisoner.[103]

On 9th March, 1463, S. Catherine of Bologna, a Poor Clare, died at the convent there, and so great was her reputation for sanctity that rather more than a fortnight after her burial, her body was disinterred and placed in the church upon an open bier for the veneration of all. The vast crowds who came were struck with the fact that her face retained a fresh and glowing colour, far more lively, indeed, than during her life. Amongst others who visited the remains was a little maid of eleven years old by name Leonora Poggi. As out of reverence she stood at some distance, it was noticed that the body not only opened wide its eyes, but made a sign with the hand, saying : "Leonora, come hither." The girl advanced trembling, but S. Catherine added : "Do not be afraid ; you will be a professed nun of this community, and all in the convent will love you. Nay, more, you shall be the guardian of this, my body." Eight years afterwards Leonora refused the hand of a wealthy suitor of high rank, and took the veil in the house of Corpus Domini. Here she lived for no less than five and fifty years, reaching an extreme old age with the love and respect of the whole sisterhood. She was indeed for half a century the guardian of the most holy relic of the body of S. Catherine.[104]

Immediately after the death of that great ecstatica, S. Maria Maddelena de Pazzi, who expired 25th May, 1607, the body of the holy Carmelite was honourably laid upon a catafalque in the nuns' church of S. Maria degli Angeli, whilst all Florence thronged thither to kiss her feet and touch were it but her raiment with medals and rosaries. Among the first who visited the convent and who were favoured by being allowed to venerate the body before the multitude won admittance was a certain pious Jesuit, Father Seripandi, and in his company chanced to be a young man of noble family whom he was striving to turn from the most dissolute courses. Whilst the good priest knelt in prayer the youth scanned intently the countenance of the Saint, but she frowning slightly gently turned away her face as if offended at his gaze. He stood abashed and dumbfounded, when Father Seripandi said : "Verily, my son, this Saint would not suffer your eyes to behold her, inasmuch as your life is so licentious and lewd." "It is true," cried the young man, "but God helping me I will amend my ways in every particular." He did so, and before long was distinguished by no ordinary piety and observance of religion.[105]

Similar cases of the resuscitation of the dead, corpses that arose from their graves, the movement of dead bodies, might indeed be almost indefinitely multiplied. And it is not at all impossible that as these extraordinary circumstances happened in the lives of the Saints, so they would be imitated and parodied by the demon, for, as Tertullian has said, "diabolus simia Dei."

It has been well remarked that man has always held the

dead in respect and in fear. The Christian Faith, moreover, has its seal upon the sanctity of death. Even from the very infancy of humanity the human intelligence, inspired by some shadow of the divine truth, has refused to believe that those whom death has taken are ought but absent for a while, parted but not for ever. It has been argued, and not without sound sense, that primitive man desired to keep the dead, to preserve the mortal shell, and what are the tomb, the cave of prehistoric man, the dolmen of the Gaulish chieftain, the pyramid of Pharaoh, but the final dwelling-place, the last home ? As for the actual corpse, this still had some being, it yet existed in the primitive idea. There can be nothing more horrible, no crime more repellent, than the profanation of the dead.

Dr. Épaulard says : " Les vraies et graves profanations, de veritables crimes, reconnaissent pour mobile les grandes forces impulsives qui font agir l'être humain. Je nommerai cela *vampirisme*, quitte à expliquer par la suite l'origine de cette appellation.

" L'instinct sexuel, le plus perturbateur de tous les instincts, doit être cité en première ligne comme l'un des facteurs les plus importants du vampirisme.

" La faim, besoin fondamental de tout être vivant, aboutit dans quelques circonstances à des actes du vampirisme. On pourait citer maint naufrage et maint siège célèbre ou la nécessité fit loi. Le cannibalisme du bien des tribus savages n'a pas d'autre origine que la faim à satisfaire.

Chez l'homme se développe énormément l'instinct de propriété. D'où le travail, d'où, chez certains, le vol. Nous venons de voir que la coutume de tous les temps fut d'orner les morts de ce qu'ils aimaient à posséder. Les voleurs n'ont pas hésité à dépouiller les cadavres. . . . Les parlements et les tribunaux eurent assez souvent à châtier des voleurs sacrilèges."[106]

Vampirism, then, in its extended and more modern sense, may be understood to mean any profanation of a dead body, and it must accordingly be briefly considered under this aspect. " On doit entendre par vampirisme toute profanation de cadavres, quel que soit son mode et quelle que soit son origine."

In France there have been many cases of sacriligious theft from the dead. In 1664 Jean Thomas was broken on the wheel for having disinterred the body of a woman and stolen

the jewels in which she was buried ; and well-nigh a century
before, in 1572, a grave-digger Jean Regnault was condemned
to the galleys for having stolen jewels and even winding-sheets
from corpses. In 1823, Pierre Renaud was sentenced at
Riom for having opened a tomb with intent to steal. Not
many years after, the police captured the band "de la rue
Mercadier," seven ruffians who made it their business to violate
graves and the vaults of rich families and who thus had stolen
gems and gold to the value of no less than 300,000 francs.
It is well-known that the notorious Ravachol forced open
the tomb of Madame de Rochetaillée in the expectation that
she had been buried in her jewels, but found nothing of this
kind, as the lady was merely wrapped in her shroud of lawn.

On 12th July, 1663, the Parliament of Paris heavily sentenced
the son of the sexton of the cemetery attached to Saint-Sulpice.
This young wretch was in the habit of exhuming corpses and
selling them to the doctors. In the seventeenth century the
Faculty of Paris was allowed one dead body a year, and the
famous physician, Mauriceau lay under grave suspicion of
having illegally procured bodies to dissect for his anatomical
studies.

In England the Resurrection Men added a new terror to
death. Even the bodies of the wealthy, when every precaution
had been taken, were hardly safe against the burgling riflers
of vault and tomb, whilst to the poor it was a monstrous
horror as they lay on their sick beds to know that their corpses
were ever in danger of being exhumed by ghouls, carted to
the dissection theatre, sold to 'prentice doctors to hack and
carve. In his novel, *The Mysteries of London*, G. W. M.
Reynolds gives a terrible, but perhaps not too highly coloured,
picture of these loathsome thefts. Irregular practitioners
and rival investigators in the anatomy schools were always
ready to buy without asking too many questions. Body-
snatching became a regular trade of wide activities. One of
the wretches who plied the business most successfully even
added a word to the English language. William Burke, of
the firm Burke and Hare, who was hanged 28th January,
1829,[107] began his career in November, 1827. This seems
to have commenced almost accidentally. Hare was the keeper
of a low lodging-house in an Edinburgh slum, and here died
an old soldier owing a considerable amount for his rent. With

the help of Burke, another of his guests, they carried the corpse to Dr. Robert Knox, of 10 Surgeon's Square, who promptly paid £7 10s. for it. The Scotch had the utmost horror of Resurrection Men, and bodies were not always easy to procure, although the vile Knox boasted that he could always get the goods he required. It is said that relations would take it in turns to stand guard over newly-dug graves, and the precaution was not unnecessary. Another lodger at Hare's fell ill, and it was decided that he should be disposed of in the same way. But he lingered, and so Burke smothered him with a pillow, Hare holding the victim's legs. Dr. Knox paid £10 for the remains. Since money is so quickly earned they do not hesitate to supply the wares. A friendless beggar woman ; her grandson, a dumb-mute ; a sick Englishman ; a prostitute named Mary Paterson, and many more were enticed to the lodgings and murdered. Quite callously Burke confessed his method. He used to lie on the body while Hare held nose and mouth ; "in a very few minutes the victims would make no resistance, but would convulse and make a rumbling noise in their bellies for some time. After they had ceased crying and making resistance we let them die by themselves." Dr. Knox contracted that he would pay £10 in winter and £8 in summer for every corpse produced. At last the whole foul business comes to light.

> Up the close and down the stair,
> But and ben with Burke and Hare,
> Burke's the butcher, Hare's the thief,
> Knox the boy that buys the beef.

So sang the street urchins. Burke confessed, and was hanged. Hare turned King's evidence, but it would seem that was hardly needed, for the suspicion which connected these ruffians with the numerous disappearances was overwhelming from the first, and soon became certainty. It was a grave scandal that both the villains and their paramours, together with Dr. Knox, who, in spite of his denials, undoubtedly was well aware of the whole circumstances, were not all five sent to the gallows. It is true that the mob endeavoured to catch them and would have torn them to pieces. To the mob they should have been duly thrown. That they escaped by some legal quibble or flaw speaks ill indeed for the age.

That species of Vampirism known as Necrophagy or Necrophagism, which is Cannibalism, is very often connected with
the religious rites of savage people and also finds a place in
the sabbat of the witches. Sir Spenser St. John, in his description of Haiti, gives curious details of the Voodoo cult when
cannibalism mingles with the crudest debauchery. Among
the Kwakiutl Indians of British Columbia the cannibals
(*Hamatsas*) are the most powerful of all the Secret Societies.
They tear corpses asunder and devour them, bite pieces out
of living people, and formerly they ate slaves who had
been killed for their banquet.[108] The Haida Indians of the
Queen Charlotte Islands practise a very similar religion of
necrophagy.[109] Among the ancient Mexicans the body of the
youth whom they sacrificed in the character of the god Tetz-
catlipoca was chopped up into small pieces and distributed
amongst the priests and nobles as a sacred food.[110] In Australia
the Bibinga tribe cut up the bodies of the dead and eat them
in order to secure the reincarnation of the deceased. The
same ceremony was observed by the Arunta.[111] Casper,
Vierteljahrschrift, viii (p. 163) mentions the case of an idiot
who killed and ate a baby in order to impart to himself
the vitality of the child. It should be remarked that necrophagy enters very largely into the passions of the werewolf,
and there are innumerable examples of lycanthropists who
have devoured human flesh, and slain men to feed upon their
bodies. Boguet recounts that in the year 1538 four persons
charged with sorcery, Jacques Bocquet, Claude Jamprost,
Clauda Jamguillaume and Thievenne Paget, confessed that
they had transformed themselves into wolves and in this shape
had killed and eaten several children. Françoise Secretain,
Pierre Gandillon and George Gandillon also confessed that they
had assumed the form of wolves and caught several children
whom they had stripped naked and then devoured. The
children's clothes were found without rent or tear in the fields,
" tellement qu'il sembloit bien que ce fust vne personne, qui
les leur eut deuestus."[112]

A remarkable instance of necrophagy which caused a great
noise in the eighteenth century is said to have given de Sade
a model for Minski, " l'ermite des Appenins," in *Juliette*, iii
(p. 313). The horrible abode of this Muscovite giant is amply
described. The tables and chairs are made of human bones,

and the rooms are hung with skeletons. This monster was suggested by Blaise Ferrage, or Seyé, who in 1779 and 1780 lived in the Pyrenees, and captured men and women whom he devoured.[113]

One of the most terrible and extraordinary cases of cannibalism was that of Sawney Beane, the son of peasants in East Lothian, who was born in a village at no great distance from Edinburgh towards the close of the fourteenth century. He and a girl in the same district wandered away in company, and took up their abode in a cave on the coast of Galloway. It is said this cavern extended nearly a mile under the sea. Here they lived by robbing travellers, and carrying off their bodies to their lair they cooked and ate them. Eight sons and six daughters they gendered, and the whole tribe used to set forth upon marauding expeditions, sometimes attacking as many as five and six persons travelling in company. Grandchildren were born to this savage, and it is said that for more than five and twenty years these cannibals killed men on the highway and dragging the prey to their lair fed upon human flesh. Suspicion was often aroused, and even panic ensued, but so skilfully had nature concealed the opening to the cave that it was long ere the gang could be traced and captured. The whole family were put to death amid the most horrible torments in the year 1435 at Edinburgh. It is probable that in the first place Beane and his female companion were driven to necrophagy by starvation, and the horrid craving for human flesh once tasted became a mad passion. The children born into such conditions would be cannibalistic as a matter of course.

Sawney Beane was made the subject of a romance—*Sawney Beane, the Man-eater of Midlothian*, by Thomas Preskett Prest, who, between the years 1840 and 1860 was the most famous and most popular purveyor of the " shocker " which circulated in immense numbers. Prest's greatest success was *Sweeney Todd*, a character who was once supposed actually to have lived, but who is almost certainly fiction. It will be remembered that Todd's victims disappeared through a revolving trap-door into the cellars of his house. Their bodies, when stripped and rifled, were handed over to be used by Mrs. Lovett, who resided next door and kept a pie-shop which was greatly frequented. Once it so happened that the supply ran short for a while, as Todd for some reason was unable to dispatch his customers, and mutton was actually used in the pies. Complaints were made that the quality of the pies had deteriorated, the meat had lost its usual succulence and flavour.

In a manuscript, which has never been printed,[114] written about 1625 by the brother of Henry Percy, ninth Earl of Northumberland,[115] George Percy, who was twice Deputy-Governor of Virginia, and entitled *A Trewe Relatyon of the Proceedings and Occurrences of Momente which have Happened in Virginia from . . . 1609 untill 1612*, details are given of the terrible conditions under which the early colonists had to live. Starvation sometimes faced them, and not only were corpses then dug out of graves and eaten, but " one of our colony murdered his wife . . . and salted her for his food, the same not being discovered before he had eaten part thereof, for which cruel and inhuman fact I adjudged him to be executed, the acknowledgment of the deed being enforced from him by torture, having hung by the thumbs, with weights at his feet a quarter of an hour before he would confess the same."

As is often recorded in history during long and terrible sieges, starvation has driven the wretched citizens of a beleagured town to devour human flesh. An example of this may be found in the Bible, which tells us of the horrors when Jerusalem was encompassed by Benadad of Syria during the reign of King Joram (B.C. 892), *Kings IV (A.V. Kings II)*, vi, 24-30 : " Congregauit Benadad rex Syriae, uniuersum exercitum suum, et ascendit, et obsidebat Samariam. Factaque est fames magna in Samaria : et tamdiu obsessa est, donec uenundaretur caput asini octoginta argenteis, et quarta pars cabi stercoris columbarum quinque argenteis. Cumque rex Israel transiret per murum, mulier quaedam exclamauit ad eum ; dicens : Salua me domine mi rex. Qui ait : Non te saluat Dominus : unde te possum saluare ? de area, uel de torculari ? Dixitque ad cam rex : Quid tibi uis ? Quae respondit : Mulier ista dixit mihi : Da filium tuum, ut comedamus eum hodie, et filium meum comedemus cras. Coximus ergo filium meum, et comedimus. Dixique ei die altera : Da filium tuum ut comedamus eum. Quae abscondit filium suum. Quod cum audisset rex, scidit uestimenta sua, et transibat per murum. Uiditque omnis populus cilicium, quo uestitus erat ad carnem intrinsecus."

(Benadad king of Syria gathered together all his army, and went up, and besieged Samaria. And there was a great famine in Samaria ; and so long did the siege continue, till the head of an ass was sold for fourscore pieces of silver, and the fourth part of a cabe of pigeon's dung, for five pieces of silver. And as the king of Israel was passing by the wall, a certain woman cried out to him, saying : Save me, my lord O king. And he said : If the Lord doth not save thee how can I save thee ? Out of the barnfloor, or out of the winepress ? And the king said to her : What aileth thee ? And she answered : This woman said to me : give thy son, that we may eat him to-day, and we will eat my son to-morrow. So we boiled my son, and ate him. And I said to her on the next day : Give thy son that we may eat him. And she hath hid her son. When the king heard this, he rent his garments, and passed by upon the wall. And all the people saw the hair-cloth which he wore within next to his flesh.)

W. A. F. Browne, sometime Commissioner for Lunacy in Scotland, has a very valuable paper *Necrophilism*, which was read at the Quarterly Meeting of the Medico-Psychological Association, Glasgow, 21st May, 1874. He points out that in Ireland, under the savagery of Queen Elizabeth, when the rich pastures were burned into a wilderness, " the miserable poor . . . out of every corner of the woods and glens came creeping forth upon thin hands, for their legs could not bear them, they looked like anatomes of death ; they spoke like ghosts crying out of their graves ; they did eat the dead carrions ; happy when they could find them ; yea, they did eat one another soon after ; insomuch as the very carcasses they spared not to scrape out of their very graves." During the Siege of Jerusalem by Titus, during the Plague in Italy in 450, cannibalism was rife. During a famine in France in the eleventh century " human flesh was openly exposed for sale in the market-place of Tournus." A man had built a hut in the forest of Mâcon and here he murdered all whom he could entice within his doors, afterwards roasting the bodies and feeding on them. Browne says that there came under his notice in the West Indies two females who frequented graveyards at night. It does not appear that they exhumed bodies but they used to sleep among the tombs, and these dark wanderings, as might be expected, thoroughly scared the native population. He also adds : "The abodes of the dead have been visited, violated ; the exhumed corpses, or parts of them, have been kissed, caressed, or appropriated, and carried to the homes of the ravisher, although belonging to total strangers." He also says : "I was much struck, when frequenting the Parisian asylums as a student, with the numbers of anæmic, dejected females who obtruded upon me the piteous confession that they had eaten human flesh, devoured corpses, that they were vampires, etc." Dr. Legrande du Saulle says that in many members of a Scottish family there appeared connate necrophagism.[116] Prochaska mentions a woman of Milan also tempted children to her house and ate them at her leisure. A girl of fourteen, belonging to Puy de Drôme, is described as having displayed on all occasions an extraordinary avidity for human blood and as sucking greedily recently inflicted wounds. The brigand Gaetano Mammone, who long terrorized South Italy, was accustomed as a regular habit to drain with his lips the blood of his unhappy captives.[117] In another instance a man who dwelt apart in a cave in the South of France seized a girl of twelve years old, strangled her, violated the corpse, and then inflicting deep gashes upon it with a knife drank the blood and devoured the flesh. He kept the remains in his retreat but subsequently interred them. He was judged insane.[118]

In the sixteenth century there dwelt in Hungary a terrible ogress, the Countess Elisabeth Ba'thory, who for her necro-sadistic abominations was known as "la comtesse hongroise sanguinaire." The comte de Charolais (1700-1760), "de lugubre mémoire," loved nothing better than to mingle murder with his debauches, and many of the darkest scenes in *Juliette* but reproduce the orgies he shared with his elder brother, the Duke of Burgundy.

Dr. Lacassagne, in his study *Vacher l'éventreur et les crimes sadiques*, Lyon-Paris, 1899, has collected many cases of necro-sadism. Joseph Vacher, who was born at Beaufort (Isère), 16th November, 1869, was guilty of a series of crimes which lasted from May, 1894, to August, 1897. He was tramping during those years up and down France, immediately after his release as cured from an asylum where he had been confined for attempting to rape a young servant who refused his hand in marriage. Vacher's first crime seems to have been committed

19th May, 1894, when in a lonely place he killed a working girl of twenty-one. He strangled her and then violated the body. On 20th November of the same year he throttled a farmer's daughter aged sixteen at Vidauban (Var), violated the body and mutilated it with his knife. In the same way on 1st September, 1895 at Bénonces (Ain), he killed a lad of sixteen, Victor Portalier, and slashed open the stomach. Three weeks later he strangled a shepherd boy of fourteen, Pierre Massot-Pellet, and mutilated the body. In all some eleven murders with violation were traced to Vacher, the last being that of a shepherd lad aged thirteen, Pierre Laurent, at Courzieu (Rhône), 18th June, 1897. The body was indescribably hacked and bitten. Probably this maniac was guilty of many more assaults which did not come to light.

In England the sensation caused by the mysterious mutilations by Jack the Ripper will not easily be forgotten. The first body was found at Whitechapel, 1st December, 1887 ; the second, which had thirty-nine wounds, 7th August, 1888. On 31st of the same month a woman's corpse was found horribly mutilated ; 8th September a fourth body bearing the same marks, a fifth on 30th September ; a sixth on 9th November. On the 1st June, 1889, human remains were dredged from the Thames ; 17th July a body still warm was discovered in a Whitechapel slum ; on 10th September of the same year the last body.

The classic instance of " vampirism," Serjeant Bertrand, will be fully dealt with in a later chapter.

Andréas Bickel killed women after having both raped and mutilated them in an indescribable manner. Dr. Épaulard quoting from Feuerbach, *Ahtenmœsigen Darstellung merk-würdzer Verbrechen* says that Bichel declared : " Je puis dire qu'en ouvrant la poitrine, j'étais tellement excité que je tress-aillais et que j'aurais voulu trancher un morceau de chair pour le manger." In the year 1825 a vine-dresser named Léger, a stalwart fellow of four and twenty, left his home to find work. He wandered about the woods for a week or more, and was then seized with a terrible craving to eat human flesh. " Il rencontre une petite fille de douze ans, la viole, lui déchire les organes génitaux, lui arrache le coeur, le mange et boit son sang, puis enterre le cadavre. Arrêté peu après, il fait tranquill-ement l'aveu de son crime, est condamné et executé."[119]

A famous case was that of Vincenzo Verzeni,[120] a necrophagist and necrosadist, who was born at Bottanuco of an ailing and impoverished stock and arrested in 1872 for the following crimes : an attempt to strangle his cousin Marianna, a girl of twelve years old ; a similar attempt to throttle Signora Aruffi ; aged twenty-seven ; a similar attempt upon Signora Gala ; the murder of Giovanna Motta (les viscères et les parties génitales sont arrachées du corps, les cuisses lacérées, un mollet detaché. Le cadavre est nu); the murder and mutilation of Signora Frizoni, aged twenty-eight ; an attempt to strangle his cousin Maria Previtali, aged nineteen. Whilst he was committing these crimes " pour prolonger le plaisir, il mutila ses victimes, leur suça le sang, et détacha même des lambeaux pour les manger."

Those vampirish atrocities which are urged by sexual mania are generally classified as necrophilia and necrosadism— " La nécrophilie est la profanation qui tend à toute union sexuelle avec le cadavre : coït normal ou sodomique, masturbation, etc. Le nécrosadisme est la mutilation des cadavres destinée à provoquer un éréthisme génital. Le nécrosadisme diffère du sadisme en ce qu'il ne recherche pas la douleur, mais la simple destruction d'un corps humain. Les nécrosadisme aboutit parfois à des actes de cannibalisme qui peuvent prendre le nom de nécrophagie . . . . Nécrophiles et nécrosadiques sont la plupart du temps des dégénéres impulsifs on debiles mentaux, ce que prouvent leur vie antérieure et leurs tares héréditaires. Ce sont en outre bien souvent des hommes auxquels un contact professionel avec le cadavre a fait perdre toute répugnance (fossoyeurs, prêtres, étudiants en médicine)." The word *nécrophilie* seems, to have been first suggested by a Belgian alienist of the nineteenth century, Dr. Guislain ; *nécrosadisme* is used by Dr. Épaulard.

Necrophilia was not unknown in ancient Egypt, and was carefully provided against as Herodotus tells us, Book II, lxxxix : Τὰςδε γυναῖκας τῶν ἐπιφάνεων ἀνδρῶν, ἐπεὰν τελευτήσωσι, οὐ παραντίκα διδοῦσι ταριχεύειν, οὐδὶ ὅσαι ἂν ἔωσι εὐειδέες κάρτα καὶ λόγου πλεῦνος γυναῖκες· ἀλλ'ἐπεὰν τριταῖαι ἢ τεταρταῖαι γένωνται, οὕτω παραδιδοῦσι τοῖσι ταριχεύουσι. τοῦτο δε ποιεῦσι οὕτω τοῦδε εἵνεκεν, ἵνα μὴ σφι οἱ ταριχευταὶ μίσγωνται τῆσι γυναιξί· λαμφθῆναι γαρ τινὰ φασὶ μισγόμενον νεκρῷ προσφάτῳ γυναικός κατειπεῖν δὲ τὸν ὁμότεχνον. " Wives of noblemen and women of great beauty and quality are not given over at once to the embalmers ; but only after they have been dead three or four days ; and this is done in order that the embalmers may not have carnal connexion with the corpse. For it is said that one was discovered in the act of having intercourse with a fair woman newly dead, and was denounced by his fellow-workman."

It was said that after Periander, tyrant of Corinth, had slain his wife he entered her bed as a husband. In the *Praxis Rerum Criminalium* of Damhouder, at the end of the sixteenth century we have : " Casu incidit in memoriam execrandus ille libidinis ardor, quo quidam feminam cognoscunt mortuam."

A very large number of cases of necrophilia has been collected by various authorities, of which it will suffice to give but a few examples. "En 1787, près de Dijon, à Cîteaux, un mien aïeul, qui était médecin de cette célèbre abbaye, sortait un jour du convent pour aller voir, dans une cabane située au milieu des bois, la femme d'un bûcheron que la veille il avait trouvée mourante. Le mari, occupé à de rudes travaux, loin de sa cabane, se trouvait forcé d'abandonner sa femme qui n'avait ni enfants, ni parents ni voisins autour d'elle. En ouvrant la porte du logis, mon grand-père fut frappé d'un spectacle monstrueux. Un moine quêteur accomplissait l'acte du coït sur le corps de la femme qui n'était plus qu'un cadavre."[121]

In 1849 the following case was reported : " Il venait de mourir une jeune personne de seize ans qui appartenait a une des premières familles de la ville. Une partie de la nuit s'était écoulée lorsqu'on entendit dans la chambre de la morte le bruit d'un meuble qui tombait. La mère, dont l'appartement était voisin, s'empressa d'accourir. En entrant, elle apperçut un homme qui s'échappait en chemise du lit de sa fille. Son effroi lui fit pousser de grands cris qui réunirent autour d'elle toutes les personnes de la maison. On saisit l'inconnu qui ne répondait que confusément aux questions qu'on lui posait. La première pensée fut que c'était un voleur, mais son habillement, certains signes dirigèrent les recherches d'un autre côté et l'on reconnut bientôt que la jeune fille avait été déflorée et polluée plusieurs fois. L'instruction apprit que la garde avait été gagnée à prix d'argent : et bientôt d'autres révélations prouvèrent que ce malheureux, qui avait reçu une éducation distinguée, jouissait d'une très grande aisance et était lui—même d'une bonne famille n'en était pas à son coup d'essai. Les débats montrèrent qu'il s'était glissé un assez grand nombre de fois dans le lit de jeunes filles mortes et s'y était livré à sa détestable passion."[122]

In 1857 the case of Alexandre Siméon, a necrophilist who was always feeble-minded—he was born in 1829, a foundling—and who eventually became wholly insane, attracted considerable attention. His habits were of the most revolting nature, and " Siméon, trompant la surveillance, s'introduisait dans la salle de morts quand il savait que le corps d'une femme venait d'y être déposé. Là, il se livrait aux plus indignes profanations. Il se vanta publiquement de ces faits."[123]

Dr. Morel, *Gazette hebdomadaire de médicine et de chirurgie*, 13th March, 1857, relates : " Un acte semblable à celui de Siméon a été commis à la suite d'un pari monstrueux, par un élève d'une école secondaire de médicine, en présence de ses camarades. Il est bon d'ajouter que cet individu, quelques années plus tard, est mort aliéné."

Dr. Moreau, of Tours, in his famous study *Aberrations du sens génésique*, 1880, quoting from the *Evénement*, 26th April, 1875, relates an extraordinary case at Paris in which the culprit, L——, was a married man and the father of six children. The wife of a neighbour having died, L—— undertook to watch in the death chamber, whilst the family were arranging the details of the interment. " Alors une idée incompréhensible, hors nature, passa par l'esprit du veilleur de la morte. Il souffla les bougies allumées près du lit, et ce cadavre, glacé, raidi, déjà au décomposition fut le proie de ce vampire sans nom." The profanation was almost immediately discovered owing to the disorder of the bed and other signs. L—— fled, but at the instance of Dr. Pousson and the husband, who was half mad with grief and rage, he was arrested and inquiry made. A quel délire a-t-il obéi ?

In *Les causes criminelles et mondaines*, 1886, Albert Bataille gives an account of Henri Blot, " un assez joli garçon de vingt-six ans, à figure un peu blême. Ses cheveux sont ramenés sur le front, à la chien. Il porte à la lèvre supérieure une fine moustache soigneusement effilée. Ses yeux, profondement noirs, enfoncés dans l'orbite, sont clignotants. Il a quelque chose de félin dans l'ensemble de la physionomie ; quelque chosi aussi de l'oiseau de nuit." " Le 25 mars, 1886, dans la soirée, entre 11 heures et minuit Blot escalade une petite porte donnant dans le cimetière Saint-Ouen, se dirige vers la fosse commune, enlève la cloison qui retient la terre sur la dernierè bière de la rangée. Une croix piquée au-dessus de la fosse lui apprend que le cercueil est le corps d'une jeune femme de dix-huit ans, Fernande Méry, dite Carmanio, figurante de théâtre, enterrée la veille.

" Il déplace la bière, l'ouvre, retire le corps de la jeune fille qu'il emporte à l'extremité de la tranchée, sur le remblai. Là, il pose, par précaution, ses genoux sur des feuilles de papier blanc enlevées à des bouquets et pratique le coït sur le cadavre. Ensuite, il s'endort probablement, et ne se réveille que pour sortir du cimitière assez à temps pour ne pas être vu, mais trop tard pour replacer le corps." A curious point is that when the profanation was discovered a man named Duhamel wrote a letter avowing that he had committed the violation. He was confined at Mazas, since he gave such full details that he was truly believed to have been guilty. Whilst under the observation of two doctors he proved to be of unsound mind. On 12th June Blot again violated a tomb, he fell asleep, was discovered and arrested. On 27th August, when brought to trial, and the judge expressed his horror of such acts, he replied callously : " Que voulez-vous, chacun a ses passions. Moi le cadavre, c'est la mienne ! " Dr. Motet was unable to certify him insane, and he was sentenced to two years' imprisonment.

Dr. Tiberius of Athens communicated the following case. A young medical student, some seven years ago, made his way at night into the mortuary chapel where lay the body of a beautiful actress who had just died, and for whom he had long nourished an insensate passion. Covering the cold clay with passionate kisses he violated the corpse of his inamorata. It should be remarked that the body had been dressed in the richest costume and covered with jewels, as it was to be carried thus in the funeral procession.

Necrophilia is said to be common in certain Eastern countries. " En Turquie, dans les endroits où les cimetières sont mal gardés, on a souvent vu, paraît-il d'abjects individus, la lie du peuple, contenter sur des cadavres qu'ils exhumaient leurs désirs sexuels."

The case of Victor Ardisson, who was called by the papers "le vampire du Muy," and who was arrested in 1901 upon multiplied charges of the exhumation and violation of dead bodies, was studied in great detail by Dr. Épaulard, who summed up his verdict in these words : " Ardisson est un débile mental inconscient des actes qu'il accomplit. Il a violé des cadavres parce que, fossoyeur, il lui était facile de se procurer des apparences de femme sous forme de cadavres auxquels il prêtait une sorte d'existence."[124]

The motive of the Leopold and Loeb case which occurred at Chicago, and which was so widely discussed throughout America in 1924 was necrosadism. Having killed the unfortunate boy the two wretched degenerates violated the body. It may not untruly be said that this morbid crime sprang in the first place from a false philosophy. With ample money at their command, their minds rotted with the backwash of Freud, these two young supermen conceived themselves above all laws. They had exhausted every erotic emotion, and sought something new to thrill their jaded nerves. These vilenesses and abominations would be ended by a return to the true philosophy, the lore of the Schoolmen and Doctors.

There are not unknown—in fact there are not uncommon— amazing cases of what may be called " mental necrophilia," a morbid manifestation for which suitable provision is made in the more expensive and select houses of accomodation.

In his study *La Corruption Fin-de-Siècle* Léo Taxil remarks : "Une passion sadiste des plus effrayantes est celle des détraqués auxquels on a donné le nom de ' vampire.' Ces insensés veulent violer des cadavres. Cette dépravation du sens génésique, dit le docteur Paul Moreau de Tours constitue le degré le plus extrême des déviations de l'appetit vénérien." He also speaks of " chambres funèbres " as being not uncommon in certain brothels. " D'ordinaire, on dispose, dans une pièce de l'établissement des tentures noires, un lit mortuaire, en un mot, tout un appareil lugubre. Mais l'un des principaux lupanars de Paris a, en permanence, une chambre spéciale, destinée aux clients qui désirent tâter du vampirisme.

" Les murs de la chambre sout tendus de satin noir, parsemi de larmes d'argent. Au milieu est un catafalque, très riche. Une femme, paraissant inerte, est là, couchée dans un cercueil découvert, la tête reposant sur un coussin de velours. Tout autour, de longs cierges, plantés dans de grandes chandeliers d'argent. Aux quatre coins de la pièce, des urnes funéraires et des cassolettes, brûlant, avec des parfums, un mélange d'alcool et de sel gris, dont les flammes blafardes, qui éclairent le catafalque, donnent à la chair de la pseudo-morte la couleur cadavérique.

" Le fou luxurieux, qui a payé dix louis pour cette séance, est introduit. Il y a un prie-dieu où'il s' agenouille. Un harmonium, placé dans un cabinet voisin, joue le *Dies irae* ou le *De Profundis*. Alors, aux accords de cette musique de funérailles le vampire se rue sur la fille qui simule la défunte et qui a ordre de ne pas faire un mouvement, quoiqu'il advienne."

It might not unreasonably be thought that the catafalque, the bier, the black pall, would arouse solemn thoughts and kill desire, but on the contrary this funeral pomp and the trappings of the dead are considered in certain circles the most elegant titillation, the most potent and approved of genteel aphrodisiacs.

NOTES. CHAPTER I.

[1] Πορευεσθε ἀπ'ἐμ̂ου, κατηραμένοι, εἰς τὸ πῦρ τὸ αἰώνιον τὸ ἡτοιμασμένον τῷ διαβόλῳ καὶ τοῖς ἀγγέλοις αὐτοῦ.   Discedite a me maledicti in ignem aeternum, qui paratus est diabolo, et angelis eius.

[2] See Sinistrari, *De Daemonialitate,* xxiv (English translation by the present writer, *Demoniality,* Fortune Press, 1927, pp. 11-12), for the coitus of witches with the demon, who assumes the corpse of a human being.

[3] *Æneid,* II, 794.   Vergil repeats this line *Æneid,* VI, 702.

[4] *S. Luke,* xxiv, 39.

[5] P. W. Hofmayr, " Religion der Schilluk," *Anthropos* (*Ephemeris Internationalis Ethnologica et Linguistica*), vi (1911), pp. 120-125.

[6] *Journal of the Anthropological Institute ;* Rev. J. Roscoe, " Notes on the Manners and Customs of the Baganda," xxxi (1901), p. 130 ; xxxii (1902), p. 46 ; and *The Baganda,* London, 1911.

[7] Hermann Rehse, *Kiziba, Land und Leute,* Stuttgart, 1910.

[8] C. Gouldsbury and H. Sheane, *The Great Plateau of Northern Rhodesia,* London, 1911, pp. 80, *seq.*

[9] Missionar J. Irle, *Die Herero, ein Beitrag zur Landes-Volks-und Missionskunde,* Gütersloh, 1906, p. 75.

[10] *South African Folk-lore Journal,* Cape Town, 1879, I, " Some Customs_of the Ovaherero," pp. 64, *sqq.*

[11] Hermann Tönjes, *Ovamboland, Land, Leute, Mission,* Berlin, 1911, pp. 193-197.

[12] *Another Grey Ghost Book.*

[13] Rev. Henry Callaway, *The Religious System of the Amazulu,* Natal, Springvale, etc., 1868-1870, Part II, pp. 144-146.

[14] The Niel Dinka, a tribe in the valley of the White Nile, regard this supreme being, Dengdit, as their ancestor, and accordingly sacrifice is offered to him at shrines builded in his honour.

[15] *The Baganda*, London, 1911, p. 271.

[16] A. Kropf, " Die religiösen Anschauungen der Kaffern," *Verhandlungen der Berliner Gesellschaft für Anthropologie, Ethnologie und Urgeschichte*, 1888, p. 46.

[17] R. H. Nassau, *Fetichism in West Africa*, London, 1904.

[18] Père Guis, " Les *Nepis* ou Sorciers," *Missions Catholiques*, xxxvi (1904), p. 370. And M. J. Erdweg, " Die Bewohner der Insul Tumleo, Berlinhafen, Deutsch-Neu-Guinea," *Mittheilungen du Anthropologischen Gesellschaft in Wien*, xxxii (1902), p. 287.

[19] Professor J. J. M. de Groot, *Religious System of China*, Leyden, 1892.

[20] J. Welhausen, *Reste arabischen Heidentumes*, Berlin, 1887.

[21] Servius on the *Æneid*, V, 77-79 :

> Hic duo rite mero libans carchesia Baccho
> Fundit humi, duo lacte nouo, duo sanguine sacro,
> Purpureosque iacit flores . . .

Also the same commentator on *Æneid*, III, 66-68 :

> Inferimus tepido spumantia cymbia lacte
> Sanguinis et sacri pateras, animamque sepulcro
> Condimus et magna supremum ucce ciemus.

[22] Cf. *Genesis*, ix, 4, and 1 *Kings* (A.V. 1 *Samuel*), xiv, 33.

[23] Both *Douai* and *A.V.*

[24] X, 487, *seq.*, and XI. This passage is dealt with in detail in chapter III.

[25] *Jeremias*, xvi, 6.

[26] *Jeremias*, xli, 5.

[27] Pierre de Labriolle, *Histoire de la Littérature Latine Chrétienne*, Paris, 1920, Tableau No. 7 (43).

[28] Migne *Patrologia Latina*, vol. xxiv, column 782.

[29] Cf. the grief of Anna at the death of Queen Dido, *Æneid*, IV, 673 :

> unguibus ora soror fœdans et pectora pugnis.

So Homer describes Briseis at the funeral of Patroelus, *Iliad*, xxiii, 284-5.

> Ἀμφ᾽ αὐτῷ χυμένη, λίγ᾽ ἐκώκυε, χερσὶ δ᾽ ἄμυσσε
> Στήθεάτ᾽, ἠδ᾽ ἁπαλὴν δειρὴν, ἰδὶ καλὰ πρόσωπα.

[30] *De Getarum (Gothorum) Origine et Rebus Gestis*, ed. Theodor Mommsen, Berlin, 1882, p. 124.

[31] A famous example is that of Innocent VIII, ob. 25th July, 1492. Infessura says that whilst the Pope lay dying a Hebrew physician proposed to reinvigorate him by the transfusion of young blood. Three boys in the prime of health and strength were selected for the experiment. Each lad received one ducat. " Et paulo post mortui sunt ; ludæus quidem aufugit, et Papa non sanatus est."

[32] F. Bonney, " On some Customs of the Aborigines of the River Darling, New South Wales." *Journal of the Anthropological Institute*, xiii (1884), p. 132.

[33] There can be no doubt that the clipping of the hair was also considered to supply the deceased with energy and vigour. The hair was regarded by many nations as the seat of strength. Cf. the history of Samson and Delilah.

[34] *Etymologie Wörterbuch des Slav. spr.*

[35] Æschylus, *Septom contra Thebas*, 820-821 :

> βασιλέοιν δ᾽ ὁμοσπόροιν
> πέπωκεν αἱμα γαῖ᾽ ὑπ᾽ ἀλλήλων φόνῳ.

[36] Aristophanes, *Uespae*, 1502 : ἀλλ᾽ οὑτός γε καταποθήσεται.

[37] l. 477.

[38] Yet in early geographical notions the Ocean, ὠκεανός, is itself ποταμός, but Homer regards Oceanus as a great River which compasses the earth's disc, returning into itself, ἀψόρροος, and to Ocean are given the epithets of a river. This idea was retained in later myths where Ocean often has the attributes of a river-god. Cf. Euripides, *Orestes*, 1377-79 :

> πόντου, ᾽Ωκεανος ὄν
> ταυρόκρανος ἀγκάλαις ἐλίσ—
> σων κυκλοῦ χθόνα.

[39] Abbott, *Macedonian Folklore*, p. 217.

[40] *Geographica*, ed. Casaubon, p. 19.

[41] Apud Schweighauser, *Epictetæ Philosophiæ Monumenta*, vol. III, and also in Coraes, Πάρεργα Ἑλλην. βιβλιοθ, vol. VIII.

[42] In MSS. sometimes μορμολύκιον.

[43] 77, E. *Platonis Opera*, " recognouit Ioannes Buenet," vol. I.

[44] Bernard Schmidt, *Das Volksleben der Neugriechen*, p. 159.

[45] Lawson, *Modern Greek Folklore*, p. 378.

[46] Ralston, *Songs of the Russian People*, p. 409.

[47] It may be remarked that the story of the murdered Pelops who was served up at a banquet to the gods by his father Tantalus when Demeter, absorbed with grief for Persephone, ate the shoulder has its locale at Elis. As soon as the lad was restored to life the goddess supplied the missing shoulder with one of ivory, and this relic was shown at Elis even in historical times as Pliny tells us : " Et Elide solebat ostendi Pelopis costa, quam eburncam adfirmabant." *Historia Naturalis*, xxviii, 4, vij, ed. Gabriel Brotier, Barbou, 1779, vol. V, p. 112. The reading " costa " is just possible in this passage, as meaning the shoulder and side. But Brotier has a gloss : " *Pelopsis costa.* Corruptè. In MSS. Reg. *Pelopis ostiliam :* in editione principe, *Pelopis hasta.* Emendauere recentiores, *Pelopis costa.* Legendum potius, *Pelopis scapula.* Est enim teste Uergilio, Georg. III, 7.

Humero Pelops insignis eburno."

One might suggest that in the editio princeps *hasta* was pro pene ; trans-latum a re militari, quod frequentissimum. Ausonius, *Cento nuptialis*, 117, has : " Intorquet summis adnixus uiribus hastam." Joannes Secundus in his *Epithalamium* writes :

Huc, illuc agilis feratur hasta,
Quam crebro furibunda uerset ictu
Non Martis soror, ast amica Martis
Semper laeta nouo cruore Cypris.

[48] This belief seems mainly confined to Elis. Curtius Wachsmutt, *Das alte Griechenland im Neuen*, p. 117.

[49] *Vampyrus* is not recorded by Du Cange ; nor by Forcellini, ed. Furlanetto and De-Vit, 1871 ; nor in the *Petit Supplement* by Schmidt, 1906.

[50] 1586-1669.

[51] *Relation de ce qui s'est passé de plus remarquable a Sant-Erini Isle de l'Archipel, depuis l'établissement des Peres de la compagnie de Jesus en icelle,* Paris, MDCLVII.

[52] Imprimatur, *Hic Liber cui Titulus*, The Present State, &c. *Car. Trumball Rev. in Christo Pat. ac Dom. Gul. Archiep. Cant. a Sac. Dom.* Ex Æd. Lamb, 8 Feb. 167⅘. Term Catalogues ; Easter (May), 1629.

[53] Rohr also wrote with John Henry Rumpel, *De Spiritibus in fodinis apparentibus, seu de Uirunculis metallicis,* the first edition of which seems to be 4to, 1668, but I have only seen those of Leipzig, 1672 and re-issue 1677.

[54] 8vo, 1739. He also wrote *Philosophicae et Christianae Cogitationes de Uampiris,* 1739.

[55] I have used the " Nouvelle édition revûe, corrigée and augmentée par l'Auteur." 2 vols., Paris, Chez Debure l'aîné, 1751.

[56] Vol. II, p. 2.

[57] Life by Gradius in Mai, *Bibliotheca Noua Patrum*, vi, Rome, 1853 ; see also Legrand's *Bibliographie hellénique du xvii siècle*, Paris, 1893.

[58] " Scuto circumdabit te ueritas eius : non timebis a timore nocturno. A sagitta uolante in die, a negotio perambulante in tenebris: ab incursu, et daemonio meridiano." *Psalm* xc.

[59] Of uncertain authorship.

[60] In Greece at the present day a funeral usually concludes with a distribu-tion of baked-meats and wine to the company assembled by the grave, and a share both of food and of drink is set aside for the dead. Frequently this is more than a light collation, and the cemetery is the scene of many a substantial meal. These repasts are generally known as μακαρία, whilst the supper to relatives and friends which follows at home in the evening is the παρηγορία " comforting," or τὸ ζεστόν, " the warming."

[61] The discourse on the temptation of Our Lord. *Homilia xvi in Evangelium.*

[62] Such apparitions are frequent. See Faber's *The Foot of the Cross : or, The Sorrows of Mary*, Fourth Edition, 1872, p. 209, Le Vicomte Hippolyte de Gouvello's *Apparitions d'une âme du Purgatoire en Bretagne*, Téqui, Paris, 4me édition, 1919, may be read with profit. Dante says, *Purgatorio*, xi, 34-36 :

> Ben si dee loro aitar lavar le note,
> che portar quinci, sì che mondi e lievi
> possano uscire alle stellate rote.

[63] W. W. Story, *Roba di Roma*, 8vo, London, 1863, remarks : "Saturday is considered lucky by the Italians, as the day of the Virgin." On a Saturday the sun always shines, if it be but for a moment. Orlando Pescetti, *Proverbi Italiani*, 12mo, Venice, 1603, has : "Ne donna senza amore ne Sabbato senza sole." The Spaniards have a similar proverb, and the French rhyme runs :

> En hiver comme en été
> jamais Samedi n'est passé
> qué le soleil n'y ait mis son nez.

Aveyron, *Proverbes et Dictous Agricoles de France*, 12mo, Paris, 1872, quotes several saws to this effect. In the Côté d'Or, Meuse, they say :

> Le soleil fait par excellence
> le Samedi la révérence.

Another proverb runs :

> Il n'y pas de Samedi sans soleil
> ni de viele sans conseil.

[64] *The Glories of Mary*. "Practices of Devotion. . . . Fourth Devotion, of Fasting."

[65] *De Passione Domini*, c. ii.

[66] Abbott, *Macedonian Folklore*, pp. 221-222.

[67] F. S. Krauss, "Vampyre im südslavischen Volksglauben," *Globus*, lxi (1892), p. 326, says that in some parts of Bosnia, when peasant women pay a visit of condolence to a house, in which a death has occurred they put a little sprig of hawthorn behind their headcloth, and on leaving the house throw away the flower into the street. The vampire will be so busy gathering together the leaves and picking up the buds that he will not be able to follow them to their own homes.

[68] 1526-1585. See G. Dejob, *Marc-Antoine Muset*, Paris, 1881.

[69] *Historia Naturalis*, VII, liii, 52.

[70] 31st October, 1885, p. 841.

[71] p. 80.

[72] Horace Welby, *The Mysteries of Life and Death*.

[73] In Monsignor's Benson's *A Winnowing*, 1910, Jack Weston dies, and returns to life. But his death would have dissolved the contract of matrimony, a point not appreciated by the author.

[74] Cooper's *The Uncertainty of the Signs of Death*.

[75] Second Edition by Walter R. Hadwen, M.D., London, 1905.

[76] *La Morte Apparente*, p. 16.

[77] *Lancet*, 22nd December, 1883, pp. 1078-80.

[78] p. 65.

[79] *De Anima*, v.

[80] As this is the feast of S. Martin some Martyrologics transfer the commemoration of S. John Eleemosinarius to 23rd January, others to 3rd February, and a few assign 13th July. Among the Greeks 11th November is the feast of S. Mennas, so S. John is transferred to the following day.

[81] Born *circa* 345 ; died 399. One of the most important ascetical writers of the fourth century. His works will be found in Migne, *Patrologia Graeca*, xl. It must be noted, however, that S. Jerome (*Epistola 133 ad Ctesiphontem*, n. 3) charges him with Originistic errors and deems him the precursor of Pelagius.

[82] S. Babylas, Bishop of Antioch, with other Christians, suffered during the Decian persecution, 250 A.D. His burial-place was very celebrated. Cæsar Gallus built a church dedicated in the Martyr's honour at Daphne to put an end to the abomination and demonism of the famous Temple and oracle there.

The bones of the Saint being transferred to the new fane Apollo's oracle ceased. When Julian the Apostate consulted his pagan god no answer was received. The Holy Relics of S. Babylas in after years were carried to Cremona. His feast is kept on 24th January ; by the Greeks 4th September.

[83] Ephraim of Antioch succeeded Euphrasius as Patriarch, 527. He distinguished himself as one of the defenders of the Faith of Chalcedon (451) against the Monophysites. Most of his writings are lost. He died in 545.

[84] First edited by Frouton du Duc in *Auctarium biblioth. patrum*, II, 1057-1159, Paris, 1624. Cotelier issued a superior text in *Ecclesiae Græcæ Monumenta*, II, Paris, 1681 ; and this has been reprinted by Migne, *Patres Graeci*, lxxxvii, 111, 2851-3112, who in the *Patres Latini*, lxxiv, 121-240, also reprints the Latin version of Blessed Ambrogio Traversari, first published at Venice, 1475 ; at Vicenza 1479.

[85] Edward Kinesman, *Lives of the Saints*, 1623, p. 591.

[86] There are two Saints of this name. Both are commemorated together by the Greeks on 19th January. *The Roman Martyrology* commemorates S. Macarius of Alexandria on 2nd January ; and S. Macarius the Egyptian on 15th January.

[87] Mgr. Guérin, *Les Petits Bollandistes*, vol. I, 2nd January.

[88] Editions by Marold in the *Bibliotheca Trubneriana*, Leipzig, 1886 ; and by Hümer *Corpus scriptorum ecclesiasticonon latinorum*, Vienna, 1891.

[89] 15 May, 334.

[90] This work may be spurious. Migne, *Patres Latini*, XIX, p. 381. (*Appendix ad opera Iuuenci*.)

[91] Arndt and Krusch, *Scriptores Renum Merouingiuanum* in *Monumenta Germ. Hist.* (1884-5), I, pt. 1, pp. 1-30. *Historia Francorum*, I, xlii.

[92] There is a poem by Guerrier de Dumast, " The Tomb of the Two Lovers of Clermont," 1836.

[93] Vol. III, p. 476.

[94] 387-493.

[95] The English Martyrologies commemorate S. Melor on 3rd January, though he was killed on 1st October, under which date he is mentioned by Usuardus, a monk of St. Germain-des-Prés, who died in 876. The best edition of Usuardus is that of Solerius, Antwerp, 1714-1717. The feast of S. Melor is 3rd October, possibly because S. Rémi is 1st October. Although I have given the old English legend it is probable that S. Melor belonged to Brittany, not Cornwall. " L'évêque de *Cornouaille* " (in Brittany) is referred to as " tuteur dévoué de Saint Mélar." The shrine of S. Melor is at Lanmeur, some ten miles from Morlaix. He is buried in the crypt of this church, and here is venerated his statue. There can be no doubt that important Relics of the Saint were given to Amesbury, and in *Les Vies des Saints de la Bretagne* we read : " Plusiers reliques de Saint Mélor passerent à differentis Eglises qui les demandèrent ; Orleans, Meaux (chez les chanoines réguliers de Notre Dame de Châyes), Ambresbury en Angleterre (dans un Monastère de religieuses), etc. " There is an old fresco of S. Melor on a pillar of Amesbury Church. I am indebted to the Vicar of Amesbury for this item of information. See *A Pilgrimage to the Shrine of S. Melor.*

[96] Valence, 1855.

[97] Duchesne puts S. Paulus in the fourth or the sixth century.

[98] This miracle forms the subject of a fine canvas by Pomarancio in the Oratorian Chiesa Nuova, S. Maria Vallicella. The room, now converted into a chapel, where the miracle took place is on the second floor of the Palazzo Massimo. Under the date 16th March is the *Diario Romano* we have the entry : " Nella chiesa entro il palazzo Massimo al Corso Vittorio Emanuele festa di S. Filippo Neri, in memoria del miracolo col quale il santo fece ritornare in vita Paolo Massimo (1583).

[99] Petra is a titular metropolitan see of Palaestrina Tertia. In the seventh century it was a flourishing monastic centre, but commercially the city had already decayed.

[100] His life was written by S. Gregory of Tours. The date of his death is uncertain. Galesinius says 524, which must be incorrect. Some Gallican

Martyrologies have 535, but S. Gregory of Langres was present that year at the Council of Clermont, and in 538 by his deputy, Evantius the priest, he signed the decrees of the third Council of Orleans. However since he did not appear at, nor send a deputy to the fourth Council of Orleans, 541, it is probable that the see was then vacant by his death.

[101] He was murdered 8th May, 1079, and canonized in 1253.

[102] *Flos Sanctorum* by Pedro de Ribadeneira, S.J.

[103] *Lives of the Saints*, 1623, by Edward Kinesman.

[104] *Vita di S. Caterina di Bologna*, by Fra Paleotti, O.M. The body of S. Catherine, which is still incorrupt, I have often venerated at the Convent of Poor Clares, Bologna.

[105] *La Santa di Firenze* da una Religiosa del suo Monastero, Firenze, 1906. The incorrupt body of S. Maria Maddalena de Pazzi now lies under the High Altar of the Carmelite Convent, Piazza Savonarola, Florence.

[106] Épaulard, *Le Vampirisme*, pp. 4-5.

[107] It is said that an old blind man who used to beg in Regent Street, London, was to be identified with Hare. He at length became a charge on the parish in London, where he was sent since he had been born at Carlingford, Co. Louth, to the workhouse at Kilheel, Co. Down, and here he ended his days, being buried among the other paupers in the " Workhouse Banks." The graves lie east and west, but Hare's grave, owing, it is said, to the doctor's directions, was dug north and south. This is a mark of infamy. It is unlucky to be buried on the north side of the churchyard, called the devil's side, says Robert Hunt in his *Popular Romances of the West of England, or the Drolls, Traditions and Superstitions of Old Cornwall*, London, 8vo, 1865. It has been noted that graves facing north and south are found at Cowden (Kent) and Bergholt (Suffolk), and are reported to be the tombs of suicides.

[108] Fr. Boas, "The Social Organization and the Secret Societies of the Kwakiutl Indians," *Report of the U.S. National Museum for* 1895, Washington, 1897 ; pp. 610 and 611.

[109] G. M. Dawson, *Report on the Queen Charlotte Islands*, 1878 ; Montreal, 1880 ; pp. 125B ; 128B.

[110] Torquemada, *Monarquia Indiana*, lib. x. c. 14, vol. II, pp. 259 *seq.* ; Madrid, 1723. See also Brasseur de Bourbourg, *Histoire des Nations civiliséco du Mexique et de l'Amérique Centrale*, Paris, 1857-1859 ; vol. III, pp. 510-512.

[111] Spencer and Gillen, *Northern Tribes of Central Australia*, pp. 473-475.

[112] Boguet, *Discours des Sorciers*, c. xlvii. Lyons, 1603, p. 163.

[113] A. Moll, *Recherches sur la " libido sexualis*," Berlin, 1898, p. 701.

[114] From Petworth House, Sussex. In Sotheby's sale, 23 and 24 April, 1928.

[115] 1564-1632.

[116] " Essai sur l'Anthropophagie," par M. le Dr. Legrande du Saulle. *Annales Medico-Psychologiques*, 3me Series ; t. viii ; p. 472, July, 1862.

[117] William Hilton Wheeler, *Brigandage in South Italy*, 1864.

[118] *Causes Célèbres*, Paris, t. vii, p. 117.

[119] Georget, *Examen médical des procès criminels des nommés Léger, etc.*, 1825.

[120] Cesare Lombroso, *Verzeni e Agnoletti*, Rome, 1873. There is a more recent study by Pasquale Ponta, *I pervertimenti sessuali nel uomo e Vincenzo Verzeni strangalatore di donne*, 1893.

[121] Michéa, *Union médicale*, 17 juillet, 1849.

[122] Brierre de Boismont : *Gazette médicale*, 21 juillet, 1849.

[123] Baillanger, " Rapport du Dr. Bédor de Troyes " ; *Bulletins de l'Académie de'médicine*, 1857.

[124] *Vampirisme*, pp. 20-37.

[125] 6me mille, pp. 236-245. It may be said that Taxil's evidence is suspect. But not upon these subjects. Moreover his statements find ample support in other writers.

CHAPTER II

The Generation of the Vampire

It may now be asked how a human being becomes or is transformed into a vampire, and it will be well here to tabulate the causes which are generally believed to predispose persons to this demoniacal condition. It may be premised that as the tradition is so largely Slavonic and Greek many of these causes which are very commonly assigned and accredited in Eastern Europe will not be found to prevail elsewhere.

The Vampire is one who has led a life of more than ordinary immorality and unbridled wickedness ; a man of foul, gross and selfish passions, of evil ambitions, delighting in cruelty and blood. Arthur Machen has very shrewdly pointed out that " Sorcery and sanctity are the only realities. Each is an ecstasy, a withdrawal from the common life." The spiritual world cannot be confined to the supremely good, " but the supremely wicked, necessarily, have their portion in it. The ordinary man can no more be a great sinner than he can be a great saint. Most of us are just indifferent, mixed-up creatures ; we muddle through the world without realizing the meaning and the inner sense of things, and, consequently our wickedness and our goodness are alike second-rate unimportant . . . the saint endeavours to recover a gift which he has lost ; the sinner tries to obtain something which was never his. In brief, he repeats the Fall . . . it is not the mere liar who is excluded by those words[1] ; it is, above all, the " sorcerers " who use the material life, who use the failings incidental to material life as instruments to obtain their infinitely wicked ends. And let me tell you this ; our higher senses are so blunted, we are so drenched with materialism, that we should probably fail to recognize real wickedness if we encountered it."[2]

Huysmans has said in _Là Bas :_ " Comme il est très difficile d'être un saint, il reste à devenir un santanique. C'est un des deux extrêmes. On peut avoir l'orgueil de valoir en crimes ce qu'un saint vaut en virtus."

It has been said that a saint is a person who always choses the better of the two courses open to him at every step. And so the man who is truly wicked is he who deliberately always choses the worse of the two courses. Even when he does things which would be considered right he always does them for some bad reason. To identify oneself in this way with any given course requires intense concentration and an iron strength of will, and it is such persons who become vampires.

The vampire is believed to be one who has devoted himself during his life to the practice of Black Magic, and it is hardly to be supposed that such persons would rest undisturbed, while it is easy to believe that their malevolence had set in action forces which might prove powerful for terror and destruction even when they were in their graves. It was sometimes said, but the belief is rare, that the Vampire was the offspring of a witch and the devil.

Throughout the trials and in the confessions of witches there are many details of the coitus of the devil and the witch, but those examples given by Henri Boguet in his great and authoritative work *Discours des Sorciers* (Third edition, Lyons, 1590) may stand for many. He devotes Chapter XII to the connexion of the devil and the witch : " L'accouplement du Demon avec la Sorciere et le Sorcier . . . 1. Le Demon cognoit toutes les Sorcieres, & pourquoy. 2. Il se met aussi en femme pour les Sorciers, & pourquoy. 3. Autres raisons pour les quelles le Demon cognoit les Sorciers, & Sorcieres." More than one witch acknowledged that Satan had known her sexually, and in Chapter XIII Boguet decides : " L'accouplement de Satan auce le Sorcier est réel and non imaginaire. . . . Les uns donc s'on mocquēt . . . mais les confessions des Sorciers que j'ay eu en main, me font croire qu'il en est quelque chose. Lautant qu'ils ont tout recogneu, qu'ils auoient esté couplez auec le Diable, & que la semeuce qu'il iettoit estoit fort froide . . . Iaquema Paget adioustoit, qu'elle auoit empoigné plusiers fois auec la main le mēbre du Demon, qui la cognoissoit, & que le membre estoit froid comme glace, lōg d'un bon doigt, & moindre en grosseur que celuy d'vn homme : Tieuenne Paget, & Antoine Tornier adioustoient aussi, qui le membre de leurs Demons estoit long, & gros comme l'un de leurs doigts." That eminent scholar and demonologist, Ludovico Maria Sinistrari, O.S.F., tells us in his *De Demonialitate* "it is undoubted by Theologians and philosophers that carnal intercourse between mankind and the Demon sometimes gives birth to human beings ; and that is how Antichrist is to be born, according to some doctors, for example, Bellarmine, Suarez, and Thomas Malvenda. They further observe that, from a natural cause, the children thus begotten by Incubi are tall, very hardy and bloodily bold, arrogant beyond words, and desperately wicked." S. Augustine, *De Ciuitate Dei*, XV, 23, says : " Creberrima fama est multique se expertos uel ab eis, qui experto essent, de quorum fide dubitandum non esset, audisse confirmant, Siluanos et Panes, quos uulgo incubos uocant, inprobos saepe extitisse mulieribus et earum adpetisse ac perigisse concubitum ; et quodsam daemones, quos Dusios Galli nuncupant, adsidue hanc immunditiam et tentare et efficere, plures talesque adseuerant, ut hoc negare impudentiae uideatur." " And seeing it is so general a report, and so many view it either from their own experience or from others, that are of indubitable honesty and credit, that the sylvans and fawns, commonly called incubi, have often swived women, desiring and acting carnally with them ; and that certain devils whom the Gauls called ' Duses ' do continually practise this uncleanness and lure others to it, which is affirmed by such persons and with such weight that it were the height of impudence to deny it." Charles René Billuart, the celebrated Dominican (1685-1757) in his *Tractatus de Angelis* tells us : " The same evil spirit may serve as a succubus to a man, and as an incubus to a woman." The great authority of S. Alphonsus Liguori in his *Praxis confessariorum*, VII, n. iii, lays down : " Some deny that there are evil spirits, incubi and succubi, but writers of weight, eminence and learning, for the most part lay down that such is verily the case." Sinistrari, as we have noted, says that the children born of the devil and a witch are " desperately wicked," and we have just seen that persons of more than ordinarily evil life are said to become Vampires.

With the exception of England,—for witches were invariably hanged among us,—the universal penalty for witchcraft was the stake ; and cremation, the burning of the dead body, is considered to be one of the few ways, and perhaps the most efficacious manner, in which vampirism can be stamped out and brought to an end. That witches were hanged in England is a fact which has often been commented upon with some surprise, and persons who travelled in France and Italy were inclined to advise the same punishment should be inflicted at home as in all other countries. It was felt that unless the body were utterly consumed it might well prove that they had not stamped out the noxious thing. In Scotland, in 1649, when Lady Pittadro, who was incarcerated upon a charge of sorcery, died before her trial, her body was buried in the usual way. But considerable excitement followed and there were instant complaints to those in high places since the Scotch General Assembly considered that the body should have been burned and the following entry occurs among the records: "Concerning the matter of the buriall of the Lady Pittadro, who, being under a great scandall of witchcraft, and bein incarcerat in the Tolbuith of this burgh during her triall before the Justice, died in prison. The Commission of the General Assembly, having considered the report of the Committee appointed for that purpose, Doe give their advyse to the Presbyterie of Dumferling to show their dislike of that fact of the buriall of the Lady Pittadro, in respect of the manner and place, and that the said Presbyterie may labour to make the persons who hes buried her sensible of their offence in so doeing ; and some of the persons who buried hir, being personallie present, are desired by the Comission to show themselvis to the Presbyterie sensible of their miscarriage therein."[3] Again in 1652 some persons who had been resident in France and who probably had followed the famous prosecutions at Louviers expressed their surprise that in England the gallows and not the stake was the penalty for this species of crime. In the Louviers case, a horrid record of diabolism, demoniac masses, lust and blasphemy, on 21 August, 1647, Thomas Boullé, a notorious Satanist, was burnt alive in the market-square at Rouen, and what is very notable the body of Mathurin Picard who had died five years before, and who had been buried near the choir grille in the chapel of the Franciscan nuns which was so fearfully haunted, was disinterred, being found (so it is said) intact. In any case it was burned to ashes in the same fire as consumed the wretched Boullé and it seems probable that this corpse was incinerated to put an end to the vampirish attacks upon the cloister. At Maidstone, in 1652, "Anne Ashby, alias Cobler, Anne Martyn, Mary Browne, Anne Wilson, and Mildred Wright of Cranbrooke and Mary Read, of Lenham, being legally convicted, were according to the Laws of this Nation, adjudged to be hanged, at the common place of Execution. Some there were that wished rather they might be burnt to Ashes ; alledging that it was a received opinion among many, that the body of a witch being burnt, her bloud is prevented thereby from becomming hereditary to her Progeny in the same evill."[4]

It is even recorded that in one case the witch herself considered that she should be sent to the stake. A rich farmer in Northamptonshire had made an enemy of a woman named Anne Foster. Thirty of his sheep were discovered dead with their "Leggs broke in pieces, and their Bones all shattered in their Skins." Shortly after his house and several of his barns were found ablaze. It was suspected that Anne Foster had brought this about by sorcery. She was tried upon this charge at Northampton in 1674, and "After Sentence of Death was past upon her, she mightly desired to be Burned ; but the Court would give no Ear to that, but that she should be hanged at the Common place of Execution."[5]

These two categories are those to which, it is generally believed, cases of vampirism may be assigned, and the remaining classes are almost entirely peculiar to Czecho-Slovakia, Jugo-Slavia, Greece and Eastern Europe.

The vampire is believed to be one who for some reason is buried with mutilated rites. It will be remarked that this idea has a very distinct connexion with the anxious care taken by the Greek and Roman of classical times that the dead should be consigned to the tomb with full and solemn ceremony. Example might be multiplied upon example and it will suffice to refer to the passage in the *Iliad* where the soul of Patroclus is represented as urgently demanding the last ceremonial observances at the tomb.

> " Sleep'st thou, Achilles, mindless of thy friend,
> Neglecting, not the living, but the dead ?
> Hasten my funeral rites, that I may pass

Through Hades' gloomy gates ; ere those be done,
The spirits and spectres of departed men
Drive me far from them, nor allow to cross
Th' abhorred river ; but forlorn and sad
I wander through the wide-spread realms of night.
And give now thy hand, whereupon to weep ;
For never more, when laid upon the pyre,
Shall I return from Hades ; never more,
Apart from all our comrades, shall we two,
As friends, sweet counsel take ; for me, stern Death,
The common lot of man, has op'd his mouth ;
Thou too, Achilles, rival of the Gods,
Art destin'd here beneath the walls of Troy
To meet thy doom ; yet one thing must I add,
And make, if thou wilt grant it, one request.
Let not my bones be laid apart from thine,
Achilles, but together, as our youth
Was spent together in thy father's house,
Since first my Sire Menœtius me a boy
From Opus brought, a luckless homicide,
Who of Amphidamas, by evil chance,
Had slain the son, disputing o'er the dice :
Me noble Peleus in his house receiv'd,
And kindly nurs'd, and thine attendant nam'd ;
So in one urn be now our bones enclos'd,
The golden vase, thy Goddess-mother's gift."
    Whom answer'd thus Achilles, swift to foot :
" Why art thou here lov'd being ? why on me
These several charges lay ? whate'er thou bidd'st
Will I perform, and all in one short embrace,
Let us, while yet we may, our grief indulge."
    Thus as he spoke, he spread his longing arms.
But nought he clasp'd ; and with a wailing cry,
Vanish'd, like smoke, the spirit beneath the earth.[6]

Having slain her husband the atrocious Clytemnestra heaps
sin upon sin and outrages not merely all decent feeling and
human respect, but in some mysterious way insults the majesty
of heaven itself in that, a supreme act of wanton insolence,
she " dared to lay her husband in the tomb without mourning
and without lamentation or dirge," for an adequate show of
outward grief was considered an essential and religious part
of any Greek funeral.   In bitter accents Electra cries :[7]

ἰὼ δαῖα
πάντολμε μᾶτερ, δαΐαις ἐν ἐκφοραῖς
ἄνευ πολιτᾶν ἄνακτ',
ἄνευ δὲ πενθημάτων
ἔτλας ἀνοίμωκτον ἄνδρα θάψαι.

As Sophocles has shown us in that great drama which some not without reason consider the supremest excellence of Greek tragedy, the heroism of Antigone carries her to heights of dauntless strength in this cause of divine charity. To scatter a few handfuls of dust upon her brother's body which lies unburied on the Theban plain, she gladly lays down her own life, she flouts the man-made law of a weak and odious tyrant, resisting him to his very face, calmly as in stern duty bound without vaunt or show of audacity, appealing against the petty and precisian tribunals of a day to the eternal judgement-seat of powers more ancient and more awful than the throne of Zeus himself, casting away her plighted troth to Hæmon as though it were a trifle, and less than a trifle of no account, going gladly and serenely to her tragic doom. This contempt of human ordinances, this icy despising of human passions, of love itself, give the figure of Antigone something statuesque, something superbly cold in the very loveliness of her nobility, and remind us, although in her utter detachment even she, the purest Greek maiden, is far far below the Spanish mystic, of S. Teresa, who in pages that are chilly as ice, yet glow like fire, descants upon the nullity of human affections and the inflexible demand of the eternal law. So in the grand yet hard enthusiasm of Antigone there is no room for sentiment. The only touches which might seem some concession to human weakness but serve to make the absence of romantic sympathies more notable and more terrible. In a passage of the Kommos she bewails her own virgin knot untied, yet she has no more than some six words to throw away upon her betrothed :

ὦ φίλταθ' Αἷμον, ὡς σ' ἀτιμάζει πατήρ.

When we consider the steadfastness and inflexible purity of her purpose we shall to some extent realise how tremendous was the ideal that inspired her, and we are able to appreciate what price it seemed fitting to a Greek should be paid for the just and ritual performance of the last duties to the dead.

Pausanias tells us that Lysander's honour was for ever smirched, not because he put to death certain prisoners of war, but because " he did not even throw handfuls of earth upon their dead bodies."[9]   It will be remarked that to the ancient Greek even this symbolism of inhumation sufficed, if nothing more could be done. Such indeed was the minimum but it was enough, and this little ceremony was by Attic Law enjoined upon all who happened to chance upon a corpse that lay unburied. To us it would seem wholly inadequate, if not nugatory and vain, but to the Greeks—and who knows how much wiser they were in this than are we ? —this act had a mystical significance, for it was as Ælian has so happily expressed it " the fulfilment of some mysterious law of piety imposed by nature."[10] It was even believed that animals when they came upon the dead of their kind, would scrape with their paws a little earth over the body. To the modern man burial in the earth, or it may be cremation, is a necessary and decorous manner for the disposal of the dead. Yet in the Greek imagination these rites implied something far more, and they involved a certain provision for the welfare of that which was immaterial but permanent, the spirit or the soul. So long as the body remains the soul might be in some way tied and painfully linked with it, a belief which as we have noted, was held by Tertullian and many other of the early writers. But the dissolution of the body meant that the soul was no longer detained in this world where it had no appointed place, but that it was able to pass without let or hindrance to its own mansion prepared for it and for which it was prepared. Of old, men dutifully assisted the dead in this manner as a pious obligation, and as we have seen in the most famous case of all, that of Antigone, they were prepared to go to any length and to make any sacrifice to fulfil this obligation. It was in later years, especially under the influence of Slavonic tradition that not only love but fear compelled them to perform this duty to the dead, since it was generally thought that those whose bodies were not dissolved might return, reanimated corpses, the vampire eager to satisfy his vengeance upon the living, his lust for sucking hot reeking blood, and therefore the fulfilment of these funeral duties was a protection for themselves as well as a benefit to the departed.

Very closely linked with this idea is the belief that those persons become vampires who die under the ban of the church, that is to say who die excommunicate. Excommunication is the principal and most serious penalty that the Church can inflict, and being so severe a penalty it naturally pre-supposes some very grave offence. It may be roughly defined as a punishment that deprives the guilty of all participation in the common spiritual benefits enjoyed by all the members of the Christian society. There are certainly other corrective measures which entail the loss of certain particular rights ; and among these are such censures as suspension for clerics, interdict for clerics and laymen and whole communities, irregularity *ex delicto*, and others. The excommunicated person does not cease to be a Christian, for his baptism can never be effaced but he is considered as an exile, and even, one may say, as non-existing, for a time at any rate, in the sight of ecclesiastical authority. But such exile comes to an end, and this the Church most ardently desires, so soon as the offender has given adequate satisfaction, yet meantime his status is that of an alien and a stranger.

Since excommunication is the forfeiture of the spiritual privileges of a certain society, it follows that those only can be excommunicated who by any right whatsoever belong to this society. Moreover, strictly speaking, excommunication can only be declared against baptized and living people, a point to be considered in detail later. Moreover, in order to fall within the jurisdiction of the *forum externum*, which alone can inflict excommunication, the offence incurring this penalty must be public and external. For there is a well-defined separation between those things appertaining to the *forum externum*, or public ecclesiastical tribunal, and the *forum internum*, or tribunal of conscience. At the same time, in the Bull " Exsurge Domine," 16th May, 1520, Leo X, rightly condemned the twenty-third proposition of Luther according to which " excommunications are merely external punishments, nor do they deprive a man of the common spiritual prayers of the Church." Pius VI, " Auctorem Fidei," 28th August, 1794, also condemned the forty-sixth proposition of the pseudo-synod of Pistoia, which maintained that the effect of excommunication is exterior only, because of its own nature it excludes only from exterior communion with the Church, as if, said the Pope, excommunication were not essentially also a spiritual penalty binding in heaven and affecting souls. The aforesaid proposition was therefore condemned as " falsa et perniciosa," false and pernicious, already reprobated and condemned in the twenty-third proposition of Luther, and, to say the very least, it incurs the technical mark

" erronea " (erroneous), since it contradicts a certain (certa) theological conclusion or truth which is clearly and necessarily deducible from two premises, of which one is an article of faith, and the other naturally certain. Most assuredly the Church cannot (nor does she seek or wish to) oppose any obstacle to the interior and personal relation of the soul with its Creator. Nevertheless the rites of the Church are the regular and appointed channel through which divine grace is conveyed, and therefore it follows that exclusion from these rites inevitably entails the privation of this grace, to whose prescribed and availing sources the excommunicated person no longer has access.

It should be mentioned that both from a moral and juridical standpoint the guilt requisite for the incurring of excommunication implies various conditions of which the three most important are, first the full use of reason ; second sufficient, if not absolute, moral liberty ; and thirdly a knowledge of the law and even of the penalty, for it follows that if such knowledge be lacking there cannot be that disregard of the ecclesiastical law known as contumacy, the essence of which consists in deliberately performing an action whilst being very fully aware and conscious not merely that the action is forbidden but also that it is forbidden under a certain definite penalty, the exact nature of which is itself defined and known. Wherefore various *causae excusantes*, extenuating circumstances, are often present, and these so mitigate the culpability that they prevent the incurring of excommunication. It is hardly necessary to enter into an examination of such circumstances as in practice there may well be, and indeed are, many considerations and exemptions which have to be taken into account, but generally speaking lack of the full use of reason, lack of liberty resulting from fear—a person who is physically constrained or morally terrorized has no freedom of will and is not responsible—or ignorance, even affected ignorance, may anyone of them be obstacles to incurring that measure of peccability which is requisite to deserve an extreme spiritual penalty. Affected ignorance is a lack of knowledge in those who might reasonably and without grave difficulty inform and enlighten themselves, but they are not bound to do so, and since every penal law is to be strictly interpreted, if such a statute positively and in set terms exacts knowledge on the part of the culprit, he is excused even by affected ignorance. Again, excommunication may be "occult," when the offence entailing it is known to no one or to almost no one at all. That is to say when no scandal has been given. This, it should be remarked, is valid in the *forum internum* only, and although he who has incurred occult communication should be absolved as soon as possible, he is not obliged to abstain from external acts connected with the exercise of jurisdiction, and moreover, since he has the right to judge himself and to be judged by his director according to the exact truth and his apprehension thereof, consequently in the tribunal of conscience he who is reasonably certain of his innocence cannot be compelled to treat himself as excommunicated, albeit he must be reasonably and justly persuaded.

It may now be briefly inquired, who can excommunicate ? The general principle is that whoever enjoys jurisdiction in the *forum externum* can excommunicate, but only his own subjects. Therefore whether excommunications be technically *a iure* or *ab homine* they may come from the supreme Pontiff alone or from a general council for the whole Church ; from the Bishop for his diocese ; from a Prelate *nullius* for quasi-diocesan territories ; and from regular Prelates for their subjects, that is to say for religious orders. Yet further anyone can excommunicate who has jurisdiction in the *forum externum* by virtue of his office even although this be delegated, for instance, legates, vicars capitular, and vicars-general can exercise this power. But a parish priest cannot inflict this penalty, nor may he even declare that it is incurred which is to say he may not pronounce this in an official manner as a judge. The right to absolve evidently belongs to him who can excommunicate and who has imposed the censure, and obviously it belongs to any person delegated by him to this effect, since the power, being of jurisdiction, may be committed to another. Technically, excommunications are divided into four classes : those particularly reserved to the supreme Pontiff ; those simply reserved to the supreme Pontiff ; those reserved to the Bishop (to the ordinary) ; and those *nemini reseruatae*, that are not reserved. Accordingly, generally speaking, only the Holy Father can absolve from the first two kinds of excommunication, although naturally his power extends to all kinds ; Bishops (and ordinaries) can rescind excommunications of the third class; whilst the fourth kind, *nemini reseruatae*, can be revoked by any priest having authority without the need of a particular delegation. Over and above this, there exist in practice certain concessions since bishops enjoy very liberal faculties and indults, which are moreover, most widely communicable whereby they are empowered to absolve *in foro interno* from all cases except those which are most definitely and *nominatim* reserved to the Supreme Pontiff. There are also the circumstances technically known as " Urgent Cases," when the power granted is valid for all cases, without exception, legally reserved though they may be to the highest authorities, even to the Pope himself, and even for the absolution of an accomplice (Holy Office, 7th June, 1899). Finally canon law lays down that at the point of death or in danger of death, all reservations cease and all necessary jurisdiction is supplied by the Church. " At the point of death," says the Council of Trent (Session XIV, c. vii), " in danger of death," says the *Rituale Romanum*, any priest can absolve from all sins and censures, even if he be without the ordinary faculty of confessor or if he himself be excommunicated. He may even do this in the presence of another priest who is duly and canonically authorized, enjoying jurisdiction (Holy Office, 29th July, 1891).

It has been said by a modern historian : " The awful import of Excommunication barely can be realized at the present time. People idly wonder why the excommunicated take their case so seriously—why they do not turn to find amusement, or satisfaction, in another channel,—why they persist in lying prone in the mire where the fulmination struck them. And, indeed, in modern times the formal sentence rarely is promulgated, and only against persons of distinction like the German Dr. Döllinger or the Sabaudo King Vittoremanuele II di Savoja, whose very circumstances provided them with the means to allay the temporal irritation of the blow."[11] The immediate effects of excommunication are summed up in the two famous verses :

> Res sacrae, ritus, communio, crypta, potestas,
> praedia sacra, forum, ciuilia iura uetantur.

It may be well now to glance very briefly at the history of the actual practice of excommunication. Among the Jews exclusion from the synagogue was a real excommunication, and it is this to which reference is made in 1 *Esdras* x, 7 and 8 : "and proclamation was made in Juda and Jerusalem to all the children of the captivity, that they should assemble together into Jerusalem. And that whosoever would not come within three days, according to the counsel of the princes and the ancients, all his substance should be taken away, and he should be cast out of the company of them that were returned from captivity." It was this exclusion which was feared by the parents of the man who was born blind, who when they were questioned by the Pharisees would give no definite answer with reference to the healing of their son, "because they feared the Jews : for the Jews had already agreed among themselves, that if any man should confess him to be Christ, he should be put out of the synagogue."[12] Again we are told, "many of the chief men also believed in him ; but because of the Pharisees they did not confess him, that they might not be cast out of the synagogue."[13]   The Apostles were told : "they will put you out of the synagogues ; yea, the hour cometh, that whosoever killeth you, will think that he doth a service to God."[14]   This penalty exercised by the Jews foreshadowed later censures, for it is said : "in the mouth of two or three witnesses every word may stand. And if he will not hear them : tell the Church. And if he will not hear the Church, let him be to thee as the heathen and Publican. Amen I say to you, whatsoever you shall bind on earth, shall be bound also in Heaven ; and whatsoever you shall loose upon earth shall be loosed also in heaven."[15] According to the Orthodox Church this power was transmitted to the successors of the apostles that is to say the bishops, so that they too had the faculty of binding and loosing. But something very definite was further implied. This faculty had actual physical consequences and the Greeks held that excommunication arrested the decomposition of a body after death.   In fact the incorruptibility of the body of any person bound by a curse was made a definite doctrine of the Orthodox Church. The very wording of the text certainly admitted of such an interpretation. ἀμὴν λέγω ὑμῖν, ὅσα ἐὰν δήσητε ἐπὶ τῆς γῆς, ἔσται δεδεμένα ἐν τῷ οὐρανῷ. Καὶ ὅσα ἐὰν λύσητε ἐπὶ τῆς γῆς, ἔσται λελυμένα ἐν τῷ οὐρανῷ. The word λύω "loose" expresses equally the ideas of dissolution and of absolution, while δέω " bind " signifies their respective and several opposites. Accordingly forms of absolution had to be provided which might be read over bodies found in such a condition, for it was thought that this might be brought about by well-nigh any curse, although an episcopal anathema was considered the most weighty and the most terrible. Nevertheless it might be that these conditions resulted from the curse of a parent even from an imprecation uttered by a man against himself, or from the ban of a priest, for in the Orthodox Church the power of excommunicating belonged to priests as well as to bishops, but they should not exercise it without episcopal sanction.[16] One such absolution runs thus : " Yea, O Lord our God, let Thy great mercy and marvellous compassion prevail ; and, whether this Thy servant lieth under curse of father or mother, or under his own imprecation, or did provoke one of Thy holy ministers and sustained at his hands a bond that hath not been loosed, or did incur the most grievous ban of excommunication by a bishop, and through heedlessness and sloth obtained not pardon, pardon Thou him by the hand of Thy sinful and unworthy servant ; resolve Thou his body into that from which it was made ; and stablish his soul in the tabernacle of saints."[17] So in the burial service an orison is made that the body may be dissolved into the dust of which it was made, διάλυσον εἰς τὰ ἐξ ὧν συνετέθη, and in a solemn Requiem, is offered the supplication, " Unbind the curse, be it of priest or of arch-presbyter," Λῦσον κατάραν, εἴτε ἱερέως εἴτε ἀρχιερέως.

Naturally, as is clearly expressed, the curse which the Orthodox Church regarded as most weighty and most effective was the ban of excommunication by a bishop, and therefore the formula of excommunication doomed the offender to remain whole after death, and the body was not freed until absolution had been read over it and the excommunication formally revoked.

However, a considerable difficulty arose. It was discovered that excommunication sometimes failed to produce the expected physical result, and the body crumbled to dust in the ordinary way. Accordingly this had to be reckoned with and explained and Leone Allacci in his *De quorundam Graecorum opinationibus* [18] cites a *nomocanon de excommunicatis* which sets out to explain how it is that sometimes excommunication can fail of its result. " Concerning persons excommunicate the which sadly incur episcopal excommunication and after death are found with their bodies ' not loosed ' (ἄλυτα)."

Certain persons have been duly, rightly, and lawfully ex·communicated by their bishops, as evil doers and transgressors of the divine law, and they have without penance and amendment, or without receiving absolution died in the state of excommunication, and so have been buried, and in a short time after their bodies have been found " loosed " (λελυμένα) and shredded joint from joint, bone from bone.

Exceeding strange and marvellous is this that he who hath been lawfully excommunicated should after his death be found with his body " loosed " (λελυμένος τὸ σῶμα) and the joints of the body separate.

So extraordinary a circumstance was immediately submitted to a conclave of expert theologians, who after long debate decided that any excommunicated person whose body did not remain whole had no more hope of salvation because he was no longer in a state to be " loosed " and absolved by the bishop who had excommunicated him, but that he was already damned in hell. If not absolutely essential, the removal of the ban was if possible to be affected by the same person who had pronounced it, and this provides, against an excommunicated person obtaining absolution too easily.[19] Of course a superior might rescind the anathema pronounced by one of his subjects, a bishop could always remove an excommunication pronounced by a simple priest, but under certain conditions this regulation must certainly prove excessively awkward. There is, for example, the well known instance told by Christophorus Angelus in his Ἐγχειρίδιον περὶ τῆς καταστάσεως τῶν σήμερον εὑρισκομένων Ἑλλήνων,[20] who relates that a bishop was excommunicated by a council of his peers, and his body remained "bound, as it were iron, for the space of a hundred years," after which time a second council of bishops at the same place pronounced absolution, and immediately as they spoke the words the body " crumbled to dust."

The *nomocanon de excommunicatis* goes on to say that " those that are found excommunicate, namely with their bodies whole and ' not loosed ' (ἄλυτα), these require absolution, in order that the body also may attain freedom from the bond (δέσμον) of excommunication.   For even as the body is found bound (δεδέμενον) in the earth, so is the soul bound (δεδεμίνη) and tormented by Satan.   And whensoever the body receives absolution and is loosed (λυθῇ), from excommunication, by the power of God the soul likewise is set free from the bondage of the Devil, and receiveth the life eternal, the light that hath no evening, and the joy ineffable."

Leone Allacci[21] considered this Orthodox dogma of the physical results of excommunication and a subsequent absolution to be certain beyond any matter of dispute, and he mentions several cases, which he says were well known and proved, which demonstrate the truth of this belief.   Athanasius, Metropolitan of Imbros, recorded that at the request of the citizens of Thasos he read a solemn absolution over several bodies, and before the holy words were even finished all had dissolved into dust.   Very similar was the example of a converted Turk who was subsequently excommunicated at Naples, and who had been dead some years before he obtained absolution from two Patriarchs, and his body dissolved, so that he was at rest.

An even more remarkable instance is that of a priest who had pronounced a sentence of excommunication, and who afterwards turned Mohammedan.   This did not affect the victim of his curse, who though he had died in the Christian faith, yet remained "bound."   This circumstance which caused the greatest alarm was reported to the Metropolitan Raphael, and at his earnest request the Mohammedan, though after much delay and hesitation consented to read the absolution over the body of the dead Christian.   As he was pronouncing the final words the body fell completely to dust, The Mohammedan thereupon returned to his former faith. and was put to death for so doing.

I do not know whether this is the same tradition as is recorded by Mr. Abbott in his *Macedonian Folk-lore*, p. 211, but I gather that the examples are not identical, although they have various points of similarity.   I quote Mr. Abbott's most striking account at length.   "How great is the dread of an ecclesiastic's wrath can be realized from the following anecdote related to the writer as a ' true story ' by a person who entertained no doubts as to its authenticity.   ' Many years ago there was an Archbishop of Salonica who once in a moment of anger cursed a man of his diocese : "May the earth refuse to

receive thee." (ἡ γῆς νὰ μή σε δεχτῇ). Years went by, and
the Archbishop embraced Islam. Owing to his erudition
and general ability, he was raised by the Mohammedans to
the office of head Mullah. Meanwhile, the individual who had
incurred the prelate's wrath died, and was buried in the usual
fashion. Now it came to pass that when, at the expiration
of three years, the tomb was opened, the inmate was found
intact, just as if he had been buried the day before. Neither
prayers nor offerings availed to bring about the desired
dissolution. He was inhumed once more ; but three years
later he was still found in the same condition. It was then
recalled to mind by the widow that her late husband had been
anathematized by the apostate Archbishop. She forthwith
went to the ex-prelate and implored him to revoke the sentence.
This dignitary promised to exert his influence, which it appears
had not been diminished a whit by his apostasy ; for once a
bishop always a bishop. Having obtained the Pasha's permission, he repaired to the open tomb, knelt beside it, lifted
up his hands and prayed for a few minutes. He had hardly
risen to his feet when, wondrous to relate, the flesh of the
corpse crumbled away from the bones, and the skeleton
remained bare and clean as if it had never known pollution.' "

It will not be impertinent here to give c. xiii, *of the Power
of Excommunication, and upon what frivolous occasions it is
made use of*, from Ricaut's *The Present State of the Greek and
Armenian Churches*, 8vo, 1679.

" The Third Command of the Church is Obedience towards
their Spiritual Pastors and Teachers, 1 *Cor. iv*, 1, *Let a man so
account of us as of the Ministers of Christ, and Stewards of
the Mysteries of God :* which is text that they often repeat in
their Churches, and raise consequences from thence of the
sublimity of their Office, and of the reverence and honour
due from the people toward their Clergy ; so that though they
want the advantages of Riches and Ornament to render them
respected in the eyes of the Vulgar ; yet their people being
affected with their divine and separated Qualifications, do not
submit only in spiritual matters, but even in Temporals refer
themselves to the determination of their Bishop, or Metropolite,
according to that of S. Paul, 1 *Cor. vi*. 1, *Dare any of you
having a matter against another, go to Law before the unjust,
and not before the Saints ?* But that which most enforces this

Duty of Obedience, is a sense of the Power of Excommunication, which rests in the Church, of which they so generally stand in fear, and the most profligate and obdurate conscience in other matters startles at this sentence, to which whilst any is subjected, he is not only expelled the limits of the Church, but his conversation is scandalous, and his person denied the common benefits of Charity and assistance, to which Christian or Humane duty doth oblige us.

"In the Exercise of this censure of Excommunication, the *Greek* Church is so ready and frequent, that the common use of it might seem to render it the more contemptible ; but that the Sentence is pronounced with so much horrour, and the same effects which have ensued thereupon, not only to the living, but also to the Corps and Carcasses of such who have dyed under Excommunication, are related with that evidence and certainty as still confirms in the people the efficacy of that Authority which the Church exercises therein. The form of Excommunication is either expressive of the party with his name and condition, secluding him from the use of Divine Ordinances, or otherwise indefinite of any person who is guilty of such or such a Crime or Misdemeanour. As for Example, if any person is guilty of Theft, which is not discovered, an Excommunication is taken out against him, whosoever he be, that hath committed the Theft, which is not to be remitted until Restitution is made ; and so the fault is published and repeated at a full Congregation, and then follows the Sentence of Excommunication in this form.

"*If they restore not to him that which is his own, and possess him peaceably of it, but suffer him to remain injured and damnifyed ; let him be separated from the Lord God Creatour, and be accursed, and unpardoned, and undissolvable after death in this World, and in the other which is to come. Let Wood, Stones, and Iron be dissolved but not they : May they inherit the Leprosie of* Gehazi, *and the Confusion of* Judas ; *may the earth be divided and devour them like* Dathan *and* Abiram ; *may they fight and tremble on earth like* Cain, *and the wrath of God be upon their heads and Countenances ; may they see nothing of that for which they labour, and beg their Bread all the days of their lives ; may their Works, Possessions, Labours, and Services be accursed ; always without effect or success, and blown away like dust ; may they have the curses of the holy and righteous Patriarchs* Abram, Isaac *and* Jacob ; *of the 318 Saints who were the Divine Fathers of the Synod of Nice, and of all other holy Synods ; and being without the Church of Christ, let no man administer unto them the things of the Church, or bless them, or offer Sacrifices for them, or give them the* Ἀντίδωρον *or the blessed Bread, or eat, or drink, or work with them, or converse with them ; and after death, let no man bury them, in penalty of being under the same state of Excommunication, for so let them remain until they have performed what is here written.*

"The effect of this dreadful Sentence is reported by the *Greek* Priests to have been in several instances so evident, that none doubts or disbelieves the consequences of all those maledictions repeated therein ; and particularly, that the body of an excommunicated person is not capable of returning to its first Principles until the Sentence of Excommunication is taken off.   It would be esteemed no Curse amongst us to have our Bodies remain uncorrupted and entire in the Grave, who endeavour by Art, and Aromatic spices, and Gums, to preserve them from Corruption : And it is also accounted, amongst the *Greeks* themselves, as a miracle and particular grace and favour of God to the Bodies of such whom they have Canonized for Saints to continue unconsumed, and in the moist damps of a Vault, to dry and desiccate like the Mummies in *Egypt*, or in the Hot sands of *Arabia*.   But they believe that the Bodies of the Excommunicated are possessed in the Grave by some evil spirit, which actuates and preserves them from Corruption, in the same manner as the Soul informes and animates the living body ; and that they feed in the night, walk, digest, and are nourished, and have been found ruddy in Complexion, and their Veins, after forty days Burial, extended with Blood, which, being opened with a Lancet, have yielded a gore as plentiful, fresh, and quick, as that which issues from the Vessels of young and sanguine persons. This is so generally believed and discoursed of amongst the *Greeks*, that there is scarce one of their Country Villages, but what can witness and recount several instances of this nature, both by the relation of their Parents, and Nurses, as well as of their own knowledge, which they tell with as much variety as we do the Tales of Witches and Enchantments, of which it is observed in Conversation, that scarce one story is ended before another begins of like wonder.   But to let pass the common and various Reports of the Vulgar, this one may suffice for all, which was recounted to me with many asseverations of its truth, by a grave *Candiot Kaloir*, called *Sofroino*, a Preacher, and a person of no mean repute and learning at *Smyrna*.

"'I knew' (said he) 'a certain person, who for some misdemeanours committed in the *Morea*, fled to the Isle of *Milo*, where though he avoided the hand of Justice, yet could not avoid the Sentence of Excommunication, from which he could no more fly, than from the conviction of his own Conscience, or the guilt which ever attended him ; for the fatal hour of his death being come, and the Sentence of the Church not being revoked, the Body was carelessly and without Solemnity interred in some retired and unfrequented place. In the mean time the Relations of the deceased were much afflicted, and anxious for the sad estate of their dead Friend, whilst the *Paisants* and *Islanders* were every night affrighted and disturbed with strange and unusual apparitions, which they immediately conclude arose from the Grave of the accursed Excommunicant, which, according to their Custom, they immediately opened, and therein found the Body uncorrupted, ruddy, and the Veins replete with Blood : The Coffin was furnished with Grapes, Apples, and Nuts, and such fruit as the season afforded : Whereupon Consultation being made, the *Kaloires* resolved to make use of the common remedy in those cases, which was to cut and dismember the Body into several parts, and to boyl it in Wine, as the approved means to dislodge the evil Spirit, and dispose the body to a dissolution : But the friends of the deceased, being willing and desirous that the Corps should rest in peace, and some ease given to the departed Soul, obtained a reprieve from the Clergy, and hopes, that for a sum of Money (they being Persons of a competent Estate) a Release might be pur·chased from the Excommunication under the hand of the Patriarch : In this manner the Corps were for a while freed from dissection, and Letters thereupon sent to *Constantinople*, with this direction, that in case the Patriarch should condescend to take off the Excommunication, that the day, hour and minute that he signed the Remission should be inserted in the Date. And now the Corps were taken into the Church (the Country-people not being willing they should remain in the Field) and Prayers and Masses daily said for its dissolution, and pardon of the Offender : When one day after many Prayers, Supplications and Offerings (as this *Sofronio* attested to me with many protestations) and whilst he himself was performing Divine Service, of a sudden was heard a rumbling noise in the Coffin of the dead party, to the fear and astonishment of all persons then present ; which when they had opened, they found the Body consumed and dissolved as far into its first Principles of Earth, as if it had been seven years interred. The hour and minute of this dissolution was immediately noted and precisely observed, which being compared with the Date of the Patriarchs release, when it was signed at *Constantinople*, it was found exactly to agree with that moment in which the Body returned to its Ashes.' This story I should not have judged worth relating, but I heard it from the mouth of a grave person, who says, 'That his own eyes were Witnesses thereof ; and though notwithstanding I esteem it a matter not assured enough to be believed by me, yet let it serve to evidence the esteem they entertain of the validity and force of Excommunication. I had once the curiosity to be present at the opening of a Grave of one lately dead, who, as the people of the Village reported, walked in the night, and affrighted them with strange Phantasmes ; but it was not my fortune to see the Corps in that nature, nor to find the Provisions with which the spirit nourishes it, but only such a Spectacle as is usual after six or seven days Burial in the Grave ; howsoever, *Turks* as well as *Christians* discourse of these matters with much confidence.'

" This high esteem and efficacy being put on Excommunication, one would believe that the Priests should endeavour to conserve the reverence thereof, being the Basis and main support of their *Authority;* and that therefore they should not so easily make use thereof on every frivolous occasion, that so familiarity might not render it contemptible and the salvation of men's Souls not seem to be played with on every slight and trivial Affair : But such is the much to be lamented poverty in this Church, that they are not only forced to sell Excommunications, but the very Sacraments ; and to expose the most reverend and mysterious Offices of Religion unto sale for maintenance and support of Priesthood.

" The taking off Excommunications after death hath been usual, but the Excommunicating after death may seem a strange kind of severity ; for so we read that *Theodosius*, Bishop of *Alexandria*, excommunicated *Origen* two hundred years after his decease.

" On the same Authority of Excommunication depends the power of re-admission again into the Church, which according to the *Greek* Canon is not to be obtained easily, or at every cold request of the Penitent, but after proof of trial first made of a hearty and serious conversion, evidenced by the constant and repeated actions of a holy life, and the patient and obedient performance of Penance imposed and enjoined by the Church. Such as have apostatized from the Faith, by becoming *Turks*, under the age of 14 years, upon their repentance, and desire of return to the Church, sought earnestly with tears, signified and attested by forty days fasting with bread and water, accompanied with continual Prayer day and night, are afterwards received solemnly into the Church in presence of the Congregation, the Priest making a Cross on the Forehead of the Penitent with the Oyl of Chrism, or the μύρον Χρίσματος usually administered to such who return from the ways of darkness and mortal sins.

" But of such who in riper years fall away from the Faith (as many Greeks do for the sake of Women, or escape of punishment) their re-admission or reception again into the Church is more difficult ; for to some of them there is enjoined a Penance of six or seven years humbling themselves with extraordinary Fasts, and continual Prayer; during which time they remain in the nature of *Catechumeni*, without the use or comfort of the Eucharist, or Absolution, unless at the hour of death ; in which the Church is so rigorous, that the Patriarch himself is not able to release a Penance of this nature, imposed only by a simple Priest ; and for receiving Penitents of this nature there is a set Form or Office in the *Greek* Liturgy.

" But now we have few Examples of those Apostates who return from the *Mohametan* to the *Christian* faith ; for none dares own such a Conversion but he who dares to dye for it; so that that practice and admirable part of Discipline is become obsolete and disused. Yet some there have been, even in my time, both of the *Greek* and *Armenian* Churches, who have afforded more Heroick Examples of Repentance, than any of those who have tryed themselves by the Rules and Canons prescribed ; for after that they denyed the Faith, and for some years have carried on their heads the Badge or distinction of a *Mohametan*, feeling some remorses of Conscience, they have so improved the same by the sparks of some little grace remaining, that nothing could appease or allay the present torment of their minds, but a return to that Faith from whence they were fallen. In this manner, having communicated their anguish and desires to some Bishop or grave person of the Clergy, and signifying with all their Courage and Zeal to die for that faith, which they have denyed; they have been exhorted, as the most ready expiation of their sin, to confess Christ at that place where they have renounced him ; and this they have resolutely performed by leaving off their Tulbants, and boldly presenting themselves in publick assemblies and at the time of publick prayers in the Church ; and when the *Turks* have challenged them for having revolted or relapsed again from them, they have owned their Conversion, and boldly declared their resolution to dye in that old Faith wherein they were baptized; and, as a Token or Demonstration thereof, being carried before the Justice of the City or Province, they have not only by words owned the Christian doctrine, but also trampled their *Turkish* Tulbants or Sashes under their Feet, and withstood three times the demand, whether they should still continue to be *Mohametans*, according as it is required in the *Mohametan* Law : For which, being condemned to dye, they have suffered death with the same cheerfulness and courage that we read of the Primitive Martyrs, who daily Sacrificed themselves for the Christian Verity.

" Considering which, I have, with some astonishment, beheld in what manner some poor *English* men, who have fondly and vilely denyed the faith of Christ in *Barbary* and the parts of *Turky*, and become, as we term them *Renegados*, have afterwards (growing weary of the Customes of *Turks* to which they were strangers) found means of escape, and returned again into *England*, and there entered the Churches, and frequented the Assembly of God's people, as boldly as if they had been the most constant and faithful of the Sheepfold : At which confidence of ignorant and illiterate men I do not so much admire, as I do at the negligence of our

Ministers, who acquaint not the Bishops herewith, to take their Counsel and Order herein : But perhaps they have either not learned, or so far forgot the ancient Discipline of ours, and all other Christian Churches, as to permit men, after so abominable a Lapse and Apostasie, boldly to intrude into the Sanctuary of God with the same unhallowed hands and blasphemous mouths, with which they denyed their Saviour and their Country. But what can we say hereunto? Alas ! Many are dissenters from our Church ; which by our divisions in Religion, hath lost much or its Power, Discipline and esteem amongst us ; and men, being grown careles and cold in Religion, little dream or consider of such methods of Repentance ; for whilst men condem the Authority, and censures of the Church, and disown the power of the Keys, they seem to deprive themselves of the ordinary means of Salvation, unless God, by some extraordinary light and eviction supplies that in a sublimer manner, which was anceintly effected by a rigorous observation of the Laws and Canons of the Church.

" It is a strange Vulgar Errour that we maintain in *England*, that the *Greek* Church doth yearly excommunicate the *Roman*, which is nothing so ; and common reason will tell us, That a Church cannot excommunicate another, or any particular Member thereof, over which it pretends no Jurisdiction or Authority ; and that the *Greek* Church hath no such Claim of Dominion or Superiority over the *Roman*, no more than it own a subjection to it, is plainly evinced in the third Chapter of this Book : and this I attest to be so, upon enquiry made into the truth thereof, and on Testimony of *Greek* Priests eminent and knowing in the Canons and Constitutions of their Church : Though we cannot deny but that anceintly one Patriarch might renounce the Communion of another, over whom he had no Jurisdiction, for his notorious Heresie ; as S. *Cyril* did to *Nestorius* before the Assembly of the Council of *Ephesus*."

It has been said that excommunication can only be incurred by living persons, but in this the belief and practice of the Orthodox Church differ from the Catholic Church, since, as has already been remarked, Theodosius of Alexandria who died in 567 excommunicated Origen who died in 253 or 254.[22] Moreover, the fact that Theodosius was deposed for heresy by Pope S. Agapitus I[23] on that pontiff's arrival in Constantinople, in 536, would not according to the Greek idea invalidate this excommunication. With regard to living persons those who have never been baptized are not members of the Christian Society, and therefore obviously they cannot be deprived of rights they have never enjoyed ; whilst as even the baptized cease, at death, to belong to the Church Militant, the dead cannot be excommunicated. This is not to say that technically, after the demise of some member of the Christian community it may be declared that such a person incurred excommunication whilst on earth. In the same strict sense he may be released from excommunication after his death, and the *Rituale Romanum* contains the following right for absolving an excommunicated person already dead.

"RITUS ABSOLUENDI EXCOMMUNICATUM IAM MORTUUM. *If it so come to pass that any excommunicated person who has departed from this life gave evident signs of contrition, in order that he shall not be deprived of ecclesiastical burial in consecrated ground, but rather that he shall be holpen by the prayers of the Church, in so far as this may be done, let him be absolved after this manner.*

"*If the body be not yet buried, let it be lightly beaten with a rod or small cords after which it shall be absolved as followeth ; and then having been absolved let it be buried in consecrated ground.*

"*But if it hath been already buried in unconsecrated ground, if it may be conveniently done, let the body be exhumed, and after it hath been lightly beaten in like manner and then absolved let it be buried in consecrated ground ; but if the body cannot conveniently be disinterred, then the grave shall be beaten lightly and the absolution shall be pronounced.*

"*And if the body be already buried in consecrated ground, it shall not be disinterred, but the grave shall be lightly beaten.*

"*Let the Priest say the Antiphon :* The bones that have been humbled shall rejoice in the Lord ; *together with the psalm* Miserere.

"*And when they have made an end of the psalm let the body be absolved, and the Priest shall say :* By the authority granted unto me I absolve thee from the bond of excommunication, which thou hast incurred (*or*, which thou art said to have incurred) on account of such and such a thing, and I restore thee to the communion of the faithful, in the Name of the Father,✝, and of the Son, and of the Holy Ghost. Amen.

" *Then shall be said the psalm,* De profundis, *and at the end thereof :*

V. Rest eternal grant unto him, O Lord.

R. And let perpetual light shine upon him.

Kyrie eleison. Christe eleison. Kyrie eleison. Our Father.

V. And lead us not into temptation.

R. But deliver us from evil.

V. From the gate of hell.

R. O Lord, deliver his soul.

V. May he rest in peace.

R. Amen.

V. O Lord hear my prayer.

R. And let my cry come to Thee.

V. The Lord be with you.

R. And with thy spirit.

Let us pray.

Prayer. Grant, we beseech Thee O Lord, to the soul of thy servant, who hath been held in the bond of excommunication, a place of refreshment, rest and repose, and the brightness of Thy eternal light. Through Christ our Lord. *R.* Amen."

It is now necessary to inquire into certain extraordinary cases which are recorded and which are true beyond all manner of doubt of persons who died excommunicated and whose bodies were seen to rise from the tomb and leave the sacred precincts where they were buried. In the first place we have the very famous account given by S. Gregory the Great[24] of the two dead nuns, generally called the " Suore Morte." Two ladies of an illustrious family had been admitted to the sisterhood of S. Scholastica. Although in most respects exemplary and faithful to their vows, they could not refrain from scandal, gossip, and vain talk. Now S. Benedict was the first to lay down the strictest and most definite laws concerning the observance of silence.[25] In all monasteries and convents, or every order, there are particular places, called the " Regular Places " (the Church, refectory, dormitory, etc.) and special times, above all the night hours, termed the " Great silence," wherein speaking is unconditionally prohibited. Outside these places and times there are usually accorded " recreations " during which conversation is not only permitted but encouraged, though it must be governed by rules of charity and moderation. Useless and idle prattling is universally forbidden at all times and in all places. Accordingly, when it was reported to S. Benedict that the two nuns were greatly given to brabble indiscreetly, the holy Abbot was sore displeased, and sent them the message to the effect that if they did not learn to refrain their tongues and give a better example to the community he must excommunicate them. At first the sisters were alarmed and penitent, and promised to amend their idle ways ; but the treacherous habit was too strong for their good resolves ; they continued to give offence by their naughty chatter, and in the midst of their folly they suddenly died. Being of a great and ancient house they were buried in the church near the high altar ; and afterwards on a certain day, whilst a solemn High Mass was being sung, before the Liturgy of the Faithful began, and the Catechumens were dismissed by the Deacon crying : " Let those who are forbidden to partake, let those who are excommunicated, depart from hence and leave us ! " Behold, in the sight of all the people the two nuns rose up from their graves, and with faces drooping and averted, they glided sadly out of the Church. And thus it happened every time the Holy Mysteries were celebrated, until their old nurse interceded with S. Benedict, and he had pity upon them and absolved them from all their sins so that they might rest in peace.[26]

S. Augustine tells us[27] that the names of the Martyrs upon the diptychs were recited, but not to pray for them, whilst the names of nuns, who were recently deceased were recited in order to offer prayers on their behalf. *Perhibet praeclarissimum testimonium Ecclesiastica auctoritas, in qua fidelibus notum est, quo loco Martyres, et quo defunctae Sanctimoniales ad Altaris Sacramenta recitantur.* It has been suggested that it was at this point the two nuns may have withdrawn from the church, but S. Gregory expressly says that it was at the moment when the Deacon chanted in a loud voice the ritual praise bidding those who were not in full communion go forth from the holy place.

S. Gregory also relates that a young monk left the monastery without permission and without receiving any blessing or dismissal from the Abbot. Unhappily he died before he could be reconciled, and he was duly buried in consecrated ground. On the next morning his corpse was discovered lying huddled up and thrown out of his grave, and his relations in terror hastened to S. Benedict, who gave them a consecrated Host, and told them to put It with all possible reverence upon the breast of the young religious. This was done, and the tomb was never again found to have cast forth the body.[28]

This custom of putting a Eucharistic Particle in the grave with a dead person may seem to many very extraordinary, but it was by no means unknown in former centuries. In the *Uita Basilii*, the *Life of S. Basil the Great*, which was often attributed to Amphilochius of Iconium,[29] but is now recognized to be spurious and of about the ninth century, we are told that S. Basil reserved a portion of a consecrated Particle, even a third part, in order that It should be buried with him. Several Synods, howbeit assemblies of no supreme authority, had already condemned this practice, and others of a later date prohibited it as contrary to the end of the Blessed Sacrament as instituted by Jesus Christ.[30]

None the less in various places the custom persisted of reverently putting Particles in the graves of persons who were much honoured for their sanctity, and thus in the tomb of S. Othmar (Audomar), who died 16th November, 759, on the island of Werd in the Rhine, and whose body was transferred ten years later to the monastery of S. Gall, being solemnly entombed in 867 in the new Church of S. Othmar at S. Gall,[31] a number of Particles were found to have been placed on the spot where his head reposed.[32]

In a life of S. Cuthbert, Bishop of Lindisfarne, Patron of Durham, which is reprinted by the Bollandists,[33] it is said that at one of the Translations of his body a number of Particles were found in the coffin. Amalarius of Metz, upon the authority of the Venerable Bede says in his great treatise *De ecclesiasticis officiis*[34] that these Particles were put upon the breast of the saint before he was buried : " oblata super Sanctum pectus posita." This circumstance however, is not mentioned by Bede, but it occurs in the *Uita S. Cuthberti*, written between 698 and 705 by a monk of Lindisfarne. Amalarius considers that this custom was doubtless derived

from the Roman Church, and that thence it was communicated to England. Nicholas-Hugues Ménard, the famous
Maurist,[35] in his glosses upon the *S. Gregorii I Papae Liber
Sacramentorum*, which he printed, Paris, 1646,[36] from a manuscript Missal of S. Eligius, states that it was not this custom
which was condemned by the various Councils, but an abuse
which had crept up and which consisted in giving communion
to the dead, and actually placing the Sacred Host in their
mouths. However that may be, we know that Cardinal
Humbert, of Silva Candida, legate of S. Leo IX, in the middle
of the eleventh century, in his answer to the various objections
and difficulties which had been raised by Michael Caerularius,
Patriarch of Constantinople, author of the second and final
schism of the Byzantine Church,[37] reproached the Greeks
with the custom of burying any Particles which might remain
over after the Communion of the people at Holy Mass.

It is said that even to-day in many places throughout Greece
upon the lips of the dead is laid a crumb of consecrated bread
from the Eucharist. Out of reverence this has often been
replaced by a fragment of pottery on which is cut the sign
of the Cross with the legend I.X.NI.KA. (Jesus Christ
conquers) at the four angles. Theodore Burt, *The Cyclades*,
informs us that locally in Naxos the object thus employed is a
wax cross with the letters I.X.N. imprinted thereon, and this
moreover still bears the name ναῦλον, fare, showing that the
tradition is closely connected with the old custom of placing
the " ferryman's coin " in the mouth of a dead man, the fee
for Charon. Now Charon, who has assumed the form Charos,
is entirely familiar to the modern Greek peasant, but his is
not merely as classical literature depicts him, Portitor Stygis,
the boatman of Styx, he is Death itself, the lord of ghosts and
shadows. Until recent years, at all events, the practice
prevailed in many parts of Greece of placing in the mouth
(more rarely on the breast) of a deceased person a small coin,
and in the district of Smyrna this was actually known as
" passage-money," τὸ περατίκιον.[38] Yet strangely enough
although both custom and name survived the reason for the
coin had been forgotten, and for a century or more (save it
might be obscurely in some very remote spot)[39] it was not
associated in any way with Charos. Possibly the original
meaning of the coin has vanished in the mists of dateless

antiquity, and even in classical days the original significance was lost, so it came then to be explained that the obol was Charon's fee, whereas this is but a late and incorrect interpretation of a custom whose meaning went deeper than that, which had existed before mythology knew of a ferryman of hell.

The soul was supposed to escape by the mouth, which as it is an exit from the body is also the entrance to the body, and naturally it is by this path that the soul, if it were to return to the body, would re-enter, or by which an evil spirit or demon would make its way into the body. The coin, then, or charm seems most likely to have been a safeguard against any happening of this kind. In Christian days the Holy Eucharist or a fragment inscribed with sacred names will be the best preventative. Moreover not infrequently the piece of pottery placed in the mouth of the dead has scratched upon it the pentacle of magic lore. It is extremely significant that in Myconos this sign is often carved on house doors to preserve the inmates from the vampire, *vrykolakas*. So in Greece at all events the custom of burying a consecrated Particle with a corpse, or of putting a crumb of the Host between the dead man's lips originated as a spell to counteract the possibility of vampirism.

It should be remarked that a consecrated Host placed in the tomb where a vampire is buried will assuredly prevent the vampire from issuing forth out of his grave, but for obvious reasons this is a remedy which is not to be essayed, since it savours of rashness and profanation of God's Body.

There are in history many other examples of excommunicated persons who have not been able to rest in consecrated ground. In the year 1030, S. Godard, Bishop of Hildesheim in Lower Saxony, was obliged to excommunicate certain persons for their crimes and filthy sacrileges. Nevertheless, so powerful were the barons and over-lords, their protectors, that they buried the bodies of their followers in the Cathedral itself, in the very sanctuary. Upon this the bishop launched the ban of excommunication against them also ; but, none the less, utterly disregarding the censures they forced their way into the various churches. Upon the next high festival in truth, the rebellious nobles were present with a throng of armed attendants in the Cathedral itself. The aisles were packed with worshippers, and afar off spanned by the vaulted roof the High Altar blazed with a myriad tapers whose glow was reflected in the mirror of polished gold and the crystal heart of great reliquaries. The Bishop, his canons around him, pontificated the Mass. But after the Gospel, S. Godard turned from the altar, and in ringing tones of command bade all those who were under any censure or ban to leave the sacred building. The living smiled contemptuously, shrugged a little and did not stir, but down the aisles were seen to glide in awful silence dark shadowy figures, from whom the crowds shrank in speechless dread. They seemed to pass through the doors out of the sacred place. When the service was done the bishop absolved the dead, and lo, the ghastly train appeared to re-enter their tombs. Thereupon the living were so struck with fear that they sought to be reconciled, and after due penance absolution was granted them.

At the instigation of Abbot Odolric of Conques the Council of Limoges held in 1031 proclaimed the " Truce of God " that is to say a temporary suspension of hostilities, and the fathers threatened with general excommunication those feudal lords who would not swear to maintain it. There thence arose a consideration of the effects of excommunication, and it was agreed by all that although so severe a sentence must not be lightly denounced, once delivered the utmost respect must be paid to its provisions. In order to illustrate this, the Bishop of Cahors related a recent event which was known to his whole diocese and which could be proved by a number of independent witnesses. For his ceaseless rapine and unrepented murders, his evil examples of a lewd and licentious life, his blasphemies and infidelity, a certain nobleman whose castle was hard by the city had been excommunicated, and not long afterwards he had fallen in some midnight foray. The friends of the deceased never doubted that the bishop would give absolution, and they made great instance that he should do so, in order that the dead man might be buried with solemn dirge and requiem, with meed of trentals hereafter sung, in the vault of his ancestors, which was one of the most striking monuments in S. Peter's Church. However, the whole territory had for so long been harried by marauding violence that the bishop considered an example must be made in order to teach the rest of the plundering nobles a lesson, and he refused either to raise the ban or to permit the wonted ceremonies at the funeral. Nonetheless in defiance of his orders an armed band of soldiers marched into the town, and buried the dead body in the tomb, carefully closing it and mortarizing it after them. However, on the following morning the body was discovered naked, bruised and banged in the market square as though it had been violently thrown out of the church, although there was no mark or sign that the tomb had been in any way tampered with or touched. The soldiers, who had buried their leader, having opened the monument found only the cerements in which the corpse had been erstwhile wound, and so they buried it there a second time, placing seals and bars upon the church door inasmuch as it was impossible for anyone to enter. On the following morning, however, the body was discovered to have been thrown forth with even more contumely than before. Nevertheless they interred it a third time, but with the same result. This was repeated no less than five times in all, and at last they huddled the poor rotting carrion as best they might into a deep hole dug in some lonely spot far from consecrated ground. These terrible circumstances filled the hearts of all with such amaze that the neighbouring barons one and all, very humbly betook themselves to the bishop, and under most solemn promises made a treaty binding themselves to respect all the privileges of the church and amend their lives in every particular.

A very remarkable incident is related in the Greek Menion[40] that is to say the collection of the twelve books, one for every month, that contain the offices for immovable feasts in the Byzantine rite, and which in some wise correspond to the *Propiuum sanctorum* in the Roman breviary. The legend, it is true, offers certain difficulties which will be considered later, but it is certainly worth repeating as showing the extreme, and indeed exaggerated views the Greeks attached to excommunication. A certain coenobite of the desert near Alexandria had been excommunicated by the archimandrite for some act of disobedience, whereupon he forsook his monastery, left the desert and came to the city. No sooner, however, had he arrived here than he was arrested by the orders of the Governor, stripped of his habit, and ordered to offer sacrifice in the temple to idols. The Coenobite refused, and after having been long tortured in vain, at length he was put to death, his head being struck off, and the trunk thrown out beyond the town walls to be devoured by the wild beasts. But the Christians took it up during the night and having embalmed it with rich spices and shrouded it in fair linen, they buried it honourably in a prominent place in the Church, since they regarded him, and with justice, as a Martyr. But upon the next Sunday when the Deacon had chanted the ritual formula, bidding the Catechumens and those who should not be present to withdraw, all were sore amazed when the tomb suddenly opened and the body of the Martyr glided there from and was seen lingering in the narthex of the church. When the Mass was done the body seemed to return once more to its grave.

The whole community was filled with fearful awe and confusion, and a Basilian nun of great piety having fasted and prayed for the space of three days received a revelation from an angel who informed her that the Coenobite was still excommunicate since he had disobeyed his superior, and that he would remain under the ban until the superior himself granted him absolution. Thereupon a company of honourable persons journeyed to the monastery, and besought the archimandrite to pronounce the words. In all haste the holy old man accompanied them to the church. Here they opened the tomb of the Martyr and a full absolution was pronounced. Thereafter he lay at rest in his appointed place.

There are several details in this account which appear very suspicious. In the first place, at the period that the desert was the resort of Coenobites, the days of persecution, so far as Alexandria was concerned, at any rate, were a thing of the past. In the city complete toleration prevailed, and indeed if there had been any prosecutions, not Christianity but the Pagan rites would have been suppressed and the heathen temples closed. Christianity in this century was honoured throughout the whole of Egypt, and Alexandria was one of the strongholds. In the second place, the monks of the desert were not Coenobites, that is to say members of a definite religious community having a Superior, but they were rather solitary hermits, belonging to no religious family, each being independent, and no hermit would have had the power to excommunicate one of his fellows. In the third place, no details are given with regard to the reasons why this monk was supposed to have incurred a major excommunication, and this, the gravest of all censures, is the only ban which excludes from participation in the sacred Mysteries. It is true, perhaps, that if a Religious broke his vows, left his monastery, abandoned his habit, and disregarding the commands of the Church betook himself to some populous city where he proceeded to live, as a secular, a life that was far from careful, such a person would presumably give great scandal and by his actions he might indeed incur the major excommunication, but we are not told that in the case of the Coenobite anything of this sort happneed, we are not informed of aggravating circumstances, and further it must be borne in mind that at the period these events were said to take place the hermits of the desert were not, as are Religious to-day, bound by vows of stability[41] and of obedience to their Superiors, who had not the right to pronounce a sentence of Major excommunication.

It should perhaps be explained that until recently excommunication was of two kinds, Major and Minor. Sabetti thus concisely explains :[42] " Excommunicatio est *censura*, *per quam quis priuatur communione Ecclesiæ ;* seu censura, qua Christianus bonis spiritualibus Ecclesiæ communibus, quorum distributio ad ipsam pertinet, uel omninio uel ex parte priuatur. Separat igitur excommunicatum a societate seu communione uisibili fidelium et bonis quæ eam, ut talis est, consequuntur.

Distinguitur excommunicatio in *maiorem*, quæ priuat omnibus bonis Ecclesiæ communibus, et *minorem*, quæ bonis aliquibus tantum priuat. *Maior* in iure nonnunquam *anathema* uocatur ; atque tunc præsertim, quando propter hæresim uel hæresis suspicionem infligitur, aut peculiaribus quibusdam adhibitis cærimoniis solemnius denuntiatur.—Insuper excommunicati excommunicatione *maiori*, alii dicuntur *tolerati*, quos fideles non tenentur uitare ; alii *non tolerati* seu *uitandi*, quos uitare debent." Briefly this is to say that minor excommunication is a prohibition from receiving the sacraments, what we call in theology the passive use of the sacraments. Major excommunication is that which we have already defined, and which now practically remains in force, whilst the technical anathema does not differ essentially from excommunication but is emphasized with special ceremonies and the most solemn promulgation of this terrible sentence.

In a life of S. Augustine the Apostle of England, which has been printed by the Bollandists,[43] John Brompton relates the following history. S. Augustine had long been endeavouring to persuade a certain nobleman of great wealth to pay the appointed tithes, but out of obstinacy these were constantly refused, which did great mischief and caused others to become discontented and impudently follow so bad an example. On a certain great feast day whilst High Mass was being solemnly sung S. Augustine was inspired to pronounce to the people that all who had been excommunicated must leave the sacred edifice. To the horror and amaze of the assistants an ancient tomb was seen to open, and there issued forth the desiccated yet incorrupt body of a man who had been buried a century and a half before. When the service was done S. Augustine in solemn procession went to the tomb whither the dead man had been seen to glide back as " ite missa est " was chanted, and here he solemnly adjured him, bidding him say why he had appeared. The dead man replied that he was excommunicate. The Saint asked where was buried the priest who had pronounced the sentence. It appeared that the tomb was in the cathedral at no great distance. Going thither the Archbishop bade the priest declare why he had excommunicated the dead man. A dark shadowy figure was seen to hover among the pillars of the nave and a low far-off voice answered : " I excommunicated him for his misdeeds, and particularly because he robbed the church of her due, refusing to pay his tithes." " Let it suffice, brother," returned the Saint, " and do you now at our bidding and at our request absolve him and free him from the censure." The shadowy figure repeated the loosening words, and faded from sight. They then returned to the tomb of the dead man, who said in a gentle whisper : " I thank you, O my father, for now at last may I find rest and repose."

Certain authorities have cast very grave doubts upon this story, for they point out that firstly, even in the time of S. Augustine himself there was no obligation in Britain to pay tithes, and these were most assuredly not required under pain of excommunication. This is very true, but there is no reason at all why the legend should not be correct in detail although very considerably antedated. It is more than probable that the incident occured in a far later century, and that the chronicler of Canterbury attributed it, perhaps in geniune error, for the tale had come down by word of mouth, or perhaps with pardonable inexactitude, to the days of S. Augustine around whose great and glorious figure had clustered so many reverend legends, so many ancient traditions.

Melchior, Abbot of the Cistercian house of Zwettl, in his work *De Statu Mortuorum* relates that a young scholar of the town of Saint-Pons, having unfortunately incurred the penalty of excommunication was killed, and shortly afterwards he appeared to one of his friends begging him to betake himself to the Bishop of Rhodez and from him to seek absolution. The friend did not hesitate to do as he was asked, and although it was mid-winter with the snow lying deep upon the ground, for it was a season of exceptional severity, he at once set out upon the journey. When he had gone some little distance the road branched, and he was undecided which path to take. With much hesitancy he proceeded towards the left, when he felt (as he thought) his cloak gently pulled, but at first he took no notice, deeming it merely the wind and the storm. A moment after his cloak was caught again and there could be no mistaking the tug. He turned and found himself gently guided into the other road. Eventually he reached the town, and obtained audience of the Bishop, who upon hearing his tale at once raised the ban with a full and plenary absolution. The young man discovered that had he continued the path to the left he must have wandered far among the snow-drifts where he would inevitably have perished of cold and exposure. That night his friend appeared to him with a glad and smiling countenance and thanking him for the pains he had been at assured him that he should by no means lose his reward.

Dom Augustin Calmet records at length a letter, dated 5 April, 1745, which he received from a correspondent who had read with great interest the manuscript of this learned writer's *Dissertation sur les apparitions des anges, des démons et des esprits.*[44] The writer says : " A man living at Létraye, a village which is not very many leagues from the town of Remiremont (Vosges),[45] lost his wife at the beginning of last

February, but married again in the week before Lent. At eleven o'clock in the evening on his marriage day, the late wife appeared and spoke to the new bride, and the result of this was that the bride declared that she must on behalf of the dead woman undertake to perform seven pilgrimages.[46] Since that day and always at the very same hour the ghost has appeared and it was distinctly heard to speak by the parish priest as well as by a number of other persons. On the 15 March, at the very moment when the woman was about to proceed to the church of S. Nicolas to which the pilgrimage was to be made, the ghost suddenly stood in her path and bade her hasten, adding that she must not allow herself to be alarmed, or in any way deterred by any accident or sickness that might befall her on the way.

Accordingly the woman set out with her husband, her brother-in-law and her sister-in-law, and she is very certain that the dead wife remained by her side until she actually came to the door of the church of S. Nicolas. When these good people arrived at a distance of some two leagues from the place, S. Nicolas' church, they were obliged to halt at an inn by the wayside which is known as " The Shelter " (*les Baraques*). Here the woman suddenly became so ill that the two men were compelled to carry her right up to the church, but no sooner had she arrived at the door than she was able to walk without any difficulty and her pain vanished in a moment. " This amazing occurrence was related to me and also to the Father Sacristan by all the four pilgrims ; and it was reported that the last thing which the dead woman told the new bride was that when one half of the pilgrimages had been duly accomplished she would be seen no more. The plain and straightforward way in which these good folk told us the story does not allow one to doubt that they were reporting actual facts." Upon this relation, Calmet comments : " It is not said that the young woman who died was under any sentence of excommunication ; but apparently she was bound by a solemn promise or a vow that she must have made to perform these pilgrimages, which she obliged her successor to discharge on her behalf. It should be remarked that the ghost did not enter the church dedicated to S. Nicolas, but apparently for some reason remained at the door."

A very extraordinary circumstance is related by Wipert, Archdeacon of the celebrated see of Toul, who wrote the life of Pope S. Leo IX, a Pontiff, who had been for more than twenty years Bishop of Toul,[47] and who died in March, 1054. The historian[48] tells us that some years before the death of S. Leo IX, the citizens of Narni, a little burgh which is picturesquely situated on a lofty rock at the point where the river Nera forces its way through a narrow ravine to join the Tiber, were one day greatly surprised and indeed alarmed to see a mysterious company of persons who appeared to be advancing towards the town. The magistrates, fearing some surprise, gave orders that the gates should be fast closed, whilst the inhabitants incontinently betook themselves to the walls. The procession, however, which was clothed in white and seemed from time to time to vanish among the morning mists and then once again to reappear, was obviously no inimical band. They passed on their way without turning to right or to left, and it is said they seemed to be defiling with measured pace almost until eventide. All wondered who these persons could be, and at last one of the most prominent citizens, a man of great resolution and courage resolved to address them. To his amazement he saw among them a certain person who had been his host many years before Ascoli, and of whose death he had been not recently informed. Calling upon him loudly by his name he asked : " Who are you, and whence cometh this throng ? " " I am your old friend," was the reply, " and this multitude is phantom ; we have not yet atoned for the sins we committed whilst on earth, and we are not yet deemed worthy to enter the Kingdom of Heaven ; therefore are we sent forth as humble penitents, lowly palmers, whose lot it is with pains and with much moil to visit the holy sanctuaries of the world, such as are appointed unto us in order. At this hour we come from the shrine of S. Martin, and we are on our way to the sanctuary of Our Lady of Farfa."[49] The goodman was so terrified at these words that he fell as in a fit, and he remained ill for a full twelvemonth. It was he who related this extraordinary event to Pope S. Leo IX. With regard to the company there could be no mistake ; it was seen not by one person or even by a few, but by the whole town. Although naturally enough the appearance of so vast a number would give rise to no little alarm since hostile designs would be suspected, so crowded a pilgrimage in the eleventh century would not by any means be a unique, even if it were an exceptional event. Whole armies of pious persons were traversing Europe from shrine to shrine, whilst the enthusiasism for the pilgrimage to Jerusalem was greatly on the increase and was, before many years had passed to culminate in the Crusades. Even by the end of the tenth century hospices had been built throughout the whole valley of the Danube, the favoured route to the Holy Land, where pilgrims could replenish their provisions. In 1026, Richard, Abbot of Saint-Vannes, led seven hundred pilgrims into Palestine, all expenses being discharged by Richard II, Duke of Normandy. In 1065, over twelve thousand Germans, who had crossed Europe, under the command of Gunther, Bishop of Bamberg, while on their way through Palestine had to seek shelter in a ruined fortress where they defended themselves against troops of marauding Bedouins.[50] Gunther actually died in this year at Odenberg (Sopron) in Hungary while engaged on a Crusade. In 1073, Pope S. Gregory VII was seriously contemplating the leading of a force of fifty thousand men to the East, military pilgrims who would repulse the Turks, rescue the Holy Sepulchre, and re-establish Christian unity. Therefore in itself the appearance of this company of pilgrims outside the walls of Narni, if remarkable, would be a very possible and understandable circumstance.

In his *Antidote against Atheism*, III, 12, Dr. Henry More relates some remarkable instances of multitudinous phantoms. He says : " Our *English Chronicles* also tell us of *Apparitions, armed men, foo*' and *horse, fighting* upon the ground in the North part of *England*, and in *Ireland*, for many evenings together, seen by many hundreds of men at once, and that the grass was trodden down in the places where they were seen to fight their *Battles :* which agreeth with *Nicolea Langbernhard* her Relation of the *cloven-footed Dancers*, that left the print of their hoofs in the *ring* they trod down for a long time after.

" But this *skirmishing* upon the *Earth*, puts me in mind of the last part of this argument, and bids me look up into the *Air*. Where, omitting all other Prodigies, I shall only take notice of what is most notorious, and of which there can by

no means be given any other account, than that it is the effect
of the *Spirits*. And this is the Appearance of *armed Men
fighting* and encountering one another in the *Sky*. There
are so many examples of these Prodigies in *Historians*, that
it were superfluous to instance in any. That before the great
slaughter of no less than fourscore thousand made by *Antiochus*
in *Jerusalem*, recorded in the second of *Maccabees* Chapter 5. is
famous. The Historian there writes, ' That through all the
City, for the space almost of fourty days, there were seen
Horsemen running in the *Air* in cloth of Gold, and arm'd
with Lances, like a band of Soldiers, and *Troops* of Horsemen
in array, *encountring* and running one against another, with
shaking of shields, and multitude of pikes, and drawing of
swords, and casting of darts, and glittering of golden ornaments, and harness of all sorts.' And *Josephus* writes also
concerning the like Prodigies that happen'd before the
destruction of the City by *Titus*, prefacing first, that they
were incredible, were it not that they were recorded by those
that were Eye-witnesses of them.

"The like *Apparitions* were seen before the Civil Wars of
Marius and *Sylla*. And *Melanchthon* affirms, that a world
of such Prodigies were seen all over *Germany*, from 1524 to
1548. *Snellius*, amongst other places, doth particularize
in *Amortsfort*, where these *fightings* were seen not much higher
than the house-tops ; as also in *Amsterdam*, where there was
also a *Sea-fight* appearing in the *Air* for an hour or two together,
many thousands of men looking on."

It is not said that it was actually the bodies of those who
were dead who were thus seen passing by the walls of Narni,
on the contrary we are given to understand that it was a
spectral host, but with regard to those persons who were
excommunicated we are to believe that physically they are
bound by the ban, and that in the cases of resuscitation it is
the actual body which appears. It is related in the life of
Libentius I, Archbishop of Hamburg-Bremen, who died
4 January, 1013, ruling his see during the reign of King
Svend Tdeskaeg,[51] that he excommunicated a number of
pirates, and that one of them having been slain was buried
on the Norwegian coast. Here by some chance well-nigh
fifty years later the body was dug up, and being found intact
most widespread terror ensued, until at length a bishop

was found who understanding the circumstances pronounced
the necessary absolutions, when the corpse crumbled to dust.
One account states that this prelate was Alured of Winchester,
although it seems difficult to suppose that this is correct.
It is related that the bodies of those who have been struck by
lightning are very often found intact, an opinion maintained
by the medical writer Zachias, but Ambroise Paré explained
this since he says that such persons are as it were embalmed
with the sulphur, which is a preventative of corruption
acting in the same way as salt. During a terrible fire at
Quebec in 1705, the Ursuline Convent was destroyed and
unhappily five nuns perished. More than twenty years later
their bodies which had been buried in a layer of hot ashes
were not merely found intact but even bled copiously in a
thick stream.

Malva relates in his *Turco-græcia*[52] that at the time of a
certain Patriarch of Constantinople, who he names Maximus
or Emanuel, and whom he places towards the end of the fifteenth century, the Ottoman Sultan was desirous of inquiring
into the truth of this belief which was so universally held by
the Greeks, namely that the body of a person who had died
excommunicate remained whole. The Patriarch caused to
be opened, the tomb of a woman, who was notorious as having
been the mistress of an Archbishop of Constantinople, and the
body was found entire. The Turkish officials then enclosed
it in a coffin which was bound round and hermetically sealed
with the Emperor's own signet. The Patriarch after having
said the appointed prayers, pronounced a solemn absolution
over the dead woman, and three days afterwards when the
coffin was opened there was only to be seen a handful of dust.
Upon this Calmet aptly remarks : " I do not see any miracle
here, since everybody knows that sometimes bodies are found
entire and complete in a monument or sarcophagus, and
that they crumble to dust immediately they are exposed to the
air," and the learned Abbot very pertinently adds : " I do not
see how the Archbishop of Constantinople could after death
validly absolve a person who was presumably impenitent and
who had died excommunicate."[53] It will readily be remembered
in this connexion that the famous vaults of S. Michan's church
in Dublin, for some reason possess the horrid property of
preserving corpses from decay for centuries. As Mr. H. F.

Berry tells us in his Preface (p. vi) to *The Registers of the Church of S. Michan*, Dublin, 1907 : " As is well-known the preservative qualities of the vaults under S. Michan's Church are most remarkable, and decay in the bodies committed to them is strangely arrested. The latest writer on the subject (D. A. Chart, *Story of Dublin*) in a short notice of the Church, speaks of being struck (among others) " by a pathetic baby corpse, from whose plump wrists still hang the faded white ribbons of its funeral." This coffin bears the date, 1679 ; yet the very finger and toe nails of the child are still distinct. The antiseptic qualities are believed to be largely attributable to the extreme dryness of the vaults and to the great freedom of their atmosphere from dust particles."

It is generally admitted that the circumstances which attend the decomposition of the human body are very difficult in their manifold complications since atmosphere, situation with other accidents play so important and obscure a part, whence these laws are still very imperfectly understood owing to the immense practical difficulties, one might almost say the impossibility, of systematic investigation. Doctors A. C. Taylor and F. J. Smith in their *Medical Jurisprudence*[54] which is universally accepted as a standard and completely authoritative work, comment on these phenomena in very plain terms, frankly acknowledging the doubts and uncertainty that still envelop the whole question. " The action of the environment, the inherent potentialities of the microbes, and the state of their vitality at any moment involve such an enormous number of varying and variable factors that it becomes quite impossible to explain on a rational basis of ascertained fact . . . the extraordinary variations in the circumstances of putrefaction that have been observed." And a little later the same authorities tell us that " sometimes one body has been found more decomposed after six or eight months burial than another which has lain interred for a period of eighteen months or two years."[55] An eminent American medical expert, Dr. H. P. Loomis, says : " I have seen bodies buried two months that have shown fewer of the changes produced by putrefaction than others dead but a week."[56]

The Greeks, as we have seen in some detail, generally regarded the fact that a body was found intact as a sign that the person had died excommunicate or under some curse, and was at any rate in a state of unhappiness, of painful detention or probation. It is now necessary to consider an aspect of the question which is diametrically and entirely opposed to this idea, namely those cases where incorruption is an evidence of extraordinary sanctity, when the mortal remains of some great saint having been exhumed after death are found to be miraculously preserved for the veneration of the faithful. It is not perhaps even to-day generally recognized how solemn and weighty, how lengthy and detailed a process is that inquiry which must precede those decrees regarding religious honour paid to a deceased person distinguished for eminent holiness of life whether it be that permissive cultus known as Beatification, or that complete preceptive universal cultus known as Canonization. The real trial of a subject proposed for Canonization may be said to begin when a number of very exhaustive examinations have already been made, which for all their rigour are preliminary and ordinary, and the Apostolic process commences which investigates the Virtues and Miracles of the person. S. Thomas defines a miracle as an effect which is beyond the " Order of the whole of created nature." And he explains this by telling us that, if a man throws a stone up into the air, such a motion is no wise miraculous, for though it exceed the powers in a nature of a stone, it is produced by the natural power of man, and therefore it does not exceed the power of the whole of created nature. Besides genuine miracles a number of marvellous phenomena may be and indeed are exhibited, many of which are due to natural powers, as yet imperfectly known or entirely unknown, to hallucination, or to fraud. Therefore miracles do not constitute sanctity of themselves, and Benedict XIV discusses in his great work *De Seruorum Dei Beatificatione et Beatorum Canonizatione*, IV, pars. I, c. iv, *De Fine Miraculorum, et de differentiis inter uera et falsa Miracula*.[57] The same great authority lays down that heroic virtues are the first and most decisive witness to sanctity ; " visions, prophecies and miracles are only of secondary importance, and they are absolutely ignored if proof of heroic virtues is not forthcoming." This is further insisted upon by Scacchus,[58] and Castellinus[59] prudently says : " Not all the just are to be canonized by the Church, but those who have shone forth with heroic virtues." However, the value of miracles must not be under-estimated, and unfortunately in many directions there seems a tendency to fall into this grave error. Benedict XIV has a very important and weighty chapter, *De Miraculorum necessitate in causis Beatificationis et Canonizationis*, which might be studied with profit and instruction. It is not possible to give in detail here the various classes of Causes whose circumstances require a various number of miracles, but it may suffice to say that if the virtues or the martyrdom of the subject are proved by eye-witnesses two miracles are required for beatification and two for canonization. If, however, the virtues or the miracles have been established by evidence which is not that of eye-witnesses (*testes de auditu*), four miracles are required for beatification and two for canonization. It should be remarked that in all cases the miracles required for canonization must be wrought after beatification, and must be proved by eye-witnesses. Among these miracles which have to be established by evidence before a decree of Beatification is pronounced, the super-natural preservation of the body of a saint is sometimes admitted, and although such a miracle is investigated with the most scrupulous care none the less it is regarded as a high and exceptional distinction. It is generally hoped that at the exhumation of a person whose cause has been begun the body may be found to be preserved incorrupt, but this is by no means invariably the case. Thus Monsignor Benson in a letter dated 4 March, 1904, written from Rome, says : " Mr. ―― and I went yesterday to the exhuming of the body of Elizabeth Sanna,[60] who died thirty-five years ago in the odour of sanctity. They hoped to find the body incorrupt ; but it was not so . . . it was very interesting to see the actual bones of the Saint, and the Franciscan habit in which she was buried as a Tertiary of S. Francis ; and to think that very possibly every one of the fragments would be a venerated relic some day."[61]

It must then be carefully borne in mind that the preserva-tion of the bodies of saints is a very remarkable miracle, and is in no wise to be compared with that preservation of bodies which may occur from time to time under conditions with which we are imperfectly acquainted. It may be well to give a few examples of this supernatural phenomenon.

Not altogether unconnected and certainly deserving of a
brief consideration are those cases of irradiation when the
bodies or the garments, or perhaps the rooms of great saints
and mystics became luminous, emitting rays of light, a fact
which although certainly it did not originate the introduction
of the nimbus or aureola into art may probably have influenced
painting to a very large extent. It is a great mistake to say
with Gerard Gietmann[62] that all such symbols are suggested
by natural phenomena, scientifically accounted for in text
books on physics. Although the nimbus was early in use in
the monuments of Hellenic and Roman art this had little,
if any, influence in the Middle Ages and in earlier Christian
times. For as Durandus tells us, and correctly, it was to
passages in the Scriptures that reference was made for authority
to depict the halo as signifying holiness and dignity.[63] " Sic
omnes sancti pinguntur coronati, quasi dicerunt. Filiae
Hierusalem, uenite et uidete martyres cum coronis quibus
coronauit eas Dominus. Et in Libro Sapientiae : Iusti
accipient regnum decoris et diadema speciei de manu Domini.
Corona autem huiusmodi depingitur in forma scuti rotundi,
quia sancti Dei protectione diuina fruuntur unde cantant
gratulabundi : Domine ut scuto bonae uoluntatis tuae coronasti
nos " (For thus are all the Saints depicted, crowned, as if
they were to say : " O daughters of Jerusalem, come ye and
see the Martyrs with the crowns with which their Lord
crowned them."[64] And in the *Book of Wisdom :* " The Just
shall receive a kingdom of glory and a crown of beauty at the
hands of the Lord."[65] Now a crown of this kind is depicted
in the form of a round buckler, because they enjoy the
heavenly protection of God, wherefore they sing in perfect
happiness : " O Lord thou hast crowned us as with the shield
of thy good-will.") It may be remarked that Pope Gregory
the Great (about 600) allowed himself to be painted with a
square nimbus, and Johannes Diaconus[66] tells us that this was
the sign for a living person and not a crown. Other examples
of this ornamentation have come down to us from the following
centuries and they show that even children were sometimes
represented with this square nimbus.

It were impertinent to trace the development of the nimbus
halo, glory, and aureola in art, but this cannot fail to have
been affected by the irradiation of the mystics and ecstaticas.

The Dominican convent of Adelhausen, which was founded by the Consort of Egon II of Urach, Count of Freiburg (1218-36), is famous in the history of German mysticism and was the theatre of the most amazing phenomena.   Christina Mechthild Tuschelin, a nun of this house who, it is said, only broke silence once during the whole of her religious life,[67] was very frequently illumined with such a glory of brightness that nobody could look upon her, and at times the community were obliged to request her to absent herself from the choir in order that they might recite their office without distraction.

Another famous Dominican, S. Vincent Ferrer, was often surrounded by light, and on more than one occasion it was thought that either he, or indeed the whole room was ablaze, and persons ran there in great alarm to extinguish the fire, Often too, his white habit was actually scorched although there was no fire in the room.

It may be worth noting that the appearance of a room or a building upon fire has been remarked under very different conditions and proceeding from a very different origin.   When the notorious Dr. John Dee was Warden of Manchester College, a position he obtained in 1595 and resigned on account of failing health in 1602 or 1603, he often excited suspicion by the extraordinary, and some whispered unhallowed, nature of his studies which he often pursued in spite of his seventy years and more until the break of day.   One mid-night, the whole college was aroused by the fierce glare of a mighty fire, and it was seen that the warden's lodgings were bursting into flame in every direction.   In a few moments a crowd had hastily rushed to the spot and buckets of water were brought, when the flames suddenly died away, and almost immediately Dr. Dee appeared from his house to thank them for their care and assure them that he had been able to subdue the conflagration.   It is said that on the next day the building bore no mark of fire, which circumstance together with the fact that he had so mysteriously extinguished the flames went far to increase his sombre reputation in the town.

The halo is by no means merely an artistic symbolism.   A bright glow was often perceived to surround the head of S. Rose of Lima, and the same was not infrequently remarked in the cases of Thomas Lombard and the lay brother Barnaby of Pistoia.   This is also recorded of S. Ravello, a Bishop of

Ferrara, and of S. Afra of Augsburg, whose *Passio* is not later than the end of the fourth century. The Olivetan chronicles in their record of the founder of this austere reform, Bernardo Ptolomei, say that he was often seen to be encircled with light, a phenomenon which also distinguished Giovanni-Battista de Lanuza, and the Poor Clare, Antonia of Florence, who died in 1472. A glory in the shape of a star was observed on the forehead of Diego Lauda, and this is also related of that marvellous ecstatic Cecilia Baldi of Bologna. The description of S. Dominic which Cecilia Cesarini used to give must be very familiar to all. She loved to tell how, save when the sorrow of others moved him to compassion, he was always joyous and happy, and very frequently a radiant light played about his temples and illumined his sweet smiles. The countenance of Dominica of S. Mary literally blazed with light when she received Holy Communion, and the same marvel was observed in the case of Ida of Louvain, a stigmatized Cistercian nun of the Convent of Valrose, who died in 1300.

There are many more recent examples of this supernatural light, as for instance in the case of S. Alphonsus Liguori whose countenance when he preached one day in the Cathedral of Foggia, a ferverino in honour of Our Lady became exceedingly luminous and beamed with rays of dazzling brilliance. Again the Venerable Antony Claret, who died 24 October, 1870, was not infrequently seen to be haloed in a great splendour of golden glory whilst saying Mass in the Royal Chapel at Madrid. This miracle was witnessed by many, and Queen Isabella II solemnly took oath to that effect, requiring it to be placed upon record. The same phenomenon was witnessed by the whole congregation when the Venerable Claret was addressing them from the pulpit in the Cathedral at Vichy.[68]

It will not appear surprising that this irradiation often seems to reach its greatest intensity at the hour of death when the last bonds which tie man to the earth are being broken. S. John of the Cross in his last moments was surrounded by so brilliant a corruscation that those who were present were bound to turn away their eyes dazzled and blinded. When a pious widow, Gentile of Ravenna was dying the whole room appeared to shine, a phenomenon which was repeated in the case of Diego Ortiz, whilst the same is recorded of the

Dominican nun, Maria Villani of Naples (1584-1670), who has
had few rivals in her profound works on mysticism.

Very many other examples might be given, but we will
now mention a few instances in which the irradiation continued
even after the soul had left the body. Such was the case with
S. Alfrida, a daughter of King Offa of Mercia ; whilst the
bodies of S. Juventius and S. Maximus reflected so penetrating
a brilliance that nobody could bear to gaze upon them.
Similar circumstances are said to have occurred at the tomb
of S. Wilfred who was enshrined in the Church of S. Peter at
Ripon, and also at the tomb of S. Kunigunde, who is buried
in the Cathedral of Bamberg.

Of Blessed Walter the Premonstratensian Abbot of Ilfeld
in Hanover, who died in 1229, the Nobertine chronicle tell us
that when the holy body was being carried on its bier to
the tomb, so great a glory shone all around it that the
religious who were inceding in solemn procession after
the remains of their dead father were fain to veil their eyes.
" B. Walterus. . . Moriens cum ad sepulchrum deferretur,
tanta lux diuinitus immissa defuncti corpus irradiauit, ut
religiosi adsistentes eam uix ferre possent." Upon this an
old poet wrote the following lines :

De B. Waltero circa cuius feretrum coposia lux resplenduit.

> Corporis hos radios pia gens stupet, immemor ante
>   Illius aetherea cor rutilasse face.
> Et quid-ni stupeat, solem dum mergitur undis,
>   Clarius exstinctam spargere posse facem ?
> Ecce suae carnis WALTERVS lege solutus,
>   Ad tumulum moestis fratribus abripitur.
> Non patitur uirtus, indignaturque sepulcro
>   Claudier, in cincres, non abitura leues :
> Ucrum oritur, radio circumfulgente Feretrum,
>   Ut solet Eois Lucifer ortus aquis.
> O uir Sancte, tuis si lux hic tanta fuisti,
>   In coelo qualis quantaque stella micas ![69]

It is not surprising that persons whose holiness and asceticism
had been so great during their lives, that their bodies were
subjected to so extraordinary a phenomenon as irradiation,
should after death have remained incorrupt. The connexion
between the two is very obvious, and it should be remarked
that incorruption is one of the commonest circumstances

recorded in hagiology. Although it is impossible to give more
than a few examples from very many, it may be mentioned
that in the case of S. Edward the Confessor, who died 5 January, 1066, when the body was examined in 1102, it was found
to be incorrupt, the limbs flexible, and the cerements fresh and
clean ; whilst two years after canonization (1161) the body,
still incorrupt, was translated to a tomb of the greatest magni-
ficence. When eighty years after the first deposition the
body of S. Hugh, Bishop of Lincoln, who died 1200 and was
buried in Lincoln Cathedral, was taken up to be translated to
a richer shrine it was found to be wholly intact. Perhaps
one of the most remarkable instances of the mortal remains of
a Saint which are yet supernaturally preserved is that of the
Poor Clare, S. Catherine of Bologna, who died 9 March, 1463
and whose body is venerated in a small yet exquisitely elegant
sanctuary attached to the convent of Corpus Domini at
Bologna. It is a remarkable circumstance that here it is not
preserved under crystal or glass but is seated, dressed in
sumptuous brocades, jewelled and crowned, in an embroidered
chair in the centre of the room. The body is desiccated, but
in no sense decayed. In the Carmelite Convent of the Piazza
Savonarola at Florence is the body of S. Maria Madalena
de'Pazzi who died 25 May, 1607. This was exhumed in
1608, on account of the damp, when it was found to be entire
and flexible, and it was officially certified to be intact in 1639
and again in 1663. It is still perfect and whole where it
reposes in an elaborate shrine of crystal and gold. In the same
Church is the incorrupt body of Maria Bartolomea Bagnesi, a
Dominican Tertiary, whose death took place on Whit-Tuesday
1577. The body of another great Saint of Florence, S.
Antoninus, which was unburied for eight days, remained
flexible. This great Archbishop died 2 May, 1459, and in 1589,
when his tomb was examined the holy remains were found to
be still intact.

In Montefalco, high among the Umbrian uplands, lies the
body of the Augustinian S. Clare, one of the glories of that
ancient Order so rich in hallowed and venerable names, and
one of the most marvellous ecstaticas of all time. Born
about 1275, perhaps a few years earlier, she became Abbess
of the Convent of Montefalco and seemed to dwell more in
Heaven than on earth. Gifted with the spirit of prophecy

and the grace of working miracles, she was the subject of extraordinary ecstasies and raptures, which were prolonged from days to weeks. She died, 17 August, 1308, at three o'clock in the morning, and when her heart was extracted from her body this was opened and therein impressed upon the very flesh were seen a figure of Christ crucified, the scourge, the Crown of Thorns, the column, the lance, three nails, the sponge and reed. This relic is venerated at Montefalco to-day. Even now her body lies there perfect and intact. The hands and face are clearly visible, exquisitely pale and lovely, untouched by any fleck of corruption. It has not been embalmed, but Lorenzo Tardy says that throughout Italy of all the bodies of Saints which are venerated incorrupt the body of S. Clare of Montefalco is the loveliest and most free from any spot or blemish during the passing years.

Moreover when her heart was opened the blood flowed forth in great abundance and was carefully collected in a glass vial. Although normally coagulated it has preserved in colour a bright fresh red as though newly spilled. At rare intervals this blood liquefies and becomes from being opaque and congealed, humid, lucent, transparent, and freely-flowing. On occasion it has been known actually to spume and bubble. There are ample records that this took place in 1495, 1500, 1508, 1570, 1600, and 1618.[70]

It is known that new blood has frequently oozed from the arm of S. Nicolas, O.S.A., which is preserved at Tolentino, but the most famous of these blood-miracles is, of course, that of S. Januarius, the Patron of Naples. Here the blood of the Saint which is contained in two phials, enclosed in a silver reliquary, is held out by the officiating priest eighteen times in the year before the congregation in the Cathedral. Upon the altar is exposed the silver bust containing the Head of the Saint. After an interval, sometimes a space of hardly more than two minutes and sometimes (but very rarely) well nigh an hour the congealed mass in the phials becomes crimson and liquid, and on occasion froths and bubbles up within the ampolla.[71] Science having exhausted itself to find some explanation of the phenomenon confesses a miracle. The same liquefaction takes place with regard to some other Relics of peculiar sanctity, the blood of S.

John Baptist, of S. Stephen, the Proto-Martyr, of S. Patricia, and especially of S. Pantaleone, Relics of whose blood preserved at the Convent of the Incoronazione, Madrid, at Naples, and at Ravello, liquefy upon the feast day of the Saint afterwards returning to a congealed substance. It would appear a relic of the blood of S. Pantaleone at Valle della Lucarina remains liquid all the year round. As one might expect, sceptics both without—and alas! within the Church have attempted to find some natural explanation, but without avail. One notoriously rationalistic writer is " strongly inclined to believe that such alleged blood-relics *always* liquefied if they were exposed long enough to light and air," a suggestion which is demonstrably false. The same maggot-monger has audaciously ventured to declare : " If we could suppose some substance or mixture had been accidentally discovered which hardened when shut up in the dark, but melted more or less rapidly when exposed to the light of day in a warmer atmosphere, it would be easy to understand the multiplication of alleged relics of this character, which undoubtedly seems to have taken place in the latter part of the sixteenth century." It is instructive to remark what wild hypotheses men will build and what shifts men will seek who endeavour to escape from facts.

On 20 May, 1444, the celebrated missionary and reformer S. Bernardine of Siena died at Aquila in the Abruzzi. It was the Vigil of the Ascension and in the choir the friars were just chanting the Antiphon to the Magnificat, *Pater, manifestaui nomen tuum hominibus . . . ad Te uenio, alleluja.* The body was kept in the Church for twenty-six days after death, and what is very remarkable there was a copious flow of blood after twenty-four days. The people of Siena requested that so great a treasure might be handed over to them, but the local magistrates refused to do this, and with obsequies of the greatest splendour, S. Bernardine was laid to rest in the Church of the Coventuals. Six years later, 24 May, 1450, the Saint was solemnly canonized by Nicolas V. On 17 May, 1472, the body, yet without speck or mar, was translated to the new Church of the Observants at Aquila, which had been especially built to receive it, and here it was enclosed in a costly shrine presented by Louis XI of France. This Church having been completely destroyed by an earthquake in 1703, was replaced by another edifice where the relics of S. Bernardine are still venerated. The body was still intact in the seventeenth century.

With regard to the flow of blood, the same phenomenon was observed and even yet continues in the case of S. Nicolas of Tolentino, who died 10 September, 1306, and who is buried in his Basilica there. Two hundred years after his death some persons who had concealed themselves in the church over night endeavoured to cut off an arm and carry it as a relic. No sooner had they commenced this operation and gashed the flesh with a knife than blood flowed freely as from a living body.

The first Patriarch of Venice, S. Lorenzo Giustiniani, died 1 January, 1455, and so great was the concourse of people to venerate his remains that the body lay in the Church of San Pietro di Castello (formerly SS. Sergio e Bacco) for no less than sixty-seven days, exposed to the air. Although it had not been embalmed the face continued of a fresh and ruddy complexion as in life. The body of the Franciscan, S. John Capistran, who died 23 October, 1456, was found to be incorrupt in 1765 ; and the body of the Augustinian nun, S. Rita of Cascia is still intact in her convent shrine among the Tuscan Hills. The body of S. Didacus, a lay brother of the Friars Minor who died at Alcala on 12 November, 1463 was exhumed four days after death and remained above ground for six months, supple and whole ; it was still without blemish in 1562. As late as 1867, the body of the foundress of the Ursulines, S. Angela Merici, who died at Brescia, 27 January, 1540, was found to be entire.

It may not impertinently be remarked here that the Orthodox Russian Church includes in its calendar a number of bishops, monks, and holy hermits, whose bodies have been discovered to be intact at some considerable period after death, and if not actually in these days an entirely necessary condition for canonization incorruption is at any rate regarded as evidence of extraordinary sanctity. At Kieff there is (or was) a famous sanctuary which contained the bodies of no less than seventy-three venerable religious. I have been told by those who have visited this shrine that these are incorrupt, although dark and mummified. They are robed in rich vestments and laid out in open coffins for general honour and worship. Hassert speaks of the body of S. Basil of Ostrog, which was entire although much desiccated.[72] At Cetienje Schwarz saw the body of S. Peter I, the Vladika, who died in 1830.[73] " Dieser dürre, steinharte Kadaver," he calls it. It should be remarked that these remains are always described as parched, sere and withered, and in no way retaining the freshness, the natural colour and complexion of life, which so often distinguishes the incorrupt bodies of Saints of the Catholic Church.

Perhaps to these mummified Relics, there could be few contrasts more striking indeed than the body of S. Catherine of Genoa—to take the first example that occurs—which, when I venerated it some years ago in the chapel of her own Ospedale seemed as though the Saint were but reposing in her shrine, as though she might open her eyes and gently smile upon her clients who knelt in humblest prayer. The extraordinary phenomena connected with the body of S. Teresa who died at Alba de Tormes, 4 October, 1582, are so well-known and have been so often described in detail that it is only necessary slightly to refer to them. The nuns fearing that this great treasure would be taken from them hastily buried her on the morrow after her death. A mass of bricks, stones, mortar and lime was hurriedly piled on the coffin lid. For many days strange knockings were heard as from the grave itself. There issued a mysterious perfume which varied not only in degree but in kind, for sometimes it was like lilies, sometimes like roses, sometimes like violets and often like jasmin. The community upbraided themselves that they had not given their mother more honourable burial, and at length it was resolved that the body should be secretly exhumed. This took place on 4 July, 1583. It was discovered that the lid of the coffin had been broken by the rubble heaped upon it, and the wood was rotten and decayed. The habit was stained and smelt of damp and earth, but the holy remains were as sound and entire as on the day they were laid in earth. They removed the mouldering clothes, washed the body, scraping off the earth with knives, and it was remarked that the scrapings of earth were redolent of the same perfumes as filled the grave. Moreover, both earth and cerements were saturated with a fragrant oil that exuded from the body. Yepes who wrote in 1614, the

year the Saint was beatified particularly draws attention to
this fragrant effusion, and later when the remains were again
examined it was found that a sheet of fair linen with which
the body had been covered was odorous from the same
defluxion. This phenomenon classes S. Teresa among the
Saints who are technically known as Myroblites ($\mu\nu\rho\delta\beta\lambda\nu\tau\epsilon\varsigma$,)
from whose Relics exude balm and aromatic ichors. Of
these perhaps S. Nicolas of Myra, who lies at Bari, is the most
famous. There may also be named S. Willibrord, the
Apostle of Holland ; S. Vitalian ; S. Lutgarde ; S. Walbruga ;
S. Rose, of Viterbo ; the Blessed Mathia de' Nazzarei, a poor
Clare of Matelica ; S. Hedwige, of Poland ; S. Eustochium ;
S. Agnes of Montepulciano, the Dominican nun ; S. Maria
Maddalena de'Pazzi ; and the ecstatic Carmelite Marguerite
Van Valkenissen, foundress of the convent of Oirschot in
Brabant.

It was this incorruptibility which was the immediate cause
of the first official steps being taken to secure the beatification and canonization of Teresa de Jesus. Before the body
was replaced after exhumation the Provincial, Father
Geronymo de la Madre de Dios, better known as Gracian, cut
off the left hand and bore it away with him to Avila in a locked
casket, when blood flowed freely from the wound. Two years
later it was decreed by the general Carmelite Chapter that the
body should be translated to the convent of Avila, which as
the birthplace of the Saint and as her first foundation undoubtedly had the best claim to these Relics. But in order
to spare the nuns of Alba the fathers decided that the trans-
ference should be performed secretly, and accordingly the
officials who were entrusted with this business opened the
tomb at nine o'clock on the night of 24th November, 1585,
and in fulfilment of their orders, whilst the sisterhood was
engaged at Matins in the choir above, exhumed the body.
To mitigate the grief of the convent it was decided that the
left arm should be severed and that they should be allowed
to retain this. Fray Gregorio de Nacianceno who was
entrusted with this overcome with emotion, drew a sharp
knife and severed the limb. He afterwards told Ribera that
it was the greatest sacrifice of himself God had ever called
upon him to make. It was remarked that the bone was
as sound, and the flesh as soft, and its colour as natural as

if the saint were alive. When the precious remains arrived at
the convent of San José of Avila it was laid on record that the
body without sign of corruption, for when they lifted it out of
the chest it seemed that of one asleep. Ribera has left us a
minute description of the remains which he examined thoroughly on 25th March, 1588, and his account is so interesting
it will not be impertinent to quote it in full. He writes :
" I saw the sainted body, greatly to my satisfaction, on 25th
March of this year of 1588, as I examined it thoroughly, it
being my intention to give the testimony I give here. I can
describe it well. It is erect, although bent somewhat forward,
as is usual with old people ; and by it, it can well be seen that
she was of very good stature. By placing a hand behind it
to lean against, it stands up, and can be dressed and undressed
as if she were alive. The whole body is of the colour of dates,
although in some parts a little whiter. The face is of a darker
colour than the rest, since, the veil having fallen over it, and
gathered together a great quantity of dust, it was much
worse treated than other parts of the body ; but it is absolutely
entire, so that not even the tip of the nose has received any
injury. The head is as thickly covered with hair as when
they buried her. The eyes are dried up, the moisture they
possessed having evaporated, but as for the rest entire. Even
the hairs on the moles on her face are there. The mouth
is slightly shut, so that it cannot be opened. The shoulders,
especially, are very fleshy. The place whence the arm was
cut is moist, and the moisture clings to the hand, and leaves
the same odour as the body. The hand exceedingly shapely,
and raised as if in the action of benediction, although the
fingers are not entire. *They did ill in taking them, since the
hand that did such great things, and that God had left entire,
ought for ever to have remained so.* The feet are very beautiful
and shapely, and, in short, the whole body is covered with
flesh. The fragrance of the body is the same as that of the
arm, but stronger. So great a consolation was it to me to see
this hidden treasure, that to my thinking it was the best day
I ever had in my life, and I could not gaze at her enough.
One anxiety I have, lest some day they should separate it,
either at the request of great personages or at the impor-
tunity of the monasteries ; for by no means should this be
done, but it should remain as God left it, as a testimony

of his greatness, and the most pure virginity and admirable
sanctity of the Mother Teresa de Jesus. To my thinking,
neither he who asks it nor he who grants it, will act like true
sons of hers."

Having dealt with so celebrated a case in some detail we
may very briefly pass in review some four or five other instances
more premising that these have been selected from a very
great many, something at random, and not because they
present any remarkable or unique phenomena which it would
not be tolerably easy to parallel in other accounts. On the
other hand they are no less memorable than is the case of
S. Teresa herself : For example, the body of S. Pascal Baylon,
who died at Villa Reale, 15th May, 1592, although covered
with quick-lime, was found nine months later to be entire
and incorrupt, and in 1611 expert surgeons declared that the
preservation was miraculous. Again the body of S. Philip
Neri, who died 25th May, 1595, was discovered perfectly intact
eight months after burial, and was still entire when examined
in 1599, 1602, and 1639. In the cases of two saints who died
in 1608, Francis Caracciolo, who expired at Agnone in the
Abruzzi, 4th June, 1608 ; and Andrea Avellino, who was struck
down by apoplexy at Naples on 10th November of the same
year, there were noticed curious blood phenomena. The
body of S. Francis remained flexible, and when an incision was
made blood freely flowed. The body of S. Andrea was found
incorrupt more than a year after he had been buried. A
quantity of blood that had been received in a phial did not
congeal, but is constantly observed to be still liquid. In
the case of S. Camillus de Lellis who died at Rome, 14th July,
1614, the body remained soft and flexible. At her convent
in the Umbrian aerie of Città di Castello reposes the unflecked
and whole body of the Capuchiness, S. Veronica Giuliani,
who died 9th July, 1727. There it may be seen, reposing as
though she were not dead, but slept.

This list might be greatly prolonged without much research
or difficulty ; however, it is no doubt already sufficiently
ample, and I have thought it worth while to treat the subject
of the incorruptibility of the bodies of saints in some detail,
as though of course, this phenomenon is in itself not to be
regarded as evidence of sanctity, the preservation of the
body of a person who has led a life of heroic virtue when this

eminent holiness has been officially and authoritatively recognized, may be admitted as a miracle, that is to say as supernatural. More than once attention has been drawn to the fact that there exist parodies of these phenomena, and as incorruptibility is often attached to sanctity so is it an essential of the very opposite of holiness, the demonism of the vampire. It has been said that the vampire, as a demon reanimates the corpses of entirely innocent people, but this is very doubtful and it is probable that the only bodies thus to be infested and preserved by dark agency are those of persons who during their lives were distinguished by deeds of no ordinary atrocity. Very often too the vampire is a corpse reanimated by his own spirit who seeks to continue his own life in death by preying upon others and feeding himself upon their vitality that is to say by absorbing their blood since blood is the principle of life.

Dr. T. Claye Shaw in his study, *A Prominent Motive in Murder*[74] has given us a most valuable and suggestive paper upon the natural fascination of blood which may be repelling or attractant, and since Dr. Havelock Ellis has acutely remarked that "there is scarcely any natural object with so profoundly emotional an effect as blood,"[75] it is easy to understand how nearly blood is connected with the sexual manifestations, and how distinctly erotic and provocative the sight or even the thought of blood almost inevitably proves. It would appear to be Plumröder, who in 1830 was the first to draw definite attention to the connexion between sexual passions and blood. The voluptuous sensations excited by blood give rise to that lust for blood which Dr. Shaw terms hemothymia. A vast number of cases have been recorded in which persons who are normal, find intense pleasure in the thought of blood during their sexual relations, although perhaps if blood were actually flowing they might feel repulsion. Yet "normally the fascination of blood, if present at all during sexual excitement, remains more or less latent, either because it is weak or because the checks that inhibit it are inevitably very powerful."[76]

Blood is the vital essence, and even without any actual sucking of blood there is a vampire who can—consciously, or perhaps unconsciously—support his life and re-energize his frame by drawing upon the vitality of others. He may be called a spiritual vampire, or as he has been dubbed a "psychic sponge." Such types are by no means uncommon. Sensitive people will aften complain of weariness and loss of spirits when they have been for long in the company of certain others, and Laurence Oliphant in his *Scientific Religion* has said : "Many persons are so constituted that they have, unconsciously to themselves, an extraordinary faculty for sucking the life-principle from others, who are constitutionally incapable of retaining their vitality." Breeders tell us that young animals should not be herded with old ones ; Doctors forbid young children being put to sleep with aged individuals. It will be remembered that when King David was old and ailing his forces were recruited by having a young maiden brought into closest contact with him, although he was no longer able to copulate. Et rex Dauid senuerat, habebatque aetatis plurimos dies : cumque operiretur uestibus, non calefiebat. Dixerunt ergo ei serui sui : Quaeremus domino nostro regi adolescentulam uirginem, et stet coram rege, et foueat eam, dormiatque in sinu suo, et calefaciat dominum nostrum regem. Quaesierunt igitur adolescentulam speciosam in omnibus finibus Israel, et inuenerunt Abisag Sunamitidem, et adduxerunt eam ad regem. Erat autem puella pulchra nimis, dormiebatque cum rege, et ministrabat ei, rex uero non cognouit eam. *III Kings* (*A.V. I Kings*) I, 1-4. (Now King David was old, and advanced in years ; and when he was covered with clothes he was not warm. His servants therefore said to him : "Let us seek for our lord the king, a young virgin, and let her stand before the king, and cherish him, and sleep in his bosom, and warm our lord the king." So they sought a beautiful young woman in all the coasts of Israel, and they found Abisag, a Sunamitess, and brought her to the king. And the damsel was exceeding beautiful, and she slept with the king ; and served him, but the king did not know her.) The vitality of the young and lovely maiden served to re-energize the old Monarch, who thus drew upon her freshness and youth, although there was no coitus.

In an article on Vampires, *Borderland*, Vol. III, No. 3, July, 1896, pp. 353-358, Dr. Franz Hartmann, mentions the "psychic sponge " or mental vampire. He says : "They unconsciously vampirize every sensitive person with whom they come in contact, and they instinctively seek out such persons and invite them to stay at their houses. I know of an old lady, a vampire, who thus ruined the health of a lot of robust servant girls, whom she took into her service and made them sleep in her room. They were all in good health when they entered, but soon they began to sicken, they became emaciated and consumptive and had to leave the service."

Vampirism in some sort and to some degree may be said to leave its trace throughout almost all nature. Just as we have the parasitic men and women, so have we the parasitic plants, and at this point there imposes itself upon us some mention of the animal which directly derives a name from habits which exactly resemble those of the Slavonic Vampire—the Vampire Bat. There has been much exaggeration in the accounts which travellers have given of these bats and many of the details would seem to have been very inaccurately observed by earlier inquirers. *The Encyclopædia Britannica* says[77] that there are only two species of blood-sucking bats known— *Desmodus rufus* and *Diphylla ecaudata*. These inhabit the tropical and part of the sub-tropical regions of the New World, and are restricted to South and Central America. Their attacks on men and other warm-blooded animals were noticed by very early writers. Thus Peter Martyr (Anghiera) who wrote soon after the conquest of South America, says that in the Isthmus of Darien there were bats which sucked the blood of men and cattle when asleep to such a degree as even to kill them. Condamine in the eighteenth century remarks that at Borja, Ecuador, and in other districts they had wholly destroyed the cattle introduced by the missionaries. Sir Robert Schomburgh relates that at Wicki, on the river Berlice, no fowls could be kept on account of the ravages of these creatures, which attacked their combs making them appear white from loss of blood.

Although long known to Europeans the exact species to which these bats belonged were not to be determined for a long time, and in the past writers have claimed many frugivorous bats, especially *Vampyrus spectrum*, a large bat of most forbidding appearance, to be the true Vampire. Charles Darwin was able to fix at least one of the blood-sucking species. He says that the whole circumstance was much doubted in

England, but "we were bivouacking late one night near Coquimbo in Chile, when my servant, noticing that one of the horses was very restive went to see what was the matter, and fancying he could detect something, suddenly put his hand on the beast's withers, and secured the vampire." (*Naturalist's Voyage Round the World*, p. 22.)

Travellers say the wounds inflicted by these bats are similar in character to a cut from a sharp razor when shaving. A portion of the skin is taken off, and a large number of severed capillary vessels being thus exposed, a constant flow of blood is maintained. From this source the blood is drawn through the exceedingly small gullet of the bat into the intestine-like stomach, whence it is, probably, gradually drawn off during the slow progress of digestion, while the animal sated with food, is hanging in a state of torpidity from the roof of its cave or from the inner side of a hollow tree.

This is exactly the Vampire who with his sharp white teeth bites the neck of his victim and sucks the blood from the wounds he has made, gorging himself, like some great human leech, until he is replete and full, when he retires to his grave to repose, lethargic and inert until such time as he shall again sally forth to quench his lust at the veins of some sleek and sanguine juvenal.

NOTES TO CHAPTER II.

[1] *Apocalypse*, xxi, 8 : " But the fearful and unbelieving, and the abominable, and murderers, and whoremongers, and sorcerers, and idolaters, and all liars, they shall have their portion in the pool burning with fire and brimstone, which is the second death." Also, xxii, 15 : " Without are dogs, and sorcerers, and unchaste, and murderers, and servers of idols, and everyone that loveth and maketh a lie."

[2] *The House of Souls*, London, 1906, pp. 113-118.

[3] *Scotch Historical Society*, xxv, p. 348.

[4] *A Prodigious and Tragicall History of the Arraignment* . . . *of six Witches at Maidstone* . . . by H. F. Gent, 1652, p. 7.

[5] *A Full and True Relation of the Tryal, Condemnation, and Execution of Ann Foster*, 1674, p. 8.

[6] *The Iliad of Homer*, " Rendered into English Blank Verse. By Edward Earl of Derby." John Murray, 1864. Vol. II, Book xxiii, ll. 82-119.

[7] *Choephorae*, 429-433.

[8] One may compare the corresponding passage in the *Antigone* of Alfieri :

Emone, ah ! tutto io sento,
Tutto l'amor, che a te portava : io sento
Il dolor tutto, a cui ti lascio.

[9] Pausanias, IX. 32. 6.

[10] Aelian, Περὶ Ζώων ἰδιότητος, V, 49.

[11] *Chronicles of the House of Borgia*, Baron Corvo, p. 283.
[12] *S. John*, ix, 22, seq.
[13] *S. John*, xii, 42.
[14] *S. John*, xvi, 2 ; and *S. Luke*, vi, 22.
[15] *S. Matthew*, xviii, 16-18.
[16] Theodore Balsamon, I, 27 and 569 ; *apud* Migne.
[17] Jacques Goar, "'Εὐχολόγιον, siue Rituale Graecorum," Paris, 1667, p. 685.
[18] C, xiii.
[19] Balsamon, I, 64-5 and 437.
[20] Cambridge, 1619.
[21] *Op. cit.*, xv.
[22] Under Justinian, Theodore Askidas and Domitian of Caesarea refused to condemn Origen. It remains an open question whether Origen and Origenism were ever anathematized. Authorities are divided, and modern writers hesitate to pronounce. The balance of opinion seems to be that Origen was not condemned, at least it does not appear that Popes Vigilius, Pelagius I, Pelagius II, S. Gregory the Great, recognized any such condemnation.
[23] Reigned 535-36.
[24] Dialogues, Book II, c. xxiii.
[25] The Holy Rule ; especially cs. vi-vii.
[26] This subject was painted by Lucio Massari, a pupil of Ludovico Caracci, in the cloisters of the Benedictine convent of San Michele-in-Bosco, Bologna. Unfortunately the fresco has perished, but it is to some extent known from engravings.
[27] *De Sancta Uirginitate*, xlv.
[28] Dialogues, Book II, c, xxiv.
[29] Born 339 or 340 ; died between 394 and 403.
[30] The Council of Constantinople held in 692 under Justinian II, commonly called the Council *in Trullo*. The Orthodox Greek Church reckons this Council to be oecumenical, but this was not so recognized in the West. S. Bede (*De sexta mundi aetate*) even terms it a reprobate synod ; and Paul the Deacon (*Hist. Lang.*, VI, p. 11) an erratic assembly.
Also the Third Council of Carthage.
[31] The cult of S. Othmar began to spread almost immediately after his death.
[32] Iso of S. Gall wrote *De miraculis S. Othmari, libri duo*, which is given by Migni *Patres Latini*, cxxi, 779-796, and in the *Monumenta Germaniae Historiae Scriptorum*, II, 47-54.
[33] The *Historia Translationis Sancti Cuthberti* as printed by the Bollandists and by Stevenson (Eng. Hist. Soc., 1838) is superseded by the fuller text in the Rolls Series and in the Surtees Society, LI, London, 1868.
[34] IV, xli.
[35] 1585-1644.
[36] This also appears in the edition of the Works of S. Gregory of 1705. Muratori (*De rebus liturgicis*, vi) highly praises the Commentary of Dom Ménard.
[37] He died 1058. See Will, *Aeta et Scripta quae de controuersiis ecclesiae graecae et latinae saeculo XI composita extant*, Leipsig, 1861 ; and Adrian Fortescue, *The Orthodox Eastern Church*, London, 1907.
[38] Or τὸ περατίκι. Schmidt, *Das Volksleben der Neugriechen* suggests that in the local dialect it may be περατίκιν.
[39] Protodikos, Περὶ τῆς παρ' ἡμῖν ταφῆς, 1860, says that in certain districts of Asia Minor the custom was still connected with Charos ; and in the same year Skordeles, Πανδώρα, xi, p. 449, stated that "until a short time ago" the coin for Charos was placed in the month of the dead at Stenimachos in Thrace.

Such a practice even prevailed in England, and in some country places was observed far later than might be supposed. I have been shown by a friend a silver coin of the reign of Queen Anne which was placed in the mouth of his great -grandmother when she lay dead, and only removed immediately before the nailing down of the coffin.

⁴⁰ Menaion (μηναῖον from μήν " month ") is the name of each separate book, whence the set of Offices is generally called Menaia. The first printed edition was made by Andrew and James Spinelli at Venice, 1528-1596 ; and reprinted, 1596-1607. The latest Greek editions were published at Venice in 1873, Orthodox rite ; and at Rome in 1888, Uniate rite.

⁴¹ The Vow of Stability, *stabilitas loci*, which unites the monk for life to the particular monastery in which his vows were made, was insisted upon by S. Benedict, who thus greatly altered the pre-existing practice and put an end to the Sarabaites and Gyrovagi against whom the holy patriarch inveighes so sternly in the first chapter of the Rule.

⁴² *Compendium Theologiae Moralis.* Sabetti-Barrett. Editio Uiccsima Quinta. Pustet, 1916, p. 984.

⁴³ sub die 26 Maii.

⁴⁴ First edition, 1746.

⁴⁵ Remiremont, a monastery and nunnery of the Rule of S. Benedict, was founded by SS. Romanicus and Amatus in 620. The monastery became a Priory of the Canons Regular of S. Augustine who, in 1623, bestowed upon the Benedictines of the Congregation of S. Vannes. Both houses were suppressed during the French Revolution. See *Gallia Christiana*, Paris, 1785, xiii, 1416 ; and Guinot's *'Etude historique sur l'abbaye de Remiremont* Epinal, 1886.

⁴⁶ The place of pilgrimage was Notre Dame du Trésor, one of the most famous sanctuaries of the diocese of Sainte-Dié (S. Deodatus).

⁴⁷ He was consecrated in 1027 ; and enthroned as Pope, 12th February, 1049.

⁴⁸ *Apud* Watterich, *Pontificum Romanorum Uitae*, I, Leipzig, 1862.

⁴⁹ The Abbey of Farfa is about twenty-six miles from Rome. It is said that in the days of the Emperor Julian or of Gratian Caesar the Syrian S. Laurentius dedicated a church to Our Lady here. Archæological discoveries in 1888 seem to show that the first monastery, devastated by the Vandals *circa* 457, had been built on the site of a heathen temple. The principal founder of Farfa was Thomas de Mauricume. He had spent three years as a humble palmer at Jerusalem, and whilst in prayer before the Holy Sepulchre, Our Lady appeared to him and bade him return to Italy, and there to restore Farfa. The Duke of Spoleto, Faroald, was also commanded to help in the good work. Since 1842 the Cardinal Bishop of Sabina, a sub-urbicarian bishop, bears also the title of Abbot of Farfa.

The body of S. Martin was venerated in his basilica at Tours. This sanctuary was famous as a place of pilgrimage until 1562, when the Protestant hordes attacked and demolished it, the shrine and the Holy Relics, the special object of their hate, being destroyed. The church was restored but again devastated under the French Revolution. Of recent years a basilica, which is unfortunately of small dimensions, has been erected and here, on 11th November, the solemnity of S. Martin is celebrated with much pomp and a great concourse of the faithful.

⁵⁰ Lambert of Hersfeld, apud *Monumenta Germaniae Historiae Scriptorum*, V, 168.

⁵¹ 960-1014.

⁵² Lib. I, pp. 26-27.

⁵³ Calmet, *op. cit.*, vol. II, c. xxx, p. 125.

⁵⁴ Vol. I, p. 282, ed. 1920.

⁵⁵ *Op. cit.*, p. 295.

⁵⁶ *Apud* Witthaus and Becker, *Medical Jurisprudence*, Vol. I, p. 446.

⁵⁷ Romas, MDCCXC, vol. VII, pp. 51-68.

⁵⁸ *De notis et signis Sanctitatis*, c. iv, 2.

⁵⁹ *De certitudine gloriae Sanctorum*, in app. ad. c. iv.

⁶⁰ The beatification of this great Servant of God is confidently awaited.

⁶¹ *The Life of Monsignor Hugh Benson*, by C. C. Martindale, S. J., London, 1916, vol. II, p. 180.

[62] Professor of Aesthetics, S. Ignatius College, Valkenburg, Holland.

[63] *Rationale diuinorum Officiorum*, I, iii, 19 *seq*.

[64] *Canticles*, iii, 2.

[65] *Wisdom*, v, 17.

[66] Migne, *Patres Latini*, LXXV, 231.

[67] One night in summer at the conclusion of Matins when the community were all surprised to see daylight, Mechtild involuntarily exclaimed : " Why, dear sisters, it is already day ! " *The Spirit of the Dominican Order*, by Mother Frances Raphael, O.S.D., Second Edition, London, 1910, p. 144.

[68] *Life of the Venerable Anthony M. Claret*, by the Rev. Eugene Sugranes, C.M.F., Texas [1921].

[69] *Epigrammata de Uiris Uitae Sanctimonia Illustribus ex Ordire Premonstrensi*, Augustini Wickmans, C.R.P., Taminiae, 1895, p. 30, and pp. 16-17.

[70] *Vita di Santa Chiara di Montefalco* . . . scritta dal Rmo. P. Maestro Lorenzo Tardy. Roma, 1881.

[71] *Memorie Istoriche della Vita, Miracoli, e Culto di S. Gianuario Martire* . . . raccolte da D. Camillo Tutini. Napoli, 1710.

[72] *Reise Luich Montenegro*, Vienna, 1893, p. 27.

[73] *Montenegro*, Leipzig, 1883, pp. 81-82.

[74] *The Lancet*, 19th June, 1909.

[75] *Studies in the Psychology of Sex*. Vol. III. " Analysis of the Sexua Impulse," pp. 120-121. Second Edition. Philadelphia. 1926.

[76] Dr. Havelock Ellis, *op. cit.*, p. 121.

[77] Whence I take the following account of the vampire bat.

CHAPTER III

THE TRAITS AND PRACTICE OF VAMPIRISM

IT was generally supposed that all suicides might after death become vampires ; and this was easily extended to those who met with any violent or sudden death. Mr. Lawson tells us that there persists a tradition in Maina, where the Vendetta is still maintained, that a man whose murder has not been avenged is liable to become a *vrykolakas*.[1] The Mainotes who derive their name from the place Maina, near Cape Taenaron (Matapan), even yet preserve many of the customs and characteristics of their ancestors, and historically are known to be of a more pure Greek descent than the inhabitants of any other district. Indeed, the peninsula which thrusts into the sea the headland of Taenaron has both social and religious customs of its own. The population is distributed into small villages, while here and there a white fortress will denote the residence of a chief. A traveller writing in 1858, remarks : " The Maina country is wild and beautiful, singularly well cultivated, considering the difficulties to be surmounted, and producing crops that put to shade the rich plains of Argos and Arcadia ; whilst the interesting mountain people exercise the highland virtues of hospitality and independance to an extent unknown in the low countries." It has been said that the last traveller who saw Maina while retaining some remains of its primitive cateran glories was Lord Carnarvon, who in 1839 explored the Morea and has left us an extraordinarily interesting account of his journey.

The population of this district continued the worship of the Pagan deities for full five hundred years after the rest of the Roman Empire had embraced Christianity, and they were not finally converted until the reign of the vigorous Emperor Basil I, 867-886. Gibbon described them as " a domestic and perhaps original race, who, in some degree, might derive their blood from the much-injured Helotes."[2] And even yet they boast of their descent from the ancient Spartans, whilst the histories of Leonidas and Lycurgus, who figure partly as saints and partly as gallant brigands, are still retold round the winter fireside. The whole district, including Kaka Voulia (the Land of Evil Counsel), is formed by the hummocks and escarpments of Mount Taygetos, and, with the exception of a long strip of coast line, which the Venetians called *Bassa Maina*, it is steep and hilly and for the most part barren. The conquest of the Morea was completed by Mahomet II in 1456-1460, but Maina could never be thoroughly subdued, and its inhabitants remained as entirely independent as were the Highlanders before Culloden.

As has been remarked, ancient traditions still persevere, and among these customs not the least obstinate is the Vendetta. A man who has been murdered is unable to rest in his grave until he has been avenged. Accordingly he issues forth as a vampire, thirsting for the blood of his enemy. In order to bring about his physical dissolution and to secure his repose it is necessary for the next of kin to slay the murderer, or at least some near relative of the murderer. Unless this is done the man upon whom the duty of avenging blood devolves is banned by the curse of the dead, and if so be that he is himself cut off before he can satify the desires of the deceased, the curse will yet cling to him even in death, and he too must become a vampire. It should be remarked that this view of blood-guilt is found in the Attic dramatists, and is in fact the mainspring of the whole story of Orestes. In the tragedy of this name by Euripides, Tyndareus, the father of Clytemnestra, remonstrates very reasonably, and indeed unanswerably with Orestes. But the hero replies and argues that if he has not avenged his father

Had not his hate's Erinyes haunted me ?[3]

Again in the *Choephoroe* of Aeschylus Orestes pursues the same idea saying that unless he avenges his father, a stern duty which has devolved upon him, he will be punished in turn by the avengers of his father's wrongs.[4] It may be remarked that in Maina to-day no recourse must be had to law for such cases, nor must the injured person satisfy himself by calling upon the aid of the police. To do this were incredibly base, the subterfuge of a recreant and a craven. Even if it be a life's whole work a man is expected, either secretly or by an open attack, to slay the murderer of his relative, and he is highly applauded when he has accomplished this pious deed. It must be appreciated that he is regarded as herein directed and inspired by the dead man who returns from his grave as a vampire craving for blood. Even if no other motive or incentive prevailed, in spite of natural shrinking and may be even cowardice, a man would undoubtedly prefer to shed blood for blood, especially when this might be done in secrecy or by craft, rather than run the terrible risk of himself becoming a vampire, finding no rest in the grave, but returning to haunt and persecute even those who were most dear to him, an unclean thing accursed of God, a foul goblin of dread most hateful to man.

So great is the horror which the act of suicide, although considered admirable in the decadence of Greece and Rome, inspires in every man of sane mind that it is not at all surprising it should be deemed that the unfortunate wretches who have destroyed themselves become vampires after death. According to the Zoroastrian creed, suicide is a most fearful crime, and is classed among the *marg-arzan*, the abominable offences. Aristotle in his *Ethics*, V, xv, terms suicide a sin against the State, and as Cicero tells us Pythagoras forbade men to depart from their guard or sentry-go in life without an order from their commanding-officer, who is God. " Uetatque Pythagoras iniussu imperatoris, id est, dei, de praesidio et statione uitae decedere." (*De Senectute*, XX, 73). The highest pagan argument against suicide will be found in Plato's *Phaedo* (61E-62E), but it is drowned in the mighty voice of the great Saint of Hippo, which peals in no unwavering tones down the centuries : " For if it be not lawful for a private man to kill any man, however guilty, unless the law have granted a special allowance for it, then surely whosoever kills himself is guilty of homicide: and so much the more guilty doth that killing of himself make himself, by how much the more guiltless he was in that cause for which he killed himself. For if the act of Judas be worthily detested, and yet the Truth saith, that by hanging of himself, he did rather augment than expiate the guilt of his wicked treachery, because his despair of God's mercy in his damnable repentance, left no place in his soul for saving repentance ; how much more ought he to

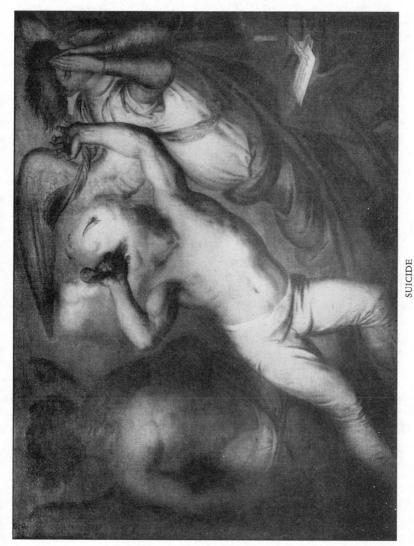

PLATE IV

SUICIDE

(From the Musée Wiertz)

[see p. 140]

PLATE V

CAUCHEMAR

By Laurence Housman

[see p. 180

forbear from being cause of his own death, that hath no guilt in him worthy of such a punishment as death ; for Judas in hanging himself, hanged but a wicked man and died guilty, not only of Christ's death, but of his own also ; adding the wickedness of being his own death, to that other wickedness of his, for which he died." (*De Ciuitate Dei*, I, xvii.)

It may be well very briefly to present the teaching of the Church concerning positive and direct suicide. If done without God's permission this always constitutes a grave injustice towards Him. To destroy a thing is in effect to dispose of it as an absolute master and to act with regard to it as one who has full and independent dominion over it. But God has reserved to Himself dominion over life. Man cannot create life, and he does not possess this full and absolute right over his own life. Consequently suicide must be reckoned as an attempt against the dominion and right of ownership of the Author of life. To this injustice is super-added a serious offence against the charity owed by man to himself, since by self-murder he deprives himself of the greatest good in his possession. Moreover this sin may be aggravated by other circumstances, such as an offence against conjugal, paternal, or filial duty ; an offence against justice or charity ; if by taking his own life a man eludes existing obligations of justice or acts of charity which he could and should perform. That suicide is unlawful is the general teaching of Holy Scripture which condemns the act as a most terrible crime, and to arouse the horror of all against Holy Church denies the suicide the rites of Christian burial. Again, suicide is directly opposed to the most natural and powerful tendency of all created things, and especially of intelligent man, the preservation of life. Indeed very large numbers of physicians, moralists, and jurists lay it down as a general rule that suicide is always due to dementia, so great is the horror which this atrocious deed inspires in every man of sane mind. As a generalization this may be admitted to be true, for it is impossible to think that those who have the calm and right use of their reason should deliberately destroy themselves, and the conditions which are necessary to incur the full culpability of an act can only in exceptional instances be conceived of as being present in the case of a suicide. Sabetti inquires : " *Quaenam ad peccatum mortale requirantur ?* " And his answer is given as follows : " *Tria* necessario requiruntur, scilicet *materia grauis* uel in se, uel ob circumstantias ; *aduertentia plena* ad malitiam grauem actus ; *consensus plenus* uoluntatis in præuaricationem. Itaque,

Requiritur 1°. *materia grauis*, secus non posset haberi lex obligans sub graui.

Requiritur 2°. *plena aduertentia* mentis, secus non habebitur plena deliberatio.

Requiritur 3°. *plenus consensus* uoluntatis, quia nisi peccator cum pleno consensu plenaque deliberatione obiectum peccati Deo præferat, et sic finem suum ultimum in creatura constituat, nequit dici a Deo totaliter recedere. Insuper a bonitate diuina prorsus alienum est, hominem æternæ damnationi addicere siue propter transgressionem leuem siue propter actum non perfecte liberum et uoluntarium.—Cf. S. Alphons, nn. 5, 6 et 53."[5]

The Christian Middle Ages were free from the terrible tendency of suicide, but with the loss of Faith it re-appeared, and Masaryk in his study *Der Selbtsmord als sociale Massenerscheinung der modernen Civilisation* (Vienna, 1881), considered it to be the special evil of these later days. Sad to relate self-destruction has fearfully increased since the Great War, but it may perhaps be mitigatingly advanced that the reason of the world tottered almost to eternal delirium during the chaos and welter of blood, and the balance is not recovered yet.

It is true that among certain nations there appears to be an indifference to human life, nay, a contempt of death itself, which often takes the most extravagant and the most outrageous forms. The Goths, the heathen Vandals, and Norse savages not only approved but sought suicide and violent death. It is, of course, only among the utterly benighted that it is possible for such abominable ideas to obtain. For example, there existed among a tribe of robbers in Southern India customs of the utmost ferocity. Such practices as the following certainly prevailed during the eighteenth century, but they have no doubt, long since been happily suppressed. If two persons had quarrelled, sometimes for the most trifling reasons, a man would kill himself merely in order to be revenged on his adversary. He believed that his ghost would be able to return and harry the surviver, or at least that some dire retribution must fall on the head of his enemy who drove him to such extreme measures.[6] Again, custom required that if a man committed suicide, letting it be known that it was on this account, the person with whom he had had the difference that led to this abominable act must immediately follow his example.[7]

Lord Avebury's statement :[8] " It is said that in China, if a rich man is condemned to death, he can sometimes purchase a willing substitute at a very small expense," has been traversed and Professor Parker would not commit himself any further than by saying : " It is popularly stated that substitutes can be bought for Taels fifty, and most certainly this statement is more than true, so far as the price of human life is concerned ; but it is quite another question whether the gaolers and judges can always be bribed."[9] Dr. W. T. A. Barber, who had been a missionary in China, relates that he had known very large numbers of persons who committed suicide out of spite against some one else, " the idea being, first, the trouble given by minions of the law to the survivor ; second that the dead would gain a vantage ground by becoming a ghost, and thus able to plague his enemy in the flesh."[10]

It is not surprising to learn that in ancient times, before the advent of Christianity, among such savage people as the Celts and the Thracians suicide was not only common but treated with the most appalling lightness and even flippancy. Thus Athenæus, speaking of the banquets of the Thracians, quotes from Seleucus as follows : " And Seleucus says, ' that some of the Thracians at their drinking parties play the game of hanging ; and fix a round noose to some high place, exactly beneath which they place a stone which is easily turned round when any one stands upon it ; and then they cast lots, and he who draws the lot, holding a sickle in his hand, stands upon the stone, and puts his neck into the halter ; and then another person comes and raises the stone, and the man who is suspended, when the stone moves from under him, if he is not quick enough in cutting the rope with his sickle, is killed ; and the rest laugh, thinking his death good sport.' "[11]

Upon the authority of the famous Stoic philosopher, Posidonius, Athenæus tells us of similar brutalities which took place among the Celts. He writes : " But Posidonius,[12] in the

third, and also in the twentieth book of his Histories, says
'The Celtæ sometimes have single combats at their entertainments. For being collected in arms, they go through the
exercise, and make feints at, and sometimes they even go so
far as to wound one another. And being irritated by this,
if the bystanders do not stop them, they will proceed even to
kill one another. But in olden times,' he continues, ' there
was a custom that a hind quarter of pork was put on the table,
and the bravest man took it ; and if any one else laid claim
to it, then the two rose up to fight till one of them was slain.
And other men in the theatre having received some silver or
gold money, and some even for a number of earthen vessels
full of wine, having taken pledges that the gifts promised
shall really be given, and having distributed them among their
nearest connexions, have laid themselves down on doors with
their faces upwards, and then allowed some bystander to cut
their throats with a sword.'

" And Euphorion the Chalcidian, in his Historical Memorials,
writes as follows : ' But among the Romans it is common for
five minæ[13] to be offered to any one who chooses to take it,
to allow his head to be cut off with an axe, so that his heirs
might receive the reward : and very often many have returned
their names as willingly, so that there has been a regular
contest between them as to who had the best right to be
beaten to death.' "[14] These atrocious examples serve to
show us something of the evil and the corruption of which
Christianity cleansed the pagan world, although it is to be
feared that the battle is not yet won, since it is a notorious
and deplorable fact that at the hour of such a crisis as the
Great War the respect due to human life became cheapened
in men's eyes, with the consequence that murder and deeds
of violence once more broke out in every direction showing
that savage instincts were dominated indeed, but in many
cases not wholly eradicated. It does not require a keen
perception to see the direct agency of the devil here, and these
atrocities which bred so callous and cruel a spirit are by no
means altogether unconnected with the recrudescence of
necromancy and black magic which foul arts once more
grew green and were almost openly pursued on every side.

The belief that a man has not complete dominion over his
own life and that it is unlawful for him to take it is certainly a

feeling naturally implanted in the human breast, and it was only when nations were entirely barbarian or had became decadent and corrupt that the notion of suicide was held up as noble and even heroic. Whatever certain among the later Greeks may have practised and taught, in earlier days, as we have seen, the act of suicide was regarded as a dark and presumptuous deed. They truly felt that there was in it something of $\dot{a}\sigma\acute{e}\beta\epsilon\iota a$,[15] something of that $\ddot{v}\beta\rho\iota\varsigma$ which so surely stirred the wrath of heaven and inevitably called down righteous vengeance. Indeed the evil and malice of suicide did not end with death but continued beyond the grave. The umbra of a man who had slain himself was dreaded and feared. So in ancient Athens it was the custom to cut off the hand of a suicide and to cremate it or at least to bury it far from his body, the object of such mutilation being to prevent his ghost from attacking the living.[16]

Similar beliefs exist among native African tribes. Thus the Wajagga of East Africa dread the spectres of suicides. When a man has hanged himself a certain complicated ceremonial becomes imperative. They take the rope from his neck and suspend a goat in the noose, after which the animal is swiftly slain. The idea seems that hereby the phantom will be in some way appeased, and he will not be so likely to tempt human beings to follow his evil example.[17]

The Baganda of Central Africa have an even greater horror of the ghosts of suicides, and the most elaborate precautions are invariably taken to protect themselves against these dangerous visitors. The body of a man who has destroyed himself is removed as far from all human habitation as possible, to waste land or to a cross-road, and there is utterly consumed with fire. Next the wood of the house in which the horrid deed has been done is burned to ashes and scattered to the winds ; whilst if the man has hanged himself upon a tree this is hewn to the ground and committed to the flames, trunk, roots, branches and all. Even this is hardly deemed to be sufficient. Curiously enough there is a lurking idea that the ghost of a suicide may survive after the cremation of the body, so horrible is this crime felt to be and so irradicated the taint that this terrible deed establishes. This is extremely significant since the cases in which cremation, a complete purgation and destruction by fire, cannot obliterate guilt and destroy the evil infection are indeed exceptional, and it might be no easy task to find a parallel instance. However, the Baganda when passing by the spot where the body of a suicide has been burned always take good care to pelt it with sticks and clods of earth to prevent the ghost from catching them. Although these places in particular are dangerous to the last degree, there are other graves that may be haunted by phantoms, which as they have no bodies are not strictly vampires, but which certainly belong to the vampire family. Such are those remote places where persons who have been accused of black magic and who failed to satisfy the ritual ordeals have been burned to death, as also those spots where persons of evil and atrocious life have been cremated or interred.[18] The Maraves, a tribe of South Africa, who also burned witches alive, whenever they had occasion to pass the place of doom, pelted it with stones, and it is said that in some instances of spots considered particularly ill-omened a regular cairn or tumulus of loose stones has arisen.[19] In Madagascar too, certain solitary graves bear an exceedingly ill-repute, so that the chance traveller with averted face throws stones at them or large lumps of earth in order to prevent the ghost following in his tracks and seizing on him.[20] It must be remarked, and this is very important, that the sticks and stones, or heavy clods of earth with which a grave is pelted are not meant merely as a symbolical insult and expression of righteous indignation, but are actually missiles which will strike and hurt the being who haunts the spot of interment. So since the haunter can be struck and injured by these very material objects,—the heavier they are the better, —he must himself possess a certain concrete substantiality, and inasmuch as objects make an impression upon him he must exist under some kind of physical condition. Doubtless the exact idea is not very clearly defined in the minds of those who are so careful to pelt the grave, yet if stones will not merely ward off an attack from the haunter, but when in the course of time they become piled up into a small cairn they serve to keep the deceased in his place, that is to say in the grave, there must be some sort of material entity which can be so materially frustrated and obstructed. Here then we have the essential and complete vampire.

It is recorded by a traveller about the middle of the last

century that when he was journeying in company with two
Mussulmans from Sidon to Tyre, as he drew near the latter
city he noticed a great pile of stones by the wayside, whereupon his companions began to pick up all the loose pebbles
that came to hand and discharged them violently at the
heap at the same time uttering the most fearful imprecations.
When they had passed and were at some little distance they
explained that a notorious brigand, whose hands were stained
with the hideous cruelties and innocent blood, had been slain
there, and buried on the spot half a century before. The
stones they threw and their curses were directed against this
villain. It might be thought in this case that the missiles
were a mark of loathing and contempt, but it seems far more
probable that they were intended to serve a very utilitarian
purpose, that is actually to keep off the wretch who would still
be haunting the pit into which his body had been cast fifty
years since.[21]

It even appears that in many parts of Syria when brigands
are killed by the highway, or vagrom murderers are dispatched
in the open country side beyond the walls of a city the body
is left to rot unburied where it lies, and after a while it is
merely covered over with a heap of stones ; moreover everyone who passes by is bound to quoit a stone or stick to add
to the pile under the penalty of incurring some dreadful
misfortune. It is supposed that heaven will horribly curse
the person who fails to throw his flinty tribute as he goes.[22]

It is not only among rude African tribes and in the East
that the graves of persons who have led cruel and anti-social
lives, particularly the spots where suicides have been buried,
are thus places of execration and fear, but in Pomerania and
in West Prussia, not to instance many other districts, the
spots where persons who have wrought their own destruction
happen to be interred are regarded as unlucky in the highest
degree, and there is no more malevolent and harmful spectre
than the suicide's ghost. A man who has destroyed himself
must not defile God's acre, in no wise may he be buried in
the churchyard but at the place where the desperate deed
was done, and everybody who passes by will cast a stone on
the spot unless he wishes the ghost of the suicide to plague
him nightly and to give him no rest until he is driven to the
same dreadful fate. It is said that, as in Africa piles of sticks

and stones accumulate to a great size, so similar cairns rise upon these haunted spots in the more remote districts along the cold shores washed by the Baltic Sea.

It is not surprising to find that in a country such as Russia, which through the ages has so often tottered to madness and of late years fallen into stark lunacy, during the seventeenth century an epidemic of suicide raged. It persisted, indeed, at spasmodic intervals throughout the eighteenth and even the nineteenth centuries, but it was somewhat earlier than this that the troubles of that luckless nation blazed out in furious frenzy. As when the year 1000 approached a fearful apocalyptic mania inflamed many parts of Europe, and men imagining that the world was about to come to an end, that almost any hour, any moment the Angel's clarion would blare, heaven and earth shrivel like some parching scroll and the Judge be set on His awful throne, in their hundreds deserted cities and homes to wander abroad preaching fevered repentance and the most extravagent forms of penance, or else in frantic despair abandoned themselves to debauchery and violence, so in Russia some mad visionary who proclaimed that the crack of doom was appointed for the year 1666[23] set the whole country aflame with terror. In many parts, men ceased to labour in the fields, relinquished their businesses and all social intercourse, barricaded themselves in their houses behind closed windows and fast-barred doors, awaiting the end with the gloomiest forebodings. As might have been expected, great numbers completely lost their senses and scores of dangerous lunatics not only infested the highroad but even invaded villages and towns preaching that the only way to escape the wrath to come was to prevent the final day by self-destruction. They were, moreover, very willing and eager to help those who shrank from so severe a test, and before long red murder was rife in every direction. Their services, however, were not required as frequently as might have been supposed for the delirium spread with such alarming rapidity that not merely households but whole communities eagerly devoted themselves to death. If in some paroxysm of wild hysteria a man had declared his intention of becoming a martyr, for so these poor wretches were deemed, the pious duty devolved upon his friends and relations of seeing that he scrupulously fulfilled his vow. Should he wish to change his mind or in any way seek to escape his fate he was pursued and saved in spite of himself by being put to death in the most atrocious torments. A veritable reign of terror ensued, and northern Russia seemed well-nigh depopulated. It were superfluous to enter into the horrible details, but it may suffice to say that at first starvation was the usual method by which these maniacs committed suicide. In the forest of Vetlouga, one fanatic at huge expense actually built a tower without doors and windows, into the body of which persons were lowered through a trap in the roof. But this was too long a process; it gave space for reflection and with the pangs of hunger reason resumed her sway. Those within yelled to be released, but all in vain. To shouts and clamour succeeded groans and fainter lamentations, until as the days passed all was still. Another remedy was found and presently the method which was preferred and which was officially prescribed as safer and more pleasing to God was immolation by fire. Accordingly, the missionaries of this horrible impiety proclaimed safety through the flame; as the prophet Elias had ascended to heaven in a blazing chariot, so the deluded wretches were taught they would ascend to a glorious and delightful eternity from the midst of the conflagration. Hundreds and even thousands perished in huge holocausts. Whole areas were strictly enclosed, the candidates took their places therein and the compound having been previously drenched with pitch, bitumen, and inflammable oils torches were applied at many points. If any overcome by agony escaped with scorched and blackened limbs they were caught and hurled back into the heart of the pyre. These immolations generally took place during the dark winter season and from midnight until the faint streaks of dawn the red glow of these horrid furnaces could be seen in every direction. For hundreds of verstas the land became a veritable Tophet. As the morning broke, hordes of wolves attracted by the stench of roasting flesh assembled to pull trunks and limbs from the embers; a dark cloud of suffocating smoke, greasy with human fat that fouled both ground and houses, hung low in the sky, and ere many days were past the plague was stalking abroad with fatal voracity. It was not until the most vigorous measures had been taken that these terrible practices could be checked, and it seems that the venom of the madness persisted long and late, for as recently as 1860, fifteen persons in the district of Olonetz committed suicide by fire, whilst during the winter of 1896-1897, twenty-four religious fanatics buried themselves alive in a pit near Tiraspol.[24] The monk, Falaley, constantly preached that death was man's only means of salvation and that he must have done with this life of sin.   One night under his influence, eighty-four persons congregated near the river Perevozinka and began to pray.   Many of them were already half-crazed through excessive fasting, and they almost covered themselves with brambles and brushwood to which fire was to be set at a given signal.   A woman, taking alarm at the thought of so horrible a death, escaped and informed the authorities. When the police arrived the fanatics shrieked that Antichrist was approaching, and setting fire to the pile most perished in the flames.   A few who were rescued received sentences of imprisonment and deportation, but a fanatic called Souchkoff, managed to escape and continued to preach the gospel of death.   Maddened by his doctrine in   one locality alone, sixty families resolved to commit suicide at a certain moment, and a peasant, named Petroff, entering a neighbour's house cut down his wife and children with a hatchet. In a barn hard by, a dozen men with their wives had assembled and amid hymns of triumph they laid their heads upon an improvised block to be hacked off by Petroff.   In another hut a woman and three children were dispatched at their own earnest request.   At length when he was weary, Petroff himself kneeled down and was slain by Souchkoff.   Between 1860 and 1870, a maniac named Chadkin, proclaimed that Antichrist was here, and all most follow him to the forests and there die of hunger.   A large number assembled and his most devoted followers saw to it that nobody could escape. After a few days the sufferings of the crowds were fearful and the place rang with their screams and groans.   Nevertheless Chadkin and his apostles did not waver.   When some poor creature, frantic with agony, managed to break away and informed the police, the devotees at once began to kill all who had gathered together, and by the time the authorities had arrived in the utmost haste there were found but three survivors.

Buddhist monks in China are often recorded to have

sought their Nirvana through an act of self-immolation by
fire, and it is said that every year among the lamaresais of
Tien-tai, in the province of Tai-chow, some half-a-dozen
bonzes thus devote themselves to death. These unfortunate
persons believe that their voluntary destruction crowns the
monastery with honours and blessing, they are aware that
they will be worshipped after their suicide, and they suppose
that they will become the divinities of the district and possess
the power to protect the whole neighbourhood, to grant fair
weather and lucky seasons, a bounteous harvest and all
prosperity. Such public incinerations are conducted with
great ceremony, and take place upon a major festival which is
bound to attract crowds of pilgrims and reverent suppliants
to the spot.[25] It is said that among the Eskimo of Bering
Strait a sorcerer has been known to burn himself alive, fully
believing that thus he will return to life as a shaman with
much greater powers and a far fuller knowledge of magic
than he had hitherto enjoyed.[26] It may be remembered
that even such low motives as vanity and a craving for mere
notoriety have proved an incentive sufficiently powerful to
induce men to seek a dramatic, if painful death by fire. Thus
the charlatan Peregrinus after a career of the most braggart
ostentation courted undying fame by self-immolation upon a
pyre at the Olympic festival, which extraordinary performance attracted throngs not only of sensible persons who
despised and mocked him but of encomiasts and apologists
who regarded him as at the least a hero, if not something
nearly approaching to deity.[27] It can hardly be argued that
higher motives inspired Empedocles if the account preserved by
Diogenes Laertius[28] to which Horace [29] makes reference be
true, namely that hoping by a sudden disappearance he
might be accounted a god, the philosopher flung himself
into the crater of Mount Aetna, but that the suicide was
revealed owing to the fact that the volcano almost immediately
after threw up one of his sandals, and thus betrayed the
manner of his death.

Josephus states that the Jews used not to bury the bodies
of those who had destroyed themselves until after sunset.
In Scotland it is still thought that the body of a suicide will
not fall to dust until the time when he should have died in the
order of nature,[30] and it is very generally held that a such

a one must be buried with the grave facing north and south. This belief also existed in England and there are graves facing north and south to be seen at Cowden (Kent) and Bergholt (Suffolk), which are locally said to be those of persons who have destroyed themselves, for it is almost universally declared that Christian burial should be with the head in west, looking eastward[31]. As is well-known, in England until the time of George IV, it was the general practice to bury suicides at the cross-roads, where a stake was driven through the body. In the year 1823, it was enacted that the body of a suicide should be buried privately between the hours of nine o'clock and twelve at night with no religious ceremony. In 1882, this law was altered, and the body may now be committed to the earth at any time and with such rites or prayers those in charge of the funeral think fit or may be able to procure. In certain country places it is still supposed that the spirit of the last person buried in a graveyard has to keep watch lest any suicide should be interred there. One explanation of the reason why persons who had taken their own lives should be buried at the cross-roads was that the ghosts of murdered persons were supposed to walk until the bodies had been recovered and committed to the church-yard with Christian rites, and since this was impossible in the case of suicides, a stake was driven through them when deposited at the cross-roads in order to keep the ghost from wandering abroad.[32] It is certain that the idea here is the same as that of driving a stake through the vampire, for sometimes this precaution was taken in the case of persons who might perchance become vampires, an operation performed not as an indignity but as a preventitive. Burchard of Worms tells us : "Cum aliquis femina parere debit, et non potest, in ipso dolore si mortem obierit, in ipso sepulchro matrem cum infante palo in terram transfigunt." And again : "Fecisti quod quaedam mulieres instinctu diaboli facere solent, cum aliquis infans sine baptismo mortuus fuerit, tollunt cadauer paruuli, et ponunt in aliquo secreto loco, et palo corpusculum transfigunt, dicentes, si sic non fecissent, quod infantulus surgeret et multos laedere posset." The reason for the selected spot of the suicide's grave being a cross-road is further explained by the belief that when the ghost or the body issues from the grave and finds that there

are four paths stretching in as many directions he will be
puzzled to know which way to take and will stand debating
until dawn compels him to return to the earth, but woe betide
the unhappy being who happens to pass by when he is lingering there perplexed and confused. Accordingly after sunset,
every sensible person will avoid all crossroads since there are
no localities more certainly and more fearfully haunted and
disturbed. It will readily be remembered that the Romans
were far more precise than we used to be in their definition
of cross-roads and employed no less than three terms,
biuium when the road branched into two, *triuium* when the
road forked into three, and *quadriuium* when the intersection
of the ways gave four arms. The prophet Ezechiel tells us
that Esarhaddon took his stand *in biuio* when he wished to
divine : " Stetit enim rex Babylonis in biuio, in capite duarum
uiarum, diuinationem quaerens, commiscens sagittas :
interrogauit idola, exta consuluit." (xxi, 21.) " For the king
of Babylon stood in the highway, at the head of two ways,
seeking divination, shuffling arrows : he enquired of the
idols, and consulted entrails." *Triuia* is the common name
given to Diana, when as Hecate she was invoked at the cross-
ways. Chariclides Comicus in Meineke's *Comicorum Fragmenta*,
IV, p. 556, has τριοδῖτις, and invokes : Ἑκάτη τριοδῖτι, τρίμορφε,
τριπρόσωπε.

Varro, *De Lingua Latina*, VII, 16, writes : " Titanis Triuia
Diana est, ab eo dicta Triuia, quod in triuio ponitur fere in
oppodis Graecis, uel quod luna dicitur esse, quae in caelo
tribus uiis mouetur in altitudinem et latitudinem et longitud-
inem." Macrobius, *Saturnalia*, I, ix, notes : " Dianae uero
ut Triuiae uiarum omnium iidem tribuunt potestatem."

In Wales it was said that witches slept by day under any
boulder that might be at a cross-road, and when dusk had
fallen they crept forth to steal little children and feast upon
their flesh. The gallows was often erected at the cross-roads,
and here the criminal hung in chains, and nourished by his
rotting flesh the mandrake grew. Many are the superstitions
which cluster around the mandrake or mandragora—" the
semi-human " as Columella (*De re rustica*, x, 19) calls it. It
was the plant of fertility, the plant of magical virtue and
occult power. In Germany it bears the name of the Little
Gallows Man, and it was believed that when a murderer or

thief was hanged and his semen or urine fell to the ground there grew up the mandrake. In England the same superstition prevailed, and in his pasquil *A Character of an Ugly Woman or a Hue and Cry after Beauty*, 1678, the Duke of Buckingham wrote : "*Imprimis*, as to her *Descent*, some *Heralds* derive her *Pedigree* from that of the *Scotch Barnacles*, and say, that she dropt from some teeming *Gallows*, or sprung up like *Mandrakes* from the S—— of some gibbitid *Raggamuffian.*" No one must dare uproot the mandrake for it moans and shrieks so fearfully that the digger will die with the yells ringing in his ears. A dog is taken and round his tail is tied a string, one end of which is attached to the plant. A man whose ears are fast stopped with wax and wool, tempts the dog away with some dainty. As the animal tugs at the cord the mandrake will be pulled from the ground, but the poor beast will fall dead at the horrid scream it gives. But there has been secured a talisman, nay, more a familiar.

Even in the mythology of Ceylon the cross-roads play an ominous part. Thus in the *Yakkun Nattanawa*, which is defined by its translator, John Callaway, as "a Cingalese poem descriptive of the Ceylon system of demonology," it is said of the Black She-Devil : "Thou female Devil, who acceptest the offerings at the place where three ways meet, thou causest the people to be sick by looking upon them at the place where four ways join together." The devil Maha-Sohon watches "to drink the blood of the elephant in the place where the two and three roads meet together." Maha-Sohon is the devil of the tombs, "therefore go not in the roads by night : if you do so you must not expect to escape with your life." Another devil, Oddy, stands where three ways meet, watching, and hot for mischief. Again the Devil of the Victim "watches and looks upon the people, and causes them to be sick at the place where three roads meet, and where four ways meet."

Ralstan[33] says that it is a common Russian belief that at cross-roads, or in the neighbourhood of cemeteries, an animated corpse often lurks watching for some unwary traveller whom it may be able to strangle and devour, eagerly quaffing the warm blood from his veins. In Cornwall to-day cross-roads are most carefully avoided after night-fall,[34] but this may be because it is commonly accepted that at the cross-roads witches from all the world over assemble for their sabbat. It seems more likely that these particular spots are avoided because of the vampires, for Henry Boguet tells us : " Les Sorciers tiennēt leurs sabbats indifferemēt en tous lieux."[35] Bernhard Ragner says that if you go to a cross-road between eleven o'clock and midnight on Christmas eve and listen, you will hear what most concerns you for the coming year.[36] It may be pointed out that this is the one night throughout the year when strange wonders happen. It is then that the thorn that sprang at Glastonbury from the Sacred Crown which the holy old man, S. Joseph of Arimathea, brought with him from Palestine, when Avalon was still an island, bourgeons into fragrant blossoms. The Cornish miners seem to hear the sound of singing choirs that arise from submerged churches by the shore, and others said that bells, beneath the ground where villages had been, upon that eve yearly ring a glad peal. At midnight the oxen, the cattle, and all the beasts kneel and adore, as they adored in the stable-cave at Bethlehem. No evil thing hath power, and as the Officer in *Hamlet*[37] tells us :

> Some say that ever 'gainst that season comes
> Wherein our Saviour's birth is celebrated,
> The bird of dawning singeth all night long ;
> And then, they say, no spirit can walk abroad ;
> The nights are wholesome ; then no planets strike,
> No fairy takes, nor witch hath power to charm,
> So hallow'd and so gracious is the time.

In certain districts of East Prussia on Christmas Eve candles are kept burning all night in the houses and no window is shuttered. It is supposed that the spirits of the dead will return in friendly-wise and the opportunity is given to them to warm themselves, so that on future occasions when they haunt the villages with more malicious intent they may remember those who are kind to them Christmas after Christmas and spare those houses from molestation and injury.[38]

Not only are those who die excommunicate, that is to say solemnly and officially cursed by the Church, liable to become vampires, but more, those who die under any kind of such ban, especially if it be the malison of a parent, or if it be a man who has perjured himself in a grave matter and called down upon his own head damnation and all manner of evil should

what he asseverate be untrue. The belief in the fearful power
of a curse, especially the curse of a father or a mother, which,
whether rightfully or wrongfully adjured, works out its
vengeance through the whole stock of kith and kin, involving
in misfortunes and destruction, innocent and guilty alike,
finds supreme illustration in the masterpieces of Greek
tragedy. It is the mighty theme of the trilogy of the *Oresteia*,
for from the very outset of the *Agamemnon* there is a brooding
and oppressive sense of multitudinous crimes, of sins done
long years ago which have swelled and accumulated their
guilt like some black cloud of transgressions about to burst
over the doomed race in a welter of tragedy and blood. The
evil wrought by Thyestes, the crimes of his grandsire Tantalus,
the atrocious banquet of Atreus, have yet to be expiated in
misery, in anguish and affliction. When the weird Trojan
woman approaches the threshold she scents the carnage of
the shambles and horrors manifold, and as the pang of inspiration thrills her she shrieks aloud : " The Furies are in this
house ; blood-surfeited, but not assuaged, they hold perpetual
revel here. It is the crime of Atreus and of Thyestes which
they hunt, and woe will follow woe."

> τὴν γὰρ στέγην τήνδ' οὔποτ' ἐκλείπει χορὸς
> σύμφθογγος οὐκ εὔφωνος· οὐ γὰρ εὖ λέγει,
> καὶ μὴν πεπωκώς γ', ὡς θρασύνεσθαι πλέον,
> βρότειον αἷμα κῶμος ἐν δόμοις μένει,
> δύσπεμπτος ἔξω, συγγόνων Ἐρινύων.

Sophocles also no less fearfully shows us the tale of Oedipus
and his children, the legend of the house of Laius, whose
family was as equally famous among the Greeks as the stock
of Atreus for its overwhelming disasters, the bitter fruit of an
undying curse which destroyed the whole race. Laius, the
son of Labdacus, had wrought a mighty evil. Lusting after the
beauty of Chrysippus, the son of Pelops, with violence he
raped the lad who belonged to another, and thus had sinned
the sin of ὕβρις since he both betrayed another's love and
used brute force in doing so.[39] For this crime his whole
progeny was involved in destruction. He married Jocasta,
the sister of Creon of Thebes, and the oracle warned him that
his son should kill him. When a boy was born to the royal
pair they cruelly exposed their child, a helpless infant, to the

wild beasts on Mount Cithaeron, but the will of heaven is
not frustrated by the impotence of man. Many years after
as King Laius is riding privately in his chariot attended by
only five servants they meet a young man upon the road.
The king bids him make way, commanding him in rough and
insolent terms. A quarrel arises. The stranger, a stalwart
warrior, strikes down the master and certain of the servants,
but one escapes and fled away for his life. Presently Oedipus
solves the riddle of the monstrous Sphinx, when the Thebans,
in gratitude, since their old monarch has been slain by robbers
on the highway elect him to rule over them, giving him the
lady Jocasta to wife. He governs the state in great prosperity,
and four children are born to him, two sons, Polyneices and
Eteocles ; two daughters, Antigone and Ismene. It is the
calm before the storm ; a fearful plague afflicts the city, and
when the divine Phoebus Apollo is consulted he answers
that the murderer of Laius must be driven from the land.
The old prophet, Teiresias, the mystic whose converse is in
heaven, but who yet in his stern pride still retains much of
humanity, is asked to rede the enigma. He answers with deep
sighs and groans, seeking to be led home again, until goaded
by the impatience and hot temper of the king he flashes forth
the truth. But it is not immediately recognized, and Oedipus
begins formally to inquire into the circumstances of the death
of his predecessor. Detail is heaped upon detail and at last
the horrible revelation forces itself upon his soul. Mad with
terror, Jocasta hangs herself within her bed-chamber, and
Oedipus tearing from her dress the buckles and clasps of
gold strikes out his eyes that are unworthy to look upon
the golden light of day. One moment a king, the next a
beggar, red with parricide, polluted with the fires of incest,
accursed of God and man, in the bitterness of utter dereliction
he must go forth desolate and alone. He dare not even bid
farewell to his sons and daughters for they are the children of
doom, seed of that admixture too fearful to be named. In
the next play, the *Oedipus Coloneus*, we find him many years
afterwards, a mysterious figure set apart by heaven in awful
loneliness. He is waiting in a place of peculiar sanctity, the
reverent groves of the Semnai Theai, the holy goddesses of
divine retribution, waiting for his silent passage to the shadowy
world. And even here the evil ambitions of his sons would

fain disturb him at the end. But he is far removed from the strife and passion of this world, and when young Polyneices, fair, false and fickle, endeavours to enlist his father's sympathies the lad receives the awful answer : " Dry were your eyes, hard as stone your heart, dumb your lips, when I went forth from Thebes friendless and alone. Here then is your reward : before the Walls of Thebes you shall perish, pierced by your brother's hand, and there your brother shall die slain by you." This terrible imprecation is only too terribly fulfilled, and defying the laws of King Creon, who would have the curse-polluted ghosts of the brothers seek for rest in vain even in Hades, Antigone meets her doom. Nor does Creon, the respectable Creon, weak and spiteful, impotent, yet a tyrant, escape scathless. His malice is sharply punished, owing to his own folly and cruelty he loses both wife and son, for he has forgotten that great truth which S. Thomas enunciated, that " reason is the first principle of all human works,"[40] and " the secular power is subject to the spiritual even as the body is subject to the soul." So owing to his impiety he is left without child to carry on his name, bereaved of all, broken and collapsed, piteously confessing himself—$\mu\acute{a}\tau\alpha\iota o\nu$ $\acute{a}\nu\delta\rho a$— a feckless and foolish old man.

It has seemed worth while thus very briefly and inadequately to review these two great themes of Greek tragedy, since in both instances they set forth in detail the terrible and relentless working of a curse, which it may be said has something of that divine vengeance that visits " the iniquity of the fathers upon the children, unto the third and fourth generation." And so something of this old Greek doctrine was very true, for who can foresee the end of the working of a curse ? Even to-day there are places and there are properties in England which owing to deeds of blood and violence in their acquisition entail some dire misfortune upon all who seek to enjoy and possess them. Such a place is the ruined Abbey of Glastonbury, and of many another house—Tintern, Newstead, Cowdray, Waverley, Barlings, Croxton, Dureford— the tale is true. *De male quaesita non gaudet tertius haeres*, says the old adage, and it is well known that lands wrested from the Church will not descend in due course owing to a failure of heirs. Such a case has come under my own observation, and Aubrey in his *Miscellanies* cites Hinton Charterhouse on Mendip and Butleigh, near Glastonbury as never having passed to the third generation. So did Cromwell's generals and adherents transmit a troubled inheritance to their descendants. Fairfax House, Putney, had its haunted chamber which was never used.

It must be remembered that a solemn curse is not merely an expletive or an imprecatory exclamation, perhaps quite meaningless, but it is far more than this ; it is significant and operative. The malediction is conceived as having a certain efficacious power, and it may be noted that this force if rightly launched does not seem to exhaust itself. No more terrible fate could be imagined than for a man to become a vampire, and this was the inevitable consequence if he were not cleared of a merited malison. The old proverb says :

> Curses are like young chicken
> And still come home to roost.[41]

This adage is terribly exemplified in the vampire who is supposed when he returns from his grave first to attack those who on earth have been his nearest and dearest. Of all curses the parental malediction is most dreaded, and curiously enough in Macedonia, Mr. Abbott tells us that a godfather is regarded with even greater respect than the actual parents and his " malediction is dreaded even more than that of a Bishop."[42] At the present day in Greece many of the usual imprecations definitely refer to the fact that the person so cursed will become a vampire after death. Such imprecations as the following are in common use. " May the earth not receive him," (Nὰ μήν τον δεχτῇ ἡ γῆς) ; " May the ground not consume him " (Nὰ μήν τον φάγῃ τὸ χῶμα) : " May the earth not digest thee " (Ἡ γῆ νὰ μή σε χωνέψῃ) : " May the black earth spew thee up " (Ἡ μαύρη γῆ νά σ' ἀναξεράσῃ) ; " Mayest thou remain incorrupt," (Nα μείνῃς ἄλυωτος) ; " May the earth not loose thee " which is to say may the body not decompose (Nὰ μή σε λυώσῃ ἡ γῆ) ; " May the ground reject thee " (Nά σε βγάλῃ τὸ χῶμα) ; " Mayest thou become in the grave like rigid wood " (Κοντούκι νὰ βγῇς) ; " May the ground reject him wholly " (Tὸ χῶμα 'ξεράσ' τόνε), which last phrase is the most terrible of all since it is nothing other than an unspeakably impious parody of the prayer which is uttered by the mourners at every Greek funeral Ὁ Θεὸς 'χωρέσ' τόνε, " May God forgive him."

Since even the curse uttered by a man in moments of anger and impatience may have such terrible effects, in Greece it is necessary that there should be some expedient which may dissipate and dispel the forces to which these words have given an impetus capable of producing the most serious and horrible results. Accordingly at a Greek death-bed there is carried out a certain ritual to attain this end. A vessel of water is brought to the bedside and he throws into it a handful of salt, and when this is dissolved the sick man sprinkles with the lymph all those who are present saying : " As this salt dissolves so may my curses dissolve " ; ὡς λυώνει τ' ἀλάτι, νὰ λυώσουν ἡ κατάραις μου. This ceremony absolves all persons whom he may have cursed in his lifetime from the evil of a ban which after death he would no longer be able to revoke. The relations and friends then solemnly forgive the dying man for ought that he may have done against them and all present declare that they bear no grudge nor anger in their hearts. It is said that if the passage be a difficult one it is supposed that somebody whom the sick man has injured has not forgiven him. If it can be guessed who this may be, he is if possible, brought to the bed-side to declare his forgiveness of any injury he may have suffered. If, however, he be dead a portion of the cerements must be sought and burned to ashes in the bed-chamber of the dying person, who is fumigated with the smoke. These elaborate precautions and the extraordinary care which is taken, for it must often be a matter of very great difficulty either to secure the attendance of the living individual or to get hold of a portion of the necessary shroud, serve to show what immense importance the modern Greek attaches to the absolution from a curse, and what horror the thought of a vampire inspires.

It is obvious that those who die unbaptized or apostate will be liable to become vampires after death, and throughout the south of Europe there still persist large numbers of ceremonies and superstitions connected with a christening whose object it is to secure the child a long, happy and healthy life.

In England as in many other countries it is thought lucky to be born on one of the great church festivals, especially if it be a Sunday. In certain districts of Yorkshire even to-day it is commonly said that " Sunday children are secure from

the malice of evil spirits."[43]   Again a child born on a Saturday,
although he may have " to work hard for his living " is considered to enjoy occult powers, to have the faculty of second
sight, to be able to see ghosts and phantoms, and indeed to
be so attuned to the supernatural that he can never be harmed
even by the vampire. It is very probable that as Saturday
is the seventh day of the week those born upon this day are
considered as akin to a seventh son, who was so popularly
believed to possess extraordinary powers of healing and the
like. The old English rhyme is well known, and perhaps
the following is one of the most usual forms :

> Monday's child is fair of face,
> Tuesday's child is full of grace,
> Wednesday's child is sour and grum,
> Thursday's child has welcome home,
> Friday's child is free in giving,
> Saturday's child works hard for his living.
> And the child that is born on Christmas Day
> Is great, and good, and fair, and gay.

Although, as we have said, in England it is considered an
omen of a happy life to be born upon some festival the exact
opposite is the case in Slav countries.[44] In Greece, particularly,
nothing could be more disastrous, and of all seasons Christmas
Day is the most unlucky. In many districts it is accounted a
terrible thing for any child to be born at any time between
Christmas and the Epiphany ; such babies are called
ἑορτοπιάσματα or "feast-blasted," and after death they will
assuredly become vampires. Even during life such a child is
a Callicantzaros.

The Callicantzaros is one of the most extraordinary and
most horrible of all the creatures of popular superstition.
Leone Allacci says that they only appear and have power during
the week from Christmas to New Year's Day,[45] but other
authorities extend this time until Twelfth Night. During
the rest of the year it is vaguely supposed that they sojourn in
some mysterious Hades or under-world. Local traditions
differ as to whether they are actually demons or whether
they are human. Allacci, who certainly inclines to the latter
view, says that children born in the octave of Christmas are
liable to be seized with a terrible mania, that they rush to and
fro with the most amazing speed, that their nails grow to a

terrible length like the talons of a bird of prey whilst their hands become as crooked claws. If they meet any person on the highway they seize him and put the question : " Tow or lead ? " If he answer : " Tow " he may escape unharmed, but if he be inadvertent enough to reply : " Lead," they grip him with terrible force, mangle him with their talons and often tear him to pieces, devouring him wholemeal.[46] During the seventeenth century this belief so strongly prevailed that the most cruel precautions were taken in the case of children who might be suspected to be liable to become Callicantzari, since the soles of their feet were exposed to a fire until the nails were singed and so their claws clipped, and even to-day in parts of Greece these practices prevail in a highly modified form, for among the Ægean islanders it is said that the small Callicantzari are particularly prone to attack and devour their own brothers and sisters, which is another strong link with the tradition of the vampire who, as we have noted before, seeks the destruction of his own kin.[47]

It is difficult to convey any idea of the popular notions concerning the appearance of a Callicantzaros, as almost every local account differs from others in almost every particular. For the most part they are considered to be very gaunt [48] and of enormous strength. On the other hand there are some who are dwarfed and stunted. The larger variety generally appear as ineffably hideous monsters with black distorted faces, eyes glaring red like fire, huge ears such as those of a donkey, great gaping mouths furnished with a slobbering scarlet tongue and sharp gleaming teeth, from which streams their fetid breath in horrid gusts. Again the pigmy Callicantzaros may appear in the shape of a child, but in this case it is usually deformed in some grotesque and painful manner. On the other hand they are sometimes harmless hobgoblins, full of mischief maybe, but objects of laughter rather than fear, though they may play many a naughty and tiresome trick not unlike the kobold and the leprechaun. A hundred tales are told of their pranks, but it is the more gruesome and the fiercer monsters with whom we are mainly concerned since it is from their ranks that the vampire is recruited, for most of them become vampires after death (a fact which seems to point to their human origin), and not infrequently they are supposed to indulge their vampirish fancies during life. It will be noticed that in the various accounts of the Callicantzari there exist many contradictions, and we must bear in mind that such diversities are often due to the original conception of these creatures, whether they are regarded as demons or monsters who are suffered to plague the countryside for a certain number of days during the Christmas season, or whether they are regarded as human beings afflicted with a terrible curse, the victims of a most horrible possession, doomed never to rest not even in the grave.

Near akin to the latter conception is the werewolf, who may be regarded as a man or woman, who either of his or her own will through black magic is able to change into the form of a wolf, or who in classical times was believed to be so changed owing to the vengeance of the gods ; and in later days was believed to be so changed owing to the enchantment of a witch or some manner of diabolic possession. Moreover, a werewolf may be a person who without any actual metamorphosis is obsessed with all the savage passions and ferocity of a wolf, so that he will attack human beings in the same way as the actual wild animal.

It may be asked, is it possible that a person should be so transformed ? Henry Kramer and James Sprenger, the learned authors of the supremely authoritative *Malleus Maleficarum*, in discussing the question distinctly answer " No, it is not possible." They allow that by horrid charms and spells a certain subjective delusion or glamour may be caused, so that by the evil art of a sorcerer a man may appear to himself and to all others who gaze upon him to be a wolf, or indeed another kind of animal, but there cannot be any actual physical change of a man into an animal. This glamour or ocular illusion is sometimes known as " sight-shifting," a convenient correlative to the accepted term " shape-shifting " which is conceived of as an objective fact. Moreover, in his *De Ciuitate Dei*, XVIII, 18, S. Augustine says : " Nor can the devils create anything (whatever shows of theirs produce these doubts) but only cast a changed shape over that which God has made, altering only in show. Nor do I think the devil can form any soul or body into bestial or brutal members, and essences ; but they have an unspeakable way of transporting man's phantasy in a bodily shape, unto other senses (this though it be not corporal, yet seems to carry itself in corporal forms through all these things) while the bodies of the men thus affected lie in another place, being alive, but yet in an ecstasy far more deep than any sleep. Now this phantasy may appear unto other senses in a bodily shape, and a man may seem to himself to be such an one as he often thinks himself to be in his dream, and to bear burdens, which if they be true burdens indeed, the devils bear them, to delude men's eyes with the appearance of true burdens, and false shapes." We must bear in mind that these explanations come from the highest authority, one of the greatest Doctors of the Church, and will, I think, very fairly cover most of the cases of the werewolf.

In early days it was recognized that a werewolf might be a person who was afflicted with a horrible mania, and Marcellus Sidetes, who lived in the reigns of Hadrian and Antoninus Pius, *circa* A.D. 117-161, wrote Περὶ λυκανθρώπου, a long medical poem in Greek hexameter verse, consisting of forty-two books, of which only a couple of fragments remain. He says that Lycanthropy is a disease, a kind of insanity or mania when the patient was afflicted with hideous appetites, the ferocity, and other qualities of a wolf. He further tells us that men are attacked with this madness chiefly in the beginning of the year, and become most furious in February; retiring for the night to lone cemeteries and living precisely in the manner of ravening wolves.

Under *Lycanthropia*, Burton[49] notes as follows : " Lycanthropia, which Avicenna calls Cucubuth, others Lupinam Insaniam, or Wolf-Madness, when men run howling about graves and fields in the night, and will not be persuaded but that they are wolves, or some such beasts. Aetius (Lib. 6, cap. 11) and Paulus (Lib. 3, cap. 16) call it a kind of melancholy ; but I should rather refer it to madness, as most do. Some make a doubt of it whether there be any such disease. Donat ab Altomari (Cap. 9, Art med.) saith, that he saw two of them in his time : Wierus (*De praestig. Daemonum*, 1, 3, cap. 21) tells a story of such a one at Padua, 1541, that would not believe to the contrary, but that he was a wolf. He hath another instance of a Spaniard, who thought himself a bear ; Forrestus (*Obseruat.* lib. 10, *de morbis cerebri*, cap. 15) confirms as much by many examples ; one amongst the rest of which he was an eye-witness, at Alcmaer, in Holland, a poor

husbandman that still hunted about graves, and kept in church-
yards, of a pale, black, ugly, and fearful look . . . this
malady, saith Avicenna, troubleth men most in February,
and is now-a-days frequent in Bohemia and Hungary, according to Heurnius (*Cap. de Man.*). Schernitzius will have it
common in Livonia. They lie hid most part all day, and go
abroad in the night, barking, howling, at graves and deserts ;
they have usually hollow eyes, scabbed legs and thighs, very
dry and pale (*Ulcerata crura, sitis ipsis adest immodica, pallidi,
lingua sicca*) saith Altomarus (Cap. 9, Art. *Hydrophobia*) ;
he gives a reason there of all the symptoms, and sets down a
brief cure of them." It is remarkable that most of these
features are found in the vampire, especially the unquench-
able thirst, " sitis immodica " which is emphasized by the
famous physician Antonio Donato Altomari, who was one of
the most learned authorities of his day. It is also remarkable that the malady is reported as being very prevalent in
Bohemia, Hungary, and Livonia, countries in which the vampire
is most frequently found. There is in fact a very close
connexion between the werewolf and the vampire, and the
lycanthropist is liable to become a vampire when he dies.

In parts of Greece, particularly in Elis,[50] it is said that even
those who eat the flesh of a sheep that has been killed by a
wolf are apt to become vampires after their death, and this
serves to show how powerful the pollution of the werewolf
was supposed to be. In Norse saga, Ingiald, the son of King
Aunund, was timid whilst a boy, but after eating the heart of a
wolf he gained strength and courage and became the boldest
of heroes.[51] It might be thought that so far from inspiring
a person with a thirst for blood the flesh of a sheep would
homœopathically infuse qualities of gentleness, and indeed
the Abipones of Paraguay were most careful to avoid mutton
lest it should make them slack and fearful in the fight.[52] But
in this instance it will be seen that the characteristics of a
sheep have been absorbed, so to speak, and infected by the
ferocity of the wolf. Curiously enough in Uganda the
Baganda greatly fear the ghosts of sheep, which they believe
would return and kill a man if they saw him give them the
fatal blow. Hence when a sheep is to be killed one man
occupies its attention in some way and another, whose presence the animal must not suspect, swiftly slaughters it before

a glimpse of him can be caught. In this way the sheep is tricked because the ghost does not know whom to haunt and punish for its death. Moreover, sheep give health and protection to cattle, and a ram is almost invariably sent into the pastures with a herd of cows. Should a sheep die in a house nobody must dare openly to mention the fact, which may only be alluded to in the most covert and circumlocutionary phrase, for were anyone to say, " the sheep is dead," its ghost sorely angered would assuredly afflict the unlucky speaker with some disease and possibly even kill him outright.[53] It is worth noting that among the ancient Greeks it was thought that any garment made from the fleece of a sheep which had been worried or torn by a wolf would have a bad effect upon the wearer and set up some roseola and an intense irritation of the skin.[54] It is certainly curious to note the whole mass of tradition which, as it would seem, the wide world over is connected with the sheep, and in particular when this animal has been attacked or slain by a wolf.

Even as some kind of vampirish infection was held to proceed from the wolf, the vampire himself will even more strongly convey this taint, and therefore, unless the most drastic and immediate remedies are applied, a person who is attacked by a vampire and whose blood has been sucked will become a vampire in turn imbued with a craving to pass on the horrible pollution. This is perhaps, and with good reason, the most dreaded quality of the vampire, and examples thereof occur again and again in legend and history.

It is far more curious that it should be thought that those over whose dead bodies a cat or any other animal has passed should become vampires. This belief widely exists amongst Slavonic peoples, and is to be found in some parts of Greece. It also prevails in China where a cat is never allowed to enter a room with a corpse for the body still contains the Kuei, the lower or inferior soul of Yin original, and by leaping over it the cat will impart something of its original savage or tigerish nature and the dead man may become a vampire.[55] It should be explained that it is a common belief among the Chinese that there are two " souls " ; the higher soul which after death seeks the divine life, the heavenly source of its being ; and the lower soul, which is gross, returning to the earth and dwelling in the grave until the complete dissolution of the corpse.

It is believed among Slavonic nations, as it was firmly believed throughout England and in many districts of France, that witches turn themselves into cats, and among the Oraons (or Uraons) a primitive hill tribe of Bengal, we have a vampire cat who is a *Chordewa*, a witch who is able to change her soul into a black cat and who then visits and frequents the houses where there are sick and dying people. Such a cat has a peculiar way of mewing quite differently from the noise of other cats, and is easily recognized. It steals quietly into a house almost like a shadow leaps lightly on the bed, eats of the food that has been prepared for the sick man and gently licks his lips. When it is able to accomplish this latter the invalid has no chance of recovering, in which connexion we must remember, as has been remarked before, that the soul is supposed to take its departure from the mouth of a dying person. Even if this cat be seen it is extraordinarily difficult to catch it, since it has a supernatural activity and will fight and scratch with the malice of a demon. However, they say that persons have sometimes succeeded, and then the woman out of whom the cat (her soul) has come remains insensible, in a state of coma as deep as death, until the cat re-enters her body. Any wound inflicted upon the cat is produced upon her. For example if they cut it, or break a leg, or destroy its sight, the woman will simultaneously suffer the same mutilation. So great a horror had the Oraons of these witches that formerly they used to burn any person that was suspected to be a Chordewa.[56]

It is a circumstance of very frequent occurrence in the witch trials of all countries that a witch who has appeared in the likeness of a cat, a hare, or any other animal and has met with an accident or been mutilated under that form is found to be marked with the same wound or to be suffering from the same harm in her human shape when this is resumed.[57]

It is not difficult then to see why, if some animal of ill-omen, —and the cat seems to be particularly unfortunate,—leaps over a corpse, the dead person should be considered in danger of becoming a vampire. In Greece, particularly in Macedonia, the most pious care is taken to prevent any such calamity. The body is watched all night long by relatives and friends and this is deemed a work of true charity by which they acquire great merit, it brings a blessing upon their own souls (ψυχικό), if, in spite of all their care some cat does jump across the body, the dead man must be pierced through with two long "sack-needles" (σακκορράφαις), in order to secure his rest and to guard against his return. It is well to scatter mustard seed on the roof and on the threshold, and the wise man will barricade his door with brambles and thorns. Should the vampire return he cannot fail to occupy himself with counting the seeds, and it will be dawn, when he must return to his grave, long before he completes the tale. Should he endeavour to pass through the bushes he will inevitably be caught and held fast by the briars. Ralston tells us that the Serbs and the Bulgarians keep this vigil even more carefully than the Greeks. "In some places the jumping of a boy over the corpse is considered as fatal as that of a cat. The flight of a bird above the body may also be attended by the same terrible results ; and so may—in the Ukraine—the mere breath of the wind from the Steppe."[58] What is extremely curious is that this tradition still lingers in the north of England, and if a cat or dog pass over a corpse the animal must be killed at once. The reason for this has been entirely forgotten, but the survival is very remarkable as showing that once there existed a dread of vampires in England which to-day is entirely forgotten. Thomas Pennant says that in Scotland: "No dog or cat must be allowed to leap over the corpse or enter the room. It is reckoned so ominous, their doing so that the poor animal is killed without mercy."[59] It is even still the custom that all animals shall be shut up till the funeral procession has left. It is believed that a cat will not remain in the house with an unburied corpse ; and rooks (we know) will abandon the place till after the funeral, if the rookery be near the mansion. The explanation given by John Jamieson[60] that if a cat has leapt over a corpse the first person on to whose lap he may afterwards jump, or who may take him up in his arms, is stricken with blindness would seem to be a later invention, a reason made up to explain the ill-omen, when the vampire tradition had disappeared, and so the real reason had been entirely forgotten.

Having investigated the various reasons why any person

should become a vampire, and discussed the fatal accident which may bring about this terrible doom various points present themselves which invite some inquiry. Although the belief varies in different parts of the world, and it is generally understood that vampires only operate by night, as King David says :[61] " Non timebis a timore nocturno " (Thou shalt not be afraid of the terror of the night), yet it is also supposed that under certain conditions vampires may wander abroad during the day, and that the vampire truly is *daemonium meridianum* (the noonday devil).[62] Therefore we may ask by what signs, if any, is a vampire to be recognized. Again, how does a vampire leave his grave ? For we must remember that the vampire is tangible, and can make his presence felt in a very unmistakable and terrible manner. This difficulty has been very clearly stated by Dom Calmet who writes as follows : " How can a corpse which is covered with four or five feet of earth, which has no room even to move or to stretch a limb, which is wrapped in linen cerements, enclosed in a coffin of wood, how can it, I say, seek the upper air and return to the world walking upon the earth so as to cause those extraordinary effects which are attributed to it ? And after all that how can it go back again into the grave, when it will be found fresh, incorrupt, full of blood exactly like a living body ? Can it be maintained that these corpses pass through the earth without disturbing it, just as water and the damps which penetrate the soil or which exhale therefrom without perceptibly dividing or cleaving the ground ? It were indeed to be wished that in the histories of the Return of Vampires which have been related, a certain amount of attention had been given to this point, and that the difficulty had been something elucidated.

"Let us suppose that these corpses do not actually stir from their tombs, that only the ghosts or spirits appear to the living, wherefor do these phantoms present themselves and what is it that energizes them ? Is it actually the soul of the dead man which has not yet departed to its final destination, or is it a demon who causes them to be seen in an assumed and phantastical body ? And if there bodies are spectral, how do they suck the blood of the living ? We are enmeshed in a sad dilemma when we ask if these apparitions are natural or miraculous.

"A priest, who is recognized as possessing intellectual qualities far beyond the ordinary, told me that some little time since when he was travelling in Moravia, Mgr. Jeanin, a Canon of the Cathedral of Olmutz, asked for his company to a village named Liebava, which the good canon was officially about to visit as Commissary of the Episcopal Court to investigate the well-authenticated reports concerning a Vampire who had recently caused much trouble and disorder in the village Liebava.

"They journeyed thither; witnesses were cited and heard; the ordinary canonical procedure was observed in every detail. The witnesses gave evidence that a certain well-known citizen who had formerly resided at Liebava after his death had sorely tormented the whole district, inasmuch as for a space of three or four years he had issued forth from the cemetery and had entered several houses. It was true these visitations were now ceased, because a certain Hungarian who passed through the village at the time when the terror was at its height avowed that he could cope with the evil and lay the Vampire to rest. In order to fulfil his promise he mounted the clock-tower of the church, and watched for the moment when the vampire came out of his grave, leaving behind him in the tomb his shroud and cerements, before he made his way to the village to plague and terrify the inhabitants.

"When the Hungarian from his coin of vantage had seen the Vampire depart on his prowl, he promptly descended from the tower possessed himself of the shroud and linen carrying them off with him back to the belfry. The Vampire in due course returned and not finding his sere-clothes cried out mightily against the thief, who from the top of the belfry was making signs to him that he should climb and recover his winding-sheet if he wished to get it back again. The Vampire, accordingly, began to clamber up the steep stair which led to the summit of the tower, but the Hungarian suddenly gave him such a blow that he fell from top to bottom. Thereupon they were able to strike off his head with the sharp edge of a sexton's spade, and that made an end of the whole business.

"The priest who related this history to me, himself saw nothing of these happenings, neither was anything witnessed by the Right Reverend Canon who was acting as Episcopal Commissioner. They only received the reports of the peasants of that district, a folk who were very ignorant, very credulous, very superstitious, and brimful of all kinds of wonderful stories concerning the aforesaid Vampire.

"For my part I think the whole history vain and utterly without foundation, and the more absurd and contradictory are the various tales which were told, the more strongly am I confirmed in the opinion which I have formed.

"Supposing, indeed, there were any truth in the accounts of these appearances of Vampires, are they to be attributed to the power of God, to the Angels, to the souls of those who return in this way, or to the Devil ? If we adopt the last hypothesis it follows that the Devil can endue these corpses with subtilty and bestow upon them the power of passing through the earth without any disturbances of the ground, of gliding through the cracks and joints of a door, of slipping through a keyhole, of increasing, of diminishing, of becoming rarified as air or water to penetrate the earth ; in fine of enjoying the same properties as we believe will be possessed by the Blessed after the Resurrection, and which distinguished the human Body of our Lord after the first Easter Day, inasmuch as He appeared to those to whom He would show Himself for ' Jesus cometh, the doors being shut, and stood in the midst, and said : Peace be to you,' *Jesus uenit ianuis clausis,* S. John, xx, 26.

"Yet even if it be allowed that the Devil can re-energize dead bodies and give them movement for a certain time can he also bestow these powers of increasing, diminishing, becoming rarified, and so subtle that they can penetrate the earth, doors, windows ? We are not told that God allows him the exercise of any such power, and it is hard to believe that a material body, gross and substantial can be endowed with this subtility and spirituality without some destruction or alteration of the general structure and without damage to the configuration of the body. But this would not be in accord with the intention of the Devil, for such a change would prevent this body from appearing, from manifesting itself, from motion and speech, ay, indeed from being eventually cut to pieces and burned as so often happens in the case of Vampires in Moravia, Poland, and Silesia."[63]

These difficulties which Dom Calmet with little perception has raised can be very briefly answered, and they are not only superficial, but also smack of heterodoxy. In the first place, the story that he tells is far from satisfactory, and even if it were—what it may be—much exaggerated one can hardly brush aside the vast vampire tradition because one instance proves to be overdrawn. In any case the business of the watcher from the belfry and the demand that the Vampire should regain his shroud by climbing the stairs to the top of the tower do not bear the mark of truth, but what is certainly significant is that the Vampire was decapitated and that then the hauntings ceased. I conceive that the story of the cerements is mere elaboration, but that the grave of the Vampire was traced, opened, and that his head was severed from his body. This eliminates some highly charged details whilst it does not touch the facts of the case. So we see that the story when divested of these trappings offers nothing impossible, that is to say nothing extraordinary or unusual in such histories.

Dom Calmet asks are the appearances of Vampires to be attributed to God, or to the souls of those who return or to the Devil ? I answer that for the hauntings of a Vampire, three things are necessary : the Vampire, the Devil, and the Permission of Almighty God. Just as we know, for we learn this from the *Malleus Maleficarum*, that there are three necessary concomitants of witchcraft, and these are the Devil, a Witch, and the Permission of Almighty God (Part I). So are these three necessary concomitants of Vampirism. Whether it be the Demon who is energizing the corpse[64] or whether it be the dead man himself who by some dispensation of Divine Providence has returned is a particular which must be decided severally for each case. So much then for Dom Calmet's question, to whom are the appearances of Vampires to be attributed.

Can the Devil endow a body with these qualities of subtilty, rarification, increase, and diminishing, so that it may pass through doors and windows ? I answer that there is no doubt the Demon can do this, and to deny the proposition is hardly orthodox. For S. Thomas says of the devil that " just as he can from the air compose a body of any form and shape, and assume it so as to appear in it visibly, so, in the same way, he can clothe any corporeal thing with any corporeal form, so as to appear therein." Moreover almost any séance will be sufficient reply to Dom Calmet's question. In his *Modern Spiritism* (1904), Mr. T. Godfrey Raupert says : " Photographs, or small drawing-room ornaments have thus been seen to change their places, and articles kept in a room other than that occupied by the sensitive, have been brought through closed doors and deposited at a spot previously indicated—in some instances placed into the hands of the person requesting the apport of the article. Many such remarkable instances of apport and of matter passing through matter have been observed under the strictest possible test conditions, and will be found recorded in the late Leipzig Professor Zoellner's deeply interesting work *Transcendental Physics*. The writer has himself observed one instance of this kind in a private house, and in circumstances entirely precluding the possibility of deception. There is, perhaps, no phenomenon which so distinctly exhibits the action of extraneous and independent intelligence as this one." (pp. 35-36.) Matter, then, can pass through matter, and the séance answers Dom Calmet. We may, if we will, adopt the ectoplasmic theory to explain the mode whereby the Vampire issues from his grave, but although this is very probably true (in some instances at all events) it is not necessarily the only solution of the problem. According to Catholic theologians evil spirits, if permitted to materialize their invisible presence, to build up a tangible and active body, do not absolutely require the ectoplasm of some medium.

Not very dissimilar to the dilemma of Dom Calmet are the views held by an eminent authority, Dr. Herbert Mayo, who was sometime Senior Surgeon of Middlesex Hospital, Professor of Anatomy and Physiology in King's College, Professor of Comparative Anatomy in the Royal College of Surgeons, London. In his well-known work, *On the Truths contained in Popular Superstitions*, he devotes his second Letter, or rather Chapter, to " Vampyrism," concerning which he says " The proper place of this subject falls in the midst of a philosophical disquisition," but he adds for the benefit of the inquirer that it is " a point on which, in my time, school-boys much your juniors entertained decided opinions." He continues to inform us that during the middle of the eighteenth century : " Vampyrism spread like a pestilence through Servia and Wallachia, causing numerous deaths, and disturbing all the land with fear of the mysterious visitation, against which no one felt himself secure.

"Here is something like a good solid practical popular delusion. Do I believe it ? To be sure I do. The facts are matter of history : the people died like rotten sheep ; and the cause and method of their dying was, in their belief, what has just been stated. You suppose, then, they died frightened out of their lives, as men have died whose pardon has been proclaimed when their necks were already on the block, of the belief that they were going to die ? Well, if that were all, the subject would still be worth examining. But there is more in it than that." He then gives an account in very full detail of a Vampire at Belgrade in the year 1732, he describes the circumstances in which the body was disinterred, It leaned to one side, the skin was fresh and ruddy, the nails grown long and evilly crooked, the mouth slobbered with blood from its last night's repast. Accordingly a stake was driven through the chest of the Vampire who uttered a terrible screech whilst blood poured in quantities from the wound. Then it was burned to ashes. Moreover, a number of other persons throughout the district had been infected with vampirism. Of the facts there can be no question whatsoever. The documents are above suspicion, and in particular the most important of these which was signed by three regimental surgeons, and formally counter-signed by a lieutenant-colonel and sub-lieutenant. Even Dr. Mayo is obliged to allow : " No doubt can be entertained of its authenticity, or of its *general* fidelity ; the less that it does not stand alone, but is supported by a mass of evidence to the same effect. It appears to establish beyond question, that where the fear of Vampyrism prevails, and there occur several deaths, in the popular belief connected with it, the bodies, when disinterred weeks after burial, present the appearance of corpses from which life has only recently departed." It is very instructive to note how the writer proceeds with the greatest subtility and no little cleverness to extract himself from logical consequences it might have seemed impossible to avoid, and how he explains an exceptional circumstance by circumstances which are far more amazing and difficult to believe. With the utmost suavity and breadth of mind he continues : " What inference shall we draw from this fact ?—that Vampyrism is true in the popular sense ?—and that these fresh-looking and well-conditioned corpses had some mysterious source of preternatural nourishment ? That would be to adopt, not to solve the superstition. Let us content ourselves with a notion not so monstrous, but still startling enough : that the bodies, which were found in the so-called Vampyr state, instead of being in a new or mystical condition, were simply alive in the common way or had been so for some time subsequently to their interment that, in short, they were the bodies of persons who had been buried alive, and whose life, where it yet lingered, was finally extinguished through the ignorance and barbarity of those who disinterred them. . . . We have thus succeeded in interpreting one of the unknown terms in the Vampyr-theorem. The suspicious character, who had some dark way of nourishing himself in the grave, turns out to be an unfortunate gentleman (or lady) whom his friends had buried under a mistake while he was still alive, and who, if they afterwards mercifully let him alone, died sooner or later either naturally or of the premature interment—in either case, it is to be hoped, with no interval of restored consciousness." I submit that Dr. Mayo has not succeeded in solving any difficulty at all connected with vampirism. No doubt, as we have already considered in some detail, cases of premature burial, which were far more common than was generally supposed, would have helped to swell the tradition, but that they can have originated it is impossible, and it is absurd to put forward the terrible accident of premature burial as an explanation to cover all the facts. It is quite impossible that a person who had been interred when in a coma or trance should have survived in the grave.

Before we deal with the signs by which it is reputed a vampire may be recognized ; the method in which a vampire presumably leaves his grave ; and the way by which a vampire may be released or destroyed, we will briefly inquire into Dr. Mayo's explanation of the actual visit of the vampire to a victim and the subsequent consequences, the terrible anæmia and hæmoplegia which may result in death followed by the vampire infection. And here we find that Dr. Mayo quite honestly and frankly confesses that he is completely at a loss to give any solution of the difficulty. It is most instructive to read those inconclusive pleas which he is driven to put forward but which his own good sense cannot accept. He writes : " The second element which we have yet to explain is the Vampyr visit and its consequences,—the lapse of the party visited into death-trance. There are two ways of dealing with this knot ; one is to cut it, the other to untie it.

" It may be cut, by denying the supposed connexion between the Vampyr visit and the supervention of death-trance in the second party. Nor is the explanation thus obtained devoid of plausibility. There is no reason why death-trance should not, in certain seasons and places, be *epidemic*. Then the persons most liable to it would be those of weak and irritable nervous systems. Again, a first effect of the epidemic might be further to shake the nerves of weaker subjects. These are exactly the persons who are likely to be infected with imaginary terrors, and to dream, or even to fancy, they have seen Mr. or Mrs. such a one, the last victim of the epidemic. The dream or impression upon the senses might again recur, and the sickening patient have already talked of it to his neighbours, before he himself was seized with death-trance. On this supposition the Vampyr visit would sink into the subordinate rank of a mere premonitory symptom.

" To myself, I must confess, this explanation, the best I am yet in a position to offer, appears barren and jejune ; and not at all to do justice to the force and frequency, or, as tradition represents the matter, the universality of the Vampyr visit as a precursor of the victim's fate. Imagine how strong must have been the conviction of the reality of the apparition, how common a feature it must have been, to have led to the laying down of the unnatural and repulsive process customarily followed at the Vampyr's grave, as the regular and proper preventive of ulterior consequences." Dr. Mayo proposes therefore " to try and untie this knot " a result which he singularly fails to achieve. He quite erroneously states " in popular language, it was the ghost of the Vampyr that haunted its future victim." This is exactly what the Vampire is not. As we have seen there is some divergence of view whether the Vampire is the actual person, energized with some horrible mystical life in death who visits his victims, and there can be no doubt at all that this is the true and proper Vampire, or whether it is a demon who animates and informs the body. But in no circumstances whatsoever is the Vampire a phantom or ghost, save by a quite inadmissible extension of the term, which then may practically be regarded (as indeed it is often most mistakenly and reprehensively regarded) as covering almost any malignant supernatural phenomenon. So an explanation which confuses a Vampire with a ghost is entirely impertinent.

We will now proceed to inquire into those physical traits by which a Vampire may be discerned.

A Vampire is generally described as being exceedingly gaunt and lean with a hideous countenance and eyes wherein are glinting the red fire of perdition. When, however, he has satiated his lust for warm human blood his body becomes horribly puffed and bloated, as though he were some great leech gorged and replete to bursting. Cold as ice, or it may be fevered and burning as a hot coal, the skin is deathly pale, but the lips are very full and rich, blub and red ; the teeth white and gleaming, and the canine teeth wherewith he bites deep into the neck of his prey to suck thence the vital streams which re-animate his body and invigorate all his forces appear notably sharp and pointed. Often his mouth curls back in a vulpine snarl which bares these fangs, " a gaping mouth and gleaming teeth," says Leone Allacci, and so in many districts the hare-lipped are avoided as being certainly vampires. In Bulgaria, it is thought that the Vampire who returns from the tomb has only one nostril ; and in certain districts of Poland he is supposed to have a sharp point at the end of his tongue, like the sting of a bee. It is said that the palms of a Vampire's hands are downy with hair,[65] and the nails are always curved and crooked, often well-nigh the length of a great bird's claw, the quicks dirty and foul with clots and gouts of black blood. His breath is unbearably fetid and rank with corruption, the stench of the charnel. Dr. Henry More in his *An Antidote against Atheism*, III, ix, tells us that when Johannes Cuntius, an alderman of Pentsch in Silesia and a witch returned as a Vampire he much tormented the Parson of the Parish. One evening, " when this *Theologer* was sitting with his wife and Children about him, exercising himself in Musick, according

to his usual manner, a most grievous stink arose suddenly,
which by degrees spread itself to every corner of the room.
Here upon he commends himself and his family to God by
Prayer. The smell nevertheless encreased, and became above
all measure pestilently noisom, insomuch that he was forced
to go up to his chamber. He and his Wife had not been in bed
a quarter of an hour, but they find the same stink in the bed-
chamber ; of which, while they are complaining one to another
out steps the *Spectre* from the Wall, and creeping to his bed-
side, breathes upon him an exceeding cold breath, of so intoler-
able stinking and malignant a scent, as is beyond all imagination and expression. Here upon the *Theologer*, good soul,
grew very ill, and was fain to keep his bed, his face, belly,
and guts swelling as if he had been poysoned ; whence he
was also troubled with a difficulty of breathing, and with a
putrid inflamation of his eyes, so that he could not well use
them of a long time after."[66] In the *Malleus Maleficarum*,
Part II, Qn. 1., Ch. 11, the following is related : " In the
territory of the Black Forest, a witch was being lifted by a
gaoler on to the pile of wood prepared for her burning and
said : ' I will pay you,' and blew into his face. And he was
at once afflicted with a horrible leprosy all over his body and
did not survive many days." Boguet, *Discours des Sorciers*,
gives as his rubric to Chapter XXV, *Si les Sorciers tuent de
leur souffle & haleine.* He tells us : " Les Sorciers tuent
& endommagent de leur souffle & haleine : en quoy Clauda
Gaillard dicte la Fribolette nous seruita de tesmoignage ;
car ayant soufflé contre Clauda Perrier, qu'elle r'encontra
en l'Eglise d'Ebouchoux, tout aussi tost ceste femme tomba
malade, & fut rendue impotente, & en fin mourut apres auoir
trainé par l'espace d'vn an en toute pauurieté, & langueur :
de mesme aussi comme Marie Perrier luy eut vne fois refusé
l'aumosne, elle luy souffla fort rudement contre, de façon
que Marie tomba par terre, & s'estant releuée ause peine elle
demeura malade par quelques iours, & iusques à tant que
Pierre Perrier son neueu eut menacé la Sorciere."
Sinistrari in his *Demoniality* (24) says that if we ask how it is
possible that the Demon, who has no body, yet can perform
actual coitus with man or woman, most authorities answer that
the demon assumes or animates the corpse of another human
being, male or female, as the case may be, and Delrio

(*Disquisitiones Magicae*, Liber II, Q. xxviii, sec. 1). comments : " Denique multae falsae resurrectiones gentilium huc sunt referendae ; & constat cum sagis ut plurimum induto cadauere diabolum sine incubum, sine succubum, rem habere ; unde & in hoc genere hominum, cadauerosus quidam faetor graueolentiae, cernitur."

Some remoter country districts, indeed, are apt to regard any poor wretch who is sadly deformed as a Vampire, especially if the distortion be altogether unsightly, prominent, or grotesque. It has even been known that a peasant whose face was deeply marked with wine-coloured pigment, owing it was thought to some accident which befell his mother during her late pregnancy,[67] was shunned and suspected of being a malignant *vrykolakas*. Chorea, they say, is a certain sign of vampirism, and it may be remarked that in Shoa this disorder is regarded as the result [of demoniacal possession, or due to the magic spell of an enemy's shadow having fallen upon the sufferer.[68] An epileptic there is also often considered as being in the power of some devil, and unless proper precautions are taken he will assuredly not rest in his grave. The Vampire is endowed with strength and agility more than human, and he can run with excessive speed, outstripping the wind.

It is curious to find that in many countries persons with blue eyes are considered extremely liable to become vampires.[69] This is the case in some parts of Greece, but there does not seem to be preserved any oral tradition to explain the particular belief. It may, of course, have arisen owing to the fact that persons with eyes of this colour would seldom, if ever, have been met with, and a stranger with blue eyes would be regarded with wonder and awe. (Thus in Ireland persons with bluish-grey eyes, especially if there be a streak of black on the pupil, which is common, are accounted to have the power of seeing ghosts.) We cannot, I think, connect the Greek idea with the Homeric epithet for the goddess Athene, γλαυκῶπις, which has been rendered " bright-eyed,"[70] " grey-eyed " or " blue-eyed," an old interpretation that proves utterly erroneous, since there can be no doubt that γλαυκῶπις means " owl-faced " (γλαύξ ;) and originally Athene was a deity who was literally imagined and represented as having the face of an owl, even if she did not, as is most probable,

actually appear in the shape of an owl. Among the Australian aborigines the owl is regarded as a sex totem of women
and is most jealously protected by them.[71] We find too,
that the owl is a sacred bird among the Indians of North-West
America, and in their ritual dances a solemnity revealed to
them, as they suppose, by their guardian spirits, wherein they
mime ancient story, the masqueraders often personate by
dress, voice, and gesture the owl. " The *dukwally* (*i.e.*,
lokoala) and other *tamanawas*[72] performances are exhibitions
intended to represent incidents connected with their mytho-
logical legends. . . An Indian, for instance, who has been
consulting with his guardian spirit, which is done by going
through the washing and fasting process before described,
will imagine or think he is called upon to represent the owl.
He arranges in his mind the style of dress, the number of
performers, the songs and dances or other movements, and,
having the plan perfected, announces at a *tamanawas* meeting
that he has had a revelation which he will impart to a select
few. These are then taught and drilled in strict secrecy,
and when they have perfected themselves, will suddenly make
their appearance and perform before the astonished tribe."[73]
The owl gives mystic qualities ; for in Northern India it is
believed that a man who eats the eyes of an owl will be able
to see, even as that bird, in the dark.[74] In Nigeria, the owl
is regarded with great awe, and the natives tremble even to
pronounce its name on account of the ill omen, preferring
to speak of " the bird that makes one afraid."[75] It may be
remembered that Vampires are credited with being able to see
in the dark, and that in many countries peasants dread to utter
the word, employing some elaborate and often not very intellig-
ible periphrasis.

Those whose hair is red, of a certain peculiar shade, are
unmistakably vampires. It is significant that in ancient
Egypt, as Manetho tells us, human sacrifices were offered
at the grave of Osiris, and the victims were red-haired men
who were burned, their ashes being scattered far and wide
by winnowing-fans. It is held by some authorities that
this was done to fertilize the fields and produce a bounteous
harvest, red-hair symbolizing the golden wealth of the corn.
But these men were called Typhonians, and were representa-
tives not of Osiris but of his evil rival Typhon, whose hair

was red.[76] Francesco Redi says : " Fra gli Egizii era tradizione
che Tifone, il genio della distruzione, simile al Arimane Persiano
al Satano Ebriaco fosse di pelo rosso, forse per memoria di
invasioni di barbari di pelo rosso e presso noi dura tutta via
la tradizione, ' Guardati dal pelo rosso nè valse a toglierla la
barba rossa del Redentore.' "[77] Red was the colour of the hair
of Judas Iscariot,[78] and of Cain, and an old Latin rhyme of
the thirteenth century has :

> Monet nos haec fabula rufos euitare
> Quos color et fama notat, illis sociare.

The Italians say :

> Capelli rossi
> o tutto foco, o tutto mosci.

John Wodroephe in *The Spared Hours of a Soldier in his
Travels*, Dort, 1623, quotes : " Garde toi bien des hommes
rousseaux, des femmes barbues, et des ceux qui sont marqués
au visage."[79] I have not met with the following tradition
save orally, but it is believed in Serbia, Bulgaria, and Rumania,
that there are certain red-polled vampires who are called
" Children of Judas," and that these, the foulest of the foul,
kill their victim with one bite or kiss which drains the blood
as it were at a single draught. The poisoned flesh of the
victim is wounded with the Devil's stigmata, three hideous
scars shaped thus, XXX, signifying the thirty pieces of silver,
the price of blood.

It is curious to note that the ancient ideas of the physio-
gnomy of amorous persons are not at all unlike the distinctive
marks of the vampire. The old belief has thus been summed
up by G. Tourdes, " Aphrodisie," *Dictionnaire Encyclopédique
des Sciences Médicales :* " The erotic temperament has been
described as marked by a lean figure, white and well-ranged
teeth, a developed hairy system, a characteristic voice, air,
and expression, and even a special odour."

Since the vampire bites his prey with sharp teeth and
greedily sucks forth the blood it is not surprising to find that
those who are born with teeth in their heads are considered
to be already marked down as vampires. Even in countries
where the vampire belief was lost this circumstance was
considered of the unluckiest,[80] and in Chapman and Shirley's[81]

Chabot, Admiral of France, V, 2, Master Advocate exposing
the villainies of the Chancellor declares : " He was born
with teeth in his head, by an affidavit of his midwife, to note
his devouring, and hath one toe on his left foot crooked, and
in the form of an eagle's talon, to foretel his rapacity. What
shall I say ? branded, marked, and designed in his birth
for shame and obloquy, which appeareth further, by a mole
under his right ear, with only three witch's hairs in it ;
strange and ominious predictions of nature ! " According to
Allacci those children who were thought likely to become
Callicantzari were taken to a fire which had been lighted in
the market-square, and here the soles of their feet were held
to the flames until the nails were singed and the danger of
their attacks averted. The allusion in *Chabot* to the " toe
on his left foot crooked, and in the form of an eagle's talon "
is particularly interesting in this connexion. It is evident
that the old physical characteristics which mark a creature
of demoniacal propensities had been remembered as of ill-
omen and horror when exactly what they portended and
betrayed had been lost in the mists of ancient lore. Moreover
it should be noted that persons and animals attack with the
hands or the claws, not generally with the feet to scratch and
rend. Accordingly the custom in the days even of Allacci
was practised but not understood, and it points to some
belief reaching back to old Greek mythology, it is probably
some link between the Callicantzaros and the Centaurs as
Lawson suggests in well-founded detail.

The vampire is, as we have said, generally believed to
embrace his victim who has been thrown into a trance-like
sleep, and after greedily kissing the throat suddenly to bite
deep into the jugular vein and absorb the warm crimson
blood. It has long since been recognized by medico-psycho-
logists that there exists a definite connexion between the
fascination of blood and sexual excitation. Owing to custom,
to inhibitions and education this emotion generally remains
latent, although a certain mental sadism is by no means a
mark of degeneracy. Dr. Havelock Ellis says : " It is
probable that the motive of sexual murders is nearly always
to shed blood, and not to cause death,"[82] an extremely
significant fact. Since the vampire is generally held to seize
the throat it is very striking that Leppmann[83] points out

that such murders are almost always produced by wounds in the neck or mutilation of the abdomen, never by wounds of the head.

Paul d'Enjoy defines the kiss as " a bite and a suction,"[84] and a high authority says : " The impulse to bite is also a part of the tactile element which lies at the origin of kissing."[85] The tactile kiss which doubtless is very primitive has developed into the olfactory and gustatory, extending thence into many elaborations and variants. Under the stress of strong sexual emotion when love is closely knit with pain there is often an overwhelming tendency to bite the partner of the act, and the love-bite is often referred to in Latin literature. Thus Plautus, *Pseudolus*, I, 1, ll. 62-66, speaks of amorous dalliance :

> Nunc nostri amores, mores, consuetudines,
> Iocus, ludus, sermo, suauis suauiatio
> Compressiones arctae amantum comparum,
> Teneris labellis molles morsiunculae,
> Papillarum horridularum oppressiunculae.

And Catullus, VIII, 17, 18, writes after a quarrel :

> Quem nunc amabis ? cuius esse diceris ?
> Quem basiabis ? cui labella mordebis ?

In a well-known Ode, Horace Carmin I, xiii, 11, 12 :

> siue puer furens
> impressit memorem dente labris notam.

which Francis Englishes :

> I burn, when in excess of wine
> He soils those snowy arms of thine,
> Or on thy lips the fierce-fond boy
> Marks with his teeth the furious joy.

Tibullus, I, vi, 14, 15, writes :

> Tunc succos herbasque dedi, queis liuor abiret,
> Quem facit impresso mutua dente Uᐱnus.

And again, I, viii, 35-38 :

> At Uenus inueniet puero succumbere furtim,
> Dum tumet, et teneros conserit usque sinus.
> Et dare anhelanti pugnantibus humida linguis
> Oscula, et in collo figere dente notas.
> But fav'ring Venus watchful o'er thy joy,
> Shall lay thee secret near th' impassion'd boy ;

His panting bosom shall be prest to thine,
And his dear lips thy breathless lips shall join ;
With active tongue he'll dart the humid kiss,
And on thy neck indent his eager bliss.

Ovid, *Amores*, III, xiv, 34, asks his mistress :

Cur plus, quam somno, turbatos esse capillos ;
  Collaque conspicui dentis habere notam ?

which is rendered by the translator in Dryden's Ovid, " by
many hands " :

Why do your locks and rumpled head-clothes show
'Tis more than usual sleep that made them so ?
Why are the kisses which he gave betray'd,
By the impression which his teeth has made ?

Many further passages from the older Latin poets might
be quoted, and amongst the moderns, Joannes Secundus[86]
and Jean Bonnefons[87] have not neglected to celebrate the love-
bite in their verses.   From the latter it will suffice to cite
the elegant Basium IV, *Execratur dentes, quibus inter osculan-
dum papillas Dominae laeserat*, which commences :

O dens improbe, dire, ter sceleste,
Dens sacerrime, dens inauspicate,
Tun' tantum scelus ausus, ut papillas,
Illas Pancharidis meae papillas,
Quas Uenus ueneratur et Cupido,
Feris morsibus ipse uulnerares ?

Of Joannes Secundus the Basium VII in the *Basiorum
Liber* is very celebrated :

Quis te furor, Neaera,
Mepta quis iubebat,
Sic inuolare nostram
Sic uellicare linguam,
Ferociente morsu ?
An, quas tot unus abs te
Pectus per omne gesto
Penetrabileis sagittas,
Parum uidentur ? istis.
Ni dentibus proteruis
Exerceas nefandum
Membrum nefas in illud,
Quo saepe solo primo,
Quo saepe solo sero,
Quo per dieisque longas
Nocteisque amarulentas
Laudes tuas canebam ?

This has been charmingly tuned by Nott :

> Ah ! what ungovern'd rage, declare,
> Neaera, too capricious fair !
> What unrevenged, unguarded wrong,
> Could urge thee thus to wound my tongue ?
> Perhaps you deem th' afflictive pains
> Too trifling, which my heart sustains ;
> Nor think enough my bosom smarts
> With all the sure, destructive darts
> Incessant sped from every charm ;
> That thus your wanton teeth must harm,
> Must harm that little tuneful thing,
> Which wont so oft thy praise to sing ;
> What time the morn has streak'd the skies,
> Or evening's faded radiance dies ;
> Through painful days consuming slow
> Through ling'ring night of amorous woe.

Dorat, *Baiser XI*, has daintily paraphrased, Secundus :

> Tes dents, ces perles que j'adore,
> D'ou s'échappe à mon oeil trompé
> Ce sourire développé,
> Transfuge des lèvres de flore ;
> Devroient-elles blesser, dis moi,
> Une organe tendre et fidelle,
> Qui t'assure ici de ma foi,
> Et nomma Thais la plus belle ?

The *Supplementum Lexicorum Eroticorum Linguae Latinae*, Paris, 1911, has : "Morsiunculae.—Gallice : Suçons.". Much Oriental erotic literature gives attention to this subject. The Indian *Kama Sutra* of Vatsyayana devotes no less than one chapter to the love-bite, and there are many references to be found in such manual as the Arabic *Perfumed Garden* of the Sheik Nefzaoui. When it is borne in mind how markedly Slavonic a tradition is the bite of the vampire it becomes extremely significant to know that biting in amorous embraces is very common among the Southern Slavs.

The peasant women of Sicily, especially says Alonzi,[88] in the districts where crimes of blood are prevalent often in their affection for their children kiss them violently, even biting them and sucking their blood until the infant wails in pain. If a child has done wrong they will not only strike it, but also bite it fiercely on the face, ears, or arms, till blood flows. Both men and women often use the threat: "I will drink your blood." There is ocular evidence that a man who had knifed another in a quarrel licked the hot blood from the victim's hand.

A very curious case was reported in the London police news of 1894. A man aged thirty, was charged with ill-treating his wife's illegitimate daughter, aged three. The acts had lasted over a period of many months ; her lips, eyes, and hands were bitten and covered with bruises from sucking, and often her little pinafore was stained with blood. "Defendant admitted he had bitten the child because he loved it." Here we have true vampirish qualities and inclinations.

The Daily Express, 17th April, 1925, gave the following : "VAMPIRE BRAIN. PLAN TO PRESERVE IT FOR SCIENCE."

Berlin. Thursday, April 16th. The body of Fritz Haarmann, executed yesterday at Hanover for twenty-seven murders, will not be buried until it has been examined at Göttingen University.

"Owing to the exceptional character of the crimes—most of Haarmann's victims were *bitten to death*—the case aroused tremendous interest among German scientists. It is probable that Haarmann's brain will be removed and preserved by the University authorities.—Central News."

The case of Fritz Haarmann, who was dubbed the "Hanover Vampire" was reported in some detail in *The News of the World*, 21st December, 1924, under the heading : "VAMPIRE'S VICTIMS." Haarmann was born in Hanover, 25th October, 1879. The father, " Olle Harmann," a locomotive-stoker, was well-known as a rough, cross-grained, choleric man, whom Fritz, his youngest son, both hated and feared. As a youth, Fritz Haarmann was educated at a Church School, and then at a preparatory school for non-commissioned officers at New Breisach. It is significant that he was always dull and stupid, unable to learn ; but it appears a good soldier. When released from military service owing to ill-health he returned home, only to be accused in a short while of offences against children. Being considered irresponsible for his actions the Court sent him to an asylum at Hildesheim, whence however he managed to escape and took refuge in Switzerland. Later he returned to Hanover, but the house became unbearable owing to the violent quarrels which were of daily occurrence between him and his father. Accordingly he enlisted and was sent to the crack 10th Jäger Battalion, at Colmar in Alsace. Here he won golden opinions, and when released owing to illness, with a pension his papers were marked " Recht gut." When he reached home there were fresh scenes of rancour whilst blows were not infrequently exchanged, and in 1903 he was examined by a medical expert, Dr. Andrae, who considered him morally lacking but yet there were no grounds for sending him to an asylum. Before long he sank to the status of a tramp ; a street hawker, at times ; a pilferer and a thief. Again and again he was sent to jail, now charged with larceny, now with burglary, now with indecency, now with fraud. In 1918, he was released after a long stretch to find another Germany. He returned to Hanover, and was able to open a small cook shop in the old quarter of the town, where he also hawked meat which was eagerly sought at a time of general hunger and scarcity. He drove yet another trade, that of " copper's nark," an old lag who had turned spy and informer, who gave secret tips to the police as to the whereabouts of men they wanted. " Detective Haarmann " he was nick-named by the women who thronged his shop because he always had plenty of fresh meat in store, and he invariably contrived to undersell the other butchers and victuallers of the quarter.

The centre of Hanover was the Great Railway Station, and Hanover was thronged especially at its centre with a vast ever-moving population, fugitive, wanderers and homeless from all parts of dislocated Germany. Runaway lads from towns in every direction made their way here, looking for work, looking for food, idly tramping without any definite object, without any definite goal, because they had nothing else to do. It can well be imagined that the police, a hopelessly inadequate force, kept as sharp a watch as possible on the Station and its purlieus, and Haarmann used to help them in their survey-ance. At midnight, or in the early morning he would walk up and down among the rows of huddled sleeping forms in the third-class waiting halls and suddenly waking up some frightened youngster demand to see his ticket, ask to know whence he had come and where he was going. Some sad story would be sobbed out, and the kindly Haarmann was wont to offer a mattress and a meal in his own place down town.

So far as could be traced the first boy he so charitably took to his rooms was a lad of seventeen named Friedel Rothe, who had run away from home. On 29th September, 1918, his mother received a postcard, and it so happened the very same day his father returned from the war. The parents were not going to let their son disappear without a search, and they soon began to hunt for him in real earnest. One of Friedel's pals told them that the missing boy had met a detective who offered him shelter. Other clues were traced and with extraordinary trouble, for the authorities had more pressing matters in hand than tracking truant schoolboys, the family obliged the police to search Cellarstrasse 27, where Haarmann lived. When a sudden entry was made Haarmann was found with another boy in such an unequivocal situation that his friends, the police, were obliged to arrest him there and then, and he received nine months imprisonment for gross indecency under Section 175 of the German Code. Four years later when Haarmann was awaiting trial for twenty-four murders he remarked : " At the time when the policeman arrested me the head of the boy Friedel Rothe was hidden under a newspaper behind the oven. Later on, I threw it into the canal."

In September, 1919, Haarmann first met Hans Grans, the handsome lad, who was to stand beside him in the dock. Grans, the type of abnormal and dangerous decadent which is only too common to-day, was one of the foulest parasites of society, pilferer and thief, bully, informer, spy, *agent provocateur*, murderer, renter, prostitute, and what is lower and fouler than all, blackmailer. The influence of this Ganymede over Haarmann was complete. It was he who instigated many of the murders—Adolf Hannappel a lad of seventeen was killed in November, 1923, because Grans wanted his pair of new trousers ; Ernst Spiecker, likewise aged seventeen was killed on 5th January, 1924, because Grans coveted his " toff shirt "—it was he who arranged the details, who very often trapped the prey.

It may be said that in 1918, Hanover, a town of 450,000 inhabitants was well-known as being markedly homosexual. These were inscribed on the police lists no less than 500 " Männliche Prostituierten," of whom the comeliest and best-dressed, the mannered and well-behaved elegants frequented the Café Kröpcke in the Georgstrasse, one of the first boulevards of New Hanover; whilst others met their friends at the andrygonous balls in the Kalenberger Vorstadt, or in the old Assembly Rooms; and lowest of all there was a tiny dancing-place, "Zur schwülen Guste," "Hot-Stuff Gussie's" where poor boys found their clientele. It was here, for example, that Grans picked up young Ernst Spiecker whose tawdry shirt cost him his life.

With regard to his demeanour at the trial the contemporary newspapers[89] write: "Throughout the long ordeal Haarmann was utterly impassive and complacent. . . The details of the atrocious crimes for which Haarmann will shortly pay with his life were extremely revolting. All his victims were between 12 and 18 years of age,[90] and it was proved that accused actually sold the flesh for human consumption. He once made sausages in his kitchen, and, together with the purchaser, cooked and ate them. . . Some alienists hold that even then the twenty-four murders cannot possibly exhaust the full toll of Haarmann's atrocious crimes, and estimate the total as high as fifty. With the exception of a few counts, the prisoner made minutely detailed confessions and for days the court listened to his grim narrative of how he cut up the bodies of his victims and disposed of the fragments in various ways. He consistently repudiated the imputation of insanity, but at the same time maintained unhesitatingly that all the murders were committed when he was in a state of trance, and unaware of what he was doing. This contention was specifically brushed aside by the Bench, which in its judgement pointed out that according to his own account of what happened, it was necessary for him to hold down his victims by hand in a peculiar way before it was possible for him to inflict a fatal bite on their throats. Such action necessarily involved some degree of deliberation and conscious purpose." Another account[91] says with regard to Haarmann: "The killing of altogether twenty-seven young men is laid at his door, the horror of the deeds being magnified by the allegation that he sold to customers for consumption the flesh of those he did not himself eat. . . With Haarmann in the dock appeared a younger man, his friend Hans Grans, first accused of assisting in the actual murders but now charged with inciting to commit them and with receiving stolen property. The police are still hunting for a third man, Charles, also a butcher, who is alleged to have completed the monstrous trio. . . . the prosecuting attorney has an array of nearly 200 witnesses to prove that all the missing youths were done to death in the same horrible way. . . He would take them to his rooms, and after a copious meal would praise the looks of his young guests. Then he would kill them after the fashion of a vampire. Their clothes he would put up on sale in his shop, and the bodies would be cut up and disposed of with the assistance of Charles." "In open court, however, Haarmann admitted that Grans often used to select his victims for him. More than once, he alleged, Grans beat him for failing to kill the ' game ' brought in, and Haarmann would keep the corpses in a cupboard until they could be got rid of, and one day the police were actually in his rooms when there was a body awaiting dismemberment. The back of the place abutted on the river, and the bones and skulls were thrown into the water. Some of them were discovered, but their origin was a mystery until a police inspector paid a surprise visit to prisoner's home to inquire into a dispute between Haarmann and an intended victim who escaped." Suspicion had at last fallen upon him principally, owing to skulls and bones found in the river Seine during May, June, and July, 1924. The newspapers said that during 1924, no less than 600 persons had disappeared, for the most part lads between 14 and 18. On the night of 22nd June at the railway station, sometime after midnight, a quarrel broke out between Haarmann and a young fellow named Fromm, who accused him of indecency. Both were taken to the central station, and meanwhile Haarmann's room in the Red Row was thoroughly examined with the result that damning evidence came to light. Before long he accused Grans as his accomplice, since at the moment they happened to be on bad terms. Haarmann was sentenced to be decapitated, a sentence executed with a heavy sword. Grans was condemned to imprisonment for life, afterwards commuted to twelve years' penal servitude. In accordance with the law, Haarmann was put to death on Wednesday, 15th April, 1925.

This is probably one of the most extraordinary cases of vampirism known. The violent eroticism, the fatal bite in the throat, are typical of the vampire, and it was perhaps something more than mere coincidence that the mode of execution should be the severing of the head from the body, since this was one of the efficacious methods of destroying a vampire.

Certainly in the extended sense of the word, as it is now so commonly used, Fritz Haarmann was a vampire in every particular.

To return to the more restricted connotation, we find that, as has been mentioned above, Dom Calmet in his famous work more than once emphasized that his great difficulty in accepting the tradition of the vampire, that is to say the vampire proper and not a mere malignant phantom, lies in the fact that it is physically impossible for a dead body to leave its grave since (he argues) if it has corporeity it cannot have subtilty, that is to say the power of passing through material objects.

Accordingly in the second volume of his great treatise he gives as the rubric to Chapter LX, *Impossibilité morale, que les Revenans sortent de leurs tombeaux.*[92] He commences : " I have already raised a serious objection, which is the impossibility that vampires should leave their graves, and should return thither, without any obvious disturbance of the ground, either when they are passing forth or when they are finding their way back again. Nobody has ever met this difficulty, and nobody ever will be able to meet it. To maintain that the devil subtilizes and renders unsubstantial the body of the vampire is merely an assertion which is made without any foundation and which is unsustained and untrue.

"The fluidity of the blood, the healthy red colour, and the absence of rigidity in the case of vampires are not circumstances which need cause us the slightest wonder, any more than the fact that the hair grows, and the bodies remain without dissolution. It is a matter of daily occurrence that bodies are found which do not crumble to dust and which for a very long time after death preserve the appearance of life. This is not in the least surprising in the cases of those who die suddenly without any illness, or indeed as the consequence of certain diseases which are well-known to medical men, sicknesses which do not affect the circulation of the blood or the elasticity of the body.

" With regard to the growth of hair this is quite a natural condition.

" One might even compare these facts with the flowers, and in general with everything which depends upon the luxuriance of vegetation among the fauna and flora of nature."

These objections thus stated may seem very weighty, but perhaps if they are impartially examined it may be found that the good Benedictine has been a little too dogmatic in his assertions. The phenomenon that the soil of the grave was almost invariably undisturbed by the exit of the Vampire, who further could make his entry through doors and windows without opening or breaking them may yet admit of an explanation which will go far to solve the difficulty Don Calmet and many others have regarded as insurmountable. In the first place it is hardly correct so sweepingly to assert that the ground is wholly undisturbed. Where careful investigation was made it was generally found that there were discovered four or five little holes or tunnels, not much larger indeed than a man's finger which pierced through the earth to a very considerable depth. And here, perhaps in this one little detail, we may find the clue to the whole mystery. The wide spread growth of spiritualism has made even the ordinary public fairly familiar with the phenomena of a séance where materialization takes place, and where physical forms are solidly built up and disintegrated again within an exceedingly short space of time. This is done by some power or entity which avails itself of the body of the passive medium and utilizes the ectoplasm which it can draw thence. Professor Ostwald writes : " Certain human beings are capable of transforming their physiological store of energy (which, as we know, is almost exclusively present in the form of chemical energy), of transmitting it through space, and of transforming it at prescribed points back into one of the known forms of energy. It results from this, that the mediums themselves are usually much exhausted, i.e., that they use up their bodily energy. A transformation into psychic energy seems also to be possible."
The extreme exhaustion of a medium after such investigation and the production of forms of organic matter is a matter of common knowledge. Of one of the most famous mediums, Eusapia Paladino it is reported : " Eusapia during the sittings fell into a deep hysterical somnambulism, and was often in

slightly dazed condition after the close. When the trance set in, she turned pale, and her head swerved to and fro, and the eyes were turned upwards and inwards. She was hyper-sensitive, especially to the touch, and also to light ; she had hallucinations, delirium, fits of laughter, weeping, or deep sleep, and showed other typical hysterical convulsions. Digestive troubles also sometimes set in, especially when she had eaten before the sitting. In a sudden light, or at a sudden rough touch, she cried out and shuddered, as she would under unexpected violent pain."[93] And again : " Eusapia Paladino used to be very exhausted after every successful sitting, especially after she had been in a state of trance. She sometimes slept until the next mid-day, and was for the rest of the day apathetic, peevish, and monosyllabic. Her skin was usually cold after the sittings, her pulse rapid (100° per minute), and she had a strong feeling of fatigue. Her subsequent sleep was often restless and interrupted by vivid dreams."[94] Speaking of another famous medium the same authority says : " In the case of Eva C. also, where the number of negative sittings is very considerable, she feels much exhausted, according to the degree of her performances, and after exhaustive positive sittings she usually needs from twenty-eight to forty-four hours to recover the deficit in her strength. Also, she is often, on the following day, dazed, and complains of headache and lack of appetite."[95] It is extremely significant, and one might say even more signifi-cant that these are the very symptoms exhibited by those who have been attacked by a Vampire.

Another fact which must be borne in mind is that the Vampire was often a person who during life had read deeply in poetic lore and practised black magic. For the connexion between spiritism and black magic one may refer to my *History of Witchcraft* when the matter is very amply discussed and made plain.[96]

With these pregnant and remarkable details in mind we may consider the explanation of vampirism given by Z. T. Pierart,[97] a well-known French spiritualist and sometime editor of *La Revue Spiritualiste*. He writes as follows : " As long as the astral form is not entirely liberated from the body there is a liability that it may be forced by magnetic attraction to re-enter it. Sometimes it will be only half-way out when the corpse, which presents the appearance of death, is buried. In such cases the terrified astral soul re-enters its casket, and then one of two things happen : the person buried either writhes in agony of suffocation, or, if he has been grossly material, becomes a vampire. The bi-corporeal life then begins. The ethereal form can go where it pleases, and as long as it does not break the link connecting it with the body can wander visible or invisible and feed on its victims. It then transmits the results of the suction by some mysterious invisible cord of connexion to the body, thus aiding it to perpetuate the state of catalepsy." Duly discounting the peculiar phraseology of "astral soul" and "ethereal form" this comment seems to point towards a possible and correct explanation.

There remain three hypotheses to be considered. Does the body of the Vampire actually dematerialize and then re-integrate outside the grave ? Or, is another body built up by the Vampire quite independently of the body which remains behind in the grave ? Thirdly, does the spirit of the Vampire withdraw ectoplasmic material from his own body, which enables him to form more permanent corporeity by drawing yet further material from his victims ? The second of these suggestions we may dismiss without much consideration since it is not borne out by any of the facts which have been investigated with regard to the subject, and the truth seems to lie between the first and the third hypotheses, partaking of both. The body of the Vampire under certain conditions acquires subtilty and therefore it is able to pass through material objects, but in order to ensure not only its vitality but the permanence of this subtile quality it must draw this energy, no doubt very often in an ectoplasmic form, from its victim, as well as what is necessary for its rejuvenescence. The continual demand which a Vampire makes both physically and spiritually upon its victims must speedily result in the death of these persons, who being infected with the poison will in their turn visit others upon whom they will prey.

It must always be remembered that the word vampire is used so loosely that there are traditions and legends which hardly require even one of these three hypotheses for their explanation, and which, one cannot too frequently repeat the caution, refer to phantoms of the vampire family rather than to the Vampire proper.

It certainly seems a possibility, and something more than a possibility, that vampiric entities may be on the watch and active to avail themselves of the chances to use the ectoplasmic emanations of mediums at séances, and this certainly constitutes a very formidable danger. It is even a fact that if a person who, consciously or unconsciously possesses the natural qualities of a materializing medium, is placed in certain nocuous circumstances, for example if he visits a house which is powerfully haunted by malefic influences, especially if he be fatigued and languid so as to offer little or no resistance, a vampirish entity may temporarily utilize his vitality to attempt a partial materializaticn. This seems clear from the many instances of persons who for no obvious reason are in certain spots, it may be a place, a house, or even a room overcome with a depression, which if they do not shake off by an act of will or by leaving the particular locality may develop into actual debility and enervation. A very striking example of an entity who in this way made an attempt at materialization is recorded by Miss Scatcherd in her contribution to *Survival*, a symposium which was published under the editorial care of Sir James Marchant. Miss Scatcherd relates : " I saw ectoplasm in solid form for the first time when looking for rooms in the neighbourhood of Russell Square. My friend, many years older than myself, was tired. She wore a black velvet cloak, and was sitting on a high chair, so that her mantle hung in long folds to the ground, while the light from the large windows fell full on her face. Suddenly I observed, on her left side, just above her waist, a patch of cloudy white substance, becoming bigger and denser as I watched its uncanny growth. Meanwhile, I was discussing terms with the landlady, a frail little woman, when a look of terror came into her eyes. She, too, was staring transfixed at the globular mass of white substance on my companion's black mantle. For out of it looked a living face, normal in size—a man's face with rolling eyes and leering grin that made one's blood run cold. When I mentally ordered him away, he grinned defiance. Fearing to startle my friend, I took the landlady aside and asked what was the matter. She burst into tears.

" ' Oh, miss ! did you not see him ? He was my first. He come like this several times, and has never forgiven me for marrying again.'

" ' What do you mean ? ' I asked again, severely.

" ' Oh ! ' she wailed. ' You must have seen his wicked face glaring at us from your friend's cloak, and now you will not take the rooms.' "[98]

In some traditions the Vampire is said to float into the house in the form of a mist, a belief which is found in countries so far separate as Hungary and China. In the latter empire wills-o'-the-wisp are thought to be an unmistakable sign of a place where much blood has been shed, such as an old battle field, and all mists and gaseous marsh-lights are connected with the belief in vampires and spectres which convey disease. Since the effluvia, the vapour and haze from a swamp or quaggy ground are notoriously unhealthy and malarial fevers result in delirium and anæmia it may be that in some legends the disease has been personified as a ghastly creature who rides on the infected air and sucks the life from his victims. But all this is mere fancy, and only deserves a passing mention as belonging to legend and story. Of the same nature is the notion that Vampires can command destructive animals and vermin such as fiies, and, in the East the mosquito, whose bite may indeed convey some fever to the veins and whose long proboscis sucks the blood of animals and man. We may remember that at Accaron Beelzebub was the Lord of flies, and these insects were often regarded as having something of a diabolical nature. Pausanias V,14, tells us that the people of Elis offered sacrifice to Zeus, Averter of Flies, a ceremony which is also mentioned by Clement of Alexandria in his Προτρεπτικὸς πρὸς ῞Ελληνας, II, 38 (ed. Potter, p. 33). Pliny *Historia Naturalis* (X, 75), says : " The Eleans invoke the fly-catching god, because the swarms of these insects breed pestilence ; and as soon as the sacrifice is made to the god the flies all perish." Pausanias (VIII, 26-7) further notes that at Aliphera in Arcadia the festival of Athene began with prayer and oblation to the Fly-catcher, and after this rite the flies gave no more trouble. Aelian (*De Animalium Natura*, XI, 8), tells us that at the festival of Apollo in the island of Leucas an ox was actually sacrificed to the flies, who when glutted with the warm blood, incontinently disappeared. Julius Solinus in his *Collectanea Rerum Memorabilium* (I, xi, ed. Th. Mommsem, Berlin, 1864), records that all flies were carefully excluded from the shrine of Hercules in the Forum Bovarium at Rome because when Hercules was handing the flesh to the priests he had prayed aloud to the Fly-catcher. It may be noted that when the demon, under whatsoever guise or name he might be adored, had received those divine honours he ever covets and filches to himself by so woefully deceiving his worshippers he withdraws his emissaries the tormenting flies who are often his imps in the form of insect. By their means he has striven to vex and molest the Saints—S. Bernard, by excommunicating the flies that buzzed about him struck them all down dead upon the floor of the church.

It now remains to inquire how the grave of a Vampire may be recognized, and in what way this terror may be checked and destroyed.

In this connexion it will not be impertinent to give a letter " d'un fort honnête homme et fort instruit de ce qui regarde les Revenants " which is cited at length by Dom Calmet. The letter is addressed to a near relative of the writer. "It is your wish, my dear cousin, that I should give you exact details of what has been happening in Hungary with regard to certain apparitions, who so often molest and slay people in that part of the world. I am in a position to afford you this information, for I have been living for some years in those very districts, and I am naturally of an inquiring disposition. From the time when I was a mere boy I have heard numbers of stories of ghosts and witches, but not once in a thousand have I believed one of them ; it seems to me that it is almost impossible to be too careful in the investigation of matters where it is so easy to be mistaken or deliberately tricked. However there are certain facts so well vouched for that one cannot but accept them as true. As to the apparitions of Hungary this is the usual account. A person is attached by a great languor and weariness, he loses all appetite, he visibly wastes and grows thin, and at the end of a week or ten days, may be a fortnight, he dies without any other symptom save anæmia and emaciation.

" In Hungary they say that a Vampire has attacked him and sucked his blood. Many of those who fall ill in this way declare that a white spectre is following them and cleaves to them as close as a shadow. When we were in our Kalocsa-Bacs quarters in the County of Temesvar[99] two officers of the regiment in which I was Cornet died from this languor, and several more were attacked and must have perished had not a Corporal of our regiment put a stop to these maladies by resorting to the remedial ceremonies which are practised by the local people. These are very unusual, and although they are considered an infallible cure I cannot remember even to have seen these in any *Rituale*.

" They select a young lad who is a pure maiden, that is to say, who, as they believe, had never performed the sexual act. He is set upon a young stallion who has not yet mounted his first mare, who has never stumbled, and who must be coal-black without a speck of white ; the stud is ridden into the cemetery in and out among the graves and that grave over which the steed in spite of the blows they deal him pretty handsomely refuses to pass is where the Vampire lies.[100] The tomb is opened and they find a sleek, fat corpse, as healthily-coloured as though the man were quietly and happily sleeping in calm repose. With one single blow of a sharp spade they cut off the head, whereupon there gush forth warm streams of blood in colour rich red, and filling the whole grave. It would assuredly be supposed that they had just decapitated a stalwart fine fellow of most sanguine habit and complexion. When this business is done, they refill the grave with earth and then the ravages of the disease immediately cease whilst those who are suffering from this marasmus gradually recover their strength just as convalescents recuperating after a long illness, who have wasted and withered. This is exactly what occurred in the case of our young officers who had sickened. As the Colonel of the regiment, the Captain and Lieutenant were all absent, I happened to be in command just then and I was heartily vexed to find that the Corporal had arranged the affair without my knowledge. I was within an ace of ordering him a severe military punishment, and these are common enough in the Imperial service. I would have given the world to have been present at the exhumation of the Vampire, but after all it is too late for that now."

It has already been remarked that in a cemetery there were often found to be a number of small passages of the size of a man's finger pierced through the earth, and it was considered that the presence of such a soupirail in a grave was a certain sign that if investigation were made a body with all the marks of vampirism would be descovered lying there.

When the corpse is exhumed, even though death has taken place long before there will be no decay, no trace of corruption, or decomposition, but rather it will be found to be plump and of a clear complexion ; the face often ruddy ; the whole person composed as if in a profound sleep. Sometimes the eyes are closed ; more frequently open, glazed, fixed, and glaring fiercely. The lips which will be markedly full and red are drawn back from the teeth which gleam long, sharp, as razors, and ivory white. Often the gaping mouth is stained and foul with great slab gouts of blood, which trickles down from the corners on to the lawn shroudings and linen cerements, the offal of the last night's feast. In the case of an epidemic of vampirism it is recorded that whole graves have been discovered soaked and saturated with squelching blood, which the horrid inhabitant has gorged until he is replete and vomited forth in great quantities like some swollen leech discharges when thrown into the brine. In Greece it is thought that the corpse's skin becomes exceedingly tough and distended so that the joints can hardly be bent ; the human pelt has stretched like the vellum tegument of a drum, and when struck returns the same sound ; whence the Greek *vrykolakas* has received the name τυμπανιαῖος (drum-like).[101] It was not infrequently seen that the dead person in his grave had devoured all about him, grinding them with his teeth, and (as it was supposed) uttering a low raucous noise like the grunting of a pig who roots among garbage. In his work, *De Masticatione Mortuorum in tumulis*, Leipzig, 1728, Michael Ranft treats at some length of this matter. He says that it is very certain that some corpses have devoured their cerements and even gnaw their own flesh. It has been suggested that this is the original reason why the jaws of the dead were tightly bound with linen bands. Ranft instances the case of a Bohemian woman who when disinterred in 1355 had devoured the greater part of her shroud. In another instance during the sixteenth century both a man and a woman seemed to have torn out their intestines and were actually ravening upon their entrails. In Moravia a corpse was exhumed which had devoured the grave-clothes of a woman buried not far from his tomb.

The authors of the *Malleus Malificarum*, Part I, Question xv, under the rubric, *It is shown that, on account of the Sins of Witches, the Innocent are often Bewitched, yea, Sometimes even for their Own Sins*, relate an instance which came under their own observation. They say :

" Also the sin of one is passed on to another in the way of desert, as when the sins of wicked subjects are passed on to a bad Governor, because the sins of the subjects deserve a bad Governor. See Job : ' He makes Hypocrites to reign on account of the sins of the people.'

" Sin, and consequently punishment, can also be passed on through some consent or dissimulation. For when those in authority neglect to reprove sin, then very often the good are punished with the wicked, as S. Augustine says in the first book *de Ciuitate Dei*. An example was brought to our notice as Inquisitors. A town once was rendered almost destitute by the death of its citizens ; and there was a rumour that a certain buried woman was gradually eating the shroud in which she had been buried, and that the plague could not cease until she had eaten the whole shroud and absorbed it into her stomach. A council was held, and the Podesta, with the Governor of the city dug up the grave, and found half the shroud absorbed through the mouth and throat into the stomach, and consumed. In horror at this sight, the Podesta drew his sword and cut off her head and threw it out of the grave, and at once the plague ceased. Now the sins of that old woman were, by Divine permission, visited upon the innocent on account of the dissimulation of what had happened before. For when an Inquisition was held it was found that during a long time of her life she had been a Sorceress and Enchantress."

If it were suspected that a man might return as a Vampire or that his ghost would prove troublesome precautions were taken to prevent this. In the first place the grave must be dug twice as deep as usual. Indeed in Oldenburg the chances are that if the grave be shallow any ghost may walk.[102] The Chuwashé, a tribe in Finland, actually nail the corpse to the coffin.[103] The Burmese tie together the two big toes, and usually also the two thumbs of the corpse.[104] The Arabs fasten the feet ; in Voigtland it is considered sufficient to secure the hands.[105] The Californians[106] and Damasas[107] break the dead man's spine. In his *Travels into Dalmatia* (English translation, London, 1778), Alberto Fortis says : "When a man dies suspected of becoming a Vampire or Vukodlak, as they call it, they cut his hams, and prick his whole body with pins, pretending that, after this operation, he cannot walk about. These are even instances of Morlacchi, who, imagining that they may possibly thirst for children's blood after death, intreat their heirs, and sometimes oblige them to promise, to treat them as Vampires when they die."

When the Vampire was tracked to his lair one of the most approved methods to render him harmless was to transfix the corpse through the region of the heart with a stake which may be of aspen or maple as in Russia, or more usually of hawthorn or whitethorn.   The aspen tree is held to be particularly sacred as according to one account of this was the wood of the Cross.   In her *Wood-walk*, Mrs. Felicia Hemans says : "The aspen-tree shivers mystically in sympathy with the horror of that mother-tree in Palestine, which was compelled to furnish materials for the Cross."[108] With regard to hawthorn de la Charbonelais Chesnil tells us : "Cet arbre est regardé comme le privilegié des fées qui se rassemblant, dit-on, sous ses rameaux embaumées. En Normandic on croit aussi que la foudre ne le frappe jamais parcequ'on suppose, mais sans aucun fondement qu'il servit à former la couronne de Christ."[109] And again : "Dans plusiers contrées, ce vegetal [Mepsilus pyraneatha] est l'objet d'une sorte de vénération parcequ'on croit que c'est dans un buisson de cette espèce qui Dieu apparut à Moïse et que c'est pour cette raison que ses feuilles demeurent toujours vertes, et que ses fruits ne se detachent point de l'arbre durant l'hiver." Of whitethorn Sir John Mandeville says :[110] "Then was our Lord yled into a gardyn, and there the Jewes scorned Hym and maden Him a crown of the branches of the Albiespyne, that is, Whitethorn that grew in the same gardyn, and setten yt upon His heved. And therefore hath the Whitethorn many virtues. For he that beareth a branch on hym thereof, no thundre, ne no maner of tempest may dere him, ne in the house that is ynne may non evil ghost enter." The ancient Greeks believed that branches of whitethorn or buckthorn (*rhamnus*) fastened to a door or outside a window prevented the entry of witches and guarded the house against the evil spells of sorcerers.[111] Hence they suspended branches of it above their lintels when sacrifices were offered for the dead lest haply any vagrom ghost should be tempted to revisit his old home or make entry into the house of some other person.[112] The atheist Bion, as atheists use, when he was dying clutched at any superstition and asked for boughs of buckthorn and branches of laurel to be attached to the door to keep out death.[113] It should be remarked that the old Greek custom is widely practised among the peasantry of Europe to-day, and in Fletcher's *The Faithfull Shepherdesse*,[114] II, when Clorin is sorting her herbs she says :

> these rhamnus' branches are,
> Which, stuck in entries, or about the bar
> That holds the door fast, kill all enchantments, charms—
> Were they Medea's verses—that do harms
> To men or cattle.

Fanshaw in his elegant translation[115] has :

> Hi rami sunt mollis *Acanthi*,
> Qui si uestibulis aut postibus affigantur,
> Unde fores pendent, incantamenta repellunt
> Omnia, pestiferæ facient licet illa MEDEÆ,
> Quae laedunt homines pecudesue.

In Dalmatia and Albania for the wooden stake is sometimes substituted a consecrated dagger, a poniard which has been laid upon the altar and ritually blessed by the priest with due sacring of holy orison, of frankincense and lustral asperges.

It is highly important that the body of the Vampire should be transfixed by a single blow, for two blows or three would restore it to life. This curious idea is almost universally found in tradition and folk-lore.[116] In *The Thousand and One Nights* (Burton, Vol. VII, p. 361) we have the story of "Sayf-al-Muluk and Badion al Jamal" where the hero cuts the ghoul in half by a single stroke through the waist. The ghost yells at him : "Oman, an thou desire to slay me, strike me a second stroke." The youth is just about to give the second slash with his scimitar when a certain old blind beggar whom he has befriended warns him. "Smite not a second time, for then will he not die, but will live and destroy us." He accordingly stays his hand and the ghoul expires.

Among Galland's manuscripts was a tale of the three sons of the Sultan of Samarcand. In the course of various adventures the third son, Badialzaman engages in a contest with the Djin Morhagean. The youngest daughter of the

Djin who loves the prince informs him that her father can only be slain if he is dealt one single blow—no more—with the sword which is hanging at his head whilst he sleeps.

When the stake has pierced the Vampire he will utter the most terrible shrieks and blood will jet forth in every direction from his convulsed and writhing limbs as he impotently threshes the air with his quivering hands. There is a tradition that when he has been dead for many years and his mysterious life in death is thus ended the corpse has been known immediately to crumble into dust.

In some countries this operation usually takes place soon after dawn, as the Vampire may only leave his grave with the dusk and must return at cock-crow, so he will be caught when he has come back torpid and heavy from his night's banquet of blood. But, as we have mentioned in another place, this belief that his ravages are confined to the dark hours is by no means universal, for Paul Lucas in his *Voyage au Levant*, speaking of Corfu says : " Des personnes qui paroissent avoir le bon sens parlent d'un fait assez singulier qui arrive souvent en ce pays, aussi bien que dans l'Isle Santeriny ; des gens morts disent-ils, reviennent, se font voir en plein jour, & vont même chez eux, ce qui cause de grandes frayeurs à ceux qui les voyent."[117] Accordingly the Vampire may walk in full daylight. Yet he may not, so they hold in Epirus, in Crete, and among the Wallachians, leave his tomb on a Saturday. " Many believe that, even in the day-time, it is only once a week, on the Saturday, that he is allowed to occupy his burial-place. When it is discovered that such a Vurvúlukas is about, the people go, on a Saturday, and open his tomb, when they always find his body just as it was buried, and entirely undecomposed."[118] Tozer, *Researches in the Highlands of Turkey* (II, p. 91) writes : " Saturday is the day of the week on which the exorcism ought by right to take place, because the spirit then rests in this tomb, and if he is out on his rambles when the ceremony takes place, it is un-availing. In most parts of the country, as the Vampire is regarded as only a night-wanderer, he has to be caught during the night between Friday and Saturday ; but in some places when he is believed to roam abroad by day as well, the whole of Saturday is allotted to him for repose, and consequently is suitable for his capture."

When the stake has been thrust with one drive through the Vampire's heart his head should be cut off, and this is to be done with the sharp edge of a sexton's spade, rather than with a sword.   Ralston [119] tells us that to transfix the Vampire with a pile is not always considered effectual.   " A *strigon* (or Istrian vampire) who was transfixed with a sharp thorn cudgel near Laibach in 1672, pulled it out of his body and flung it back contemptuously ".[120] The only certain methods of destroying a Vampire appear to be either to consume him by fire, or to chop off his head with a grave-digger's shovel. The Wends say that if a Vampire is hit over the back of the head with an implement of that kind, he will squeal like a pig."   It may be noted that the heads of murderers or warlocks were often struck off and destroyed, or else set between the legs or directly underneath the body.[121]

To burn the body of the Vampire is generally acknowledged to be by far the supremely efficacious method of ridding a district of this demoniacal pest, and it is the common practice all over the world.   The bodies of all those whom he may have infected with the vampirish poison by sucking their blood are also for security sake cremated.   Leone Allacci writes :   " Quare ciues, cum uident homines, nulla grassante infirmitate, in tanta copia emori ; suspicati quod est, sepulchra, in quibus recens defunctus sepultus est, aperiunt ; aliquando statim, aliquando etiam tardius, cadauer nondum corruptum, inflatumque comperiunt ; quod e sepulchro extractum, precibusque effusis a sacerdotibus, in rogum ardentem coniiciunt ; et nondum completa supplicatione, cadaueris iuncturae sensim dissoluuntur, et reliqua exusta in cineres conuertuntur."[122] Any animals which may come forth from the fire—worms, snakes, lice, beetles, birds of horrible and deformed shape— must be driven back into the flames for it may be the Vampire embodied in one of these, seeking to escape so that he can renew his foul parasitism of death.   The ashes of the pyre should be scattered to the winds, or cast into a river swiftly flowing to the sea.

Sometimes the body was hacked to pieces before it was cast into the fire ; very often the heart was torn from the breast and boiled to shreds in oil or vinegar.   Quantities of boiling water or boiling oil were also poured into the grave.   Mr. Abbott in his *Macedonian Folklore* (1903) tells us of a ceremony which took place when a Vampire had been tracked. He writes : [123] " I was creditably informed of a case of this description occurring not long ago at Alistrati, one of the principal villages between Serres and Drama. Someone was suspected of having turned into a Vampire. The corpse was taken out of the grave, was scalded with boiling oil, and was pierced through the navel with a long nail. Then the tomb was covered in and millet was scattered over it, that, if the Vampire came out again, he might waste his time in picking up the grains of millet and be thus overtaken by dawn. For the usual period of their wanderings is from about two hours before midnight till the first crowing of the morning cock. At the sound of which " fearful summons " the Vrykolakas like the Gaelic *sithehe*, or fairy, vanishes into his subterranean abode."

The Turks on occasion have had recourse to the remedy of burning to put to rest a Greek Vampire, for Crusius in his *Turco-Graecia* relates : [124] ' In sabbato pentecostes Turcae combusserunt Graecum, biennio ante defunctum : quod uulgo crederetur noctu sepulcro egredi, hominesque occidere. Alii autem ueram causam perhibent, quod quindecim pluresue homines spectrum eius uidentes mortui sint. Sepulcro extractus, consumpta carne cutem ossibus adhaerentem integram habuit."

William of Newbury speaking of the vampires which infested England in the twelfth century says that similar molestations had often happened and there were on record very many famous cases. The only way in which a district could be completely secured and an end put once and for all to these hideous visitations was by exhuming the body and burning the Vampire to ashes.[125]

The following form of exorcism is described as having been employed in Rhodes on a woman who returned as a Vrykolakas. " The priest of the village laid on the ground one of the dead woman's shifts, over the neck of which he walked, held up by two men, for fear the vampire should seize him. While in this position he read verses from the New Testament, till the shift swelled up and split. When this rent takes place the evil spirit is supposed to escape through the opening."[126]

The first precaution taken by the Wallachians to prevent the Vampire from ravaging is to drive a long nail through the skull and to lay the thorny stem of a wild rose bush upon the body, so that its winding sheet may become entangled with it should there be any attempt to rise.[127]

In Bulgaria " There is yet another method of abolishing a Vampire—that of *bottling* him. There are certain persons who make a profession of this ; and their mode of procedure is as follows : The sorcerer, armed with a picture of some saint, lies in ambush until he sees the Vampire pass, when he pursues him with his *Eikon ;* the poor Obour takes refuge in a tree or on the roof of a house, but his persecutor follows him up with the talisman, driving him away from all shelter, in the direction of a bottle specially prepared, in which is placed some of the vampire's favourite food. Having no other resource, he enters this prison, and is immediately fastened down with a cork, on the interior of which is a fragment of the *Eikon*. The bottle is then thrown into the fire, and the Vampire disappears for ever."

With reference to this enclosing of the Vampire in a bottle it may be remembered that it was once a common practice of sorcery to imprison familiar spirits in a vial. Among the articles put forth by Don Alfonso Manriquez, who on 10 September, 1523, succeeded as Grand Inquisiter Adrian, Bishop of Tortosa,[128] was the following which a man in duty bound must reveal to the Holy office should he become aware of any such offence : " If any person made or caused to be made mirrors, rings, phials of glass or other vessels therein to contain some spirit who should reply to his inquiries and aid his projects."[129]

Newton in his *Travels and Discoveries in the Levant* (Vol. I., p. 213) says that in Mitylene the bodies of those who will not lie quiet in their graves are transported to a small adjacent island, a mere eyot without inhabitants where they are re-interred. This is an effectual bar to any future molestation for the Vampire cannot cross salt water. Running water too he can only pass at the slack or the flood of the tide.

As all other demoniacal monsters the Vampire fears and shrinks from holy things. Holy Water burns him as some biting acid ; he flies from the sign of the Cross, from the Crucifix, from Relics, and above all from the Host, the Body of God. All these, and other hallowed objects render him powerless. He is conquered by the fragrance of incense.

Certain trees and herbs are hateful to him, the whitethorn (or buckthorn) as we have seen, and particularly garlic. Often when the Vampire is decapitated his mouth is stuffed full with garlic ; garlic is scattered in and all over the coffin by handfuls ; and he can do no harm. In China and among the Malays to wet a child's forehead with garlic is a sure protection against vampires. The West Indian negroes to-day smear themselves with garlic to neutralize the evil charms of witches and obeah men. It may be noted that the Battas or Bataks of Sumatra ascribe pining and wasting away, sickness, terror and death to the absence of the soul (*Tendi*) from the body and the soul must be lured back to his tenement. One of the most powerful soul-compelling herbs which is used by them in their mystic rites on these occasions is garlic.[130] At the S. John (Midsummer) Festival of fire, on the Vigil of the Major solemnity of that Saint, 23rd June, at Dragingnan, Var, the people roasted pods of garlic by the bonfires. These pods were afterwards distributed to every family, and were believed to bring good luck.[131]

In countries which are non-Christian the practices are naturally somewhat different, although it should be remarked that burning the body of the Vampire is universal. In China, corpses suspected of potential vampirism were allowed to decay in the open air before burial, or, when buried, were exhumed, as in other countries, and cremated. In the absence of the corpse from its grave the lid of the coffin was removed, since it was thought that the circulation of fresh air would prevent the Vampire from returning to it. Rice, red peas and scraps of iron were also scattered round the grave. These formed a mystical barrier the dead man could not surmount, he fell to the ground stiff and stark, and then could be taken up and burned to ashes.[132]

In some Slavonic countries it is thought that a Vampire, if prowling out of his tomb at night may be shot and killed with a silver bullet that has been blessed by a priest. But care must be taken that his body is not laid in the rays of the moon, especially if the moon be at her full, for in this case he will revive with redoubled vigour and malevolence.

It should perhaps be mentioned that the Macedonians believe in the existence of a vrykolakas of sheep and cattle as well as the more formidable vrykolakas who drains human blood. The vrykolakas of animals rides upon their shoulders and as the ordinary vampire sucks a vein, killing the unfortunate beasts and leaving them a mere fibrous mash of skin and bone. Vagrant Mohammedan dervishes profess to have the power of exterminating these inferior vampires, whence they are often saluted as " vampire-killers," and they tramp the countryside ostentatiously exhibiting an iron rod which ends in a sharp point (*shish*) to pierce through and destroy the pest, or a long lance-like stick furnished at the top with a small axe to strike him down.[133] But here we have descended to mere quackery. Although as we have seen there are many methods and many variants, it is certain that an effectual remedy against the Vampire is to transfix his heart with a stake driven through with one single blow, to strike off his head with a sexton's spade, and perhaps best of all to burn him to ashes and purge the earth of his pollutions by the incineration of fire.

NOTES TO CHAPTER III.

[1] *Modern Greek Folklore*, p. 375.

[2] c. liii.

[3] οὐκ ἄν με μισῶν ἀνεχόρευ' 'Ερινύσιν ;   *Orestes*, 581.

[4] ll, 924-925.

Κλ.   ὅρα, φύλαξαι μητρὸς ἐγκότους κύνας.

Ορ.   τὰς τοῦ πατρὸς δὲ πῶς φύγω, παρεὶς τάδε ;

[5] *Compendium Theologiae Moralis*, Sabetti-Barrett.   Editio Uiccsima Quinta ; Pustet ; 1916. p. 115.

[6] " Rache als Selbstmordmotiv," R. Lasch ; *Globus*, lxxiv (1898), pp. 37-39.

[7] *Lettres édifantes et curieuses*, Nouvelle édition, xi, Paris, 1781, pp. 246-248.   The letter in question was written by Fr. Martin, S.J., at Marava, in the mission of Madura, 8th November, 1709.

[8] *Origin of Civilization*, pp. 378 *seq.*

[9] *China Past and Present*, London, 1903, pp. 378, *seq.*   Professor Parker was Professor of Chinese at the Owens College, Manchester.

[10] In a letter, 3rd February, 1902, to Sir James George Frazer, which is cited by the latter.

[11] I quote the translation by C. D. Yonge, Bohn's Classical Library, London, 1854, vol. I, pp. 250-251, *The Deipnosophists*, IV, 42.

[12] Of Apamea in Syria.   He was born *circa* B.C. 135, and died at Rome soon after B.C. 51.   His knowledge was very varied and remarkable.   None of his writings have come down to us entire, but the fragments were collected by Bahe, Lugduni Batauorum, 1810.

[13] About £20.

[14] *Deipnosophists*, IV, 40, Yonge's translation, vol. I, pp. 248-249.

[15] Impiety ; and later, as in Dio Cassius lvii, 9, *disloyalty* to the Emperor (as θεός).

[16] Aeschines, *Contra Ctesiphontem* ; 244, p. 193. Ed. F. Franke, Leipzig, 1863.

[17] " Trauer und Begrabnissitten der Wadschagga," B. Gutmann. *Globus.* (Illustrierte Zitschrift für Länder—und Völkerkunde). lxxxix ; 1906; p. 200.

[18] *The Baganda ;* Rev. J. Roscoe, London, 1911.

[19] " Der Muata Cazembe und die Völkerstämme der Maraves, Chevas, Muembas, Lundas, und andere von Süd-Afrika," *Zeitschrift für allgemeine Erdkunde,* vi, (1856), p. 287.

[20] *Les Missions Catholiques,* vii (1875), p. 328. Article by Fr. Finaz, S.J.

[21] A note by G. P. Badger, p. 45, *The Travels of Ludovico di Varttema,* Hakluyt Society, 1863.

[22] " Beiträge zur Kenntniss abergläubischer Gebräuche in Syrien," Eijūb Abēla. *Zeitschrift des Deutschen Palaestina-Vereins,* 1884, vii, p. 102.

[23] Satan is bound for a thousand years ; *The Apocalypse,* xx, 1-3, " And after that, he must be loosed a little time." The number of the beast " is six hundred sixty-six." *Apocalypse,* xiii, 18.

[24] Ivan Stchoukine, *Le Suicide collectif dans le Raskol russe,* Paris, 1903.

[25] *The Chinese Recorder and Missionary Journal,* xix, 1888, pp. 445-451 ; 502-521. " Self-immolation by Fire in China," by D. S. Macgowan, M.D.

[26] *Eighteenth Annual Report of the Bureau of American Ethnology,* Part I, pp. 320 ; 433, *seq.* (Washington, 1899). " The Eskimo about Bering Strait," by E. W. Nelson.

[27] Lucian, *De morte Peregrini.* Cf. Tertullian, *Ad Martyres,* iv : " Peregrinus qui non olim se rogo immisit."

[28] VIII, 57-74.

[29] *Ars Poetica,* 464-466 :
deus immortalis haberi
dum cupit Empedocles, ardentem frigidus Aetnam
insiluit.

[30] *Notes and Queries,* vi, 216.

[31] S. Bede, *In Die S. Paschae,* writes : " Debet autem quis sic sepeleri, ut capite ad occidentem posito, pedes dirigat ad orientem, in quo quasi ipsa positione orat : et innuit quod promptus est ut de occasu festinet ad ortum : de mundo ad saeculum."

[32] John Brand, *Popular Antiquities of Great Britain ;* Preface dated London, 1795. (First edition, 2 vols., 1813.) Edited by W. E. Hazlitt, 3 vols., London, 1870. Vol. iii, 67.

[33] *Folk Tales of the Russians,* p. 311.

[4] *Folk Lore Journal,* v, 218.

[3] *Discours des Sorciers,* Lyons, 1603, p. 58, cxx. Marginal note : " Du lieu du Sabbat." There were, of course, favourite spots for the rendezvous of witches.

[36] *Legends and Customs of Christmas* in *The Chicago Tribune,* European edition, Christmas Number, 1925.

[37] I, i, 158-164.

[38] Dr. A. Wuttke ; *Der Deutsche Volksaberglaube der Gegenwart,* Hamburg, 1860.

[39] Athenaeus, xiii, 79, notes : " The fashion of making favourites of boys was first introduced among the Grecians from Crete, as Timaeus informs us. But others say that Laius was the originator of the custom, when he was received in hospitality by Pelops ; and that having become passionately enamoured of his Chrysippus, he put the lad in his chariot and so bore him away and fled with him to Thebes. But Praxilla the Sicyonian says that Chrysippus was carried off by Jupiter." Plato, *Laws,* i, 636, speaks of ὁ πρὸ τοῦ Λαιοῦ νόμος, but Plutarch in his *Life of Pelopidas* (Clough, vol. ii, p. 219) argues against the view. Aeschylus wrote a *Laius* which probably dealt with this incident, and we know that it formed the subject of a tragedy by Euripides, *Chrysippus,* of which one only line is preserved :

γνώμην ἔχοντα μ᾽ ἡ φύσις βιάζεται.

Cicero, *Tusculanarum Disputationum,* Liber iv, xxxiii, writes : " Atque ut muliebres amores omittam, quibus maiorem licentiam natura concessit :

quis aut de Ganymedis raptu dubitat, quid poetae uclint ; aut non intelligit quid apud Euripidem et loquatur et cupiat Laius ? "

[40] S. Thomas, *Summa*, i-ii, 58, a. 2.

[41] Quoted in Kwong Ki Chiu, *A Dictionary of English Phrases*, etc., London and New York, 1881, 8vo.

[42] Abbott, *Macedonian Folklore*, Cambridge, 1903.

[43] William Henderson, *Notes on the Folk-lore of the Northern Counties of England and the Borders*, London, 1866, 8vo.

[44] In the case of many superstitions and omens a diametrically opposed explanation is often given in several countries. Thus for an English girl to dream of roses means the best of good luck, but roses if seen in sleep by a Breton maid bode dire misfortune.

[45] *De quorumdam Graecorum opinationibus*, ix.

[46] Allacci, *op cit.*, x.

[47] " Ce rédivive ou Oupire sorti de son tombeau, ou un Démon sous sa figure, va la nuit embrasser & serrer violemment ses proches ou ses amis, & leur suce le sang, jusqu'à les affoiblir, les exténuer & leur causer enfin la mort. Cette persécution ne s'arrête pas à une seule personne ; elle s'étend jusqu'à la dernière personne de la famille."—Calmet, *Traité sur les Apparitions* . . ., ed. 1751 ; II, c. xiii ; pp. 60-61.

[48] So metaphorically the name "Callicantzaros" is sometimes applied to a very lean man. Πολίτης, Παραδόσεις, II, p. 1293.

[49] *Anatomy of Melancholy*, Part I ; Sect. 1 ; Mem. 1 ; Subs. 4.

[50] The belief is Slavonic, and Elis being particularly subject to Slav influence, acquired the tradition.

[51] P. E. Müller, Saxo Grammaticus, *Historia Danica*, Copenhagen, 1839-1858, vol. ii. p. 60.

[52] M. Dobrizhoffer, *Historia de Abiponibus*, Vienna, 1784 ; I, 289, *sqq.*

[53] Rev. J. Roscoe, *The Baganda*, London, 1911 ; pp. 288 *sqq.*

[54] Aelian, *Le natura animalium*, I, 38 (ed. R. Hercher. Paris, Didot, 1858).

[55] G. Willoughby-Meade, *Chinese Ghouls and Goblins*, 1928 ; chap. ix, p. 223.

[56] " Religion and Customs of the Uraons," by the Rev. P. Dehon, S.J., *apud* the *Memoirs of the Asiatic Society of Bengal*, vol. i, No. 9, (Calcutta 1906), p. 141.

[57] Well-nigh innumerable examples might be cited, for the belief seems universal. In Petronius the soldier who was a werewolf when wounded one night in his animal form by a thrust in the neck from a pike, on the next morning lay in bed " like an ox in a stall " whilst the surgeon dressed a gash in his neck. Delrio, *Disquisitiones Magicae*, Liber II, q. xviii, discussing lycanthropy says : " Hoc autem ultimo casu nihil mirum est, si postmodum uere inueniantur saucii illis membris humanis quae in ferino corpore exceperant. Nam & leuiter cessit circumiectus aër, & uulnus uero corpori inhaesit. Uerum quando uerum corpus abfuit, tune Diabolus in absentium corpore eam partem consauciat quam scit in ferino corpore sauciatam fuisse." Bartolomeo de Spina in his *De strigibus*, xix, relates a case which came to his knowledge when at Ferrara, a hideous cat entered a house but was attacked, wounded and driven from a high window. The next day, an old hag, long suspect of witch-craft, was discovered in bed with bruised and broken limbs. " Etenim per-cussiones & plagae, quae in catto infixae sunt, in illa uetula sunt inuentae quoad membrorum correspondentium." Bodin, *De la Demonomanie des Sorciers*, II, vi, writes : " veu que ceux qui ont esté blessez en forme de bestes, se sont apres estre rechangez, trouuez blessez en forme humaine." In the *Malleus Maleficarum*, Part II, Qn. 1, Ch. 9. (translation by the present author, John Rodker, 1928, pp. 126-127) is told the history of the three cats who attacked a woodcutter. He drove them away with many blows, and after-wards it came to light how three respected matrons who were so bruised that they had to keep their beds complained that the workman had assaulted and beaten them. Glanvil in his *Saducismus Triumphatus*, London, 1681, Part II, p. 205, when relating the famous case of Julian Cox, a Somersetshire witch who was hanged at Taunton in 1663, speaks of " *the Body of* Julian

being wounded by a stab at her Astral Spirit, *as it is found also in* Jane Brooks, *and an old woman in* Cambridgeshire, *whose* Astral Spirit *coming into a* Mans *house, (as he was sitting alone at the fire) in the shape of a huge cat, and setting her self before the fire, not far from him, he stole a stroke at the back of it with a Fire-fork, and seemed to break the back of it, but it scrambled from him, and vanisht he knew not how.   But such an Old Woman, a reputed Witch, was found dead in her Bed that very night, with her Back broken, as I have heard some years ago credibly reported.*" J. Ceredig Davies, *Folk-lore of West and Mid-Wales,* Aberystwyth, 1911, p. 243, says that throughout Wales " the possibility of injuring or marking the witch in her assumed shape so deeply that the bruise remained on her in her natural form was a common belief."

⁵⁸ W. R. S. Ralston. *Songs of the Russian People.* London, 1872.

⁵⁹ Thomas Pennant, *A Tour in Scotland,* 1769. 8vo. Chester, 1771.

⁶⁰ *Etymological Dictionary of the Scottish Language,* 2 vols. Edinburgh, 1808 ; (and supplement, 2 vols., 1824).

⁶¹ Psalm xc.

⁶² Delrio, *Disquisitiones Magicae,* Liber II, Q. xxvii, sec. 2, speaks of the especial ferocity of the noonday devil : " A tempestate diei dicitur meridianus, eo quod hoc genus daemonum meridiano tempore & apparere solitum, & homines crudelius acriusque infestare ; tum spirituali tentatione ac praelio, maxime luxuriae & acediae stimulis, quae duo peccata urgent uchementius hominem cibis distentum plenumque ut recte Nicetas in *Nazian,* orat. citatam [*De sacro Baptismate*], & Euthy. ac Theodoret, *in Psal.* tum etiam corporeis afflictionibus, quod potest collegi ex ucterum gentilium opinione qui Pana (daemonum meridianorum hic unus) tum maxime iracundum & formidabilem credebant, ut testatur Theocritus *eidyl,* 1 & colligitur ex historiis."

⁶³ *Op. cit.* ed., 1751, vol. II, c. 11.

⁶⁴ The Devil can effect no real resurrection of a dead person, that is he cannot restore to life, for this is the power of God alone. Delrio *Disquisitiones Magicae,* Liber II, q. xxix, sec. 1, asks : *An diabolus possit facere ut homo uere resurget ?* This great scholar says some very valuable things in this connexion. He writes : " *Censeo minimam, uel nullam daemonis esse potestatem.* Non potest facere ut homo a mortuis resurgat : siue non potest facere, ut anima hominis suum corpus subintret, & illud uiuificet, informetque . . . Posset daemon, si Deus permitterit, cogere animam damnatam subire corpus, ut illud moucat, & in illo actiones aliquas demonstret ; quia sic ipse potest subire, & hanc animam inuitam cruciatu ad hoc posset compellere. Possunt etiam magi (ex pacto) per superiores daemones cogere inferiores, ut cadauer ingressi, illud gestent, moueant, ceteraque ad tempus faciant, quibus uideantur uiuere."

⁶⁵ Venette in his *Géneration de l' Homme* remarks that men who have much hair on the body are usually very amorous. It is indeed a widespread belief that in ardent natures the pilous system is notably luxuriant.

⁶⁶ 1653 ; Second edition with Appendix, 1655.

⁶⁷ The phenomenon of the psychic state in pregnancy, the French *envie* and German *Versehen,* has been fully discussed by Dr. Havelock Ellis, *Studies in the Psychology of Sex,* vol. v, Philadelphia, 1927.

⁶⁸ W. Cornwallis Harris, *The Highlands of Aethiopia,* i, p. 158, London, 1844.

⁶⁹ Ottolenghi, *Archivio di Psichiatria,* facs. vi, 1888, p. 573 notes that whilst normal persons only show twenty per cent. of blue eyes and criminals generally thirty-six per cent., the sexual offenders show fifty per cent. of blue eyes.

⁷⁰ Dr. Georg Autenrieth, *An Homeric Dictionary,* translated by Robert Porter Keep. London, 1896, *s.u.*

⁷¹ James Dawson, *Australian Aborigines,* p. 92. Melbourne, Sydney, and Adelaide, 1881,

⁷² A Chinook term signifying " guardian spirits."

⁷³ James G. Swan, *The Indians of Cape Flattery,* p. 66. *Report of the United States National Museum for* 1895. Washington, 1897.

[74] W. Crooke, *Popular Religion and Folk-lore of Northern India*, i, p. 279. Westminster, 1896.

[75] A. F. Mockler-Ferryman, *British Nigeria*, p. 285 ; London, 1902.

[76] Plutarch, *Isis et Osiris*, 33, 73 ; Diodorus Siculus, i, 88.

[77] Francesco Redi, *Bacco in Toscana*, London, 12mo, 1804.

[78] In Middleton *A Chaste Maid in Cheapside*, 4to, 1630 (acted perhaps twenty twenty years before), iii, 2, at the christening we have the prattle of the gossips :

> *Third Gossip :* Now, by my faith, a fair high-standing cup
> And two great postle spoons, one of them gilt.
> *First Puritan :* Sure, that was Judas then with the red beard.

Cf. Dryden's lines on Jacob Tonson, the publisher :

> With two left legs and Judas-coloured hair.

In *As You Like It*, iii, 4, Rosalind says : " His own hairs of the dissembling colour," to which Celia replies : " Something browner than Judas's."
Martial, xii, liv, has an epigram :

> Crine ruber, niger ore, breuis pede, lumine laesus
> Rem magnam praesta, Zoile, si bonus es.

Upon which Lemaire glosses (*Martialis Epigrammata* ; Parisūs 1825, iii, p. 48) : " *Crine ruber.* Hoc semper in malam partem acceptum, et ut pulchritudini, ita bonae indoli contrarium uisum. Et apud nos hodie exstat tritum prouerbium quo improbitatis arguuntur qui crinem rubrum habent." In folk-lore red hair is regarded as a mark of great sexuality, Κρυπτάδια, vol. ii, p. 258.

[79] p. 276.

[80] Cf. Shakespeare, 3 Henry *VI*, v. 6 :

> Thy mother felt more than a mother's pain,
> And yet brought forth less than a mother's hope ;
> To wit, an indigest deformed lump . . .
> Teeth hadst thou in thy head when thou wast born,
> To signify thou camest to bite the world.

And again :

> For I have often heard my mother say
> I came into the world with my legs forward . . .
> The midwife wonder'd, and the women cried
> " Oh ! Jesus bless us ! he is born with teeth ! "
> And so I was : which plainly signified
> That I should snarl, and bite, and play the dog.

[81] *The Tragedie of Chabot Admirall of France : As it was presented by her Majesties Servants, at the private House in Drury Lane. Written by George Chapman and James Shirley.* 4to, 1639. This Tragedy was licensed by the Master of the Revels 29 April, 1635.

[82] *Studies in the Psychology of Sex*, vol. iii. Philadelphia, 1926, p. 121. n².

[83] *Bulletin Internationale de Droit Pénal*, vol. vi, 1896, p. 115.

[84] " Le Baiser en Europe et en Chine," *Bulletin de la Société d'Anthropologie*, Paris, 1897, fasc. 2.

[85] *Studies in the Psychology of Sex*, vol. iv, Philadelphia, 1927, p. 216.

[86] Johannes Secundus Everard, 1511-1536.

[87] Jean Bonnefons, born at Clermont in Auvergne, 1554 ; died 1614.

[88] G. Alonzi, *Archivio di Psichiatria*, vol. vi., fasc. 4.

[89] *News of the World*, 21 December, 1924. Under heading, " Vampire's Victims."

[90] This is hardly correct. Hans Sennenfeld, who frequented " Zur Schwülen Guste " was twenty years old. Another victim, Hermann Bock, aged twenty-three, was a young rough, " a fellow well able to take care of himself."

[91] *News of the World*, 7 December, 1924.

[92] *Traité sur les Apparitions*, . . . Tome ii, Paris, 1751, p. 299.

[93] *Phenomena of Materialisation* by Baron von Schrenck Notzing. Translated by E. E. Fournier d'Albe. London. Kegan Paul, 1923, p. 10.

[94] *Op. cit, p.* 26.

⁹⁵ *Op cit.*, p. 26.

⁹⁶ London, 1926. c. vi. "Diabolic Possession and Modern Spiritism," especially pp. 248-269.

⁹⁷ M. Pierart was a professor at the College of Maubeuse, and afterwards secretary to Baron du Potet. He founded *La Revue Spiritualiste* in 1858, and was esteemed as the rival of Allan Kardec. He died in 1878.

⁹⁸ *Survival.* By various Authors. Edited by Sir James Marchant, K.B.E., LL.D. Putnams, London and New York.

⁹⁹ See Schwicker, *Geschichte des Temeser Banates*, Nagy-Becskerek, 1861.

¹⁰⁰ Afanasief, *Poeticheskiya Vozzryeniya Slavyan na Prirodu* ["Poetic Views of the Slavonians about Nature"], 3 vols., Moscow, 1865-69, 8vo, vol. iii, p. 576, quotes Vuk Haradjic to this effect.

¹⁰¹ Leone Allacci, *De quorumdam Graecorum opinationibus*, cap. xii, sqq.

¹⁰² L. Strackerjan, *Aberglaube und Sagen aus dem Herzogthum Oldenburg*, Oldenburg, 1867, I, p. 154.

¹⁰³ M. Alex. Castron, *Vorlesungen über die finnische Mythologie*. St. Petersburg. 1853. p. 337.

¹⁰⁴ Shway Yoe (Sir T. G. Scott), *The Burman; His Life and Notions*, London, 1882, ii, p. 338. Captain C. J. F. S. Forbes, *British Burma*, London, 1878, p. 93.

¹⁰⁵ J. A. E. Köhler, *Volksbrauch Aberglauben, Sagen und andre alte Überlieferungen im Voigtland;* Leipzig, 1867, p. 251.

¹⁰⁶ Adolf Bastian, *Die Mensch in der Geschichte*. Leipzig, 1860. ii, p. 331.

¹⁰⁷ C. J. Anderson, *Lake Ngami*, Second Edition, London, 1856, p. 226.

¹⁰⁸ An old line runs: *Ligna Crucis palma, cedrus, cupressus, oliva.* The gipsies say that the Cross was of ash-wood. According to Wiliam Ellis, *The Timber-tree Improved*, London, 1738, 8vo, p. 178, there was a local belief in Herefordshire that the Cross was of service wood. Some think the Cross was of pine.

¹⁰⁹ *Dictionnaire des Superstitions, Erreurs, Préjuges et Traditions populaires, Troisième et dernière Encyclopedic Théologique.* 2 vols., 4to, 1855.

¹¹⁰ *The Voyage and Travails*, first printed Westminster, 4to, 1499. A convenient edition is London, 8vo, 1725.

¹¹¹ Dioscorides, περὶ "Ὕλης 'Ιατρικῆς, *De arte medica*, I, 119, Ed. Sprengel, Leipzig, 1829-30.

¹¹² The scholiast on the Θηριακά (l. 861) of Nicander of Claros. Keil's revision (1856) of the 1816 edition of Schneider, Leipzig.

¹¹³ Diogenes Laertius, *Uitae philosophorum*, iv, 54-57. Ed. C. G. Cobet, Paris (Didot), 1878.

¹¹⁴ The first quarto has no date, but is probably 1609-10. I quote from Dyce's recension.

¹¹⁵ *La Fida Pastora.* 12 mo. Londoni, 1658, p. 21.

¹¹⁶ E. S. Harland *The Legend of Perseus*, London, 1896. Vol. iii., p. 23.

¹¹⁷ *Voyage du Sieur Paul Lucas au Levant.* A la Haye. MDCCV. Vol. ii, p. 209.

¹¹⁸ R. Pashley, *Travels in Crete*, Cambridge and London, 1837. Vol. ii, p. 201.

¹¹⁹ *Russian Folk Tales.* London, 1873, p. 323.

¹²⁰ Cf. c. vii. p.

¹²¹ The Cardinal Bishop of Olmutz gave Gioseppe Davanzati, Archbishop of Trani, the following account of the methods of dealing with vampires in his German diocese. Tribunals were summoned to take information and decide upon the course of action. "I ministri di questi predendone esatta informazione, e formandone un giuridico processo ne vengono ad una sentenza finale contro al sudetto Vampiro, mediante la quale viene solennemente e con tutte le formole legali decretato : che il publice Carnefice portandosi al luogo, ove si trova il Vampiro, apra il sepolcro, e con una sciabla o larga spada a vista di tutto il popolo spettatore recida il Vampiro il capo, e dopo con una lancia gli apri il petto, e trapassi col ferro da parte a parte il cuore del Vampiro strappandoglielo dal seno e poi ritorni di nuovo a chiudere l'avello. In tal maniera, mi disse il Porporato, cessava affatto di più comparire il

Vampiro, quantunque molti altri di questi, che non erano stati ancora giustiziati, nè esecutoriati non cessavano di comparire, e di produrre i calamitosi effeti come i primi. Ma quel, ch'era da notarsi, e di maraviglia insieme, secondo il medesimo Autore si era, che molti de'detti Vampiri giustiziati, si trovano ben colorati, rubicondi, con occhi aperti, e turgidi di vivo sangue, come se fossero attualmente vivi, e di prospera salute ; a segno tale, che alcuni di questi al colpo della lanciata, che loro veniva inflitta, mandavano uno spaventoso grido, e scaturivano dal petto un copioso ruscello di sangue, il quale per la copia arrivava ad innaffiare non solo il catalette, ma spargendosi al di fuori guingeva a bagnare il prossimo terreno. Cosa non men orrida, e spaventosa a vedersi, che orribile a descriversi ed a concepirsi."

[122] *De Quorundam Graecorum Opinationibus*, p. 142.

[123] pp. 218-219.

[124] vii, p. 490. Compare Heineccius, *De absolutione mortuorum* . . ., p. 20.

[125] *Chronica rerum Anglicarum*, Liber V, c. xxii. " Talia saepius in Anglia contigisse, et crebis clarere exemplis, quietem populo dari non posse, nisi miserrimi hominis corpore effosso et concremato."

[126] H. F. Tozer, *Highlands of Turkey*, ii, 91, quoting Newton, *Travels and Discoveries in the Levant* (i. p. 212).

[127] Arthur and Albert Schott. *WalachischeMaehrehen*, p. 298.

[128] Who ascended the Papal Chair as Adrian IV, 9 January, 1522.

[129] In the *Uniculum Spirituum* it is related that Solomon imprisoned three millions of infernal spirits with seventy-two of their kings in a bottle of black glass, which he cast into a deep well near Babylon. The Babylonians, however, hoping to find a treasure in the well, descended, and broke the bottle, thus releasing these legions of darkness. The story of the Djin and the Fisherman is one of the most familiar tales of *The Thousand and One Nights*. The idea of enclosing spirits in a bottle would seem to be Oriental. Don Cleofas, the hero of *El Diabolo Coxuelo*, by Luis Velez de Guevara (first printed in 1641) having accidentally entered the house of an astrologer, delivers from a bottle where he had been confined by a potent charm el diabolo coxuelo who appropriately rewards his liberator. The situation is even better known owing to *Le Diable Boiteux* and the release of Asmodée, which Le Sage has amply borrowed from the Spanish romance. In China there is the story of a Vampire who is caught and imprisoned in a jar which is thrown into Lake T'ai. See G. Willoughby-Meade, *Chinese Ghouls and Goblins*, pp. 235-37.

[130] Dr. R. Römer, " Bijdrage tot de Geneeskunst du Karo-Batak's," *Tijdschrift voor Indische Taal-Land-en Volkenkunde*, i, (1908), pp. 212, *sqq.*

[131] Aubin-Louis Millin, *Voyage dans les Départemens du Midi de la France*, Paris, 1807-1811. Vol. iii, p. 28.

[132] J. J. M. de Groot, *The Religious System of China*, v. 725, 744, 749, *sqq.*

[133] G. F. Abbott, *Macedonian Folklore*, p. 221.

CHAPTER IV

THE VAMPIRE IN ASSYRIA, THE EAST, AND SOME ANCIENT COUNTRIES

AMONG the elaborate and extensive demonology of Babylonia and Assyria the Vampire had a very prominent place. From the very earliest times Eastern races have always held that belief in the existence of dark and malignant powers, evil spirits and ghosts which is, we cannot doubt it, naturally implanted in the heart of man and which it remains for the ignorance and agnosticism of a later day to deny. The first inhabitants of Babylonia, the Sumerians, recognized three distinct classes of evil spirits, any one of whom was always ready to attack those who by any accident or negligence laid themselves open to these invasions. In particular was a man who had wandered far from his fellows into some haunted spot liable to these onsets, and Dr. R. Campbell Thompson tells us that this " is the interpretation of the word *muttaliku*, ' wanderer,' which occurs so often in the magical text to indicate the patient."[1] Of the Babylonian evil spirits the first were those ghosts who were unable to rest in their graves and so perpetually walked up and down the face of the earth ; the second class was composed of those horrible entities who were half human and half demon ; whilst the third class were the devils, pure spirits of the same nature as the gods, fiends, who bestrode the whirlwind and the sand-storm, who afflicted mankind with plagues and pestilence. There were many subdivisions, and in fact there are few evil hierarchies so detailed and so fasciculated as the Assyrian cosmorama of the spiritual world.

The evil spirit who was known as *Utukku* was a phantom or ghost, generally but perhaps not invariably of a wicked and malevolent kind, since it was he whom the necromancers raised from the dead, and in an ancient Epic when the hero, Gilgamish, prays to the god, Nergal to restore his friend

Ea-bani, the request is granted, for the ground gapes open and the *Utukku* of Ea-bani appears "like the wind,"[2] that is, says Dr. Campbell Thompson, "probably a transparent spectre in the human shape of Ea-bani, who converses with Gilgamish." The *Ekimmu* or Departed Spirit, was the soul of the dead person which for some reason could find no rest, and wandered over the earth lying wait to seize upon man. Especially did it lurk in deserted and ill-omened places. Dr. Thompson tells us that it is difficult to say exactly in what respect the *Ekimmu* differed from the *Utukku*,[3] but it is extremely interesting to inquire into the causes owing to which a person became a *Ekimmu*, and here we shall find many parallels with the old Greek beliefs concerning those duties to the dead which are paramount and for which a man must risk his life and more. It was ordinarily believed among the Assyrians that after death the soul entered the Underworld, "the House of Darkness, the seat of the god, Irkalla, the House from which none that enter come forth again." Here they seem to have passed a miserable existence, enduring the pangs of hunger and thirst, and if their friends and relatives on earth were too niggardly to offer rich meats and pour forth bountiful libations upon their tombs they were compelled to satisfy their craving with dust and mud. But there were certain persons who were yet in worse case, for their souls could not even enter the Underworld. This is clear from the description given by the phantom of Ea-bani to his friend, the hero Gilgamish :

> The man whose corpse lieth in the desert—
> Thou and I have often seen such an one—
> His spirit resteth not in the earth ;
> The man whose spirit hath none to care for it—
> Thou and I have often seen such an one,
> The dregs of the vessel— the leavings of the feast,
> And that which is cast out into the street are his food.[4]

"The *Ekimmu*-spirit of an unburied corpse could find no rest and remained prowling about the earth so long as its body was above ground."[5] This is exactly one phase of the Vampire, and in the various magical texts and incantations are given lists of those who are liable to return in this manner. As well as the ghosts of those whose bodies were uncared for or unburied, that is to say those who were lost or forgotten, there

were the spirits of men and women who died violent or premature deaths, or who had left certain duties undone, and even
youths or maidens who had loved but who had been snatched
away before they had known happiness. In an exorcism
various spirits are addressed individually :

> Whether thou art a ghost unburied,
> Or a ghost that none careth for,
> Or a ghost with none to make offerings to it.
> Or a ghost that hath none to pour libations to it,
> Or a ghost that hath no prosperity.

Other phantoms who can obtain no rest are :

> He that lieth in a ditch .. . .
> He that no grave covereth . . .
> He that lieth uncovered,
> Whose head is uncovered with dust,
> The king's son that lieth in the desert,
> Or in the ruins,
> The hero whom they have slain with the sword.

And again :

> He that hath died of hunger in prison,
> He that hath died of thirst in prison,
> The hungry man who in his hunger hath not smelt the
>   smell of food,
> He whom the bank of a river hath made to perish,
> He that hath died in the desert or marshes,
> He that a storm hath overwhelmed in the desert,
> The Night-wraith that hath no husband,
> The Night-fiend that hath no wife.[6]
> He that hath posterity and he that hath none.

If the spirit of the dead man be forgotten and no offerings
were made at the tomb, hunger and thirst would compel
it to come forth from its abode in the Underworld to seek the
nourishment of which it has been deprived, and, according
to the old proverb, since a hungry man is an angry man it
roams furiously to and fro and greedily devours whatsoever
it may. " If it found a luckless man who had wandered far
from his fellows into haunted places, it fastened upon him,
plaguing and tormenting him until such time as a priest should
drive it away with excorcism." This is clear from two
tablets which have been translated as follows :

> The gods which seize (upon man)
>   Have come forth from the grave ;
> The evil wind-gusts
>   Have come forth from the grave ;
> To demand the payment of rites and the pouring out
>   of libations,
>   They have come forth from the grave ;
> All that is evil in their hosts, like a whirlwind
>   Hath come forth from their graves.

Or again :

> The evil Spirit, the evil Demon, the evil Ghost, the evil
>   Devil,
> From the earth have come forth ;
> From the Underworld unto the land they have come forth ;
> In heaven they are unknown,
> On earth they are not understood,
> They neither stand nor sit,
> Nor eat nor drink."

Even as the Vampire of Eastern Europe to-day, the Babylon-ian *Ekimmu* was the most persistent of haunters and the most difficult to dislodge. If he could find no rest in the Under-world he would speedily return and attach himself to anyone who during life had held the least communication with him. Man's life was certainly surrounded with dangers when the mere act of sharing just once food, oil, or garments with another person gave the spirit of this individual a claim to consort with his friend, or it might be even the casual acquaint-ance, who had shown him some slight kindness. The link could be slighter yet than that since in a long and elaborate formula of priestly conjuration, a particularly solemn and ritual incantation for the exorcizing of evil spirits, especially Vampires, it is plainly said that merely to have eaten, to have drunk, to have anointed oneself, or dressed oneself in the society of another was enough to forge an extraordinary spiritual copula. In this imprecatory orison, which assumes a strictly liturgical character, various kinds of vampirish spectres are banned :

> Whether thou are a ghost that has come from the earth,
> Or a phantom of night that hath no couch,
> Or a woman (that hath died) a virgin,
> Or a man (that hath died) unmarried,
> Or one that lieth dead in the desert,

Or one that lieth dead in the desert, uncovered with earth,
Or one that in the desert . . .
      (hiatus)
Or one that hath been torn from a date palm,
Or one that cometh through the waters in a boat,
Or a ghost unburied,
Or a ghost that none careth for,
Or a ghost with none to make offerings,
Or a ghost with none to pour libations,
Or a ghost that hath no posterity,
Or a hag-demon,
Or a ghoul,
Or a robber-sprite,
Or a harlot (that hath died) whose body is sick,
Or a woman (that hath died) in travail,
Or a woman (that hath died) with a babe at her breast,
Or a weeping woman (that hath died) with a babe at her
    breast,
Or an evil man (that hath died),
Or an (evil) spirit,
Or one that haunteth (the neighbourhood),
Or one that haunteth (the vicinity),
Or whether thou be one with whom on a day (I have eaten),
Or whether thou be one with whom on a day (I have drunk),
Or with whom on a day I have anointed myself,
Or with whom on a day I have clothed myself,
Or whether thou be one with whom I have entered and
    eaten,
Or with whom I have entered and drunk,
Or with whom I have entered and anointed myself,
Or with whom I have entered and clothed myself,
Or whether thou be one with whom I have eaten food when
    I was hungry,
Or with whom I have drunk water when I was thirsty,
Or with whom I have anointed myself with oil when I was
    sore,
Or with whom when I was cold I have clothed his naked-
    ness with a garment,
(Whatever thou be) until thou art removed,
Until thou departest from the body of the man, the son
    of his god,
Thou shalt have no food to eat,
Thou shalt have no water to drink,

    .   .   .   .   .

If thou wouldst fly up to heaven
Thou shalt have no wings,
If thou wouldst lurk in ambush on earth,
Thou shalt secure no resting-place.
Unto the man, the son of his god— come not nigh,

Get thee hence !
Place not thy head upon his head,
Place not thy (hand) upon his hand,
Place not thy foot upon his foot,
With thy hand touch him not,
Turn (not) thy back upon him,
Lift not thine eyes (against him),
Look not behind thee,
Gibber not against him,
Into the house enter thou not,
Through the fence break thou not,
Into the chamber enter thou not,
In the midst of the city encircle him not,
Near him make no circuit ;
By the Word of Ea,[7]
May the man, the son of his god,
Become pure, become clean, become bright !

. . . . .

May his welfare be secured at the kindly hands of the
gods.[8]

This incantation is extremely important as here we see many
of the ideas which have persisted through the ages. The
Vampire, or restless spirit might be a man whose lay body
dead in the desert, uncovered with earth, " a ghost unburied,"
and it is readily remembered that among the ancient Greeks
there was no more reverent duty than to bury the dead.
Again, to-day, the Slavs consider that brigands and high-
waymen whose lives are passed in deeds of violence and rapine
after death will probably in another mode continue their
predatory habits as Vampires ; so the Assyrian Vampire
might be " a robber-sprite." It will be remarked that the
threat which drives away the *Ekimmu* is that until he has
departed no libation shall be poured over his grave, no baked
meats offered there, and no saving rites performed.

It was even held that if a man but looked upon a corpse he
established that mysterious psychic connexion which would
render him liable to be attacked by the spirit of the deceased.
Among the Ibo people in the district of Awka, Southern
Nigeria, one of the most important taboos which has to be
preserved by the priest of the Earth is that he may not see a
corpse, so terrible is held to be the spiritual contagion. Should
he by an unlucky chance meet one upon the road he must
at once veil his eyes with his wristlet.[9] This wrist-band or
bracelet is a most important periapt or charm since it is

regarded as a spiritual fetter keeping the soul in the body, and to bind such a talisman upon the wrist is particularly appropriate, since many peoples believe that a soul resides wherever a pulse is felt beating. Moreover, not only does this amulet guard the soul securely within the body but it also keeps evil spirits and demons out of it, and therefore at the ceremonies of the cutting of hair of Siamese children, which is an extremely important and symbolical rite, a magic cord is tied round the wrist of the child to protect him from malignant and foul spectres who would invade him.[10] Accordingly by shrouding his eyes with his wristlet the Ibo priest protects himself against any molestation by the spirit of the corpse. Very similar protective powers are also ascribed to finger rings, and among the Lapps the person whose business it is to shroud a corpse receives from some relative of the departed a brass ring which he must wear fastened to his right arm until the funeral rites are over. This ring is believed to shield him from any onset on the part of the ghost.[12] In the Tyrol a woman—particularly if she be pregnant or in travail—must never take off her wedding-ring, or else witches and vampires will have power over her.[13] In England it is considered to be courting disaster if a woman takes off her wedding-ring, whilst actually to lose the wedding-ring is one of the worst possible misfortunes. It may be mentioned that to-day the Greeks of the Isle of Karpathos (Scarpanto) never bury a body which has rings upon it; " for the spirit, they say, can even be detained in the little finger, and cannot rest."[14] It is not suggested that anything so horrible might happen as that the spirit should become evil or a Vampire, but certainly it would not be in the full enjoyment of happiness and peace.

Among the Assyrians the *Ekimmu* might appear in a house. Just as the Vampire, it would pass through walls or doors, and whether it merely glided about as a silent phantom, or whether it gibbered uttering unintelligible and mocking words with hideous mop and mow, or whether it seemed to ask some question that required a response, in any case such an apparition was terribly unlucky. The direst misfortunes followed, certainly involving the destruction of the house, and it was seldom that the owner, if not many of his family as well would not die within very short space of time. It seems, indeed, that the *Ekimmu* would drain the life out of a household, which is purely a vampirish quality, although perhaps it does not appear that this was always a physical operation, the actual sucking of blood, as is believed to be the case with the *vrykolokas*. But Dr. Campbell-Thompson tells us that there were few superstitions which had obtained such a hold over the Assyrians as the belief in the *Ekimmu*-spirit.

One incantation speaks of the meat and drink of the evil spirit :

> Thy food is the food of ghosts,
> Thy drink is the drink of ghosts.

In another " Prayer against the Evil Spirits " the Vampires are spoken of in the plainest terms. This incantation is as follows :

> Spirits that minish heaven and earth,
> That minish the land,
> Spirits that minish the land,
> Of giant strength,
> Of giant strength and giant tread,
> Demons (like) raging bulls, great ghosts,
> Ghosts that break through all houses,
> Demons that have no shame,
> Seven are they !
> Knowing no care,
> They grind the land like corn ;
> Knowing no mercy,
> They rage against mankind :
> They spill their blood like rain,
> Devouring their flesh (and) sucking their veins.
> Where the images of the gods are, there they quake
> In the Temple of Nabû, who fertilises the shoots of
>   wheat.
> They are demons full of violence
> Ceaselessly devouring blood.
> Invoke the ban against them,
> That they no more return to this neighbourhood.
> By heaven be ye exorcised ! By Earth be ye exor-
>   cised ![15]

These Seven Spirits re-appear both in Syriac and in Palestinian magic. In his exhaustive and authoritative work *Semitic Magic* (p. 52) Dr. Campbell Thompson says : " Their predilection for human blood, as described in the cuneiform incantation, is in keeping with all the traditions of the grisly mediaeval Vampires." An Ethiopic charm pre- scribes the following invocation : " Thus make perish, O

Lord, all demons and evil spirits who eat flesh and drink blood : who crush the bones and seduce the children of men ; drive them away, O Lord, by the power of these thy names and by the prayer of thy holy Disciples, from thy servant." In an even more curious Syriac exorcism the Seven Spirits are described in detail almost exactly as they were pictured by the earlier inhabitants of Mesopotamia. The charm is to protect the flocks and herds, and it may be noted that there has come down to us an Assyrian protective incantation which is almost exactly similar. The Syriac runes go thus : " *For the fold of cattle.* ' Seven accursed brothers accursed sons ! destructive ones, sons of men of destruction ! Why do you creep along on your knees and more upon your hands ? ' And they replied, ' We go on our hands, so that we may eat flesh, and we crawl along upon our hands, so that we may drink blood.' As soon as I saw it, I prevented them from devouring, and I cursed and bound them in the name of thy Father, the Son, and the Holy Ghost, saying : ' May you not proceed on your way, nor finish your journey, and may God break your teeth, and cut the veins of your neck, and the sinews thereof, that you approach not the sheep nor the oxen of the person who carries (sc. these writs) ! I bind you in the name of Gabriel and Michael, I bind you by that Angel who judged the woman that combed (the hair of) her head on the eve of Holy Sunday. May they vanish as smoke from before the wind for ever and ever, Amen ' "

The twenty-second formula of the *Cuneiform Inscription of Western Asia,* which was published by Sir Henry Rawlinson and Mr. Edwin Morris in 1866 contains the following curse against a Vampire :

> The phantom, child of heaven,
> Which the gods remember,
> The Innin (hobgoblin) prince
> Of the lords
> The . . .
> Which produces painful fever,
> The vampire which attacks man,
> The *Uruku* multifold
> Upon humanity,
> May they never seize him !

The earliest Vampire known is that depicted upon a prehistoric bowl, an engraving of which has been published in the *Délégation en Perse* [16] where a man copulates with a vampire whose head has been severed from the body. Here the threat of cutting off her head is supposed to frighten her away from the act represented and Dr. R. Campbell-Thompson suggests[17] that "quite probably the man may have drunk from this bowl as helping the magic (although this is a doubtful point)." A vampire is depicted among the Babylonian cylinder seals in the *Revue d'Assyriologie*, 1909,[61] concerning which the same great authority has given me the following note : "The idea is, I presume, to keep off the nocturnal visits of Lilith and her sisters. Just as the prehistoric or early people showed pictures of enemies with their heads cut off (in order that what they were there showing might by sympathetic magic actually happen), so will the man troubled by nightly emissions attributed to Lilith, depict on his amulet the terrors which are in store for these malignants."

The Hebrew Lilith is undoubtedly borrowed from the Babylonian demon Lilîtu, a night spirit, although it is not probable that the Lilith has any connexion with the Hebrew Laîlah, "night." It was perhaps inevitable that the Rabbis should assume some such derivation, and it must be allowed that the comparison seemed plausible enough, although it has been shown, on the evidence of the Assyrian word *Lilû*, that the old theory must no longer be maintained, and Lilith is almost certainly to be referred to *lalû*, "luxuriousness," and *lulti*, "lasciviousness, lechery." This night ghost is mentioned in *Isaias* xxxiv, 14, where the Vulgate has : "Et occurrent daemonia onocentauris, et pilosus clamabit alter ad alterum : ibi cubauit lamia, et inuenit sibi requiem." Which *Douay* translates : "And demons and monsters shall meet, and the hairy ones shall cry out one to another, there hath the lamia lain down, and found rest for herself." The *Authorised Version* has : "The wild beasts of the desert shall also meet with the wild beasts of the island, and the satyr shall cry to his fellow ; the screech owl also shall rest there, and find for herself a place of rest." Upon *screech owl* there is a marginal note : "Or, night monster." The *Revised Version* prefers : "And the wild beasts of the desert shall meet with the wolves, and the satyr shall cry to his fellow ; yea, the night-monster shall settle there, and shall find her a place of rest." There are marginal notes ; satyr, "or, *he-goat*" ; the night-monster, "Heb. *Lilith*." In classical Latin, *lamia* is defined by Lewis and Short as "a *witch* who was said to suck children's blood, a *sorceress*, *enchantress*." I doubt whether this is a very accurate definition, although possibly it will cover the meaning in Horace, *Ars Poetica*, 340 :

> Ne quodcumque uelit poscat sibi fabula credi,
> Neu pransae lamiae puerum uiuum extrahat aluo.

Which Francis translates :

> The probable maintain,
> Nor force us to believe the monstrous scene,
> Which shows a child, by a fell witch devour'd,
> Dragg'd from her entrails, and to life restor'd.

Apuleius, *Metamorphoses*, I, has : "Quo (odore spurcissimi humoris) me lamiae illae infecerunt." Here *lamia* is hardly the equivalent of anything more than "witch." So the meaning of Vampire had been to a large extent lost or submerged. This idea, however, seems to have remained in Aristophanes, when in the *Wasps* (1177) Philocreon boasts what tales he can tell :

πρῶτον μὲν ὡς ἡ Λάμι᾽ ἁλοῦσ᾽ ἐπέρδετο.

Liddell and Scott define Λάμια as : "*a fabulous monster said to feed on man's flesh*, a bugbear to frighten children with," referring to this passage in Aristophanes, which does not seem a very satisfactory or scholarly explanation. Tertullian, *Aduersus Ualentinianos*, which de Labriolle dates at 208-211, uses the phrase *lamiae turres* as nursery tales, *Contes de nourrice*, *contes bleus*. Theil in his *Grand Dictionnaire de la Langue Latine* terms *lamia* by "lamie, sorcière, qui suçait, disait-on, le sang des enfants ; magicienne." These lexicographers for some extraordinary reason do not appear to have remarked the use of the word in the Vulgate. Gervase of Tilbury in his *Otia Imperialia* has some account of lamias, so called, he states, because they lacerate children : "lamiae uel laniae, quia laniant infantes." In country places even yet many an old nurse dares not trust a child in a cradle without a candle or lamp in the room for fear of the night-hag.

Rabbinical literature is full of legends concerning Lilith. According to tradition she was the first wife of Adam and, the

mother of devils, spirits, and *lilin,* which is the same word as
the Assyrian *Lilu.* From Jewish lore she passed to mediæval
demonology, and Johann Weyer says that she was the princess
who presided over the Succubi. It is true that the *LXX*
translates in this passage of the prophet Isaias the Hebrew
Lilith by Lamia, but it has been suggested that the nearest
Latin equivalent might be *strix,* for although *strix* may be
properly a screech owl, yet the Latins believed that these
drained the blood of young children, and Ovid, *Fasti,* VI,
131-140 has :

> Sunt auidæ uolucres ; non quæ Phineia mensis
>   Guttura fraudabant : sed genus inde trahunt.
> Grande caput : stantes oculi : rostra apta rapinæ :
>   Canities pennis, unguibus hamus inest.
> Nocte uolant, puerosque petunt nutricis egentes ;
>   Et uitiant cunis corpora rapta suis.
> Carpere dicuntur lactentia uiscera rostris ;
>   Et plenum poto sanguine guttur habent
> Est illis strigibus nomen : sed nominis huius
>   Causa ; quod horrenda stridere nocte solent.

But it is clear that the Strix was not always a bird, for in
the Lombard Code we find the expression " Strix uel masca."
Thiel has : " masca (mascha), *sorcière, ML. De là le français :
masque.*" In fact *masca* has the same meaning as *Larua*
which signifies a ghost, or as in the well-known line of Horace,
a mask :

> Nil illi larua et tragicis opus esse cothurnis.[18]

In the *Breuiarium Romanum,* pars aestiua, die 30 Augusti,
ad Matutinum, in 11 Nocturno, lectio V, it is said of S. Rose of
Lima, " laruas daemonum, frequenti certamine uictrix,
impauide protriuit ac superauit."

Moreover, the Strix was a vampire, and it may not be
superfluous again to quote the well-known Saxon Capitulary of
Charlemagne, 781, Liber I, 6 : " Siquis a diabolo deceptus
crediderit secundum morem Paganorum, uirum aliquem aut
feminam Strigem esse, et homines comedere, et propter hoc
ipsum incenderit, uel carnem eius ad comedendum dederit,
uel ipsam comederit, capitis sententia puniatur."

As has been remarked the earliest known representation of
a vampire shows her in the act of copulation with a man and
we have just observed that Weyer regards the Hebrew Lilith

as queen of the Succubi, The connexion here is very plain, for Martin Delrio, 5, 7, in his *Disquisitionum Magicarum Libri Sex*, I, 178, (Louvain, 1599), definitely states : " Axioma I sit, solent Malefici et Lamiae cum daemonibus, illi quidem succubis, hae uero incubis, actum Uenerium exercere. . . . Axioma II potest etiam ex huiusmodi concubitu daemonis incubi proles nasci." Michael Psellus (Μιχαὴλ ὁ Ψελλός), the famous Byzantine scholar of the tenth century, in his treatise, *De Operatione daemonum dialogus* (graece et latine cum notis Gaulmini, Paris, 1615), says that a monk of Mesopotamia, named Marcus, informed him that demons here capable of sensual passions, " Quemadmodum et sperma nonnulli eorum emittunt et uermes quosdam spermate procreant. At incredibile est, inquam, excrementi quicquam daemonibus inesse, uasaue spermatica et uitalia. Uasa quidem eis, inquit ille, huiusmodi nulla insunt, superflui autem seu excrementi nescio quid emittunt hoc mihi asserenti credito." The learned authors of the *Malleus Maleficarum* discuss, " Whether Children can be Generated by Incubi and Succubi " (Part I, Question iii), and " By which Devils are the Functions of Incubus and Succubus Practised " (Part I, Question iv). Appeal is made to the authority of S. Augustine, who, *De Trinitate*, III, says " That devils do indeed collect human semen, by means of which they are able to produce bodily effects : but this cannot be done without some local movement, therefore demons can transfer the semen which they have collected and inject it into the bodies of others." Moreover, Sprenger and Kramer inquire : " Is it Catholic to affirm that the functions of Incubi and Succubi belong indifferently and equally to all unclean spirits ? " They reply : " *It seems* that it is so ; for to affirm the opposite would be to maintain that there is some good order among them." Now the vampire is certainly an unclean spirit, whether it be that the body is animated by some demon, or whether it be the man himself who is permitted to enter his corpse and energize it and accordingly it is Catholic to believe that a vampire can copulate with human beings. Nor are there lacking instances of this. We have the well-known history related by Phlegon of Tralles where Machates enjoys Philinnion, who has returned (albeit he knows it not) from her tomb ; and in modern Greece it is quite commonly held that the *vrykolakas* will revisit his widow and know her, or he even seduces other women whilst their husbands are away, or what is more striking still he will betake himself to some town where he is not recognized, and he will even wed, children being born of such unions. Mr. Lawson (*Modern Greek Folklore*) informs us that in Thessaly he was actually told of a family in the neighbourhood of Domoko, who reckoned a *vrykolakas* among their ancestors of some two or three generations ago, and by virtue of such lineage they inherited a certain skill which enables them to deal most efficaciously with the *vrykolakas* who at intervals haunt the country-side, indeed so widely was their power esteemed that they had been on occasion summoned as specialists for consultation when quite remote districts were troubled in this manner.

Alardus Gazaeus in his *Commentary* on Cassian's *Collationes*, VIII, 21, (Migne, *Patrologia Latina*, xlix) plainly teaches: " Devils, although incorporeal and spiritual, can take to themselves the bodies of dead men, and in such bodies can copulate with women, as commonly with *striges* and witches, and by such intercourse can even beget children." The Strix we have just considered, and in the passage quoted from Gazaeus it would not, I think, be far amiss simply to translate *striges* as "vampires." If it be asked how an incubus or succubus, or a vampire, can fornicate with human beings we may refer to the famous treatise by the learned Ludovico Maria Sinistrari, the *De Daemonialitate* where that great Franciscan theologian has in detail discussed and admirably resolved these difficulties.

It has been said that "there is no trace of vampires in Jewish literature," but this would not appear to be strictly accurate for, *Proverbs* xxx, 15, we have: " Sanguisugae duae sunt filiae, dicentes: Affer, Affer." The *LXX* has βδέλλη for the equivalent of the Hebrew עֲלוּקָה which the Vulgate renders *sanguisuga*. *Douay* translates: " The horseleach hath two daughters that say: Bring, bring." The *Authorised Version* renders: " The horse-leach hath two daughters, *crying*: Give, give." The *Revised Version* prefers: " The horseleach hath two daughters, *crying*, Give, give." There are marginal notes, upon horseleach, " Or, *vampire*." Upon crying ; " Or, called." This sanguisuga is probably a vampire or blood-sucking demon, and thus the passage is explained by

Mühlau, *De Prouerbiis Aguri et Lemuelis* (42 sqq.), Leipzig, 1849 ; and Wellhausen, *Reste arabische Heiderstums*, p. 149 ; (2te Auflage), Berlin, 1897.

In ancient Egypt we can trace certain parallels to the Assyrian beliefs, for the ancient Egyptians held that every man had his *ka*, his double, which when he died lived in the tomb with the body and was there visited by the *khu*, the spiritual body or soul which at death departed from the body, and although it might visit the body, could only be brought back from its habitation in heaven by the ceremonial performance of certain mystic rites. Yet from one point of view the soul was sufficiently material to partake of the funeral offerings which were brought to the tomb for the refreshment of the *ka*. One of the chief objects of these sepulchral oblations was to maintain the double in the tomb so that it should not be compelled to wander abroad in search of food. But, as in Assyria, unless the *ka* were bountifully supplied with food it would issue forth from the tomb and be driven to eat any offal or drink any brackish water it might find. The *ka* occupied a special part of the tomb, " the house of the *ka*," and a priest called " the priest of the *ka* " was appointed specially to minister to it therein. The *ka* snuffed up the sweet smell of incense which was very agreeable to it when this was burned on certain days each year with the offerings of flowers, herbs, meat and drink in all of which it took great delight. The *ka* also viewed with pleasure the various scenes which were sculptured or richly painted on the walls of the tomb. In fact it was not merely capable, but desirous of material consolations. It would appear even that in later times the *khu* was identified with the *ka*.

In Arabic the word for horse-leach is عَلَق , while مَوَلَّق , formed from the same root " to hang," means the kind of Jinn called Ghoul (غُول). The Ghoul appears as a female-demon who feeds upon dead bodies and infests the cemeteries at night to dig open the grave for her horrid repasts. Sometimes she would seem to be a woman, half-human, half-fiend, for in story she is often represented as wedded to a husband who discovers her loathsome necrophagy. She can bear children, and is represented as luring travellers out of the way to lonely and remote ruins where she falls upon them suddenly and devours them, greedily sucking the warm blood from their veins. The Ghoul is familiar from *The Thousand and One Nights* as is the story of the Prince who having pursued a strange beast whilst hunting was carried to a great distance, and chanced to see by the wayside a lovely maiden who sat and wept. She told him that she was the daughter of an Indian king who had been lost in this desert spot by her caravan. The chivalrous youth takes her upon his horse, and a little later pleading a certain necessity she descends—latrines are particularly considered to be haunts of evil spirits and malignant entities, and Jean de Thévenot in his *Travels into the Levant* ("Newly done out of French, folio, London, 1687), says : "*The Kerim Kiatib*, merciful scribes wait upon him [the Turk] in all places, except when he does his needs, when they let him go alone, staying for him at the door till he comes out, and then they take him into possession again ; wherefore when the Turks go to the house of office they put the left foot foremost, to the end the Angel who registers their sins may leave them first ; and when they come out they set the right foot before, that the Angel who writes down their good works may have them first under his protection."

The young man hears voices in the haunted latrine, the feigned Indian lady cries : "Children, to-day I have brought you a fat and comely juvenal." And several answer : "Bring him along, Mother, bring him along for our bellies cry for food." At these words he trembled exceedingly for he saw he had to do with a ghoul and when she returned he lifted up his voice in prayer : "O thou who art ever ready to hearken to the oppressed who calls upon Thee and Who dost unveil all deceit, grant me to triumph over mine enemy, and keep all evil far from me, for Thou canst all that Thou dost desire." When the ghoul heard these words she vanished from sight, and the prince is able to make his way back home. (The Fifth Night. *Les Mille Nuits et Une Nuit.* trs. Dr. J. C. Mardrus, Vol. I, 1899, pp. 57-59, "Histoire du Prince et de la Goule.")

In the story of Sidi Nouman a young man marries a wife named Amine, who to his surprise when they are set at dinner only eats a dish of rice grain by grain, taking up each single grain with a bodkin, and "instead of partaking of the other dishes she only carried to her mouth, in the most deliberate manner, small crumbs of bread, scarcely enough to satisfy

HUNGER, MADNESS AND CRIME

(From the Musée Wiertz)

PLATE VI

[see p. 232]

PLATE VII

MALAY VAMPIRES

(From *Skeat's Malay Magic*)
(*By permission of Messrs. Macmillan & Co., Ltd.*)

[see p. 254

a sparrow. The husband discovers that Amine steals out at nights and on one occasion he follows her. Sidi Nouman is relating these adventures to the Caliph Haroun Alraschid and he continues: "I saw her go into a burying place near our house; I then gained the end of a wall, which reached the burying place, and after having taken proper care not to be seen, I perceived Amine with a female Ghoul. Your Majesty know that Ghouls of either sex are demons, which wander about the fields. They commonly inhabit ruinous buildings, whence they issue suddenly and surprise passengers, whom they kill and devour. If they fail in meeting with travellers, they go by night into burying places, to dig up dead bodies, and feed upon them. I was both surprised and terrified, when I saw my wife with this Ghoul. They dug up together a dead body, which had been buried that very day, and the Ghoul several times cut off pieces of the flesh, which they both ate, as they sat upon the edge of the grave. They conversed together with great composure, during their savage and inhuman repast; but I was so far off that it was impossible for me to hear what they said, which, no doubt, was as extraordinary as their food, at the recollection of which I still shudder. When they had finished their horrid meal, they threw the remains of the carcase into the grave, which they filled again with the earth they had taken from it." (*Arabian Nights Entertainments*, translated by the Rev. Edward Forster. New Edition. London, 1850, p. 399.)

When they are next at dinner Sidi Nouman remonstrating with his wife asks if the dishes before them are not as palatable as the flesh of a dead man. In a fury she dashes a cup of cold water into his face and bids him assume the form of a dog. After various adventures as a mongrel cur, he is restored to his original shape by a young maiden skilled in white magic, and this lady also provides him with a liquid which when thrown upon Amine with the words: "Receive the punishment of thy wickedness" transforms this dark sorceress into a mare. This animal is promptly led away to the stable.

This tale is not dissimilar to a history which is related by the Dominican, Mathias de Giraldo, who was an exorcist of the Inquisition, in his *Histoire curieuse et pittoresque des sorciers, devins, magiciens, astrologues, voyants, revenants âmes en peine, vampires, spectres, esprits malins, sorts jetes exorcismes, etc., depuis l'Antiquité jusqu'à nos jours.* (Ed. Fornari Paris, 1846.)

It may be taken as an example of many Oriental fictions which are significant since they show the popular belief in vampires. About the beginning of the fifteenth century there lived in a pleasant suburb of Bagdad an elderly merchant who by his diligence throughout the years amassed a very considerable fortune, and who had no heir to his wealth save a son whom he tenderly loved. Wishing to see the young man happily married, he decided that he would arrange a match with the daughter of another merchant, a friend of old standing, who like himself had prospered exceedingly in commerce. Unfortunately the lady was far from comely, and upon being shown her portrait the youth, Abdul-Hassan by name, asked for a certain delay that he might consider the proposed union.

One evening when, according to his wont, he was rambling alone in the light of the moon through the country near his father's house, he heard a voice of enchanting sweetness which rendered with great skill and tenderness certain love lyrics to the accompaniment of a lute. The youth, leaping a garden wall, found that the singer was a maiden of extraordinary beauty, who was seated in the balcony of a small but elegant house and who, unconscious of her audience, continued to fascinate him by her enchanting voice almost as much as by her dazzling charms. On the following morning, after his devotions, Abdul-Hassan proceeded to make inquiries concerning the lady. But so retired a life did she lead that it was not for some while he was able to ascertain that she was unmarried and the only daughter of a philosopher, whose learning was said to be of the most profound, although he could bestow scant dowry upon his child, a paragon instructed in every art and science. From this moment the marriage which had been suggested became impossible to the young man, and realizing that concealment would be useless he boldly approached his father, confessed his love and besought that he might be allowed to choose his own wife. As until that time he had in every way obeyed his doting parent and the father found it impossible to deny a first request in so important a particular. Accordingly he determined to put

no obstacle in the way of his son's happiness, and paying a
visit to the house of the philosopher he formally demanded for
his son the hand of this sage's daughter. After a brief courtship the marriage was celebrated with much splendour,
and several weeks passed in an extreme of happiness. Abdul-
Hassan presently noted that his wife, Nadilla, would never
partake of an evening meal, for which singularity she excused
herself on account of the somewhat frugal and severe regimen
she had always followed under her father's roof. One night,
however, after but a few weeks had passed, Abdul-Hassan,
awakening from a deep sleep found that he was alone in the bed.
At first he took no heed, but he grew anxious as the hours
wore away, and his bride did not return until shortly before
dawn. Resolved to fathom the mystery he still feigned to be
fast in slumber, but on the following night when he had
pretended to close his eyes he carefully watched the actions
of his wife. After a little while, no sooner did she deem herself
unobserved than throwing over her a long dark cloak she
silently slipped away. He rose, hastily dressed himself,
and followed her at some little distance. To his surprise
she soon left the main streets of the town and made her way
to a remote cemetery which had a very ill repute as being
darkly haunted. Tracking her very carefully he perceived
that she entered a large vault, into which with the utmost
caution he ventured to steal a glance. It was dimly lighted
by three funerary lamps, and what was his horror to behold
his young and beautiful wife seated with a party of hideous
ghouls, about to partake of their loathsome feast. One of
these monsters brought in a corpse which had been buried that
day, and which was quickly torn to pieces by the company,
who devoured the reeking gobbets with every evidence of
satisfaction, recreating themselves meanwhile with mutual
embraces and the drone of a mocking dirge. Fearing that he
might be caught and even destroyed, as soon as possible the
youth escaped back to his home, and when his wife returned
he appeared deep in unbroken sleep until the morning.
Throughout the whole of that day he gave no sign of what he
had discovered, but in the evening as Nadilla was excusing
herself from joining him at supper, according to her custom,
he insisted that she should eat with him. None the less
she steadfastly declined, and at last filled with anger and

disgust he cried : " So then you prefer to keep your appetite for your supper with the ghouls." Nadilla turned pale, her eyes blazed, and she shook with fury, but she vouchsafed no reply and retired in silence. However, about midnight when she thought that her husband was fast asleep she exclaimed : " Now wretch receive the punishment for thy curiosity." At the same time she set her knee firmly on his chest, seized him by the throat, with her sharp nails tore open a vein and began greedily to suck his blood. Slipping from beneath her he sprung to his feet, and dealt her a blow with a sharp poniard wherewith he had been careful to arm himself, so that she sank down dying at the side of the bed. He called for help, the wound in his throat was dressed and on the following day the remains of this vampire were duly interred.

However, three nights afterwards, although the doors were locked, Nadilla appeared exactly at twelve o'clock in her husband's room and attacked him with superhuman strength and ferocity, tearing at his throat. His weapon proved useless now and the one chance of safety lay in speedy flight. On the following day they caused her tomb to be opened, and the body was discovered apparently asleep since it seemed to breathe, the eyes were open and glared horribly, the lips were blub and red, but the whole grave was swimming in newly-spilled blood. After this they repaired to the house of the old philosopher and he, when pressed revealed a most remarkable history. He said that his daughter, who, as he suspected, had devoted herself to the study of black magic, had been married some few years previously to an officer of high rank at the court of the Caliph. She forthwith, however, gave herself over to the most abominable debauchery and had been killed by her outraged husband, but coming to life again in the grave she returned to her father's house and dwelt there. Upon hearing this tale it was determined that the body must be exhumed and cremated. A great pyre of dry wood was built with frankincense, aloes, and costly spices, the corpse, writhing and foaming at the mouth, was placed thereon and reduced to ashes, which were collected and scattered in the Tigris to be borne away and dispersed amid the waves of the Persian Sea.

This is an extremely typical legend of an Oriental vampire, and we find the same details repeated again and again both in Eastern stories, and in those imitations which were so popular throughout Europe when once Antoine Galland had given France his adaptation of *The Arabian Nights*. Thus in *Les Contes Orientaux* of the Comte de Caylus, which are related to a King of Persia, afflicted with insomnia, in order to lull him to sleep, there is the story of a vampire who is only able to prolong this existence by devouring from time to time the heart of a comely young man. It would not be difficult to quote similar fictions but they are often derived at second, or even third hand, and accordingly are of little evidential value merely being devised for the entertainment of the reader.

Throughout the ancient Empire of China and from the earliest times the belief in vampires is very widely spread, and sinologists have collected many examples, some of which occur in myth and legend and some of which were related as facts, showing us that the Chinese Vampire lacks few, if any of the horrible traits he exhibits in Greek and Slavonic superstition.[19]

The Chinese Vampire, Ch'ing Shih, is regarded as a demon who by taking possession of a dead body preserves it from corruption owing to his power of preying upon other corpses or upon the living. The Chinese believe that a man has two souls : the *Hun*, or superior soul, which partakes of the quality of good spirits ; and the *P'o*, or inferior soul which is generally malignant and may be classed among the Kuei, or evil spirits. It is thought that whilst any portion of a body, even if it be a small bone, remained whole and entire the lower soul can ulilize this to become a vampire, and particularly should the sun or the moon be allowed to shine fully upon an unburied body the P'o will thence acquire strength to issue forth and obtain human blood to build up the vitality of the vampire. The belief,—which has some natural foundation,—that the sun can convey strength and vitality, is to be found, in one form or another, in very many lands.

Thus among the Chacu Indians of South America a newly married couple must sleep the first night on a mare's or bullock's skin with their heads towards the west, for the marriage was not fully ratified, nor would the wife conceive until the rays of the sun had touched their feet the following morn.[20] During the Impregnation-rite (*Garbhādhāna*) which was a part of old

Hindoo marriages, the bride was required to look towards the sun or to be exposed to its rays so that she might become fruitful, and bear her husband stout boys.[21] In parts of Siberia it was the custom for a young couple to be led forth with some ceremony and rejoicing on the morning after the nuptials to greet the sun and bask in his rays. This is still observed in Iran and Central Asia where it is believed that the clear beams of the sun will impregnate the bride.[22]

There is an old myth amongst the Indians of Guacheta that the daughter of a certain chief having climbed a hill top when she was touched by the first rays of the sun conceived and gave birth to an emerald, which in a day or two became a child who grew to be a mighty hero, Garanchacha, the Son of the Sun.[23] In Samoan legend a damsel named Manga-mangai finds herself pregnant through gazing at the Sun at dawn, and bears a male baby, the Child of the Sun.[24]

The Phrygians thought of the Moon as a Man,[25] and the same idea prevails or formerly prevailed among the Green-landers who imagined that the Moon was a brisk youth and he " now and then comes down to give their wives a visit and caress them ; for which reason no woman dare sleep lying upon her back without she first spits upon her fingers and rubs her belly with it. For the same reason the young maids are afraid to stare long at the moon, imagining they may get a child by the bargain."[26] It is said that in some parts of Brittany it was once supposed by the peasants that a girl who exposed herself naked in the moonlight might find herself pregnant by it and give birth to a monster.[27] In England the same belief existed, and the old term "moon-calf," *partus lunaris*, signified a false conception—*mola carnea*, or foetus imperfectly formed, being supposed to be occasioned by the influence of the moon.[28]

In appearance the Chinese monster is very like the European vampire, for he has red staring eyes, huge sharp talons or crooked nails, but he is also often represented as having his body covered with white or greenish white hair. In his standard work on *The Religious System of China*, Dr. de Groot suggests that this last characteristic may be due to the fungi which grow so profusely on the cotton grave-clothes used by the Chinese. In some cases, if he be particularly potent for ill, the Vampire is able to fly with speed through the air, which may be compared with the faculty ascribed to vampires by Serbian legend, that of penetrating a house or vanishing away in a swiftly floating mist or vapour.

A few anecdotes, which I owe to Mr. G. Willoughby-Meade's *Chinese Ghouls and Goblins*,[29] will show the close similarity of vampirish activities in China to those which are recorded in the tales of other lands. In the South-West of China a man added to his other villainies the study of black magic which enabled him to perpetrate the most abominable crimes. Having been caught in the very act of murder he was executed but within three days he had returned to earth and was terrorizing the whole neighbourhood. With infinite difficulty he was yet again made a prisoner, and this time he was drowned in a mighty river, which, it was hoped, would bear his body away on its foaming stream. Yet the third day had hardly come when it was reported that he was scouring the country-side and committing fresh deeds of violence and blood. Once more was he taken and put to death, only to re-appear and infest both hamlets and villages. At last when he had been seized and his head struck from his body, this was buried on the spot where he had fallen, whilst the severed head was conveyed to a great distance. Within forty-eight hours he was again seen, apparently as powerful and savage as ever, but it was noted that his neck was marked around by a thin streak of red. At last his mother, whom he had beaten, resorted to a mandarin of great honour and worship and gave him a mysterious vase, which was hermetically sealed. She explained that she had reason to believe that this through enchantment contained the superior soul of her son, whilst the inferior soul continued to animate and would persist in re-energizing his body, influencing him to commit these atrocities. "If you but break this little vase," said she, "you can dissipate both souls, and then you may execute him once and for all." The vessel, tied fast and painted with cabalistic signs, was forthwith shattered into a thousand pieces. The offender was caught with far less difficulty than had been supposed possible, he was put to death, and in a few days the body crumbled to dust, nor did he ever again re-visit the earth.

Although this story may be held strictly not to be a Vampire legend it is certainly closely analogous, and the following

narrative contains details which we meet in a thousand traditions of Hungary and Moldavia. A tutor named Liu, who
was resident in a family that lived at some distance from his
native place, was granted a holiday in order that he might
perform his devotions at the tomb of his ancestors. On the
morning when he was to resume his duties his wife entered his
chamber very early to call him so that he might set forth in
good time on his journey, but to her horror when she approached
the bed she saw stretched thereon a headless body, although
there was no spot or stain of blood. Half mad with fear she
at once gave the alarm, yet the circumstances were so surprising that the Magistrate gave orders for her arrest upon the
suspicion of having murdered her husband, and in spite of the
fact that she vehemently protested her innocence she was
detained in custody until the fullest inquiries had been made.
However, nothing immediately transpired to throw light
upon the mystery, and it was not until two or three days later
that a neighbour who was gathering firewood on a hillside
hard by perceived a great coffin with the lid partly raised,
that seemed to have been curiously placed near an old and
neglected grave. His utmost apprehensions being aroused
he called a number of persons together from the village before
he dared investigate the cause of this unusual circumstance.
They approached the coffin and quickly removed the cover.
Within reposed a corpse which had the face of a living man,
unspeakably brutish and horrible. Its angry red eyes glared
fiercely upon them, long white teeth champed the full red lips
into a foam of blood and spittle, and within its lean bony hands,
armed with long nails like the claws of a vulture it held the
missing head of the unfortunate Liu. Some at once ran to
the authorities, who upon hearing the report hastened to the
hill with an armed guard, reaching the place well before
sunset. It was found impossible to detach the head without
severing the arms of the corpse, and when this was done
the crimson gore gushed out in a great flood swilling the
coffin. The head of Liu was found to be desiccated, sucked
dry, and bloodless. Command was forthwith given that the
coffin and its contents should at once be burned to ashes on
a mighty pyre, whilst the tutor's widow was immediately
released from custody.

Another story, which for its macabre details might have

come from the pages of Apuleius and indeed something reminds us of the adventures of Aristomenes in the hostelry at Hypata, is that of four travellers who, late one night, when very weary and almost fainting for want of food, knocked at the door of an inn at Ts'ai Tien, Shan Tung. There was no accommodation to be had, every room was full, the place was crowded from cock-loft to cellar. However, our travellers were so wayworn that they refused to budge, and they pressed Boniface to find them at least some nook or corner, they were not nice and they did not mind what or where. At last after being persuaded with many words and well-nigh as many coins he very reluctantly led them to a lonely house at a little distance where, so he curtly muttered, his daughter-in-law had recently died. The room was only lighted by the flicker of one poor lamp which was all he could allow them and behind a heavy curtain was laid the uncoffined body of the girl. Four pallets, not altogether uncomfortable, with blankets and a rug or two had been provided, and in a very few minutes three of the travellers were fast asleep. A strange sense of evil seemed to oppress the fourth, and in spite of his fatigue fear prevented him from shutting his eyes for some little while. Yet the leaden weight that lay heavy on his lids could not be resisted long and he had already fallen into a doze when he heard what seemed to be an ominous rustling sound behind the curtain as though somebody was stirring very softly. Cold with horror, he peered out from half-closed eyes and he distinctly saw a horrible stealthy hand thrust itself from behind the curtain which was noiselessly drawn aside. There stood the livid corpse gazing into the room with a baleful glare. It approached softly and stooping over the three sleepers seemed to breathe thence upon their faces. The man who was awake horror-struck buried his head under the quilt. He felt that the corpse was bending over him, but after a few moments as he lay in an agony of terror there was the same gentle rustle as before, and anon cautiously peeping he noticed that it had returned to its bier and was stretched out stark and still.

He crept from his place and not daring to whisper shook each one of his comrades, but could not make them move. He then reached for his clothes, but the gentle rustling sounded once more and he realized that he had been observed.

In a moment he flung himself back on the bed and drew the coverlet tightly over his face. A few moments later, he felt that the awful creature was standing by his side. However, after a scrutiny it seemed to retire again, and at length half-mad with fright he put out his hand, grasped some clothes which he huddled on and rushed bare-foot from the house, the door of which he was able to bolt and bar just as the corpse leaped at him with demoniacal fury. As he ran at full speed under the light of a waning moon to put as great a distance between himself and the haunted house as possible, he chanced to glance back and shrieked aloud with fear to find that the corpse was not only hard at his heels but gaining upon him rapidly. In desperation he fled behind a large willow-tree which grew at the side of the road, and as the corpse rushed in one direction he darted rapidly in the other. Fire seemed to glint from its red eyes, and as it swooped upon him with hideous violence he fell senseless to the ground, so that missing its aim it clasped the tree in a rigid gripe. At daybreak they were found, and when the corpse was pulled away it was seen that its fingers had impaled and riddled the tree with the force of a sharp wimble. The traveller after many months recovered his health, but his companions were all found to be lying dead, poisoned by the fetid breath of the Vampire. It should be remarked that here we have a detail, repulsive enough but altogether in keeping, which we also find in Hungary, namely the carrion stink of a vampire's breath. This certainly seems to be one of the most horrible, as it is one of the most significant stories in the whole library of Chinese vampire legend.

It hardly seems necessary to give in detail the history of Lu, who whilst watching one night in his orchard saw a terrible spectre, a hideous hag clothed in red. (It may be remarked that among certain tribes, such as the Borâna Gallas and the Masai, warriors who have slain a foe in fight are painted with vermilion,[30] but it is curious to find that in China this evil apparition should have worn red since this is the lucky Yang, or solar colour, and considered to be of efficacy against the darker powers.) A thief who entered Lu's garden to rob the fruit was discovered mad with terror since in one of the alleys he had encountered a man without a head. That part of the ground whence these phantoms seemed to spring was dug up, and they soon came across a red coffin containing the body of a woman, together with a black coffin in which was the corpse of a man who had been decapitated. Both bodies were as perfectly preserved as though they had been buried that very day. The coffins and bodies were burned to ashes, whereupon the hauntings ceased.

This story might be paralleled from ghost tales the whole wide world over, but the following seems more particularly to belong to the Vampire legends. In the year 1751, a courier called Chang Kuei was sent express from Peking with a most urgent government dispatch. Late one night after he had passed through Liang Hsiang a fierce storm arose, and the gusts of wind completely extinguished his lantern. Fortunately he perceived at some little distance a humble khan whither he made his way as it was absolutely impossible to proceed in the darkness. The door was opened by a young girl who ushered him in and led his horse to a little stable. That night she admitted him to her bed promising to set him well on his way at dawn, but he did not wake in fact until many hours after, when he was not only benumbed with cold but to his surprise found himself lying stretched upon a tomb in a dense thicket, while his horse was tied to a neighbouring tree. His dispatch was not delivered until twelve hours after the time when it was due, and accordingly, being questioned and asked what accident had delayed him, he related the whole circumstance. The magistrate ordered that inquiries should be made locally, and they discovered that a girl, named Chang, a common strumpet, had hanged herself in the wood some years before, and that several persons had been led aside to enjoy her favours, and so been detained in the same way as the imperial courier. It was presently ordered that her tomb should be opened, and when this had been done the body was found therein perfectly preserved, plump and of a rosy complexion, as though she were but in a soft slumber. It was burned under the direction of the authorities, and from that time the spot ceased to be so terribly haunted.

These particulars are in some respects not altogether unlike a legend which is related of a certain S. Hilary,[31] who was one of the earliest missionaries in the Alpine districts of North Italy. The story goes that after they had journeyed for many days into the heart of a most desolate country they came one eve of S. John[32] to a remote village of some size as it appeared where the people were holding a midsummer festival, but with strange pagan rites. Here at eventide they were greeted by a grave man saluting them most courteously and saying that he was the steward of the Lady Pelagia, who wished to give them entertainment in her palace. The missionaries, grateful of this kindness, were received with gracious welcome, and the mistress of the house, a patrician who was of the most surpassing beauty, led them to a banquet which had been made ready. Here Hilary sat beside her and she talked of many things, so that the good Bishop was moved with a great tenderness at her youth and her beauty. She thanked them in all humility for the honour they had done her villa, pressed them to sojourn long as her guests, and asked them many questions which the learned man was delighted to answer, whilst his companions sat as it were spell-bound by her charms. Presently, however, the conversation took a deeper turn and the lady poised shrewd problems in science and in theology, difficulties which S. Hilary was well-nigh hard put to it to solve neatly and in simple words. Yet she spake with such modesty and with such an air of seeking to know more of divine things that the holy Hilary was glad to expound these matters, albeit he thought the argument savoured somewhat of sophistry and wordy skill. At length she said in honeyed phrase, " I pray thee, good father, rede me this question aright : What is the distance between heaven and earth ? " The Saint gazed in some wonder, when suddenly a voice, menacing and loud, was heard to thunder through the hall : " Who can tell us that more certainly than Lucifer who fell from heaven ? " The Lady Pelagia arose and flung up her lovely white arms with an exceeding bitter cry, but the voice continued : " Breathe on her, Hilary, breathe upon her the breath of the Name of Christ ! " And the Bishop, rising, fortified himself with the sign of redemption and breathed upon the beautiful woman in the name of the Lord. Instantly the light died from her eyes and the life left her limbs, and there was no longer the Lady Pelagia but a statue of marble which glistened exceeding white and fair. And Hilary knew it to be a statue of the goddess whom men worshipped in Greece as Aphrodite, but in Rome as Venus, who is also Pelagia, born of the sea. At that moment the statue fell prone in a thousand pieces, the lamps were extinguished, and they saw in the east the grey of dawn. As the sun rose they beheld they were in the midst of the ruins of an ancient Roman city, and their feet stood in the courts of a marble temple, broken and decayed, o'ergrown with high grass and rankest weeds. This had been the fair hall where they feasted,[33] and all around were scattered the fragments of the statue of the Lady Pelagia. So they bent the knee in prayer and in thanksgiving that they had been delivered from the wiles of the Temptress, and anon they passed on their way lauding Christ in sweet hymns and melody of many canticles.

A Chinese story which is referred to the eighteenth century tells us of a Tartar family living at Peking, a house of the highest importance, whose son was betrothed to a lady of lineage equally aristocratic and equally ancient. Upon the wedding day, as is the Chinese custom, the bride was brought home in the ceremonial sedan-chair and this according to wont was carefully curtained and closed. It so happened that just as they were passing an old tomb there sprung up for a moment a sharp breeze which raised a cloud of thickest dust. When the *cortège* reached the bridegroom's house there stepped out of the sedan two brides identical in every detail both of feature and dress. It was impossible at that point to interrupt the nuptials, but later in the evening the most piercing screams were heard from the bridal chamber. When the door of the room had been quickly broken open the husband was stretched unconscious on the ground, while one of the brides lay with her eyes torn out and her face covered with blood. No trace of the second bride could be seen. But upon search being made with lanterns and torches a huge and hideous bird, mottled black and grey, armed with formidable claws and a beak like a vulture was discovered clinging to a beam of the roof. Before they could fetch weapons to attack it, the monstrous thing disappeared with exceeding swiftness through the door. When the husband recovered his senses he related that one of the brides had suddenly struck him across the face with her heavily embroidered sleeve and that the jewels and passementerie stunned him for the moment. A second afterwards a huge bird swooped upon him and pecked out his eyes with its beak. So this horrible Vampire blinded the newly married pair. The circumstance of the dust-cloud is exactly similar to the mist wherein the Slavonic Vampire conveys himself, but the transformation of the Vampire into a bird is scarcely to be met with in European tradition. Crows, rooks, and ravens may sometimes vaguely held to be unlucky, but they are generally associated with weather-lore, although Justus Doolittle in his *Social Life of the Chinese*[34] says that the appearance of a crow at a wedding in China was always considered most ominous. In various parts of England, particularly in Essex, to see a crow flying alone, or if a crow flies towards you, it is considered a sign of bad luck. In Worcestershire they say that : " When a single crow flies over you, it is the sign of a funeral ; two are a certain prognostication of a wedding."[35] The old saw is well-known with reference to crows :[36]

> One's unlucky,
> Two's lucky,
> Three is health,
> Four is wealth,
> Five is sickness,
> Six is death.

The raven was often held to denote sickness and death and his croak sounded a knell. So in *The Jew of Malta*, Marlowe has :

> Let the sad presaging raven that tells
> The sick man's passport in her hollow beak,
> And in the shadow of the silent night
> Doth shake contagion from her sable wings.[37]

On the other hand rooks are far more lucky. In East Anglia, and indeed in many other parts of England, it bodes good fortune if rooks settle near a house,[38] for this bird always begins to build on a Sunday, and when rooks desert a rookery, it foretells the downfall of the family owning the property ;[39] in some counties even they are said as a sign of grief to abandon their nests at the approach of death to the head of the family, and not to return to the ancestral domain until after the funeral at soonest. An actual instance was given of this occurrence as having happened in 1874, on the death of Sir John Walsham, at his seat, Knill Court, in Herefordshire.[40] In Cornwall rooks are believed to forsake an estate if on the death of the proprietor no heir can be found to succeed him.

So it will be seen that a black bird need by no means invariably be of ill-omen. Propertius speaks of the crow as "innocent" (*cornix immerita*). In his denunciation of the bawd and witch Acanthis [41] he mentions that the eyes of the crow were often used to confect a magical charm.

> Posset ut intentos astu caecare maritos,
> Cornicum immeritas eruit ungue genas,
> Consuluitque stryges nostro de sanguine, et in me
> Hippomanes foetae semina legit equae.

This passage is to be taken literally, although no doubt there is also an allusion to the proverb *cornicum oculos configere* "to delude or deceive the most wary," as we say "to catch a weasel asleep," which no doubt arose from its custom of attacking prey first in the eyes. Beroaldus and Passerat would explain the allusion of Propertius metaphorically, but this is only a secondary allusion.

There is related a curious story of a Chinese temple which was haunted by a Vampire. This fane was dedicated to three heroes of the third century A.D., who had been deified on account of their prowess during the civil wars of that most troubled period. It seems that the place was always kept locked except on the great solemnities of the spring and autumn sacrifices, and not even a priest would venture to sleep there. In the year 1741 a shepherd asked and obtained permission to spend his nights in the shelter of the temple. Many people told him that it was terribly haunted, but nobody seemed exactly to know in what manner. Accordingly taking his big leather whip and having provided himself with a lantern, after he had collected his flock at evening he entered and proceeded to settle for the night. However, when all was darkest and most still it seemed that something stirred near the three statues. On a sudden there rose up out of the ground near the pedestal a very tall man of hideous aspect, gaunt and lean, his body covered with matted green hair. His glowing eyes seemed to flash fire when he caught sight of the intruder, and darting forth a claw-like hand armed with the nails of a bird of prey he almost succeeded in seizing the shepherd, who leapt nimbly to one side and lashed out with his heavy whip. The spectre, however, grinned hideously showing rows of shark-like teeth and the heavy leather fell harmlessly upon him. Rushing to the door the shepherd was just in time to evade a second clutch. Hardly knowing what he did he clambered up a large tree in the courtyard, and looking down he saw that the horrible figure was standing in the doorway glowering with rage, but did not appear able to advance beyond the threshold. All night the poor wretch clung there, and as the day broke the spectre vanished into the recesses of the building. It was early when various persons came to inquire how the bold man had fared, and finding him half distraught with terror they soon learned what had happened during the night. The next proceeding was to examine the base of the statute, and when this had been cautiously done it was remarked that a curious black vapour rose from the ancient fissures in the stone. The local authorities investigated these circumstances, and gave instructions that the pedestal should be broken down to discover what was lurking beneath it. After digging a little depth they found the body of a tall man of most hideous appearance, fetid and desiccated, covered with a green pile, just as the shepherd had described. The magistrates immediately commanded that a pyre should be built. The corpse was set thereon, and torches applied at every corner. The Vampire writhed and whistled with a screeching sound; blood poured from it in streams, and the bones crackled sharply. Once the body had been consumed, the hauntings entirely ceased but it was long before the temple lost its sombre reputation.[42]

It will be seen that the Chinese beliefs are linked with the Babylonian ideas on the one hand, for as the *Ekimmu* was driven from the Underworld by hunger and thirst, when no offerings were made at the tomb, and it came forth to wander on earth and attack those whom it might devour, so ghosts enduring the Buddhist purgatory of physical want are obviously imagined to seize living persons that they may refresh and energize themselves with human blood. Again, as in Western Europe to-day, so in China, the Vampire is most powerful for evil between sunset and sunrise. His dominion commences when the sun sinks to rest, and he is driven back to the lair of his grave with the first rays of the dawn. One prominent feature of the European Vampire, a circumstance which affords an additional reason why he is dreaded and shunned, perhaps even more than any other demon or phantom of the night is that he infects with his pollution his luckless victim who in his turn also becomes a vampire. In China this does not appear to be a feature of the Vampire manifestation. Something of the kind, however, may be traced among the Karens of Burma. For a Karen wizard will snare the wandering soul of a sleeper and by his art transfer it to the body of a dead man. The latter, accordingly, returns to life as the former expires. But the friends of the sleeper in their turn engage another sorcerer who will catch the soul of another sleeper, and it is he who dies as the first sleeper comes to life. Apparently this process may be continued almost indefinitely, and so it may be presumed that there takes place an indeterminate succession of death and resuscitations.

With regard to another Chinese Ghoul, Mr. Willoughby-Meade tells us : " the Prêta, or suffering soul of a suicide seeking a substitute, is not quite a parallel to the true vampire."[43]

The Prêta also appears in Southern India, but the Indian Vampire which may now be briefly considered, however interesting, will hardly be found to have those features in common with the Western Vampires as are so strikingly to be noticed in the Chinese variety. Indeed, it may be said that the Indian Vampire is practically a demon, and that only in a few minor details does he essentially approximate to the true European species. Mr. N. M. Penzer in a note upon *The Ocean of Story* says : " As far as the *Ocean of Story* is concerned, the ' Demons ' which appear are Rakshasa, Pisacha, Vetala, Bhuta, Dasyus, Kumbhanda and Kushmanda. Of these that most resembling the European Vampire is probably the Rakshasa," of which a very horrible description is given.

" Now the Vetala, which is seen in all its glory in the present work (*The Ocean of Story*) is a curious individual. He is the Deccan Guardian, in which capacity he sits on a stone smeared with red paint, or is found in the prehistoric stone circles scattered over the hills. In fiction, however, he appears as a mischievous goblin, and that is how we find him in the *Ocean*. A study of his actions will show him to be quite above the ordinary run of such demons. He is always ready to play some rather grim practical joke on any unwary person who chances to wander near burning-ghats at night, for here are corpses lying about or hanging from stakes, and what more effective means could be formed to frighten the life out of humans than by tenanting a corpse!

"I would describe the Vetala as 'sporting,' in that he has an inate admiration for bravery and is perfectly ready to own himself beaten, and even to help and advise. In the Vetala tales . . . we shall see that as soon as the Vetala discovers the persistence and bravery of Trivikramasena, he at once warns him of the foul intents of the mendicant. We have also seen that even the Rakshasa can become quite tame, and act the part of a kind of Arabian *jinn* who appears on thought. Thus we see that the Vetala of Hindu fiction is by no means an exact counterpart of the blood-sucking vampire of Eastern Europe who never had a good intention or decent thought in his whole career."[44]

In a private letter to myself Mr. Penzer writes : " It is the Rakshasas who are the more prominent among malicious demons. Their name means ' the harmers ' or ' destroyers ' as their particular delight is to upset sacrifices, worry ascetics, animate dead bodies, etc. They date in India from *Rig-Vedic* days.

" In the *Atharva Veda* they are described as deformed, of blue, green, or yellow colour, with long slit eyes. Their nails are poisonous and are dangerous to the touch. They eat human and horse flesh, the former of which they procure by prowling round the burning-ghats at night. They possess great wealth, and bestow it on those they favour. Their chief is Ravana, the enemy of Rama. See Crooke, *Folk-Lore of Northern India*, Vol. I, p. 246 *sqq*.

" The Pisachas are very similar to the above, while the Vetalas are perhaps more like Vampires."

In the Preface to *Vikram and the Vampire*, " Tales of Hindu Devilry " (Adapted by Richard F. Burton), London, 1870, p. xiii, Sir Richard Burton says : " The *Baital-Pachisi*, or *Twenty-five* (tales of a) *Baital*—a vampire or evil spirit which animates dead bodies—is an old and thoroughly Hindu repertory. It is the rude beginning of that fictitious history which ripened to the *Arabian Nights' Entertainments*, and which, fostered by the genius of Boccaccio, produced the romance of the chivalrous days, and its last development, the novel—that prose-epic of modern Europe." *Baital* in Sankrit is *Vetāla-pancha-Vinshati*. " Baital " is the modern

form of " Vetala." When the Raja encounters the Baital it
was hanging " head downwards, from a branch a little above
him. Its eyes which were wide open, were of a greenish-
brown, and never twinkled ; its hair also was brown and
brown was its face—these several shades which, notwithstanding, approached one another in an unpleasant way, as
in an over-dried cocoa-nut. Its body was thin and ribbed
like a skeleton or a bamboo framework, and as it held on to a
bough, like a flying-fox, by the toe-tips, its drawn muscles
stood out as if they were ropes of coir. Blood it appeared
to have none, or there would have been a decided determination of that curious juice to the head ; and as the Raja
handled its skin, it felt icy cold and clammy as might a snake.
The only sign of life was the whisking of a ragged little tail
much resembling a goat's. Judging from these signs the
brave king at once determined the creature to be a Baital—
a Vampire."

A belief in Vampires is very firmly established among the
Malays of the Peninsula, and there are a number of magic
rites which must be performed to protect both women and
children.[45] Probably the spirit most resembling a European
Vampire is the Pĕnanggalan, which is supposed to resemble
a trunkless human head with the sac of the stomach attached
thereto, and which flies about seeking an opportunity of sucking
the blood of infants. There are, however, other spectres which
are dangerous to children. There is the Bajang, which
generally takes the form of a polecat[46] and disturbs the
household by mewing like a huge cat. The Langsuir is seen
as an owl with hideous claws which perches and hoots in a most
melancholy way upon the roof, Her daughter, a still-born
child, is the Pontianak or Madi-anak, who is also a night-owl.
The Polong is a kind of goblin, and the Pĕlĕsit corresponds
most closely to the familiar of the English witches.

The Bajang is generally said to be a male demon and the
Langsuir is considered as the female species. Both of these
spirits are supposed to be a kind of demon-vampire, and are
often handed down in certain families as heirlooms, in exactly
the same way as in English trials we find that the familiar
descended from mother to daughter. Thus at Chelmsford
" at an examination and confession of certaine Wytches,"
26 July, 1566,[47] Elizabeth Francis confessed to various

"vilanies," amongst the rest that "she learned this arte of witchcraft at the age of xii yeres of hyr grandmother whose nam mother Eue of Hatfyelde Peuerell, disseased. Itm when shee taughte it her, she counseiled her in the lykenesse of a whyte spotted Catte." In 1582, during the celebrated St. Osyth prosecutions Ales Hunt confessed that she entertained two familiars, and "saith, that her sister (named Margerie Sammon) hath also two spirites like Toads, the one called Tom, and the other Roddyn : And saith further, her sayde Syster and shee had the sayd spyrites of their Mother, Mother Barnes." That a familiar should have been handed down in this manner seems to have been a well-known custom among the Lapps, for in his notes upon the *De Prodigiis* of Julius Obsequens,[48] J. Scheffer[49] quoting Tornaeus says : "the Laplanders bequeath their Demons as part of their inheritence, which is the reason that one family excells another in this magical art."

With regard to the Bajang, Sir Frank Swettenham further gives the following account : " Some one in the village falls ill of a complaint the symptoms of which are unusual ; there may be convulsions, unconsciousness, or delirium, possibly for some days together or with intervals between the attacks. The relatives will call in a native doctor, and at her (she is usually an ancient female) suggestion, or without it, an impression will arise that the patient is the victim of a *bajang*. Such an impression quickly develops into certainty, and any trifle will suggest the owner of the evil spirit. One method of verifying this suspicion is to wait till the patient is in a state of delirium, and then to question him or her as to who is the author of the trouble. This should be done by some independent person of authority, who is supposed to be able to ascertain the truth.

" A further and convincing proof is [then to call in a ' *Pawang* ' skilled in dealing with wizards (in Malay countries they are usually men), and if he knows his business his power is such that he will place the sorcerer in one room, and, while he in another scrapes an iron vessel with a razor, the culprit's hair will fall off as though the razor had been applied to his head instead of to the vessel ! That is supposing that he *is* the culprit ; if not, of course he will pass through the ordeal without damage.

"I have been assured that the shaving process is so efficacious that, as the vessel represents the head of the person standing his trial, wherever it is scraped the wizard's hair will fall off in a corresponding spot. It might be supposed that under these circumstances the accused is reasonably safe, but this test of guilt is not always employed. What more commonly happens is that when several cases of unexplained sickness have occurred in a village, with possibly one or two deaths, the people of the place lodge a formal complaint against the supposed author of these ills, and desire that he be punished.

"Before the advent of British influence it was the practice to kill the wizard or witch whose guilt had been established to Malay satisfaction, and such executions were carried out not many years ago.

"I remember a case in Perak less than ten years ago, when the people of an up-river village accused a man of keeping a *bajang*, and the present Sultan, who was then the principal Malay judge in the State, told them he would severely punish the *bajang* if they would produce it. They went away hardly satisfied, and shortly after made a united representation to the effect that if the person suspected were allowed to remain in their midst they would kill him. Before anything could be done they put him, his family, and effects on a raft and started them down the river. On their arrival at Kuala Kangsar the man was given an isolated hut to live in, but not long afterwards he disappeared."[50]

The same authority tells us: "*Langsuior*, the female familiar, differs hardly at all from the *bajang*, except that she is a little more baneful, and when under the control of a man he sometimes becomes the victim of her attractions, and she will even bear him elfin children." The original Langsuir, legend says, was a woman of the most superb beauty, who died from the shock of hearing that her child was still-born, and had taken the shape of the Pontianak. When this terrible news was reported to her, she "clapped her hands," and without further warning "flew whinnying away to a tree, upon which she perched." She always wears a robe of exquisite green. Her tapering nails are of extraordinary length, which is considered among the Malays a mark of distinction and beauty, and which may be compared with the talons of the European Vampire. She has long jet black tresses which flow down even as far as her ankles, but these serve to conceal the hole in the back of her neck through which she sucks the blood of children. Yet her vampirish qualities can be destroyed if the right means are adopted, and in order to effect this she must be caught, and her nails and flowing hair cut quite short, the tresses being stuffed into the hole of her neck, in which case she will become quiet and domesticated, just like an ordinary woman, and she will be content to lead a normal life for many years together. Story relates that the Langsuir returned to civilization until she was allowed to dance at a village festival, when for some reason her savage nature re-asserted itself and with wild screams she flew off into the depths of the dark forests from whence she had come. Dr. Skeat says that a Malay peasant once told him how exceedingly fond of fish these women-vampires are, and how not infrequently they may be seen " sitting in crowds on the fishing-stakes at the river mouth awaiting an opportunity to steal the fish." This seems completely to explain the following rune by the recital of which a Langsuir may be laid :

> O ye mosquito-fry at the river's mouth
> When yet a great way off, ye are sharp of eye,
> When near, ye are hard of heart.
> When the rock in the ground opens of itself
> Then (and then only) be emboldened the hearts of my foes
>   and opponents !
> When the corpse in the ground opens of itself
> Then (and then only) be emboldened the hearts of my foes
>   and opponents !
> May your heart be softened when you behold me,
> By grace of this power that I use, called Silam Bayu.

The " mosquito-fry at the river's mouth " is no doubt an allusion to the Langsuir who were swarming round the fishing-stakes, endeavouring to devour the fish.

Sir William Maxwell in the *Journal of the Straits Branch of the Royal Asiatic Society*, Singapore (1878-1899), No. VII, p. 28, thus describes the Langsuir : " If a woman dies in childbirth, either before delivery or after the birth of a child, and before the forty days of uncleanness have expired, she is popularly supposed to become a *langsuyar*, a flying demon of the nature of the 'white lady' or 'banshee.' To prevent this a quantity of glass beads are put in the mouth of the corpse, a hen's egg is put under each arm-pit, and needles are placed in the palms of the hands. It is believed that if this is done the dead woman cannot become a *langsuyar*, as she cannot open her mouth to shriek (*ngilai*) or wave her arms as wings, or open and shut her hands to assist her flight."

The Penanggalan is a sort of monstrous Vampire who delights in killing young children. One legend says that long ago in order to perform a religious penance (*dudok bertapa*) a woman was seated in one of the large wooden vats which are used by the Malays for holding the vinegar which proceeds from draining off the sap of the thatch-palm (*menyadap nipah*). Quite unexpectedly a man came along, and finding her seated there, asked : "What are you doing here ? " She replied very shortly : "What business is that of yours ? " But being very much startled, she leaped up and in the excitement of the moment kicked her own chin with such force that the skin split all round her neck and her head with the sac of the stomach hanging to it actually became separated from the body, and flew off to perch upon the nearest tree. Ever since that time she has existed as a malign and danger-ous spirit, brooding over the house, screeching (*mengilai*) whenever a child is born, or trying to force her way up through the floor in order to drain its blood.

Among the Karens of Burma we meet with the *Kephn*, a demon which under the form of a wizard's head and a stomach attached devours human souls.

Mr. Hugh Clifford in his study *In Court and Kampong*, London, 1897, speaks of "The Penangal, that horrible wraith of a woman who has died in child-birth, and who comes to torment small children in the guise of a fearful face and bust, with many feet of bloody, trailing entrails in her wake."

The following description which is almost entirely parallel to that of the most deadly European Vampires is quoted by Dr. Skeat in his *Malay Magic*, London, 1900, p. 328, n.1. : "He " (Mr. M.) said, "Very well then, tell me about the *penanggalan* only, I should like to hear it and write it down in English so that Europeans may know how foolish those persons are who believe in such things." I then drew a picture representing a woman's head and neck only, with the intestines hanging down. Mr. M. caused this to be engraved on wood by a Chinese, and inserted it with the story belonging to it in a publication called the *Anglo-Chinese Gleaner*. And I said, " Sir, listen to the account of the *penanggalan*. It was originally a woman. She used the magic arts of a devil in whom she believed, and she devoted herself to his service night and day until the period of her agreement with her teacher had expired and she was able to fly. Her head and neck were then loosened from the body, the intestines being attached to them, and hanging down in strings. The body remained where it was. Wherever the person whom it wished to injure happened to live, thither flew the head and bowels to suck his blood, and the person whose blood was sucked was sure to die. If the blood and water which dripped from the intestines touched any person, serious illness followed and his body broke out in open sores. The *penanggalan* likes to suck the blood of women in child-birth. For this reason it is customary at all houses where a birth occurs to hang up *jeruju* [a kind of thistle] leaves at the doors and windows, or to place thorns wherever there is any blood, lest the *penanggalan* should come and suck it, for the *penanggalan* has, it seems, a dread of thorns in which her intestines may happen to get caught. It is said that a *penanggalan* once came to a man's house in the middle of the night to suck his blood, and her intestines were caught in some thorns near the hedge, and she had to remain there until daylight, when the people saw and killed her.

" The person who has the power of becoming a *penanggalan* always keeps at her house a quantity of vinegar in a jar or vessel of some kind. The use of this is to soak the intestines in, for when they issue forth from the body they immediately swell up and cannot be put back, but after being soaked in vinegar they shrink to their former size and enter the body again. There are many people who have seen the *penanggalan* flying along with its entrails dangling down and shining at night like fire-flies.

" Such is the story of the *penanggalan* as I have heard it from my forefathers but I do not believe it in the least. God forbid that I should." (*Hikayat Abdullah*, p. 143.)

It may be remembered that the Greeks thought that branches of buckthorn (*rhamnus*) fastened to doors and windows kept out witches, as Discorides tells us, *De Materia*

Medica, I, 119. At the time of woman's delivery also they smeared pitch upon the houses to keep out the demons (εἰς ἀπέλασιν τῶν δαιμόνων) who are wont to attack mothers at this period, which the patriarch, Photius, notes in his *Lexicon* (ninth century) when he discusses the word ῥάμνος. The Serbians to-day paint crosses with tar on the doors of houses and barns to guard them from vampires. On Walpurgis Night the Bohemian peasant never neglects to strew the grunsel of his cow-sheds and stables with hawthorn, branches of gooseberry bushes, and the briars of wild rose-trees so that the witches or vampires will get entangled amid the thorns and can force their way no further. The tar of the Serbian will glue them fast in like manner. It was formerly believed among the Scotch Highlanders, and the custom may yet linger that tar daubed on a door kept away the witches. The horse shoe, at any rate, is still commonly to be seen so affixed, not as in England for good luck, but with the very definite object of protecting the house against warlocks and witches. Alexander Burnes, *Travels in Bokhara*, 1834, I, p. 202, says : " Passing a gate of the city of Peshawur I observed it studded with horse-shoes, which are as superstitious emblems in this country as in remote Scotland." The bawds of Amsterdam believed that a horse-shoe, which had either been found or stolen, placed on the chimney-hearth would bring many clients to their stew and keep away witches, say the author of *Le Putanisme d'Amsterdam*, 1687. " The horse-shoe," writes William Henderson in his *Notes on the Folk-lore of the Northern Counties of England and the Borders*, London, 1866, " is said to owe its virtue chiefly to its shape. Any other object presenting two points or forks, even the spreading out of the two forefingers, is said to possess similar occult power, though not in so high a degree as the rowan wish-rod. In Spain and Italy forked pieces of coral are in high repute as witch-scarers. A crescent formed of two boars' tusks is frequently appended to the necks of mules as a charm." In many countries mountain ash (or rowan) is held to be most efficacious against witches and vampires. If an Irish housewife ties a sprig of rowan on the handle of the churn-dash when she is churning no witch can steal her butter. In a local ballad made on the case of Mary Butters, the Carnmoney witch, when in August, 1807, Alexander

Montgomery's cow was enchanted so no butter could be made from her milk the following lines occur :

> It happened for a month or two
>> Aye when they churn'd they got nae butter.
> Rown-tree tied in the cow's tail,
>> And vervain glean'd about the ditches ;
> These freets and charms did not prevail,
>> They could not banish the auld witches.

Gay in his *Fables*, XXIII, " The Old Woman and her Cats " mentions the horse-shoe as a protection against witches :

> Straws laid across, my pace retard ;
> The horse-shoe's nail'd (each threshold's guard) ;
> The stunted broom the wenches hide,
> For fear that I should up and ride.
> They stick with pins my bleeding seat,
> And bid me show my secret teat.

In Polynesia we pretty generally find the *tü*, who under some aspects is a kind of vampire-demon and Dr. R. H. Codrington in his *The Melanesians : Studies in their Anthropology and Folk Lore*, says, " There is a belief in the Banks Islands in the existence of a power like that of Vampires. A man or a woman would obtain this power out of a morbid desire for communion with some ghost, and in order to gain it would steal and eat a morsel. The ghost then of the dead man would join in a close friendship with the person who had eaten, and would gratify him by afflicting any one against whom his ghostly power might be directed. The man so afflicted would feel that something was influencing his life, and would come to dread some particular person among his neighbours, who was, therefore, suspected of being a *talamaur*. This latter when seized and tried in the smoke of strong-smelling leaves would call out the name of the dead man whose ghost was his familiar, often the names of more than one, and lastly the name of the man who was afflicted. The same name *talamaur* was given to one whose soul was supposed to leave the grave and absorb the lingering vitality of a freshly dead person. There was a woman, some years ago, of whom the story is told that she made no secret of doing this, and that once on the death of a neighbour she gave notice that she would go in the night and eat the vitality. The friends of the deceased therefore kept watch in the house where the corpse lay, and at dead of night heard a scratching at the door, followed by a rustling noise close by the body. One of them threw a stone and seemed to hit the unknown thing ; and in the morning the *talamaur* was found with a bruise on her arm, which she confessed was caused by a stone thrown at her whilst she was eating the vitality. Such a woman would feel a morbid delight in the dread which she inspired, and would also be secretly rewarded by some whose covert spite she gratified."

In his *Ashanti Proverbs*, "Translated from the Original (*The Primitive Ethics of a Savage People*)," p. 48, Mr. R. Sutherland Rattray speaks of the *Asasabonsam*, "a monster of human shape, which living far in the depths of the forest, is only occasionally met by hunters. It sits on tree tops, and its legs dangle down to the ground and have hooks for feet which pick up any one who comes within reach. It has iron teeth. There are female, male, and little *sasabonsam*." Mr. Rattray also describes the *obayifo*, which word is derived from *bayi*, "sorcery." This is "a kind of human vampire whose chief delight is to suck the blood of children, whereby the latter pine and die. Men and women possessed of this power and credited with volitant powers, being able to quit their bodies and travel great distances in the night. Besides sucking the blood of their victims, they are supposed to be able to extract the sap and juices of crops. Cases of coco blight are ascribed to the work of the *obayifo*. These witches are supposed to be very common, and a man never knows but that his friend or even his wife may be one. When prowling at night they are supposed to emit a phosphorescent light. An *obayifo* in every day life is supposed to be known by having sharp, shifty eyes, that are never at rest, also by showing an undue interest in food, and always talking about it, especially meat, and hanging about when cooking is going on, all of which habits are therefore purposely avoided."

A striking similarity to the beliefs of the Malay Peninsula is to be traced among the horrible superstitions of ancient Mexico. The Mexican religion presents an extremely complex system with a crowded pantheon and displays a corresponsive ceremonial of the most elaborate nature and exacting service. There existed a certain kind of monachism, and the sacerdotal caste is particularly distinguished by being deeply learned in myth and symbolism reduced to the most unyielding dogma, thus involving practices, sometimes pleasing and poetical, sometimes abhorent in their excess of savagery and barbarism, but which one and all were not merely so much upheld as rigorously enforced by the state authorities of a great empire, which determined an essential unity of religious conception throughout its furthermost borders. There were of course, beneficent deities such as the Sun god, Tonatiuh, who was also called Xipilli " the Turquoise," whose festival Clavigero tells us[51] " which was celebrated every fifty-two years, was by far the most splendid and most solemn, not only among the Mexicans, but likewise among all the nations of that Empire, or who were neighbouring to it . . . every place resounded with the voice of gladness and mutual congratulations on account of the new century which heaven had granted him. The illuminations made during the first nights were extremely magnificent ; their ornaments of dress, entertainments, dances, and public games were superiorly solemn." But even here we find that human sacrifice was offered. There were also goddesses such as Xochiquetzal, " Flower Feather " who is considered by Diego Muñoz Camargo as corresponding to Venus, and whom he thus describes : " She dwells above the nine heavens in a very pleasant and delectable place, accompanied and guarded by many people and waited on by other women of the rank of goddesses, where are many delights of fountains, brooks, flower-gardens, and without her wanting for anything."[52] There was also Macuilxochitl, " Five Flower," the god of pleasure, whose festival, one of the movable feasts, was the *Xochilhuitl*, the Feast of Flowers, concerning which Sahagun says that : " the great folk made a feast, dancing and singing in honour of this sign, decorating themselves with their feathers and all their grandeur for the *areyto* [sacred dance]. At this feast the king bestowed honours upon warriors, musicians and courtiers."[53] There exists an elegant little song of this debonair god who is the Lord of Music and Games, which commences thus :

> Out of the place of flowers I come,
> Priest of the Sunset, Lord of the Twilight.

Quails were offered to him at midday, but even this solemnity was not without some sombre incident, for it was the occasion when all the nobles in Mexico who lived near the frontiers of an enemy brought the slaves whom they had captured to the capital for sacrifice.

When we find that some circumstance of cruelty even intrudes upon the worship of the kindliest and most joyous gods it may well be supposed that the demonology of Mexico is grim in the extreme, nor can we be at all astonished that the first explorers and the earlier Spanish authors again and again expressed their horror of the terrible imagination and primitive fears which peopled the gloom of a Mexican midnight with the abominable shapes of foulest devils and vengeful dead. Probably the most horrible, as he is possibly the most powerful, of the Mexican gods was Tezcatlipocâ of whom Bernal Diaz says : "And this Tezcatepuca was the god of hell and had charge of the souls of the Mexicans, and his body was girt with figures like little devils with snakes' tails."[54] This hideous figure, it is very significant to remark, particularly favoured cross-roads, where the *Ciuateteo*, who are vampire-witches, held their sabbat. Tezcatlipocâ was also known as *Yaotzin*, "The Enemy" and in a thousand horrid phantom shapes he haunted the woods during the dark hours. He bore in his hand a magical instrument. From him proceeded those eerie and mysterious sounds which are heard at night and which fill with strange forebodings not only luckless travellers but even those who shudder when sheltered in their homes. He would often utter the howl of the jaguar, and the ill-omened cry, "yeccan, yeccan" the screech of the *uactli* bird, a species of hawk, whose note sounded a swift death to him who heard it. Another of his guises was the *Youaltepuztli*, or "ax of the night." When all was most silent and most still there might be heard near some remote temple a sound as if an ax were being laid to the roots of the trees. Should anyone dare to investigate the cause of the noise he was suddenly caught by Tezcatlipocâ who appeared as a decomposing headless corpse in whose mouldering breast were set "two little doors meeting in the centre," and it was the swift opening and shutting of these which produced the sound of a man hewing down the trees. If some brave hero could plunge his hand into the aperture and clutch the black heart he might demand what ransom he would ere he let the demon go. But he must be one to whom fear was unknown for most persons who caught sight of this hideous phantom perished in an extremity of terror.

The true Mexican Vampires were the Ciuateteo whom we have mentioned above, women who had died in their first labour,[55] and over whose revels this devil-deity presided. They were also known as the *Ciuapipiltin*, or princesses, in order to placate them by some honourable designation, as in the same way Ciuateteo signifies " Right honourable mother." Of these Sahagun says : " The Ciuapipiltin, the noble women, were those who had died in childbed. They were supposed to wander through the air, descending when they wished to the earth to afflict children with paralysis and other maladies. They haunted cross-roads to practise their maleficent deeds, and they had temples built at these places where bread offerings were made to them, also the thunder stones which fall from the sky. Their faces were white, and their arms and hands were coloured with a white powder *ticitl* (chalk)." These haunting women celebrated their own sabbat, and it is curious to remark that it was thought of as being a meeting of the dead rather than, as in Europe, an infernal company of the living. The representations of the Ciuateteo in the ancient paintings are extremely hideous and repulsive. They often wear the dress and are distinguished by the characteristics of the goddess, Tlazolteotl, whose priests were the *Cuecuesteca*, and who was the goddess of all sorcery, lust, and evil. The learned friar who interpreted the *Codex Telleriano-Renensis* certainly speaks of the Ciuateteo as witches, who flew through the air upon their broom-sticks and met at cross-roads, a rendezvous presided over by their mistress Tlazolteotl. It may be remarked that the broom-stick is her especial symbol, and that she is often associated with the snake and the screech-owl. Under one aspect, also, she is regarded as a moon-goddess, and may, indeed, be fairly closely parallelled with the Greek Hecate. These animals, which were considered unlucky also often accompanied the Ciuateteo, who, moreover, carried a witch's broom, and upon whose garments crossbones were painted. They were essentially malignant, and sought to wreak their vengeance upon all whom they might meet during the dark hours. In the native huts the doors were carefully barred and every crack or cranny carefully filled up to prevent

these vampire-witches from obtaining entrance. Occasionally, however, they would attack human dwellings, and did
they obtain ingress the children of the household would pine
and dwindle away owing to the blight that these loathsome
creatures cast upon them. Accordingly in their shrines
where four cross-roads met men heaped up enticing and
substantial food offerings, in order that these malignant dead
might so satisfy their hunger that they would not seek to
make an onset upon the living. One explanation why the
shrine should be at cross-roads was in order that the Ciuateteo
might be confused and not knowing which way to take to
the nearest human habitation, be surprised by dawn before
she could set out to seize her prey. We find this exact reason
is given in Greece and in other countries for burying the
body of a suicide, who will almost certainly become a vampire,
at four cross-roads.

With regard to Mexican Vampire-witches, who it appears
partook in almost equal quantities the nature of both these
evil things, Sahagun records : " It was said that they vented
their wrath on people and bewitched them. When anyone
is possessed by the demons, with a wry mouth and disturbed
eyes, with clenched hands and inturned feet, wringing his
hands and foaming at the mouth, they say that he has linked
himself to a demon ; the Ciuateteo, housed by the cross-ways,
has taken his form."

But this was not the only vampire known to the mythology
of Mexico. The Lord of Mictlampa (the Region of the Dead)
certainly has vampirish attributes. He is often depicted as a
complete skeleton (*Codex Borgia*, sheet 14), and sometimes
he has a bunch or broom of *malinalli* grass, which was associated
with witchcraft. In another representation he appears with
a skeleton head but a black body, and at the side is seen a
skull swallowing a man who falls into its bony jaws. In the
Codex Magliabecchiano[56] he is depicted as a blue-grey form
with enormous talons upon his hands that are markedly reminis-
cent of the claws of a Vampire. He sits in the portico of a dark
temple and before him are his worshippers, a number of men
and women, who feast upon human flesh, tearing heads, legs,
and arms which they snatch from several earthen vessels.
His wife was Mictecaciuatl, " Lady of the Place of the Dead,"
and she is often represented as wearing for ornaments the paper

flags, which were generally put upon corpses prepared for cremation. She is sometimes seen to be thrusting a mummy into the earth, and there is a reference to her as the " earth-monster."

It would, perhaps, be hardly too much to say that in ancient Mexico all magicians were regarded as Vampires, a tradition which long survived even after the conversion of the country so that one of the regular questions which the Spanish priests used to put to those of whose faith they were suspicious was : " Art thou a sorcerer ? Dost thou suck the blood of others ? " That such interrogations were not superfluous is shown by the terrible occurrence at the end of the sixteenth century when Cosijopii, formerly King of Tehuantepec, was discovered amid a throng of his ancient courtiers and a concourse of people taking part in an idolatrous ceremony of peculiar horror. Even in the seventeenth century the priests of the Province of Oaxaca learned that numbers of Indians congregated secretly at night to worship their idols. It is true that the famous letter of Bishop Zumárraga to the Chapter of Tolosa, written in 1531 says that : " quingenta deorum templa sunt destructa et plusquam uicesies mille figurae daemonum, quas adorabant, fractae et combustae." But Fray Mendieta mentions certain idols of paper[57] which seemed to have been for a while preserved, and possibly new figures were clandestinely sculptured in the traditional manner to supply the place of those which had been so properly and so religiously destroyed. Such ceremonials were, of course, clear witchcraft, and the Mexican sorcerer or *naualli* seems to have been credited with taking the shape of a wer-coyote, the prairie wolf, as well as to have practised vampirism. So here too in Mexico we find a close connexion between the wer-animal and the Vampire. Sahagun notes : " The *naualli* or magician is he who frightens men and sucks the blood of children during the night." It appears that these sorcerers lived in separate huts built of wood very brightly painted, and that those who wished to bargain with them were wont to resort to these accursed houses under the cover of dark. Not superfluously then does the *Vade mecum* of a missionary who was engaged in the work of evangelizing the native Mexicans include such questions as : " Art thou a diviner ? " " Dost thou suck the blood of others, or dost thou wander about at night, calling upon the demons to help thee ? "

Of all the many and dark superstitions that prevail in the West Indies none is more deeply rooted than the belief in the existence of vampires, and as this tradition was brought from Guinea and the Congo and maintained for more than two centuries by the hundreds of thousands of African slaves who were so constantly being imported from this native continent it may not impertinently be considered here. In Grenada, particularly, the vampire is known as a "Loogaroo," a corruption of *loupgarou*, and the attributes generally assigned to the loogaroo as well as the current stories told of these ghastly beings not infrequently recall the pages of De Lanere, clearly showing that the demonology of the French colonists of the seventeenth century was soon welded with negro witch-craft and voodoo. The West Indian natives, and above all the black, Quashee as he is called, hold that loogaroos are human beings, especially old women, who have made a pact with the devil, by which the fiend bestows upon them certain magic powers on condition that every night they provide him with a quantity of rich warm blood. And so every night the loogaroos make their way to the occult silk-cotton-tree (*bombax ceiba*, often known as the Devil's tree or Jumbie[58] tree), and there, having divested themselves of their skins, which are carefully folded up and concealed, in the form of a ball of sulphurous fire they speed abroad upon their horrid businesses. Even to-day visitors to Grenada have been called out of the house late at night by the servants to see the loogaroos, and their attention is directed to any solitary light which happens to flash through the darkness, perhaps the distant lantern of some watchman who is guarding a cocoa piece. Until dawn the loogaroos are at work, and any Quashee who feels tired and languid upon awaking will swear that the vampire has sucked his blood. Doors and shutters are no barrier to the monster who can slip through the tiniest chink, but if only rice and sand are scattered before a cabin the loogarroo must perforce stay until he has numbered every grain, and so morning will assuredly surprise him ere the tale is told.

Mr. H. J. Bell recounts the following anecdote which is sufficiently striking as reproducing in actual belief of to-day more than one of the old witch traditions. A native gardener pointed out to Mr. Bell a hideous beldame walking along the highway. This hag, who wore a bandage over one eye, was reputed to be a loogaroo of the most infamous and evil kind. It happened that one day upon awakening the gardener had felt extraordinary weak and supine. To his horror he remarked a slight stain of blood on his clothes, and he at once realized he had been the victim of a vampire. The following night he refrained from sleep, preserving a silent vigil. A little after twelve-o'clock there came a faint scratching in the thatch of the roof. As this grew louder the man guessing that the loogaroo was about to enter thrust through the spot with his cutlass. A stifled screech fell to hideous moans, and rushing out of the hut he heard the sound die away in the distance, whilst a blue marish light vanished into the house where this ancient sibyl dwelt. The next day she was found lying in bed, half blind from an injury to one of her eyes. This she vowed had been caused during the night owing to a fall over the sharp stump of a tree whilst she was chasing some strayed chickens. Nobody believed her, and the gardener was praised for having so deservedly punished the vampire for her foul sorceries.

It is said that the human skin of a loogaroo has been found hidden in the bushes under a silk-cotton-tree. In this case it must be seized fast and pounded in a mortar with pepper and salt. So the vampire will be unable to assume a human shape and will perish miserably.

Now and again negroes have been discovered bold enough to play the loogaroo in order to cover up their nightly depredations. Two confederates will plan the robbing of a cocoa piece, and whilst one fellow will climb the tree to strip off the pods his friend will pass softly up and down in the vicinity waving a lantern fashioned from an empty dry calabash cut to imitate grotesque and gargoyled features, and lighted by a candle set in a socket which has been cleverly inserted.

The tradition, however, has its more serious sides and obscene, if not bloody, rites are practised in secret places where the white man will hardly venture. On one occasion a witch was seen at midnight dancing naked round a fire, and as she leaped to the drone of foul incantations she ever and anon cast strange substances into the flame which blazed up into a myriad colourings.

The loogaroo is particularly obnoxious to dogs, and any person at whom apparently without cause dogs will bark furiously or even endeavour to attack is incontinently accounted infect with the vampire taint.

It is supposed that the loogaroo will frequently molest animals of all kinds, and indeed in Trinidad and especially on the Spanish Main the horses suffer greatly from the attacks of large vampire bats. It is necessary that all the windows and ventilation holes of the stables and cattle pens should be firmly secured by wire netting to prevent the entrance of the bats, which are able greatly to harm any animal in whose flesh they manage to fasten their teeth.

It may seem that the superstition of the Quashee, although grosser and more ignorant, lacks some of the crueller and more abominable traits of the tradition in other countries. This is merely owing to the fact that it has largely been driven under ground by energetic and repressive measures. Père Labat in his *Nouveaux voyages aux Isles d' Amérique* (1712) gives the story of a vampirish black sorceress who used to threaten to eat the hearts of those who offended her, and almost invariably they soon after began to waste away in great agony. When their bodies were opened it was seen that the heart and liver were drained dry as parchment. He further says : " Nearly all the negroes who leave their country, having attained the age of manhood, are sorcerers, or, at all events, are much tainted with magic, witchcraft and poison." Even half a century ago an important ordinance was passed in all the West Indian colonies imposing heavy penalties on any person found guilty of dealing in Obeah. Writing as lately as 1893, Mr. H. J. Bell says of Hayti, one of the most beautiful of the West Indies, an island possessing an area almost equal to that of France : " Dreadful accounts reach us of thousands of negroes having gone back to a perfectly savage life in the woods, going about stark naked, and having replaced the Christian religion by Voodooism and fetish worship. Cases of cannibalism have even been reported, and nowhere in the West Indies has Obeah a more tenacious hold on high and low than in Hayti."

By a comparison of the beliefs in these many lands, in ancient Assyria, in old Mexico, in China, India and Melanesia, although details differ, but yet not to any marked degree, it will be seen that the superstition and the tradition of the Vampire prevail to an extraordinary extent, and it is hard to believe that a phenomenon which has had so complete a hold over nations both old and young, in all parts of the world, at all times of history, has not some underlying and terrible truth however rare this may be in its more remarkable manifestations.

NOTES TO CHAPTER IV

[1] R. Campbell Thompson. *The Devils and Evil Spirits of Babylonia*, London, 1903, vol. I, p. xxviii, n.

[2] Leonard W. King. *Babylonian Religion*, p. 75.

[3] *Op. cit.*, p. **xxv**.

[4] King, *Babylonian Religion*, p. 176 ; Gilgamish Epic, Tablet xii.

[5] Campbell Thompson, *op. cit.*, p. xxx.

[6] The Night-fiend *idlu lili* is the male counterpart of the Night-wraith, *ardat lili*. *Idlu* is the word used for a grown man of full strength.

[7] Ea was the great god whose emanation always remained in water, and accordingly who was invoked with lustrations and aspersions of lymph.

[8] Campbell Thompson, *op. cit.*, pp. 37-49.

[9] Northcote W. Thomas, *Anthropological Report on the Ibo-speaking Peoples of Nigeria*, London, 1913, I, 57*sqq.*

[10] Le Sieur de la Borde, " Relation de l'Origine, Moeurs, Coustumes, Religion, Guerres et Voyages des Caraibes sauvages des Isles Antilles de l'Amerique," *Recueil de divers Voyages faits en Afrique et en l'Amerique, qui n'ont point esté encore publiez.* Paris, 1684.

[11] E. Young, *The Kingdom of the Yellow Robe*, Westminster, 1898.

[12] Y. Scheffer, *Lapponia*, Frankfort, 1673, p. 313.

[13] Ignaz V. Zingerie, *Sitten, Braüche und Meinungen des Tiroler Volkes*, 2nd edition. Innsbruck, 1871.

[14] " On a Far-off Island," *Blackwood's Magazine*, February, 1886 ; p. 238.

[15] Campbell Thompson, *op. cit.*, I, pp. 69-71.

[16] Among the illustrations of prehistoric utensils.

[17] In a private letter to myself, 24th March, 1928.

[18] *Satirae*, I, v, 64.

[19] For much relating to Chinese Vampires I am indebted to Mr. G. Willoughby-Meade's *Chinese Ghouls and Goblins*, Constable, London. Published March, 1928.

[20] Thomas J. Hutchinson, " On the Choco and other Indians of South America," *Transactions of the Ethnological Society of London*, N.S. iii (1865), p. 327.

[21] Monica Williams, *Religious Thought and Life in India*, London, 1883, p. 354.

[22] H. Vambery, *Das Türkenvolk*, Leipsic, 1885, p. 112.

[23] H. Ternaux-Compans, *Essai sur l'ancien Cundinamara*, Paris, (*s.d.*), p. 18.

[24] George Turner, LL.D., *Samoa, a Hundred Years ago and long before*, London, 1884, p. 200.

[25] W. Drexler *apud* W. H. Roscher, *Ausführliches Lexikon der griechischen und römischen Mythologie, s.u.* " Men."

[26] Hans Egede, *A Descriptign of Greenland*, London, 1818, p. 209.

[27] *Revue des Traditions Populaires*, xv (1900), p. 471.

[28] Cf. *The Tempest*, II, 2, where Caliban is alluded to as a " moon-calf."
Stepheno : " How cam'st thou to be the siege of this moon-calf ? "
Trinculo : " I hid me under the dead moon-calf's gaberdine for fear of the storm." In Dryden and Davenant's *The Tempest, or the Enchanted Island*, 4to, 1670, II, Trincalo calls Caliban " perverse Moon-calf."
The same phrase is reproduced in Shadwell's operatic *The Tempest or, The Enchanted Island*, 4to, 1674.

[29] Constable's, London, 1928.

[30] Ph. Paulitschke, *Ethnographie Nordost-Afrikas : die materielle Cultur des Danakil, Galla, und Somâl*, Berlin, 1893.
A. C. Hollis, *The Masai*, Oxford, 1905.
[31] Apparently not S. Hilary of Arles, nor S. Hilary of Poictiers.
[32] The custom of gathering various herbs, especially S. John's Wort, hawkseed, and mugwort on S. John's eve, 23 June, as a protection against magical spells was almost universal throughout Europe as it was believed that then warlocks and witches were especially active. An immense library of folk-lore is concerned with this day. R. Kühnau, *Schlesische Sagen*, Berlin, 1910-1913, iii, p. 39, n.1394, says : " On S. John's Night (between the 23rd and 24th of June) the witches busily bestir themselves to force their way into the houses of men and the stalls of cattle."
[33] The deception was wrought by glamour. Algernon Blackwood has made excellent use of such a magical delusion in his occult studies, *Dr. John Silence*, 1908, Case iv, " Secret Worship."
[34] Two vols. New York, 1862. Vol. II, p. 327.
[35] J. Noake, *Worcestershire Notes and Queries*, London, 12 mo, 1856, p. 169.
[36] I quote the version given by J. O. Halliwell, but there are many variants.
[37] Act II. The soliloquy of Barabas as he is prowling outside the convent toward midnight. One may compare Shakespeare's " The nightly owl or fatal raven," *Titus Andronicus*, II, iii. 97. Also in *Othello*, IV, i, 21 :

Oh ! it comes o'er my memory
As doth the raven o'er the infected house,
Boding to all.

And Lady Macbeth's (*Macbeth*, I, v, 35) :

The raven himself is hoarse
That croaks the fatal entrance of Duncan
Under my battlements.

Tickell, *Colin and Lucy*, has :

Three times, all in the dead of night,
A bell was heard to ring,
And at her window, shrieking thrice,
The raven flapp'd his wing ;
Full well the love-lorn maiden knew,
The solemn-boding sound. . . .

Much of interest might be written on this subject of which it has been possible for me *en passant* barely to touch the fringe.
[38] Robert Forby, *Vocabulary of East Anglia*, 2 vols., London, 8vo, 1830.
[39] William Henderson, *Notes on the Folk-lore of the Northern Counties of England and the Borders*, London, 8vo, 1866. Harrison Ainsworth's fine romance, *Rookwood*, first published in April, 1834, may be noted in connexion with this tradition.
[40] *The Animal World*, vi, p. 29.
[41] V, v.
[42] G. Willoughby-Meade, *Chinese Ghouls and Goblins*, pp. 234-35.
[43] *Op. cit.*, p. 236.
[44] *The Ocean of Story*, pp. 139-140. Note II, Chapter LXXIII.
[45] W. W. Skeat, *Malay Magic*, London, 1900, pp. 320-331.
[46] In 1644, Elizabeth Clarke, a notorious witch, confessed to Matthew Hopkins that amongst other familiars she entertained our " Newes, like a Polcat."
[47] *The examination and confession of certaine Wytches at Chelmsforde in the Countie of Essex before the Quenes Maiesties Judges the XXVI daye of July anno 1566.*
[48] Nothing is known of this writer who probably compiled his book in the fourth century. The *De Prodigiis* or *Prodigiorum Libellus* contains a record of the phenomena classed by the Romans under the general heading of *Prodigia* or *Ostenta*. The series extends in chronological order from the consulship of Scipio and Laelius, B.C. 190, to the consulship of Fabius and Aelius, B.C. 11. The materials are derived from an abridgement of Livy, whose very phrases are continually employed.

[49] Amsterdam, 1679.

[50] W. W. Skeat, *op. cit.*, p. 234.

[51] Francesco Saverio Clavigero, *Storia Antico del Mexico*, Cesona, 1780. English translation by Charles Cullen, 2 vols., London, 1787.

[52] Diego Muñoz Camargo, *Historia de Tlascala*, Book I, c. xix. Edited by A. Chavero, Mexico, 1892.

[53] Bernardino de Sahagun, *Historia Universal de Nueva-España*. Mexico, 1829 ; London, 1830, in vol. vi of Lord Kingsborough's *Antiquities of Mexico*. French translation by Jourdanet and Siméon, Paris, 1880.

[54] Bernal Diaz del Castillo. *Historia Verdadera de la Conquista de Nueva-España*. Translated by A. P. Maudslay as *The True History of the Conquest of Mexico*. Hakluyt Society, London, 1908.

[55] In Ireland hagiographical lore mention is made of a special burying-place for women who die in childbirth. *Lives of the Cambro-British Saints*, Ed. Rev. W. J. Rees, 1853, p. 63.

[56] Reproduced by the Duc de Loubat, Rome, 1904. And also reproduced by Zelia Nuttall as *The Book of the Life of the Ancient Mexicans*, Berkeley, California, 1903. This codex is accompanied by a contemporary gloss in Spanish.

[57] G. de Mendieta, *Historia Ecclesiastica Indiana*. Icazbalceta, Mexico, 1870.

[58] The West Indian " Jumbies " or " Duppies " are ghostly visitants, malignant and terrific spectres. Many of the old houses in the West Indies have the reputation of being haunted in a most unpleasant way.

CHAPTER V

THE VAMPIRE IN LITERATURE

A CONSIDERATION of the Vampire theme in literature must of necessity be somewhat eclectic, if not even arbitrary in the selection of works which it reviews and with which it sets out to deal. Any exhaustive inquiry is well-nigh impossible, and this not so much, perhaps, on account of the wealth of the material, although indeed there is a far vaster field than might generally be supposed, as owing to the very vague definition and indeterminate interpretation one is able to give to vampirism from a purely literary point of view. It is the craft of an artist in the telling of ghost-stories to see that his colours should not be too vivid and too clear, and no mean skill is required to suggest without explanation, to mass the shadows without derangement, to be occult yet not to be obscure. Accordingly it would be a matter of extreme difficulty to differentiate the malignant and death-dealing spectre or it may be even corpse who returns to wreak his foul revenge from the Vampire,—using this latter word in its widest sense, as one must employ it when speaking of literature, a caution which here given as regards this Chapter will serve once for all. In such a story, for example, as Dr. M. R. James' *Count Magnus*[1] is the horrible revenant a ghost or a vampire ? The writer has left the point ambiguous. It is of the very essence of his happy invention that he should do so, and the deftly veiled incertitude adds to the loathly terror of the thing. It will be readily remembered that the story relates how a traveller in Sweden about the middle of the last century whilst staying near an ancient manor house in Vestergothland obtains permission to examine the family papers and among these he comes upon the traces of a certain Count Magnus de la Gardie who in the year 1600 had built the house or *herrgård*. Even after the lapse of two and a half centuries dark traditions are still lingering concerning this mysterious nobleman, whose body lies in a richly ornate copper sarcophagus that stands the principal feature of a domed mausoleum at the eastern end of the church. Reluctantly the landlord tells a story which happened in the time of his grandfather ninety-two years before. Two men determined to go at night and have a free hunt in the woods upon the estate. They are warned : " No, do not go ; we are sure you will meet with persons walking who should not be walking. They should be resting, not walking." The two men laughed and cried : " The Count is dead ; we do not care for him." But in the night the villagers " hear someone scream, just as if the most inside part of his soul was twisted out of him." Then they hear a hideous laugh, " it was not one of those two men that laughed, and, indeed, they have all of them said that it was not any man at all." In the morning they go out with the priest, and they find one of the men dead, killed in so terrible a fashion that they buried him on the spot. " He was once a beautiful man, but now his face was not there, because the flesh of it was sucked away off the bones." The other man is standing with his back against a tree, " pushing with his hands—pushing something away from him which was not there."

There was some vague gossip that the Count had been " on the Black Pilgrimage, and had brought something or someone back with him." During his investigation of the papers the English traveller, Mr. Wraxall, found a *Liber nigrae peregrinationis*, or at least a few lines of such a document indicating that the Count had once journeyed to the city of Chorazin and there adored the prince of the air. In careless mood as he is passing near the mausoleum, Mr. Wraxall exclaims : " Ah, Count Magnus, there you are. I should dearly like to see you." He is indiscreet enough to cry out thus flippantly on two further occasions, and at last he is thoroughly alarmed by hearing the sound of metal hinges creaking and he knows that the sarcophagus is slowly opening wide. In a state of frenzied fear he sets out for England the next day, yet turn and double as he will he is everywhere haunted by two hideous figures, a man in a long black cloak and a broad-leafed hat and something in a dark cloak and hood. Upon landing at Harwich he makes his way across country to a neighbouring village, when on looking out of the carriage window he sees at a cross-road the two horrible creatures. He finds a lodging, but within the next forty-eight hours his pursuers fall upon him. He is discovered dead, and in the district it is still remembered how " the jury that viewed the body fainted, seven of 'em did, and none of 'em wouldn't speak to what they see, and the verdict was visitation of God ; and how the people as kep' the 'ouse moved out that same week and went away from that part."

This story may, I think, certainly be considered as Vampire lore, and although it must, of course, be perfectly familiar to all who delight in tales of the supernatural I have related it at some little length here, partly because it is told so excellently well, and partly because it so admirably fulfils and exemplifies the qualities that this kind of literature should possess. It is brief and succinct, although there are many details, but every touch tells. No ghost story should be of any length. The horror and the awe evaporate with pro-lixity. The ghost is malevolent and odious. In fiction a helpful apparition is a notable weakness, and the whole narrative becomes flabby to a degree. The authentic note of horror is struck in the eerie suggestion which, as we have noticed, is of intent left ill-defined. Nothing could be more crude than an explanation, and it is this banality that often ruins a story which otherwise might be of the very first order.

To review the traces of vampire legends which appear in sagas, and which are in truth but few and unimportant, seems to be outside our province here, and even more foreign to our purpose would be the present examination of the vampire legend in folk-lore since this has already been dealt with in the course of the preceding chapters, and to regard such traditions merely as literature would be not only to look at them from a wrong perspective but to misrepresent their quality and essentially to pervert their purpose.

Since some point must be chosen at which to consider vam-pirism in literature we may most fairly recall to mind the many academic and philosophical treatises upon the Vampire which were rehearsed and discussed in German Universities during the earlier part of the eighteenth century, and these startling themes soon began to attract the attention of poets and literary men. Thus among the poems of Heinrich August Ossenfelder[2] we have a short piece entitled *Der Vampir*, which is as follows :

> Mein liebes Mägdchen glaubet
> Beständig steif und feste,
> An die gegebnen Lehren
> Der immer frommen Mutter ;
> Als Völker an der Theyse
> An tödtliche Vampiere
> Heyduckisch feste glauben,
> Nun warte nur Christianchen,
> Du willst mich gar nich lieben ;
> Ich will mich an dir rächen,
> Und heute in Tockayer
> Zu einem Vampir trinken.
> Und wenn du sanfte schlummerst,
> Von deinen schönen Wangen
> Den frischen Purpur saugen.
> Alsdenn wirst du erschrecken,
> Wenn ich dich werde küssen
> Und als ein Vampir küssen :
> Wann du dann recht erzitterst
> Und matt in meine Arme,
> Gleich einer Todten sinkest
> Alsdenn will ich dich fragen,
> Sind meine Lehren besser,
> Als deiner guten Mutter ?

The poet Wieland[3] has a passing reference to the Vampire :

> Der Jüngling aus den Wolken
> Herab gefallen, stumm und bleich,
> Als hätt' ein Vampyr ihm die Adern ausgemolken,
> Steht ganz vernichtet von dem Streich.[4]

It would be an exaggeration to say that the Vampire entered German literature with Goethe's famous ballad *Die Braut von Korinth*, but it would be difficult to over-estimate the influence and the popularity of this piece, the subject of which is directly derived from Phlegon of Tralles. The young Athenian who visits his father's old friend to whose daughter he has been betrothed receives at midnight the Vampire body of the girl whom death has prevented from becoming his bride, and who declares :

> Aus dem Grabe werd' ich ausgetrieben,
> Noch zu suchen das vermifste Gut,
> Noch den schon verlornen Mann zu lieben

Und zu saugen seines Herzens Blut.
Ist's um den geschehn,
Muss nach andern gehn,
Und das junge Volk erliegt der Wut.[5]

Even more famous are the charnel horrors of Bürger's *Lenore* which was first printed in 1773 in the *Gottinger Musenalmanach* and which notwithstanding the legions of hostile comments and parodies whereof Brandl gives an ample list[6] has remained a household word.

In spite of the immense enthusiasm at that date in contemporary England for German romantic literature it is remarkable that no translation of *Lenore* was published here until 1796, when William Taylor of Norwich printed in the *Monthly Review* of March his rendering which in some respects must be called an adaptation. He had, however, by his own account written the translation as early as 1790,[7] and there can be no doubt that very shortly after its completion it was declaimed, applauded and much discussed in Norwich literary circles. We know that Mrs. Barbauld who visited Edinburgh " about the summer of 1793 or 1794 "[8] read aloud Taylor's version to a number of enthusiastic admirers. This event was described to Sir Walter Scott by Miss Cranstoun, afterwards Countess Purgstall,[9] although Scott himself mentions that his curiosity " was first attracted to this truly romantic story by a gentleman, who, having heard *Lenore* once read in manuscript, could only recollect the general outline, and part of a couplet, which, from the singularity of its structure, and frequent recurrence,[10] had remained impressed on his memory."[11] This gentleman was Mr. Cranstoun, the brother of Countess Purgstall, and so her statement is no doubt accurate as Scott might well have received his account both from the brother as well as from the sister. It was in the course of 1794, or at any rate early in the following year that Scott made his own rendering of the ballad. The account of Taylor's version, *Ellenore*, which " electrified " the assembled company at Dugald Stewart's house when read by the famous Anna Letitia Barbauld had given him the strongest desire to see the original. Just about this time, however, it was a difficult matter to procure books from the continent, and it was not until after some delay that a copy of Bürger's works was conveyed to him from Hamburg. He immediately devoured the German ballad and was so impressed that he forthwith set about Englishing it. "I well recollect" he writes, "that I began my task after supper, and finished it about daybreak next morning."[12] Scott's friends privately printed a few copies of the poem as a surprise for the author,[13] and as it went from hand to hand it met with the most flattering reception. In 1796, besides the public issue of the translations from Bürger by Taylor and by Scott, no less than three other versions appeared, from the several pens of W. R. Spencer, H. J. Pye and J. T. Stanley. The translation by the last named author was given to the public in an *édition de luxe* at five shillings, as well as in the ordinary edition of half a crown.[14] In 1797, a pasquil followed, *Miss Kitty : a Parody on Lenora, a Ballad*, " Translated from the German, by several Hands," whilst in the following year, Mrs. Taylor turned the popular poem into Italian as a " Novella Morale."[15] Probably the most faithful, if not the most spirited translation, was that by the Rev. J. Beresford which was published in 1800.

It was in 1797 that Coleridge wrote the first part of *Christabel*, and German critics have somewhat superfluously endeavoured to emphasize herein the influence of *Lenore*, since upon examination it would hardly seem that such is present even in the smallest degree. For example, if the narrative of Geraldine be carefully read[16] it must be evident that the following judgment of Professor Brandl is without foundation. This critic writes : " Ihre Vorgeschichte (of Geraldine) schöpfte er grossentheils aus Bürgers ' Lenore ' in Taylors Uebersetzung : die Dame ist, wenigstens ihrer Erzählung nach, auf einem windschnellen Ross entführt und halbtodt vor Furcht hier abgesetzt worden ; statt des schwarzen Leichenzuges, der Lenoren auf ihrem Ritt durch die Mondnacht aufstiess, will sie 'den Schatten der Nacht ' gekreuzt haben ; noch zittert das verdorrte Blatt neben ihr wie aus Herzenangst."[17]

As we might expect, the young Shelley was enchanted by *Lenore*, and Medwin relates how the poet long treasured " a copy of the whole poem, which he made with his own hand."[18] Dowden tells the story how one Christmas Eve Shelley dramatically related the Bürger ballad with appropriate intonation and gesture " working up the horror to such a height of fearful interest" that the company fully expected to see Wilhelm stalk into the parlour.[19] In his study of Shelley, Charles Middleton has remarked: "It is hinted, somewhat plausibly, that the *Leonora* of Bürgher first awakened his poetic faculty. A tale of such beauty and terror might well have kindled his lively imagination, but his earliest pieces, written about this time, and consisting only of a few ballads, are deficient in elegance and originality, and give no evidence whatever of the genius which soon after declared itself."[20] To suggest, as Zeiger would have it,[21] that *Lenore* influenced the poem which in the romance *St. Irvyne*[22] Megalina inscribes on the wall of her prison, and which commences :

> Ghosts of the dead ! have I not heard your yelling
> Rise on the night-rolling breast of the blast, . . .

is the merest ineptitude, since these verses are taken almost word for word from "Lachin y Gair" in Byron's *Hours of Idlen.ss*, and that had been published some four years previously.[23]

As I have elsewhere shown in some detail, Shelley's two juvenile romances owe not only their inspiration but a great deal of their phrasing and noctivagations to Charlotte Dacre's *Zofloya : or The Moor*, which appeared in 1806, and which, as the poet himself declares "quite enraptured" him.[24] It is a very remarkable circumstance that in spite of the extremely plain hint which might profitably have been taken from such poems as *Die Braut von Korinth* and *Lenore* the novelists of the Gothic school, soaked though they were in German literature, searching the earth and the depths of the earth for thrills and sensation of every kind, do not seem to have utilized the tradition of the Vampire. It is a puzzle indeed if we ask how it was that such writers as Monk Lewis, "Apollo's sexton," who would fain "make Parnassus a churchyard ";[25] and Charles Robert Maturin who, as he himself confessed, loved bells rung by viewless hands, daggers encrusted with long shed blood, treacherous doors behind still more treacherous tapestry, mad nuns, apparitions,[26] *et hoc genus omne ;* the two lords of macabre romance, should neither of them have sent some hideous vampire ghost ravening through their sepulchral pages. In the Gothic romance we have horror heaped on horror's head ; mouldering abbeys, haunted castles, banditti, illuminati, sorcerers, conspirators, murderous monks and phantom friars, apparitions without number until the despairing reviewers cried aloud : " Surely the *misses* themselves must be tired of so many stories of ghosts and murders." We have such titles as the famous *Horrid Mysteries ; The Midnight Groan ; The Abbot of Mont-serrat, or, The Pool of Blood ; The Demon of Venice ; The Convent Spectre ; The Hag of the Mountains ;*[27] and a hundred such lurid nomenclatures, but until we come to Polidori's novel which will be considered later, nowhere, so far as I am aware, do we meet with the Vampire in the realm of Gothic fancy. So vast, however, is this fascinating library and so difficult to procure are these novels of a century and a quarter ago that I hesitate sweepingly to assert that this theme was entirely unexploited. There may be some romance which I have not had the good fortune to find where a hideous vampire swoops down upon his victims, but if such be the case I am at least prepared to say that the Vampire was not generally known to Gothic lore, and had his presence made itself felt in the sombre chapters of one votary of this school I think he would have re-appeared on many occasions, for the writers were as accustomed to convey from one another with an easy assurance, as they were wont deftly to plunder the foreign mines. Inevitably one of the band, T. J. Horseley Curties, Francis Lathom, William Herbert, Edward Montague, Mrs. Roche, Eliza Parsons, Miss M. Hamilton, Mrs. Helme, Mrs. Meeke, Isabella Kelley, and many another beside insatiably agog for horrid phantasmagoria would have utilized the Vampire in some funereal episode.

One might even have supposed that the notes to Southey's *Thalaba the Destroyer,*[28] must have put them on the track, and surely stanzas eight, nine and ten in Book VIII could not have passed unnoticed :

> A night of darkness and of storms !
> Into the Chamber of the Tomb
> Thalaba led the Old Man,
> To roof him from the rain.
> A night of storms ! the wind
> Swept through the moonless sky,
> And moan'd among the pillar'd sepulchres ;

And in the pauses if its sweep
   They heard the heavy rain
Beat on the monument above.
In silence on Oneiza's grave
Her father and her husband sate.
The Cryer from the Minaret
Proclaim'd the midnight hour.
" Now, now ! " cried Thalaba ;
And o'er the chamber of the tomb
   There spread a lurid gleam,
Like the reflection of a sulphur fire ;
   And in that hideous light
Oneiza stood before them. It was She   . . .
Her very lineaments. . . .   and such as death
Had changed them, livid cheeks and lips of blue ;
   But in her eye there dwelt
   Brightness more terrible
Than all the loathsomeness of death.
" Still art thou living, wretch ? "
In hollow tones she cried to Thalaba ;
  " And must I nightly leave my grave
   To tell thee, still in vain,
  God hath abandoned thee ? "

" This is not she ! " the Old Man exclaim'd ;
  " A Fiend ; a manifest Fiend ! "
And to the youth he held his lance ;
  " Strike and deliver thyself ! "
" Strike HER ! " cried Thalaba,
  And palsied of all power,
Gazed fixedly upon the dreadful form.
" Yea, strike her ! " cried a voice, whose tones
Flow'd with such a sudden healing through his soul,
  As when the desert shower
  From death deliver'd him ;
But obedient to that well-known voice,
  His eye was seeking it,
  When Moath, firm of heart,
Perform 'd the bidding : through the vampire corpse
  He thrust his lance ; it fell,
  And howling with the wound,
  Its fiendish tenant fled.
A sapphire light fell on them,
And garmented with glory, in their sight
  Oneiza's spirit stood.

It is important to remark that in his notes[29] upon this passage Southey cites at considerable length various cases of vampirism, particularly from the *Lettres Juives*, the Vampires of Gradisch, also the history of Arnold Paul, and the very ample account given by Tournefort. He further says: "The Turks have an opinion that men that are buried have a sort of life in their graves. If any man makes affidavit before a judge, that he heard a noise in a man's grave, he [*i.e.*, the body] is, by order, dug up and chopped all to pieces. The merchants (at Constantinople) once airing on horseback, had, as usual, for protection, a Janisary with them. Passing by the burying place of the Jews, it happened that an old Jew sat by a sepulchre. The Janisary rode up to him, and rated him for stinking the world a second time, and commanded him to get into his grave again.—*Roger North's Life of Sir Dudley North.*"[30]

It might perhaps not unfairly be argued that the two notorious romances of the Marquis de Sade *Justine, on les Malheurs de la Vertu* and *Juliette* depict scenes of vampirism, and if we are to take the word in any extended sense this is certainly the case. In the first place it must be remembered that as it passed through various editions—it was first issued in 1791, 2 vols., 8vo,—until it appeared in its final and complete form in 1797 as *La Nouvelle Justine, on les Malheurs de la Vertu, suivie de l'Histoire de Juliette, sa soeur*, 10 vols., 18mo (of which *Justine* occupies four and *Juliette* six) *Justine* was added to and augmented until the last version is practically double the length of the first, and the book has been entirely re-written. In *Justine* we have the episodes in the house of Monsieur Rodin, and more particularly the orgies of the Comte de Gernade who takes a lustful pleasure in watching the blood flow from the veins of his victims, as also the cruelties of the monster Roland all of which may well be esteemed vampirism. Many similar scenes are described with great prolixity in *Juliette*, and this romance is distinguished by such horrible figures as the Muscovite giant Minski, whose favourite meat is human flesh, and in whose castle the table and chairs are made of bleaching bones, and Cordelli, the necrophilist of Ancona.

In *The New Monthly Magazine*,[31] 1 April, 1819, was published *The Vampyre : a Tale by Lord Byron*, which although it may seem to us—steeped in Le Fanu and M. R. James— a little old-fashioned, at the time created an immense sensation and had the most extraordinary influence, being even more admired and imitated on the Continent than in England. It was almost immediately known that actually the story did not come from the pen of Lord Byron, but had been written by Dr. John William Polidori, physician-companion to the poet. Byron had, as a matter of fact, been writing a work of the same title in imitation of Mrs. Shelley's *Franken-stein*, but he denied the authorship of this piece in the famous letter facsimilied in Galignani's edition of his works. A first printed, *The Vampyre* forms a part of extracts from "A letter from Geneva, with Anecdotes of Lord Byron." Here is to be read that "among other things which the lady, from whom I procured these anecdotes, related to me, she mentioned the outline of a ghost story by Lord Byron. It appears that one evening Lord Byron, Mr. P. B. Shelley, the two ladies and the gentleman (the daughters of Godwin and Dr. Polidori) before alluded to after having perused a German work, which was entitled Phantasmagoriana[32] began relating ghost stories ; when his lordship having recited the beginning of Christabel, then unpublished, the whole took so strong a hold of Mr. Shelley's mind, that he suddenly started up and ran out of the room. The physician and Lord Byron followed, and discovered him leaning against a mantlepiece with cold drops of perspiration trickling down his face. After having given him something to refresh him, upon enquiring into the cause of his alarm, they found that his wild imagina-tion having pictured to him the bosom of one of the ladies with eyes (which was reported of a lady in the neighbourhood where he lived) he was obliged to leave the room in order to destroy the impression. It was afterwards proposed in the course of conversation, that each of the company present should write a tale depending upon some supernatural agency, which was undertaken by Lord Byron, the physician, and Miss M. Godwin. My friend, the lady above referred to, had in her possession the outline of each of these stories, I obtained them as a great favour, and herewith forward them to you, as I was assured you would feel as much curiosity as myself, to peruse the *ébauches* of so great a genius, and those immediately under his influence." Upon this the Editor has the following note : "We have in our possession the Tale of Dr.—— as well as the outline of that of Miss Godwin. The latter has already appeared under the title of

' Frankenstein, or the modern Prometheus ' ; the former, however, upon consulting this author, we may, probably, hereafter give to our readers."

The Vampyre is introduced by several paragraphs which deal with the tradition. This preamble commences : " The superstition upon which this tale is founded is very general in the East. Among the Arabians it appears to be common ; it did not, however, extend itself to the Greeks until after the establishment of Christianity ; and it has only assumed its present form since the division of the Latin and Greek churches ; at which time, the idea becoming prevalent, that a Latin body could not corrupt if buried in their territory, it gradually increased, and formed the subject of many wonderful stories, still extant, of the dead rising from their graves, and feeding upon the blood of the young and beautiful. In the West it spread, with some slight variation, all over Hungary, Poland, Austria, and Lorraine, where the belief existed, that vampyres nightly imbibed a certain portion of the blood of their victims, who became emaciated, lost their strength, and speedily died of consumptions ; whilst these human blood-suckers fattened—and their veins became distended to such a state of repletion as to cause the blood to flow from all the passages of their bodies, and even from the very pores of their skins."

The Editor then recounts the famous instance of Arnold Paul, and continues : " We have related this monstrous rodomontade, because it seems better adapted to illustrate the subject of the present observations than any other instance we could adduce. In many parts of Greece it is considered as a sort of punishment after death, for some heinous crime committed whilst in existence, that the deceased is doomed to vampyrise, but be compelled to confine his visitations solely to those beings he loved most while on earth—those to whom he was bound by ties of kindred and affection. This supposition is, we imagine, alluded to in the following fearfully sublime and prophetic curse from the ' Giaour.'[33]

> But first on earth, as Vampyre sent,
> Thy corse shall from its tomb be rent ;
> Then ghastly haunt thy native place,
> And suck the blood of all thy race ;
> There from thy *daughter, sister, wife,*

At midnight drain the stream of life ;
Yet loathe the banquet, which perforce
Must feed thy livid living corse,
Thy victims, ere they yet expire,
Shall know the demon for their sire ;
As cursing thee, thou cursing them,
Thy flowers are withered on the stem.
But one that for *thy crime* must fall,
The youngest, best beloved of all,
Shall bless thee with a *father's* name—
That word shall wrap thy heart in flame !
Yet thou must end thy task and mark
Her cheek's last tinge—her eye's last spark,
And the last glassy glance must view
Which freezes o'er its lifeless blue ;
Then with unhallowed hand shall tear
The tresses of her yellow hair,
Of which, in life a lock when shorn
Affection's fondest pledge was worn—
But now is borne away by thee
Memorial o thine agony !
Yet with thine own best blood shall drip
Thy gnashing tooth, and haggard lip ;
Then stalking to thy sullen grave
Go—and with Ghouls and Afrits rave,
Till these in horror shrink away
From spectre more accursed than they."

After an allusion to Southey's *Thalaba*, Tournefort's *Travels*, and Dom Calmet's classical work, the editor concludes : " We could add many curious and interesting notices on this singularly horrible superstition, and we may, perhaps, resume our observations upon it at some future opportunity ; for the present, we feel that we have very far exceeded the limits of a note, necessarily devoted to the explanation of the strange production to which we now invite the attention of our readers ; and we shall therefore conclude by merely remarking, that though the term Vampyre is the one in most general acceptation, there are several other synonimous with it, which are made use of in various parts of the world, namely, Vroucolocha, Vardoulacha, Goul, Broucoloka, &c."

The story tells how at the height of a London season " there appeared at the various parties of the leaders of the *ton* a nobleman, more remarkable for his singularities, than his rank. He gazed upon the mirth around him, as if he could not participate therein. Apparently, the light laughter of the

fair only attracted his attention that he might by a look
quell it, and throw fear into those breasts where thoughtless-
ness reigned. Those who felt this sensation of awe, could
not explain whence it arose ; some attributed it to the dead
grey eye, which fixing upon the object's face, did not seem
to penetrate, and at one glance to pierce through to the inward
working of the heart ; but fell upon the cheek with a leaden
ray that weighed upon the skin it could not pass." This
original is invited to every house, and in the course of the
winter he meets " a young gentleman of the name of Aubrey "
he was an orphan left with an only sister in the possession of
great wealth, by parents who died while he was yet in child-
hood." Aubrey is greatly fascinated by Lord Ruthven, for
this is the name of the mysterious nobleman, and intending
to travel upon the Continent he mentions this intention to my
Lord, and is " surprised to receive from him a proposal to
join him. Flattered by such a mark of esteem from him who,
apparently, had nothing in common with other men, he gladly
accepted it, and in a few days they had passed the circling
waters."

As they travelled from town to town, Aubrey notices the
peculiar conduct of his companion who bestows largess upon
the most worthless characters, broken gamblers and the like,
but refuses a doit to the deserving and virtuous poor. However
the recipients of this charity " inevitably found that there
was a curse upon it, for they all were either led to the scaffold
or sunk to the lowest and the most abject misery." Eventually the travellers arrive at Rome, and here Aubrey receives
letters from his guardians who require him immediately
to leave his companion as since their departure from London
the most terrible scandals, adulteries and seductions, have
come to light. At Rome Aubrey is able to foil Lord Ruthven's
plans, frustrating an intrigue designed to ruin a heedless young
girl, and then he " directed his steps towards Greece, and,
crossing the Peninsula, soon found himself at Athens."
Here he lodges in the house of a Greek, whose daughter Ianthe
is a paragon of the most exquisite beauty. As he sketches the
ruins of the city she is wont to entertain him with Greek legend
and tradition, and " often, as she told him the tale of the
living vampyre, who had passed years amidst his friends, and
dearest ties, forced every year, by feeding upon the life of a

lovely female to prolong his existence for the ensuing months, his blood would run cold, whilst he attempted to laugh her out of such idle and horrible fantasies ; but Ianthe cited to him the names of old men, who had at last detected one living among themselves, after several of their relatives and children had been found marked with the stamp of the fiend's appetite ; and when she found him so incredulous, she begged of him to believe her, for it had been remarked, that those who had dared to question their existence, always had some proof given, which obliged them, with grief and heart-breaking to confess it was true. She detailed to him the traditional appearance of these monsters, and his horror was increased, by hearing a pretty accurate description of Lord Ruthven ; he, however, still persisted in persuading her, that there could be no truth in her fears, though at the same time he wondered at the many coincidences which had all tended to excite a belief in the supernatural power of Lord Ruthven."

Before long it becomes evident that Aubrey is in love with Ianthe, "and while he ridicules the idea of a young man of English habits, marrying an uneducated Greek girl, still he found himself more and more attached to the almost fairy form before him." He endeavours to occupy his time with antiquarian excursions which lead him farther and farther afield, and at length he determines to proceed to a point beyond any he has as yet visited. When Ianthe's parents hear the name of the place he proposes to visit they most earnestly implore him on no account to return when once dusk has fallen, "as he must necessarily pass through a wood, where no Greek would ever remain after the day had closed, upon any consideration. They described it as the resort of the vampyres in their nocturnal orgies, and denounced the most heavy evils as impending upon him who dared to cross their path. Aubrey made light of their representations, and tried to laugh them out of the idea ; but when he saw them shudder at his daring thus to mock a superior, the very name of which apparently made their blood freeze, he was silent."

Having given his promise to Ianthe that he will be back well before evening he sets out very early. The exploration, however, takes longer than he has supposed, and when he turns his horse homeward the darkness is already hurrying on urged by a terrific storm. The steed, alarmed at the battle of the elements dashes off at breakneck pace and only halts trembling and tired before a distant hovel in the heart of a solitary wood. " As he approached, the thunder, for a moment silent, allowed him to hear the dreadful shrieks of a woman mingling with the stiffled exultant mockery of a laugh, continued in one almost unbroken sound." With a terrific effort Aubrey burst open the door and rushing into the darkness " found himself in contact with someone, whom he immediately seized, when a voice cried " again baffled," to which a loud laugh succeeded, and he felt himself grappled by one whose strength seemed superhuman : determined to sell his life as dearly as he could, he struggled ; but it was in vain ; he was lifted from his feet and hurled with enormous force against the ground ; his enemy threw himself upon him, and kneeling upon his breast, had placed his hand upon his throat, when the glare of many torches penetrating through the hole that gave light in the day, disturbed him—he instantly rose and, leaving his prey, rushed through the door, and in a moment the crashing of the branches, as he broke through the wood was not longer heard." Several peasants now hastened into the hut bearing flambeaus which illuminate the scene, and to the horror of all there is discovered hard by, the lifeless body of Ianthe. A curious dagger lies near, but her death was not the result of a blow from this weapon. " There was no colour upon her cheek, not even upon her lip ; yet there was a stillness about her face that seemed almost as attaching as the life that once dwelt there : —upon her neck and breast was blood, and upon her throat were the marks of teeth having opened the vein :—to this the men pointed, crying, simultaneously struck with horror, ' a Vampyre, a Vampyre ! ' " It appears that Ianthe had followed the traveller to watch over his safety. Aubrey is carried back to the city in a raging fever, and the parents of the unfortunate girl die brokenhearted owing to so terrible a loss.

Whilst Aubrey lies ill Lord Ruthven arrives in Athens and establishing himself in the same house nurses the invalid with such care that past differences are forgotten, since Aubrey not only becomes reconciled to his presence but even seeks his company. Together they travel into the wildest interior of Greece, and here in some mountain pass they are attacked by brigands, from whose guns Lord Ruthven receives a shot in the shoulder. His strength strangely decreasing, a couple of days later it is plain to all that he is at the point of death. He now exacts a terrific oath that his companion shall conceal all that is known of him and that the news of his death shall not be allowed to reach England. "Swear!" cried the dying man, "Swear by all your soul reveres, by all your nature fears, swear that for a year and a day you will not impart your knowledge of my crimes or death to any living being in any way, whatever may happen, or whatever you may see." Aubrey binds himself most solemnly by the prescribed oath, and in a paroxysm of hideous laughter Ruthven expires.

According to a promise which has been obtained from the robbers by a heavy bribe the body was conveyed to the pinnacle of a neighbouring mount, that it should be exposed to the first cold ray of the moon which rose after his death. Aubrey insists that it shall be interred in the ordinary way, but when he is conducted to the place it is found that the body has disappeared, and in spite of the protestations of the band he is convinced that they have buried the corpse for the sake of the clothes. One circumstance, however, gives Aubrey much food for thought. Among the effects of the deceased he discovered a sheath of most curious pattern and make which exactly fits the dagger that had been found in the deserted hut upon the occasion of Ianthe's death.

Returning to England, as he retraces his journey through Rome to his horror Aubrey discovers that in spite of the precautions he had so carefully taken, Lord Ruthven succeeded only too well in his bad designs and now there is bitter sorrow and distress where once reigned peace and happiness. The lady had not been heard of since the departure of his lordship, and Aubrey instinctively divines that she has "fallen a victim to the destroyer of Ianthe."

Upon his arrival in London the traveller is greeted by his sister, whose presentation into society had been delayed until her brother's return from the Continent, when he might be her protector. "It was now, therefore, resolved that the next drawing room, which was fast approaching, should be the epoch of her entry into the busy scene." Upon this gay occasion the crowd was excessive, and as Aubrey heedless and distracted is watching the gay throng a voice which he recognizes only too well, whispers in this ear : "Remember your oath." Turning he sees Lord Ruthven standing near him. A few nights later at the assembly of a near relation among the crowd of admirers by whom his sister is surrounded —the most prominent of the throng—he again perceives the mysterious and horrible figure. Hurrying forward he seizes his sister's arm and requests her immediately to accompany him home. However, before they have had time to retire again does the voice whisper close to him : " Remember your oath ! "

Aubrey now becomes almost distracted. He sees no remedy against a monster who has already once mocked at death. Even if he were to declare all that he knew it is probable that he would hardly be believed. Whenever he attends a social gathering his looks as he scans the company become so suspicious and strange that he soon acquires a reputation for great eccentricity. As the months go on his loathing and his fears drive him well-nigh to madness, so that eventually a physician is engaged to reside in the house and take charge of him. He is a little consoled by the thought that when the year and the day have passed he will at least be able to unburden his mind and be at any rate freed from his terrible oath. It so happens that he overhears a conversation between the doctor and one of his guardians who enlarges upon the melancholy circumstance of her brother being in so critical a state when Miss Aubrey is to be married on the following day. He instantly demands the name of the bridegroom and is told the Earl of Marsden. He requests to see his sister and in an hour or two she visits him. As they are conversing she opens a locket and shows him a miniature of the man who has won her affections. To his horror he perceives that it is a portrait of Lord Ruthven and falling into convulsions of rage he tramples it under foot. In twenty-four hours the period of his oath will have expired, and he implores them to delay the wedding at least for that time. Since there seems no good reason for doing this the request is disregarded, upon which Aubrey falls into so sad a state of utter depression succeeded by an outburst of fury that the physician concludes him to be not far removed from lunacy and doubles the restraint. During the night the busy preparations for the nuptial are ceaselessly continued. It appears that upon the pretext of being her brother's dearest friend and travelling companion Lord Ruthven had visited the house to inquire after Aubrey during his supposed derangement, and from the character of a visitor gradually insinuated himself into that of an accepted suitor. When the bridal party has assembled Aubrey, neglected by the servants, contrives to make his way into the public apartments which are decorated for the nuptials. Ere he can utter a cry, he is, however, at once perceived by Lord Ruthven who with more than human strength thrusts him, speechless with rage, from the room, at the same time whispering in his ear : " Remember your oath, and know, if not my bride to-day, your sister is dishonoured. Women are frail ! " The attendants at once secure the unhappy man, but he can no longer support his distress. In his agonies a blood vessel breaks and he is incontinently conveyed to bed. This sad accident is kept from his sister ; the marriage was solemnized, and the bride and bridegroom left London.

" Aubrey's weakness increased ; the effusion of blood produced symptoms of the near approach of death. He desired his sister's guardians might be called, and when the midnight hour had struck, he related composedly what the reader has perused—he died immediately after.

" The guardians hastened to protect Miss Aubrey ; but when they arrived it was too late. Lord Ruthven had disappeared, and Aubrey's sister had glutted the thirst of a Vampyre ! "

It were not easy to overestimate the astounding sensation which was caused by this story, and the narrative is certainly not without considerable merit, for in places the eerie atmosphere is well conveyed, Nor is it difficult to understand the extraordinary influence of the tale, since it introduced a tradition which had been long forgotten and which promised infinite possibilities in the way of that sensation and melodramatic calentures which the period craved. The first separate edition of *The Vampyre* appeared in 1819, and was published by Sherwood. The first issue of this, which is now very rare, contains a certain amount of preliminary matter concerning the Shelleys, Byron and Godwin. This was omitted in later issues, and accordingly one often finds that copies of *The Vampyre* are described as First Edition, which is strictly quite correct, although they are the Second Issue,

and naturally of far less value in a bibliographer's eyes. A
large number of reprints increased with amazing rapidity
and in the same year the novel was translated into French
by Henri Faber, *Le Vampire, nouvelle traduite de l'anglais de
Lord Byron*, Paris, 1819. In February, 1820, there followed
under the aegis of Charles Nodier a very obvious imitation,
or rather continuation by Cyprien Bérard, *Lord Ruthwen
ou les Vampires.* "Roman de C. B. Publié par l'auteur de
Jean Sbogar et de *Thérèse Aubert.*[34] Paris, 1820." In 1825,
a new translation of Polidori's story was given by Eusèbe de
Salles. Nor was Germany behind hand, for *The Vampyre*
was first translated in 1819 : *Der Vampyr. Eine Erzahlung
aus dem Englischen des Lord Byron. Nebst einer Schilderung
seines Aufenthaltes in Mytilene.* Leipzig, 1819. In the
following year there appeared at Frankfort a version by J.V.
Adrian of Byron's poems and prose, wherein was included
Der Blutsuger. In a collection of Byron's work the first
volume of which was published at Zwickau in 1821, *The
Vampyre* again found a place in volume V (1821), translated
by Christian Karl Meifsner as *DerVampyr.* The tale has also
been included in various other continental collections and
translations of Byron's work even until a recent date.

Yet it was well-known all the while that Polidori was the
author of the story, but as Byron's was by far the greater
name, so this sensational novella must be attributed to the
cavaliero whose romantic adventures and the scandal of whose
amours were thrilling the whole of Europe. Writing in
the same year as the great poet's death Amédée Pichot of the
University of Marseilles in his *Essai sur le génie et le caractère
de Lord Byron*[35] declared that this spurious issue " a autant
contribué à faire connaître le nom de lord Byron en France,
que ses poëmes les plus estimés." Publishers insisted upon
Le Vampire, "nouvelle," being included among Byron's
works, and it is said that Ladvocat was furious when it was
represented to him that since it was openly acknowledged
that Polidori had written *The Vampire*, the translation should
properly be no longer given among the poet's work nor put
forth under his name.

As might have been expected it was not long before the
Vampire appeared upon the stage, and the first play of this
kind would seem to be the famous melodrama by Charles

Nodier (with Achille Jouffroy and Carmouche) which with music by Alexandre Piccini and scenery by Ciceri, was produced in Paris on 13th June, 1820, at the Théâtre de la Porte-Saint-Martin, whose directors were the popular M. M. Croznier and Merle. The rôle of Lord Rutwen was taken by M. Philippe; the celebrated Madame Dorval was Malvina;[36] and the new play had an extraordinary success.

It was immediately published as *Le Vampire, mélodrame en trois actes avec un prologue, Par MM. . . . ; Musique de M. Alexandre Piccini; Décors de M. Ciceri*. This might be purchased at 1 fr. 25cs. "au magasin général de pièces de Théâtre, Chez J.-N. Barba, Libraire, Palais Royal, derrière le Théâtre Français, No. 51." The characters in the Prologue are Ituriel, ange de la Lune, Mlle. Descotte; Oscar, génie des Mariages, M. Moëssard; and Un Vampire, M. Philippe. The scene opens in "une grotte basaltique," the Caledonian caves of Staffa. Oscar and Ituriel discourse of Vampires, and the latter asks: "Serait-il vrai que d'horribles fantômes viennent quelquefois, sous l'apparence des droits de l'hymen, égorger une vierge timide, et s'abreuver de son sang?" This is indeed the case, and it is signifcant that on the morrow Malvina (Miss Aubray) is to wed "le comte de Marsden." A vision of the sleeping Malvina appears when "Un spectre vêtu d'un linceuil s'échappe de la plus apparente de ces tombes" and rushes upon her. He is swiftly repulsed by Oscar, the good genius and the curtain falls. The characters in the play are: Lord Rutwen, M. Philippe; Sir Aubray, M. Perrin *ou* Théringy; Malvina, Mad. Dorval; Brigitte, Mad. St. Amand; Edgar, M. Edmon; Scop, M. Pierson; Petterson, M. Dugy; Lovette, Mlle. J. Vertpré; Oscar, M. Moëssard; with attendances of *Domestiques* and *Villageois*. The drama to a certain extent adroitly follows the lines of the Polidori novel, but with notable changes, which are well contrived and introduced. Lord Rutwen and Aubray have been fellow travellers, but the latter has no suspicion of Rutwen's real nature. In fact he holds him in the dearest affection since once he was saved from death by his friend who, whilst shielding him from a brigand's attack, fell by a chance shot. When Lord Rutwen arrives to claim Malvina's hand it is with delight Aubray hails his preserver on whom he supposed killed by the bandit's gun. It is cleverly explained how the wound did not after all prove fatal, whereupon "Rutwen, mes desirs sont remplis" cries Aubray, "nous allons être frères" (*Ils s'embrassent*). Lovette a farmer's daughter of the Marsden estate is to wed Edgar, and Rutwen graciously presents himself at the marriage feast. As Lord of the Manor he is received with every respect and homage, but he immediately proceeds to attempt Lovette's virtue. Oscar "un viellard dont la tête vénérable inspire le respect. Sa démarche a quelque chose d'imposant et de mystérieux," has already warned the maiden, and she coldly avoids such ardent importtunities. Whilst Rutwen is actually pursuing the coy lass who shuns his embrace, Edgar in a fury fires a pistol at the seducer and he falls crying, "Je meurs." Aubray hastening to the spot is barely in time to receive him in his arms, and with dying lips Rutwen adjures him to swear the following oath. "Promets-moi que Malvina ne saura point ce qui m'est arrivé ; que tu ne feras rien pour venger ma mort avant que la première heure de la nuit n'ait sonné. Jure-moi le secret sur ce coeur expirant." Aubray much moved cries, "Je te le jure," and as Rutwen expires they lay the body gently on the ground. "A`ce moment on voit la lune planer entièrement sur le corps de Rutwen, et éclairer les glaçons de la montagne. La toile tombe."

Act III. "représente un grand vestibule gothique, la porte de la chapelle se voit au fond." Oscar solemnly utters words of warning to Brigitte, who is already full of fears which are not unnoticed by Malvina. When Aubray meets his sister she speaks joyfully of her marriage but as he is about to tell her of the fatal happening suddenly Rutwen appears and seizing his arm "lui dit d'une voix sombre : ' Songe à ton serment ' ! " Aubray now realizes that there is some horrid secret and displays violent emotion crying out in broken tones : " 'Eloigne-toi fantôme !   . .   ma soeur . . .   dérobe-toi, aux poursuites de ce monstre . . .   il te dira qu'il est ton époux . . .   refuse ton serment . . .   cet hymen est un crime ! " At length he is carried off by the servants who fear that he has lost his senses, an idea Rutwen encourages. In spite of this disorder the bridegroom now hotly presses on the nuptials ; the great doors are opened " et laisse voir la chapelle éclairée," Rutwen and Malvina approach the altar. With a wild cry Aubray rushes in to intercept the ceremony, upon which the monster drawing his dagger is about to plunge it deep into Malvina's heart when one o'clock strikes,— his power is gone." Il laisse tomber son poignard et cherche à s'enfuir, des ombres sortent de la terre et l'entraînent avec elles ; l'Ange exterminateur paraît dans un nuage, la foudre éclate et les Ombres s'engloutissent avec Rutwen. Pluie de feu. TABLEAU GÉNÉRAL."

The dialogue of this melodrama is spirited, the situations striking and well managed, and even in reading the play, one can clearly visualize that upon the stage it must have been extraordinarily effective, especially when set off with all the attractions of the scene painter's glowing perspectives, the magic craft of the subtle machinist, and the richest adornment of romantic costume.[37] Even before he had introduced the Vampire on to the boards Nodier had prophesied that this macabre monster would win a veritable triumph, and his prediction was amply fulfilled. "Le Vampire épouvantera, de son horrible amour, les songes de toutes les femmes, et bientôt sans doute, ce monstre encore exhumé prêtera son masque immobile, sa voix sépulcrale, son oeil d'un gris mort, . . . tout cet attirail de mélodrame à la Melpomène des boulevards ; et quel succès alors ne lui est pas réservé ! "[38] On 1st July, 1819, writing in the *Drapeau Blanc* he was far more serious and far more emphatic : "La fable du vampire est peut-être la plus universelle de nos superstitions. . . Elle a partout l'autorité de la tradition : elle ne manque ni de celle de la théologie ni de celle de la médicine. La philosophie même en a parlé."

All Paris flocked to see *Le Vampire*, and nightly the Porte-Saint-Martin was packed to the doors. Philippe and Madame Dorval were applauded to the echo by enthusiastic audiences who recalled them again and again after the final tableau. Even the book of the play had an immense circulation and every morning Barba's counter was freshly stocked with huge piles of the duodecimo, which rapidly diminished during the day.

Not a few critics, however, adopted a very uncompromising attitude, and were unsparing in their condemnation of so popular a melodrama. In *Les Lettres Normandes*, 1820, (tome XI, p. 93) *Le Vampire* was thus noticed : " Le mélo-drame du *Vampire* dans lequel on voit paraître un monstre qui suce le sang des petites filles et qui offre des Tableaux qu'une honnête femme ne peut voir sans rougir, est l'ouvrage de MM. Ch. Nodier, rédacteur du *Drapeau Blanc* ; Achille Jouffroy, rédacteur de *La Gazette* et auteur des *Festes de l'anarchie* ; et Carmouche autre rédacteur du *Drapeau Blanc*." This censure is, however, wholly inspired by political feeling which thus inveighed against the royalist Nodier, and which not unmingled with green jealousy we also find prominent in the *Conservateur littéraire* of April, 1820 (Tome II, p. 245) where we had : " Pour balancer le succès du *Vampire* mélodrame dégoûtant et si monstreux que les auteurs MM. Ch. Nodier et Carmouche m'ont pas osé se faire connaître, le théâtre de la Porte-Saint-Martin se prépare à représenter la traduction littérale, en prose, de la *Marie Stuart* de Schiller."

Yet another critic is even more trenchant and severe :" Le Vampire Ruthwen veut violer ou sucer dans les coulisses une jeune fiancée qui fuit devant lui sur le théâtre : cette situation est-elle morale ? . . .   Toute la pièce représente indirectement Dieu comme un être faible ou odieux qui abandonne le monde aux génies de l'enfer."[39]

Yet all these attacks served but to enhance the attraction, and it is remarkable for how many years this continued undiminished. In 1823 a revival of *Le Vampire* with Philippe and Madame Dorval again thronged the Porte-Saint-Martin to excess. Alexandre Dumas, who was present at this production has recorded how vast was his delight, how ineffable his thrills during the sombre scenes of this sepulchral melodrame. How the theatre applauded the lean livid mask of the Vampire, how it shuddered at his stealthy steps ! There are, perhaps, to be found throughout the whole of the many works of Alexandre Dumas few pages more entertaining than those chapters in his *Memoires* which relate with rarest humour and not a few flashes of brilliant wit his adventures at a performance of *Le Vampire* at the Porte-Saint-Martin in 1823. It would be difficult to find a livelier, and yet at the same time entirely serious and even critical, account of a theatrical performance. Unfortunately it is too long to give in full. In the edition of *Mes Mémoires*, Troisième Série, Michel Lévy, Paris, 1863, it occupies no less than five chapters, LXXIII-LXXVII, and these are none of the shortest, (pp. 136-193). One is tempted to quote some delicious passages, but the account might lose thereby ; it must be read as a delightful whole. Yet there is one extract which may certainly be made without impertinence, the story of the Vampire which was related to Dumas by his neighbour " le monsieur poli qui lisait un Elzévir." They have discussed the tradition at some length, and incidentally the good bibliophile refers his young acquaintance to the work of Dom Calmet, from whom he gives ample citations. He further remarks that he has resided in Illyria for three years, and he very sharply animadverts upon certain details on Nodier's melodrama which are foreign to the vampire tradition. " You speak of vampires as though they really existed," remarks Dumas. " Of course they exist," said his neighbour dryly. " Have you ever seen one then ? " " Most certainly I have." " That was whilst you were in Illyria ? " " Yes."

" Et vous y avez vu des vampires ? "

" Vous savez que c'est la terre classique des vampires, l'Illyrie, comme la Hongrie, la Servie, la Pologne.

" Non, je ne sais pas . . . je ne sais rien. Où étaient ces vampires que vous avez vus ?

" A Spalatro. Je logeais chez un bonhomme de soixante-deux ans. Il mourut. Trois jours après avoir été enterré, il apparut la nuit à son fils et lui demanda à manger ; son fils le servit selon des desirs ; il mangea et disparut. Le lendemain, le fils me raconta ce qui lui était arrivé, me disant que bien certainement son père ne reviendrait pas pour une fois, et m'invitant a me mettre, la nuit suivante, à une fenêtre pour le voir entrer et sortir. J'étais curieux de voir un vampire. Je me mis à la fenêtre ; mais, cette nuit-la, il ne vint pas. Le fils me dit, alors, de ne pas me décourager, qu'il viendrait probablement la nuit suivante.—La nuit suivante, je me remis donc à ma fenêtre, et, en effet, vers minuit, je reconnus parfaitement le vieillard. Il venait du côté de cimetière ; il marchait d'un bon pas ; mais son pas ne faisait aucun bruit. Arrivé à la porte, il frappa ; je comptai trois coups ; les coups résonnèrent secs sur le chêne, comme si l'on eut frappé avec un os, et non avec un doigt. Le fils vint ouvrir la porte, et le vieillard entra. . . .

" J'écoutais ce récit avec la plus grande attention, et je commençais à preférer les entr'actes au mélodrame.

" Ma curiosité était trop vivement excitée, reprit mon voisin, pour que je quittasse ma fenêtre ; j'y demeurai donc. Une demi-heure après, le vieillard sortit ; il retournait d'où il était venu, c'est-a-dire du côté du cimetiere. A l'angle d'une muraille, il disparut. Presque au même instant, ma porte s'ouvrit. Je me retournai vivement, c'était son fils. Il était fort pâle. ' Et bien, lui dis-je, votre père est venu ?—Oui . . . L'avez-vous vu entrer ? Entrer et sortir. . Qu'a-t-il fait aujourd'hui ? Il m'a demandé à boire et à manger, comme l'autre jour. Et il a bu et mangé ? Il a bu et mangé . . . Mais ce n'est pas le tout. . . voici ce qui m'inquiète. . . Il m'a dit . . . Ah ! il vous a parlé pour autre chose que pour vous demander à boire et a manger ? . . . Oui, il m'a dit : ' Voici deux fois que je viens manger chez toi. C'est à ton tour maintenant de venir manger chez moi.' Diable ! . . . Je l'attends après demain à la même heure. Diable ! Diable ! Eh ! oui, justement, voilà ce qui me tracasse.' Le surlendemain, on le trouva mort dans son lit ! Ce même jour, deux ou trois autres, personnes du même village qui avaient vu aussi le vieillard, et qui lui avaient parlé, tombèrent malades et moururent à leur tour. Il fut donc reconnu que le vieillard était vampire. On s'informa auprès de moi ; je racontai ce que j'avais vu et entendu. La justice se transporta au cimetière. On ouvrit les tombeaux de tous ceux qui étaient morts depuis six semaines ; tous ces, cadavres étaient en décomposition. Mais, quand on en vint au tombeau de Kisilova,—c'était le nom du vieillard,—on le trouva les yeux ouverts, la bouche vermeille, respirant à pleins poumons, et cependant immobile, comme mort. On lui enfonça un pieu dans le coeur ; il jeta un grand cri, et rendit le sang par le bouche ; puis on le mit sur un bûcher, on le réduisit en cendre, et l'on jeta la cendre au vent. . . . Quelque temps après, je quittai le pays ; de sorte que je ne pus savoir si son fils était devenu vampire comme lui.

" Pourquoi serait-il devenu vampire comme lui ? demandai-je.

" Ah ! parce que c'est l'habitude, que les personnes qui meurent du vampirisme deviennent vampires.

" En vérité, vous dites cela comme si c'était un fait avéré.

" Mais c'est qu'aussi c'est un fait avéré, connu, enregistré ! "

It will readily be remembered that in *Monte-Cristo* when

during the performance of *Parisina* at the Teatro Argentino, Rome, the Count and Haidée enter their box, the Countess G—— directing her opera-glass in that direction asks Franz d'Epinay who they may be remarking that as for herself, " All I can say is that the gentleman whose history I am unable to furnish seems to me as though he had just been dug up ; he looks more like a corpse permitted by some friendly grave-digger to quit his tomb for a while, and revisit this earth of ours, than anything human. How ghastly pale he is ! " " Oh, he is always as colourless as you now see him," said Franz. " Then you know him ? " almost screamed the countess. " Oh ! pray do, for Heaven's sake, tell us all about— is he a vampire or a resuscitated corpse, or what ? " A few moments later when the lady has carefully studied the *loge* of their mysterious *vis-à-vis*, Franz demands : " Well, what do you think of our mysterious neighbour ? " " Why, that he is no other than Lord Ruthven himself in a living frame," was the reply. This fresh allusion to Byron drew a smile to Franz's countenance ; although he could not but allow that if anything was likely to induce belief in the existence of vampires, it would be the presence of such a man as the mysterious personage before him. . . . " Is it possible," whispered Franz, " that you entertain any fear ? " " I'll tell you," answered the countess. " Byron had the most perfect belief in the existence of vampires, and even assured me he had seen some. The description he gave me perfectly corresponds with the features and character of the man before us. Oh ! it is the exact personification of what I have been led to expect. The coal-black hair, large bright, glittering eyes, in which a wild, unearthly fire seems burning,—the same ghastly paleness ! "[40]

Nearly thirty years after Dumas in collaboration with Maquet utilized the theme of *Le Vampire* for his own drama of the same name which was given at the Ambigu-Comique, 20th December, 1851, and which may conveniently be considered here.

Le Vampire is described as a " Drame Fantastique en Cinq Actes, en Dix Tableaux " and there are very many characters in this remarkable play. The principal parts were taken as follows : Lord Ruthwen, M. Arnault ; Gilbert de Tiffauges, M. Goujet ; Juan Rozo, a Spanish inn-keeper, M. Coquet ;

Botaro, his son-in-law, M. Curcy ; Lazare, M. Laurent ; Lahennée, M. Thierry ; Jarwick, M. Lavergne ; the Ghoul, Mme. Lucie Mabire ; Hélène de Tiffauges, Mlle. Jane Essler ; Juana, Mlle. Marie Clarisse ; Antonia, Mlle. Daroux ; Petra, Rozo's daughter, Mlle. Heloïse ; and the mystic fairy Mélusine, Mlle. Isabelle Constant. Lazare is a capital character, but the intrusion from Oriental legend of the ghoul cannot be considered happy. On the other hand the appearance of Mélusine, whose legend was collected about the end of the fourteenth century by Jean d'Arras, is certainly effective and entirely in keeping with the history, since according to Paracelsus she was an occult power, and in folk lore she is often represented as protecting ancient houses—in Belgium she is the guardian of the old family de Gavre,—whilst one of her four sons became King of Brittany.

It is hardly necessary to do more than give the very briefest outline of the story as Dumas tells it. The play opens with a crowded scene of merrymakers in the patio of Juan Rozo's inn. They are celebrating the nuptials of his daughter with young Botaro, and every room is occupied by his friends and acquaintance in festive mood. Juana, who is staying at the hostlery seeks for a guide to the castle of Tormenar, which lies at some little distance, for there she is to meet Don Luis de Figuerroa, whom she will wed upon the following day. She has secretly left the convent of Annunciades, where she was a boarder, since her father has other designs for her hand, and accordingly it is necessary that she should meet her betrothed in some lonely spot. But nobody, not even the good-natured Lazare, the servant of the inn, will conduct her to the haunted castle, " un château qui est en ruine, un château qui ne loge que des reptiles, et qui n'héberge que des fantômes." However, a numerous company, amongst whom is Gilbert de Tiffauges, arrives at the inn, and these travellers on being told that they cannot be accommodated in spite of the fact that night is falling, incontinently resolve to take up their quarters in Tormenar, so in spite of the warnings about ghosts and goblins, having once well stocked themselves with wine and food they merrily set forth, Gilbert taking charge of Juana who has confided to him her story. However, a mysterious figure, a lady, apparently of rank, who has been staying at the inn watches them as they take their departure and mutters to herself as she fixes her gaze upon Juana : " Il te faut deux heures pour aller retrouver ton beau fiancé. . . . Je l'aurai joint dans trois minutes ! " She is in fact the ghoul, a female vampire, and with the speed of lightning she has gone to destroy the unfortunate Don Luis.

In the second Act we see the huge Gothic hall of the old castle. A door opens and from an inner chamber the ghoul rushes out exclaiming : " Il était jeune ! Il était beau ! . . . Me voilà redevenue jeune et belle ! " The voice of Gilbert is now heard, and with the cry, " À l'an prochain, Gilbert." she disappears from sight. It will be remarked that in his treatment of the vampire tradition Dumas has adopted the legend that the vampire must year by year rejuvenate his waning forces by absorbing the life of another and sucking from another's veins fresh blood, a detail which although it may recommend itself to, and legitimately be used by, the dramatist and the writer of romances is actually inexact and but rarely to be met with, and only then in folk-lore not of the first value. The travellers, no small party, spread their provisions upon the huge tables in the old hall and laughing at the stories of ghosts and apparitions are soon in convivial mood. The conversation, however, eventually turns on the supernatural and Gilbert tells of his old home in Brittany, where one room in the castle is hung with the tapestry of the Fairy Mélusine, representing this lady and all her attendants. The story goes that if any of the family sleeps in that room she will descend from the tapestry and reveal his fortune, warning him of danger should such threaten. Another companion who has sojourned in Epirus speaks of the vampires, the women who will attack men and leave them dead and sapless ; the men who will attack women to drink their blood. Just as the words are uttered Lord Ruthwen enters and announces himself as a belated traveller, who finding no room at Rozo's inn down in the village has made his way thither,—he has even taken Lazare into his service. Presently the company disperse to their several rooms to make themselves as comfortable as may be for the night in such difficult circumstances. To his horror Gilbert discovers in the chamber he is to occupy the body of a young man, strangely pale, with a slight wound in the throat. By a letter he finds near upon the body it is plain that this can be none other than the unfortunate Don Luis. At the same moment a piercing cry is heard, and Juana ghostly pale and dying totters from her room. Gilbert rushes to her assistance just in time to see Lord Ruthwen dart out after her as she falls dead at his feet. In a moment he has drawn his sword and strikes Ruthwen to the heart, before he recognizes who it may be. In faltering accents Ruthwen explains that hearing a cry he has gone to the assistance of the lady, and with his last breath he implores Gilbert, who is well-nigh distracted at the unhappy accident, to bear his body to the hillside, where it may be bathed in the earliest rays of the new moon. This Gilbert promises, and in the final tableau we see the body of Lord Ruthwen laid upon the mountain. The moon slowly issues from the clouds, and as its silver light falls upon the corpse it seems as though the eyes opened and the mouth smiled. A moment more and the Vampire leaps to his feet re-vitalized and with fresh energy for some new demoniac enterprise.

In Act III. we find ourselves in Brittany, about a year later, at the château de Tiffauges where Hélène awaits her brother's return. After an affectionate greeting he confides to her the secret of his love for Antonia a lady of Spalatro in Dalmatia, and she in her turn informs him that she is about to give her hand to the Baron de Marsden. This latter proves to be none other than Lord Ruthwen, who informs Gilbert that he was sore wounded indeed at Tormenar, but that certain kindly shepherds finding him on the mountain side nursed him back to life. Moreover, he explains his change of name by informing them that his elder brother having recently died, he has succeeded to the title and estates. Visiting Tiffauges in the hope of meeting Gilbert once more, he has fallen a victim to the charms of Hélène. The explanation is cleverly contrived, but at the same time Gilbert is hardly convinced ; he feels that there is some mysterious and terrible secret lurking in the background. A happy idea strikes him. He will sleep that night in the tapestry chamber of the lady Mélusine. The scene that follows must have been extraordinarily effective upon the stage. Gilbert is slumbering, and from their places in the tapestry step forth Mélusine and her court to warn the scion of her house that danger is near. From the framed canvas and the panels descend with stately stride

the old barons to tell their descendant of the horror that
encompasses him, Mélusine reveals the secret :

> "Prions, pour qu' à Gilbert Dieu tout-puissant inspire
> Un généreux effort.
> Ruthwen est un démon, Ruthwen est un vampire;
> Son amour, c'est la mort ! "

(One cannot but recall the famous scene in Gilbert and
Sullivan's *Ruddigore* with its subtle admixture of beauty,
fantasy and humour.)

In Act IV of *Le Vampire* we are shown the accomplishment
of Ruthwen's designs against Hélène. Gilbert's frenzied
warnings and denunciations are heard with alarm but with un-
belief. They whisper that he is a lunatic, and when Ruthwen
relates a cunning story of a mischance in Spain which temporarily unsettled Gilbert's reason, a story that seems borne out
in every detail by the unhappy brother's horror and despair,
the attendants for his own safety seek to restrain their young
master. Ruthwen triumphs. But now the ghoul appears
and bids him take heed how he seeks Gilbert's life for that is
hers, and she will not likely relinquish her prey. Ruthwen
defies her and the two vampires part in horrid enmity. Lazare
cautions Hélène that her brother's story is no figment, but it
is too late, the vampire seizes his victim and as midnight strikes
he destroys his hapless bride and quaffs his fill from her veins.
Too late Gilbert succeeds in forcing an entrance. There is a
terrific struggle, and Ruthwen is hurled from the window
into the depths of a tremendous valley.

In the last act we find that in order to escape the pursuit
of Ruthwen, who has extricated himself unhurt but filled with
designs of even more malignant vengeance, Gilbert has transported Antonia to Circassia. Here, however, we meet the
ghoul who, disguising herself under the name of Ziska, obtained
admittance to the castle in the quality of an attendant upon
Antonia. She informs Gilbert that she alone can save his
betrothed from the vampire, and at that moment the ghastly
face of Ruthwen is actually seen peering through the window.
She demands that he shall relinquish Antonia's hand, and
accept her love though it be to death. He refuses to betray
Antonia, and at length by a supreme act of renunciation
she divulges the secret whereby the Vampire may be annihil-
ated, although this revelation must put an end to her own

existence. Ziska explains how Gilbert's sword is to be blessed
by a priest with a certain occult formula and if the weapon
thus consecrated be driven through the Vampire's heart it
will once and for all rid the world of this infernal pest. Yet
as she speaks she seems to vanish in flames and they hear her
last sad sigh ; " Adieu pour ce monde ! Adieu pour l'autre !
Adieu pour l'éternité " !

The final scene is a deserted cemetery. " Tombes, cyprès.
Fond sombre et fantastique ; neige sur la terre ; lune rouge
au ciel." The Vampire lies half in and half out of his grave,
grinning hideously. Gilbert is standing near. " Pour la
dernière fois, adore Dieu ! " he adjures. " Non," yells the
monster. " Alors, desespère et meurs " ! cries Gilbert and
plunges the hallowed sword into the monster's heart. The
Vampire falls back into the grave, howling fearfully, and a
heavy stone closing him in fast seals him there in the womb
of the earth for ever and ever. " Au nom du Seigneur,
Ruthwen, je te scelle dans cette tombe pour l'éternité ", et
Gilbert trace sur la pierre une croix que devient lumineuse.
A great aureola fills the sky and multitudes of rejoicing
angels are seen. Among them are Hélène and Juana, smiling
in happiest benison, whilst there rises from the earth the body of
Ziska, radiant and beautiful, to join the glorious throng
among whose immortal ranks she is enrolled by the merits of
her great act of renunciation and unselfish love.

This drama of Dumas is infinitely more elaborate than the
play of Nodier, but I am not altogether certain whether
it is in some respects so good a work. The first two acts
attain a high level ; the scene in the tapestry chamber would
be most picturesque upon the stage ; there are several other
telling situations and effective speeches, but as a whole it is
too prolix, and we feel that the episode of Antonia in particular is an anti-climax. Nor, as I have remarked before,
although material use is made of the character, can one
consider the figure of the ghoul entirely in keeping with the
rest. Had the level of the opening scenes been maintained
we should possess an excellent piece of work. But without
concentration and compression that was hardly possible,
and here we have the secret of Nodier's success. Although
he has an occasional crudity, it may be, which Dumas might
not have tolerated, so swift is his action, as is essential to

melodrama, so cleverly does he engage the interest of his
audience, that we have no time to criticize a roughness here
and there, but are rather intent to follow the next turn of
the tale.

Immediately upon the furore created by Nodier's *Le
Vampire* at the Porte-Saint-Martin in 1819 vampire plays of
every kind from the most luridly sensational to the most
farcically ridiculous pressed on to the boards. A contemporary critic cries : " There is not a theatre in Paris without its
Vampire ! At the Porte-Saint-Martin we have *le Vampire* ;
at the Vaudeville *le Vampire* again ; at the Variétés *les trois
Vampires ou le clair de la lune*."

Jean Larat[41] further mentions a play by Paul Féval, *Le
fils Vampire*. The version by John Wilson Ross of *The Loves of
Paris*, a romance, published by G. Vickers, 3, Catherine Street,
Strand, 1846, is said to be " Translated from the French of
Paul Féval, author of ' The Vampire,' ' The Loves of the
Palais-Royal,' ' The Receipt at Midnight,' ' Stella,' ' The
Son of the Devil,' etc., etc.", but it does not appear whether
" The Vampire " mentioned here is a play or a romance.
Probably it is the latter but no such translation is known.

Le Vampire which was produced at the Vaudeville, 15 June,
1820,[42] is a *comédic-vaudeville* in one act by Scribe and
Mélesville. The scene is laid in Hungary, " une salle d'un
château gothique," and the characters are as follows : Le
Comte de Valberg, feld-maréchal, M. Guillemin ; Adolphe de
Valberg, son néveu, M. Isambert ; le Baron de Lourdorff,
M. Fontenay ; Saussmann, concierge du château, M. Hippolyte ; Charles, valet du comte, M. Fichet ; un Notaire,
M. Justin ; Hermance de Mansfred, Madame Rivière ; Nancy,
sa soeur, Madame Lucie ; Péters, filleul de Saussmann,
Madame Minette ; with attendance of domestics and wedding
guests. This elegant little piece opens with nuptials of Hermance de Mansfred at the castle of the Baron de Lourdorff,
to whom she is betrothed. It appears that she has something
trifled with the affections of Adolphe de Valberg, now supposed
dead. Her sister, Nancy, acknowledges that she loved
Adolphe, but kept silence owing to his courtship of Hermance.
Adolphe's uncle, the Count de Valberg, who knows nothing of
the two ladies, fearing his nephew is unworthily entangled
has had him held in military detention at Temesvar, whence

however he has disappeared. The intrigue of the seventeen
scenes, although clearly unravelled in the play, is a little
complicated, and it must suffice to relate by an accident
Adolphe appears at the castle. Upon being asked his name
he answers : " Lord Ruthwen. An Englishman," whereupon
he is immediately taken to be a Vampire and the servants are
thrown into a state of panic. Eventually he is reconciled to
his uncle who recognizes him as the brave young hero by whom
his life was saved on a recent battlefield ; Nancy's fidelity is
rewarded with the hand of the man she loves, and who now
realizes that Hermance's heart was never his ; so that the
curtain falls upon a double wedding.

Several pretty lyrics are interwoven with the dialogue and
Nancy's first song, to the air " De sommeiller, encor ma chère "
from *Fanchon la vielleuse*, is as follows :

> Oui, ces paysans respectables
> Nous rapellent le bon vieux temps :
> Chez eux on croit encore au diable,
> Aux vampires, au revenants ;
> On croit à toutes les magies,
> Aux amours, aux soins assidus,
> Aux grands sorciers, aux grands genies . . .
> Bref à tout ce qu'on ne voit plus !

Les Trois Vampires, ou le clair de la lune[43] which was being
played at the Variétés is a thoroughly amusing farce in one
act by Brazier, Gabriel, and Armand. It shows the adventures
of a *bon bourgeois*, M. Gobetout, who has so distracted his brain
by reading stories of Vampires and ghosts that when one night
he sees in his garden three shadowy figures he is well nigh
beside himself with terror as he supposes they can be no
other than three vampires infesting his house. A little later
he catches sight of his two daughters and their abigail who
appear actually to be eating with the mysterious strangers.
" Les vampires qui soupent avec mes filles ! " he groans in
accents of despair. However it proves that the supper is
very material, cold chicken and a glass of good wine, whilst
the rendezvous is of an amorous nature, since the visitors
are two young sparks and their valet. So the play ends with
a triple marriage. One remark of the worthy M. Gobetout was,
it is said, nightly greeted with a hurricane of applause. He
was wont to murmur in pensive accents : " Les vampires

. . . il nous viennent d'Angleterre . . . C'est encore
une gentilesse de ces Messieurs . . . ils nous font de jolis
cadeaux ! "

Another farce, *Encore un Vampire*, which when produced
in 1820 at Paris, met with considerable success, was published
as by Emile B. L., and yet another vampire burlesque was
contributed by A. Rousseau. *Les Etrennes d'un Vampire*
at a minor theatre was billed as from a manuscript " trouvé
au cimitière de Père-Lachaise."

More amusing is the work of Désaugiers who in August,
1820, gave *Cadet Buteux, vampire, avec relation véridique
du prologue et des trois actes de cet épouvantable mélodrame
écrit sous la dictée de ce passeux du Gros Caillou, par son secré-
taire, Désaugiers.* When published by Rosa, 1820, this
libretto bore the motto : " *Vivent les morts !* "

Yet another burlesque published by Martinet, 1820, is
*Le Vampire, mélodrame en trois actes, paroles de Pierre de la
Fosse de la rue des Morts.*[44]   A few verses from this vaudeville
may be interesting to quote, particularly as showing the long
continued popularity of Nodier's melodrama.

> Lisant pour un sou d'politique
> Plac' Royale, sur un banc,
> J'tombe, le tour est diabolique,
> A' point nommé, sur l'Drapeau blanc.
>
> J'prends un billet, non pas pour le parterre,
> Ces places sont réservées aux amis,
> Sans l'secours de l'abbé Saint-Pierre,
> Avec treiz sous' j'monte au paradis.
>
> Au dernier banc, paix, qu'chacun s'taise !
> A' bas la gueule on crie du premier rang,
> L'rideau s'lève et quoique très mal à l'aise,
> Le croirez-vous, j'vois le Père Lachaise,
> Du dernier banc.

The Vampire is described as " d'échappé de corbillard,"
One sees everywhere

> Des fantôms, des revenans,
> Mettant la tête a la fenêtre,
> Afin d'regarder les passans.

There was even a *Polichinel Vampire* which when performed
at the Circus Maurice in 1822 attracted all who had a mind

for a hearty laugh, and a contemporary visitor[45] to Paris merrily wrote that "Polichinel is the very jolliest fellow in the world."[46]

A comic operetta in one act, *Le Vampire* by Martin Joseph Mengals which was produced at Ghent, 1 March, 1826, deserves no more than passing mention.

James Robinson Planché speedily adapted Nodier's *Le Vampire* as *The Vampire, or, The Bride of the Isles,* and his version with music by Joseph Binns Hart[47] was brought out at the English Opera House, 9th August, 1820, with T. P. Cooke[48] as Ruthven, Earl of Marsden, the Vampire. Owing to his fine acting in the part, and perhaps a little to the scenic effects—the scene is laid in the Caverns of Staffa—the play was given nightly to packed houses. It is interesting to remark that for this piece the celebrated vampire trap was invented. Of this I quote the following simple description : " A vampire trap consists of two or more flaps, usually india-rubber, through which the sprite can disappear almost instantly, where he falls into a blanket fixed to the under surface of the stage. As with the star trap, this trap is secured against accidents by placing another piece or *slide*, fitting close beneath when not required, and removed when the prompter's bell gives the signal to make ready."

The following account of the production of *The Vampire* is given by Planché in his *Recollections and Reflections*, Chapter III.[49] Having just spoken of an Easter piece with which he had furnished Drury Lane, *Abudah, or, The Talisman of Oromanes,*[50] founded upon one of the *Tales of the Genii*[51] and which although it had a run of nine nights Planché calls a very poor piece, " miserably put on the stage," he continues to speak of a subsequent success, and tells us : " A more fortunate melodrama of mine, " The Vampire, or The Bride of the Isles," was produced at the Lyceum, or English Opera House, as it was then called, 9th August, 1820. Mr. Samuel James Arnold, the proprietor and manager, had placed in my hands, for adaptation, a French melodrama, entitled " Le Vampire," the scene of which was laid, with the usual recklessness of French dramatists, in Scotland, where the superstition never existed. I vainly endeavoured to induce Mr. Arnold to let me change it to some place in the East of Europe. He had set his heart on Scotch music and dresses—

the latter, by the way, were in stock—laughed at my scruples, assured me that the public would neither know nor care—and in those days they certainly did not—and therefore there was nothing left for me but to do my best with it. The result was most satisfactory to the management. The situations were novel and effective ; the music lively and popular ; the cast strong, comprising T. P. Cooke, who made a great hit in the principal character, Harley, Bartley, Pearman, Mrs. Chatterley and Miss Love. The trap now so well known as " the Vampire trap " was invented for this piece, and the final disappearance of the Vampire caused quite a sensation. The melodrama had a long run, was often revived, and is to this day a stock piece in the country. I had an opportunity many years afterwards, however, to treat the same subject in a manner much more satisfactory to myself, and, as it happened, in the same theatre, under the same management ; but of that anon."

The full cast of *The Vampire, or, The Bride of the Isles* was originally as follows : " In the Introductory Vision " ; Unda, Spirit of the Flood, Miss Love ; Ariel, Spirit of the Air, Miss Worgman ; The Vampire, Mr. T. P. Cooke ; Lady Margaret, Mrs. Chatterly. " In the Drama " : Ruthven, Earl of Marsden, the Vampire, Mr. T. P. Cooke ; Ronald, Baron of the Isles, Mr. Bartley ; Robert, an English Attendant on the Baron, Mr. Pearman ; M'Swill, the Baron's Henchman, Mr. Harley ; Andrew, Steward to Ruthven, Mr. Minton ; Father Francis, Mr. Shaw ; Lady Margaret, Daughter of Ronald, Mrs. Chatterly ; Effie, Daughter of Andrew, Miss Carew ; Bridget Lord Ronald's Housekeeper, Mrs. Grove. With regard to the costumes of which Planché speaks it is interesting to remark that the principal characters Ruthven and Lady Margaret are described as follows : *Ruthven*, Silver breast plate, studded with steel buttons ; plaid kilt ; philibeg ; flesh arms and leggings ; sandals ; Scotch hat and feathers ; sword and dagger. *Lady Margaret*, white satin dress, trimmed with plaid and silver ; plaid silk sash ; Scotch hat and feather. This is in the true transpontine tradition of Ossianic attire. The play is timed to take one hour and thirty minutes in representation—and Planché has done his work of adaptation very well, although I doubt whether his few slight departures from the original are improvements. Nevertheless he has given the dialogue a native turn and an ease which were at this period too often lacking in similar versions from the French.

In 1825, T. P. Cooke visited Paris and appeared as Le Monstre at the Porte-Saint-Martin in Planché's melodrama which proved a remarkable success, running for no less than eighty nights.

The Vampire or The Bride of the Isles has its place among the repertory of Hodgson's " Juvenile Drama," and this in itself is an indication of no small popularity.

In *The Second Maiden's Tragedy*,[52] a Globe play of 1611, licensed for the stage by Sir George Buc on 31st October of that year, a macabre drama now generally attributed to Tourneur,[53] there are some remarkable scenes which culminate in something very like necrophilia, and a perverse ill-omened melancholy pervades the whole action.   In Act IV the Tyrant, a usurper, ordering soldiers to attend him with " Lanthornes and a pickax " makes his way at midnight to the Cathedral, crying :

> Death nor the marble prison my love sleeps in
> Shall keep her body lockt up from mine arms.
> I must not be so cozened.

A little later : " Enter the Tirant agen at a farder dore, which opened, bringes hym to the Toombe wher the Lady lies buried ; The Toombe here discouered ritchly set forthe." He adjures the sepulchre :

> The house of silence and the Calms of rest
> After tempestuous life, I claim of thee
> A mistress one of the most beauteous sleepers
> That ever lay so cold.

The vault is forced, whilst the lover soliloquizes :

> O the moon rises ; what reflection
> Is thrown about the sanctified building,
> E'en in a twinkling, how the monuments glisten
> As if *Death's* palaces were all massy silver
> And scorned the name of marble.   Art thou cold ?
> I have no faith in't, yet I believe none.
> Madam ; 'tis I, sweet lady, pry'thee speak
> 'Tis thy love calls on thee ; thy king, thy servant.
> No! not a word, all prisoners to pale silence
> I'll prove a kiss.

First Soldier :

    Here's chill venery !

    'Twould make a pandar's heels ache. I'll be sworn

    All my teeth chatter in my head to see't.

Tyrant :

    By th' mass, thou'rt cold indeed. Beshrew thee for't,

    Unkind to thine own blood ? Hard hearted lady,

    What injury hast thou offered to the youth

    And pleasure of thy days : refuse the Court

    And steal to this hard lodging, was that wisdom ?

      .   .   .   . Since thy life has left me

    I'll clasp the body for the spirit that dwelt in't,

    And love the house still for the mistress' sake.

    Thou art mine now spite of destruction

    And *Govianus* ; and I will possess thee.

    I once read of a *Herod* whose affection

    Pursued a virgin's love as I did thine,

    Who for the hate she owed him killed herself

    (As thou too rashly didst), without all pity :

    Yet he preserved her body dead in honey,

    And kept her long after her funeral :

    But I'll unlock the treasure house of art

    With keys of gold and bestow all on thee ;

    Here slaves receive her humbly from our arms,

      .   .   .   . So reverently

    Bear her before us gently to our palace.

    Place you the stone again where we first found it.

After a while the scene is in the palace : " They bringe the
Body in a Chaire drest up in black veluet which setts out the
pailenes of the handes and face, And a faire Chayne of pearle
crosse her brest and the Crucyfex aboue it ; He standes silent
awhile letting the Musique play, becknyng the soldiers that
bringe her in to make obeisaunce to her, and he hym self makes
a lowe honour to the body and kisses the hande. A song
within in Voyces.

Song :

    O what is Beauty that's so much adored

    A flattring glass that cozens her beholders.

    The Night of Death makes it look pale and horrid

    The Daynty preseru'd flesh how soone it molders

      To loue it lyuinge it bewitchett manye

      But after life is seldom heard of any."

Tyrant :

    How pleasing art thou to us even in death

    I love thee yet, above all women living

    And shall do seven years hence.

I can see nothing to be mended in thee
But the too constant paleness of thy cheek.
I'd give the kingdom, but to purchase there
The breadth of a red *Rose*, in natural colour,
And think it the best bargain that ever king made yet,
But Fate's my hinderer,
And I must only rest content with Art,
And that I'll have in spite on't.

Accordingly an artist in painting and perfumery is summoned to adorn the face of the corpse and give it a fresh lively red colour. However this merchant of cosmetics is none other than Govianus, the rightful heir, disguised, and he fucuses the dead cheeks and lips with a peter which is confected with a strong poison, so that when the Tyrant lustfully kisses the cold flesh, he is blasted with the venom and falls in the agonies of death. The incident is extremely powerful, if extremely horrible. As the Tyrant expires Govianus taunts him thus :

O thou sacrilegious villain,
Thou thief of rest, robber of monuments,
Cannot the body after funeral
Sleep in the grave for thee ?   Must it be raised
Only to please the wickedness of thine eye ?
Does all things end with death and not thy lust ?
Hast thou devised a new way to damnation,
More dreadful than the soul of any sin
Did ever pass yet between earth and hell ?

A very large number of plays are founded upon what may be termed the "Romeo and Juliet" motive, the awakening, or the restoration to life in some sort, of a loved one supposed dead, arousing from a trance, it may be, or a coma, a theme admitting almost innumerable variants. In the Italian, French and German theatres alone—nor does this rough list pretend to be exhaustive—we have Sforza d' Oddi's *Imorti vivi* (1576) ; Pagnini's *Imorti vivi* (1600) ; Rota's *La morta viva* (1674) ; Douville's *Les morts vivans* (1654) ; Quinault's *Le fantôme amoureux* (1659) ; Boursault's *Le mort vivant* (1662) ; Sedaine's *Der Tote ein Freyer* (1778) ; Kurländer's *Der tote Neffe* ; Friedrich Rambach's *Der Scheintote* ; Leopold Huber's *Der Scheintote*; Theodore Friedrich's *Die Scheintoten*; F. L. W. Meyer's *Der Verstorbene* ; G. Lebrun's *Die Verstorbenen* ; Tenelli's *Der Verstorbene* ; Holbein's "romantisches Gemälde" *Der Verstorbene*; Paers' opera *Die lebenden Toten* ; and a ballet

(1803) *Der lebendige Tote* ; *cum multis aliis quae nunc perscribere longum est.*

It may be convenient here briefly to review the progress of the Vampire in the theatre, at least in his most important appearances.

An Italian opera, *I vampiri*, the work of the much applauded Neapolitian composer Silvestro di Palma, which was performed at the Teatro San Carlo[54] in 1800 did not of course take anything from the novel by Polidori which indeed, it preceded by nearly twenty years. but was rather inspired by the famous treatise of Guiseppe Davanzati : *Dissertazione sopra i Vampiri di Gioseppe Davanzati Patrizio Fiorentino e Tranese, Cavaliere Gerosolimitano, Arcivescovo di Trani, e Patriarca d'Alessandria. (Seconda edizione.) Nalopi. M.D.CC.LXXXIX. Presso Filippo Raimondi. Con licenzi de' Superiori.*

On 28th March, 1828,[55] at Leipzig, was produced an opera, "Grosse romantische Oper," *Der Vampyr*, founded on the original French melodrama, the scene being changed from Scotland to Hungary. The libretto is by Wilhelm August Wohlbrück and the music by his yet more famous brother-in-law Heinrich August Marschner. *Der Vampyr* was an enormous success. A free adaptation of this being made by J. R. Planché, and produced at the Lyceum, 25th August, 1829, it ran for sixty nights. In his *Recollections and Reflections* which have before been quoted, Planche commences Chapter X by some account of this. " In the summer of 1829 I had the opportunity of treating the subject of ' The Vampire ' in accordance with my own ideas of propriety. The French melodrama had been converted into an opera for the German stage, and the music composed by Marschner.

" Mr. Hawes, who had obtained a score of it, having induced Mr. Arnold to produce it at the Lyceum, I was engaged to write the libretto, and consequently laid the scene of action in Hungary, where the superstition exists to this day, substituted for a Scotch chieftain a Wallachian Boyard, and in many other respects improved upon my earlier version. The opera was extremely well sung, and the costumes novel as well as correct, thanks to the kindness of Dr. Walsh, the traveller,[56] who gave me some valuable information respecting the national dresses of the Magyars and the Wallachians.

" I am surprised that Marschner's most dramatic and melodious works, ' Der Vampyr,' ' Die Judin,' &c., have not been introduced to our more advanced musical audiences at one or other of our great operatic establishments.

" The production of ' Der Vampyr ' was followed by that of ' The Brigand ' at Drury Lane."

Polidori's tale formed the basis of a romantic opera in three acts, the libretto of which was from the pen of C. M. Heigel, and the music by P. von Lindpaintner. This was seen at Stuttgart on 21st September, 1828, and it proved a remarkable success. It was announced as being from " Byron's famous tale," although at this date such an attribution can hardly have deceived any.

On 25th May, 1857, there was produced in Berlin a "Komischen Zauber-Ballet *Morgano* " by Paul Taglioni with music by J. Hertzel. The scene is laid in Hungary during the seventeenth century, and in the sixth tableau Elsa dances an infernal lavolta with the vampires in their haunted castle, but she is rescued by her lover, Retzka, who slays the vampire Morgano with a consecrated poniard. In 1861 at Milan appeared a ballet by Rotta, *Il vampiro*, with music by Paolo Giorza. *Guten Abend Herr Fischer ! oder, Der Vampyr* is a light vaudeville in one act by G. Belly and G. Löffler, with music by W. Telle, which had some success in its day. *Ein Vampyr* by Ulrich Franks (Ulla Wolf) given at Vienna in 1877 is a farce taken from Scribe.

In England Dion Boucicault's[57] *The Vampire*, in three acts was produced at the Princess's Theatre, London, 19th June, 1852, when the author made his first appearance before a metropolitan audience. Of this drama the following criticism, if criticism it may be called, was given by Henry Morley in his *Journal of a London Playgoer*.[58] It must be remembered that Morley continually shows himself extremely prejudiced and his censure must not be taken any more seriously than we regard the ill-word of many critics to-day, for example, the shrill petulant piping and the childish miffs of St. John Ervine in the sullens. Under 19th June Morley writes : " If there be any truth in the old adage, that ' when things are at the worst they must mend,' the bettering of Spectral Melodrama is not distant ; for it has reached the extreme point of inanity in the new piece which was produced on

Monday at the Princess's Theatre, under the attractive title of *The Vampire*.

" Its plot is chiefly copied from a piece which some years ago turned the Lyceum into a Chamber of Horrors ; but it has been spun out into three parts, facetiously described as ' Three Dramas ' : the little period of a century has been interposed between each part; and, in order that the outrage on the possible shall be complete, the third part is projected forward into the year that will be 1860 ! By this ingenious arrangement, the resuscitation of the original *Vampire* has been enabled to supply the lovers of the revolting at the Princess's with three acts of murder—that is, two consumated, and one attempted ; but, as the delicate process of vampirical killing is exactly after the same pattern in each case, the horror is quite worn out before the career of the creature terminates. Nothing but tedious trash remains.

" To ' an honest ghost ' one has no objection; but an animated corpse which goes about in Christian attire, and although never known to eat, or drink, or shake hands, is allowed to sit at good men's feasts ; which renews its odious life every hundred years by sucking a young lady's blood, after fascinating her by motions which resemble mesmerism burlesqued ; and which, notwithstanding its well-purchased longevity, is capable of being killed during its term in order that it may be revived by moonbeams—such a ghost as this passes all bounds of toleration.

" The monster of absurdity was personated by its reviver Mr. Boucicault, with due paleness of visage, stealthiness of pace, and solemnity of tone ; the scenery, especially a moonlit ridge amidst the heights of Snowdon, was beautiful, and the costumes were prettily diversified ; but the dreary repetition of fantastical horror almost exhausted even the patience which a benefit enjoins. Unfortunately, the mischief of such a piece, produced at a respectable theatre, does not end with the weariness of the spectators, who come to shudder and remain to yawn ; for it is not only ' beside the purpose of playing,' but directly contravenes it ; and though it may be too dull to pervert the tastes of those who witness its vapid extravagances, it has power to bring discredit on the most genial of arts."

It may be pointed out that this account, probably through ignorance, possibly of intent, is deliberately inaccurate.

Although confessedly a poorer play than Planché's *The Vampire* Dion Boucicault's drama is not derived from the earlier piece, but both are taken from the same source, Polidori's romance. Seeing that Henry Morley was Emeritus Professor of English Literature in University College, London, it were reasonable to suppose that he should have been acquainted with Polidori's novella. Or perhaps I rather ought to say that therefor it was not to be expected he should have known of this famous work.

Boucicault afterwards revived *The Vampire* as *The Phantom*, and this was given in London with good applause. The American cast of the characters of *The Phantom*, "As Produced at Wallack's Theatre, New York City," is as follows : In Act I (1645), The Phantom, Dion Boucicault ; Lord Albert Clavering, Mr. J. B. Howe ; Sir Hugh Neville of Graystock Mr. Ralton ; Sir Guy Musgrave, Mr. Etynge ; Ralph Gwynne, Mr. Levere ; Davy, Mr. T. B. Johnstone ; Lucy Peveryl, Miss Agnes Robertson ; Ellen, Miss Alleyne ; Maud, Miss Ada Clare ; Janet, Mrs. H. P. Grattan. In Act II (1750), Alan Raby, Dion Boucicault ; Colonel Raby, Mr. Ralton ; Edgar, his nephew, Mr. J. B. Howe ; Dr. Rees, Mr. Burnett ; Curate, Mr. Paul ; Corporal Stump, Mr. Peters ; Ada Raby, Miss Agnes Robertson ; Jenny, Mrs. L. H. Allen.

Subsequently, I presume when *The Phantom* was given in London, some modifications were made which seem to me most decidedly to be improvements. The first act was placed in the latter part of the reign of Charles II, and two hundred years were supposed to elapse between the first and the second acts. This necessitated trifling changes in the dialogue at certain points ; and naturally a complete alteration of costume to a modern style for Act II. In fact the script of the play which is printed in Dicks' Standard Plays, No. 697, (*c.* 1887) under " Costume " gives the following direction[59] : " The costumes in the First Act are of the period of the latter part of the reign of Charles the Second. In the Second Art the respective characters are dressed in the provincial costume of Wales at the middle of the present century. The following description of Alan Raby's costume for each act will show the necessity of a complete change in the style of dress which this drama requires.

Alan Raby.—*First Act :* A Puritan's suit of black serge, bound with black velvet—cloak and breeches to match—black belt and buckle—black gauntlets—shirt collar thrown back so as to show the throat bare—black stockings—black velvet shoes with strap across the instep—black sugar-loaf hat and broad riband and steel buckle—phosphoric livid countenance—slightly bald head—long black lank hair combed behind the ears—bushy black eyebrows and heavy black moustache. *2nd dress :* Black dress coat and overcoat of the same colour—black trousers—black waistcoat—black kid gloves, white wristbands over them—white cravat and black German hat—all modern, and such as would be worn by a gentleman at the present time." In the theatre such a contrast would have proved very effective.

I notice that Boucicault has in certain scenes borrowed his situations pretty freely from *Le Vampire* of Dumas, and occasionally he has even conveyed actual dialogue from the French play.

At the commencement of *The Phantom* we are shown a room in a Welsh inn, and it appears that Davy and Janet the hostess have just been married. A sudden storm sends Lucy Peveryl thither for shelter, and she confides to Janet that she is on her way to meet at sundown her cousin Roland Peveryl, who is a fugitive and proscribed. On this account he dare not openly seek her hand, but the lovers are secretly betrothed. He has promised to meet her, in order to bid her farewell for a time, in the most unfrequented spot, the ruins of Raby Castle. No sooner does Janet hear that name than she cries out with horror, and speaks of a fearful story connected with the place. They are interrupted by the arrival of Lord Clavering with a party of guests, amongst whom are friends of Lucy. She frankly informs them of her rendezvous, and they decide to accompany her, more especially as the inn has not sufficient accommodation for the travellers, who resolve to take provisions and wine and spend the night in the deserted chambers of the old castle. Davy endeavours to prevent them, nor are his efforts altogether selfish. He tells them : " No one ever sought a night's shelter in the ruins of Raby Castle, that ever lived to see the morning. . . . Within the ruins of Raby dwells some terrible thing—man or fiend ! . . . No traveller that knows the road will ever venture near that spot after nightfall ; but strange wayfarers, benighted in the storm have wandered to this place of shelter, and the next morning they are found—dead—each with a wound in his throat in the right side, from which they have evidently bled to death ;—but no blood is spilt around, the face is white and fixed, as if it had died of horror." " And he, my betrothed," cries Lucy, " Roland is there." Nevertheless the company laugh at these old stories and determine to make their way to the old castle. This they actually find in far better state than they have been led to expect, and their servants who have insisted upon Davy showing them the way soon get a very fair supper from the provisions they have purchased at his inn. Roland Peveryl is not to be found, but whilst they are eating a stranger enters, a Puritan, and announces himself as Gervase Rookwood, a traveller who has lost his way in the mountains. Davy, however, almost collapses with terror. He recollects that many years before the castle belonged to Sir Owen Raby, a noble cavalier, while Alan Raby, his younger brother had joined the forces of Cromwell. Taking advantage of this difference the traitor one midnight with a band of Puritan soldiers surprises the castle, and butchers the sleeping garrison, killing his brother with his own hand. About a year later, however, the tables are turned, the Royalists recapture the place, Alan Raby is seized, and in their rage they hurl the fratricide from a window which hung shudderingly over a fearful precipice. Curiously enough no trace of the body could ever be recovered. But Davy recognizes that Gervase Rookwood is none other than Alan Raby. Here we have the old belief that a man guilty of some monstrous crime, in this case rebellion against the King and the murder of a brother, is compelled to return as a vampire. When the company disperse to their various apartments for the night Lord Clavering is horrified to discover in his room the dead body of young Roland Peveryl, " a wound deep in his throat, but bloodless." At the same moment a piercing scream is heard and Lucy Peveryl rushing from her chamber with her hands wildly clasping her neck falls dead in Lord Clavering's arms. Seeing as he thinks a shadowy form that steals from her room he draws a pistol and fires. When the company hurry in with lights they discover Alan Raby has been shot. In faltering accents the dying man explains that hearing a cry for help he hastened to the lady's assistance. He will only forgive Lord Clavering on one condition. " When I have breathed my last, let my body be conveyed amongst the peaks of Snowdon, and there exposed to the first rays of the rising moon which touch the earth." This is done, and the first act concludes with a tableau of the peaks of Snowdon, whilst from behind the clouds there sails high in the heaven a silver sickle that strikes the corpse with her argent shaft of mystic light. The vampire wakes, and leaps to his feet crying in exultant tones : " Fountain of my life : once more thy rays restore me. Death ! I defy thee ! "

It cannot escape notice that in this act there are many parallels with *Le Vampire* of Dumas.   Raby Castle is the Castle of Tormenar ; Lucy Peveryl is Juana ; Roland Peveryl, Don Luis de Figuerroa ; Lord Clavering, Gilbert de Tiffauges ; and Davy the *gracioso* Lazare.

Two centuries have flown.   Raby Castle is now inhabited in possession of Colonel Raby, whose daughter is betrothed to her cousin Edgar.   It has been falsely reported that this latter fell in battle, but the scene opens with his return.   When the sad news first arrived Ada Raby was stricken almost to death, and, as they believed, actually died ; but she was recalled to life by a mysterious stranger, since which hour she seems to have fallen completely under his influence and in some extraordinary way only to respond to his power.   This is none other than Gervase Rookwood, who now appears and informs Colonel Raby that he and none other is the lawful lord of Raby Castle.   The Colonel's claim lies in the fact that when years before the last of the old Raby family, Sir Alan Raby died, or rather was killed, and no will could be found, the estate reverted to a distant branch of the Rabys, now represented by the Colonel.   However, a document is produced in the handwriting of Alan Raby, his will, wherein he bequeaths the estate to Gervase Rookwood and the Rookwood successors.   It seemed as though such a title cannot be resisted, but Doctor Rees, a scholar of occultism, is filled with the gravest suspicions of the stranger.   In a " Dictionary of Necromancy, a rare work by Dr. Dee," he has read of vampires, and he divines the demoniac nature of the pretended Rookwood.   In a trancelike state Ada Raby has rejected Edgar and is to be given to the stranger, when Dr. Rees examining the documents discovers that the will of Sir Alan Raby, which must be some two hundred years old, although the hand is doubtless that of Raby as the archives prove, is written upon paper which has a watermark of 1850, " scarcely five years old." The vampire who

endeavours to assassinate Edgar, is killed by a charmed bullet.
Whilst his limbs relax in death the hypnotic spell vanishes
from Ada's mind and she is united to her lover. But to their
horror they notice that as the moonlight touches the body of
Alan Raby where he has fallen, his members begin to twitch
anew with life. Dr. Rees seizes the vampire and hurls the body
into the darkest chasm of the mountain side, where no beam
nor ray can ever penetrate or find the smallest chink of entrance.

The Phantom is, of course, somewhat old-fashioned and a
little stilted, as was the mode, in its diction. No doubt some
of the situations could be revised and far more neatly turned,
yet on the whole I conceive that it should prove of its kind
excellent fare in the theatre, and some scenes, at least, in
capable hands were not without emotional appeal, I had almost
said a certain impressiveness. Far worse dramas have (not
undeservedly) earned their meed of approbation and applause.

On 15th August, 1872, was advertised : " Royal Strand
Theatre. Production of a Bit of Moonshine in Three Rays,
entitled ' The Vampire,' written by R. Reece." There was
indeed a bounteous bill of fare. At seven was given a farce,
The Married Bachelor ; at 7.30 Byron's *Not Such a Fool as He
Looks ;* " At Half Past Nine the new and original Burlesque,
a little Bit of Moonshine in Three Rays, called *The Vampire,*
written by R. Reece. The new Music by John Fitzgerald, the
New Scenery Painted by H. P. Hall ; Dresses by May, Mrs.
Richardson and Assistants ; Machinery by Wood ; Properties
by Ball. The Piece produced under the direction of Mrs.
Swanborough, Mr. J. Wallace, and Mr. Reece." The house,
says the *Era,* 18th August, 1872, was crowded for this "satirical
burlesque." His play, the author wrote, was founded upon
" a German legend, Lord Byron's story, and a Boucicaultian
drama." The Vampire, according to Reece, is a plagiarist
who lives on other people's brains. The title rôle was acted
by Edward Terry who kept the audience in roars of laughter.
" Mr. Terry's make-up as the Vampire was something extraordinary, and he worked with unflagging energy to add ' go '
to the novelty." During a picnic in the ruins of Raby Castle
the Vampire endeavours to steal the note books of Ada Raby
(Miss Emily Pitt) and Lady Audley Moonstone (Mrs. Raymond)
two lady novelists, so that he may utilize their efforts for his
weekly instalment of the " penny dreadful " and other fiction.

He is attacked by the two lovers of the ladies, Lord Albert
Clavering (Miss Bella Goodall) and Edgar (Miss Topsy Venn),
and a good deal of broadest farce follows. " The author was
cordially greeted upon his appearance before the curtain, and
the latest Strand burlesque may be noted as an undoubted
success." *The Illustrated London News*, 24th August, 1872,
although very justly doubting the propriety of the subject as a
theme for travesty highly praised Edward Terry " as the
Hibernian plagiarist with the broadest of brogues and the most
ghastly of faces." As Allan Raby he haunts the ruins of Raby
Castle, Raby Hall, and the Peak of Snowdon, seeking to filch
the notebooks of tourists, "from which he may gather materials
for a three-volume novel which he has been engaged by a
publisher to compose."

On Monday, 27th September, 1909, at the Paragon Theatre
was produced *The Vampire*, a " two-scene sketch," adapted by
Mr. José G. Levy from the French of Mme. C. le Vylars and
Pierre Souvestre. " It is a capitally written little piece conceived in the grand Guignol vein;" *The Stage*, 30th September,
1909. The first scene is Harry le Strang's smoking-room.
Harry has been infatuated with a demi-mondaine named
Sonia, who shot herself in a fit of remorse. The despairing
lover is in communication with a Hindoo spiritualist Seratsih,
who has evoked the spirit of the dead woman, now become a
vampire and preying upon Harry's vitality and reason. An
old friend, Jack Harlinger, in order as he thinks to save the
situation persuades his own fiancée, Olga Kay, to personate
the ghost of Sonia. The result is swift tragedy, for the
maddened Harry le Strang shoots her dead destroying the
vampire, whilst he himself falls at the revolver of Jack
Harlinger. Harry le Strang was played by Charles Hanbury ;
Jack Harlinger, Lauderdale Maitland ; Seratsih, Clinton
Barrett ; and Olga Kay, Janet Alexander. The piece was very
well received.

The Vampire, a Tragedy in Five Acts, by St. John Dorset
(the Rev. Hugo John Belfour), Second Edition, 1821,[60] does
not appear to have been acted. It was dedicated to W. G.
Macready, Esq., whose kindness the author acknowledges in
most grateful terms. The story is Oriental, the same being
laid in Alexandria, and it is a " moral " vampire that is shown
by the poet. In his " advertisement " he quotes a passage

from the *Examiner*, when noticing Planché's melodrama wrote :
" There are Vampires who waste the heart and happiness of
those they are connected with, Vampires of avarice, Vampires
of spleen, Vampires of debauchery, Vampires in all the shapes
of selfishness and domestic tyranny." This is his theme, and
although his pages have considerable merit I do not conceive
that his scenes would have been entirely successful on the stage,
since they are poetical and reflective rather than dramatic.

In Germany sensational fiction was long largely influenced
by Polidori, and we have such romances as Zschokke's *Der tote
Gast*, Spindler's *Der Vampyr und seine Braut*, Theodor Hilde-
brand's *Der Vampyr, oder die Totenbraut*. Edwin Bauer's
roman à clef the clever *Der Baron Vampyr*,[61] which was
published at Leipzig in 1846, hardly concerns as here, whilst
Ewald August König's sensational *Ein moderner Vampyr*,[62]
which appeared in 1883, or Franz Hirsch's *Moderne Vampyr*,[63]
1873, productions which only use in their titles the word
" Vampire " to attract,—one might say, to ensnare attention,
are in this connexion no more deserving of consideration than
mere chap-books and pedlar's penny-ware such as Fiorelli's
Der Vampyr, and Dr. Seltzam's pornographic *Die Vampyre
der Residenz*.

Undoubtedly the vampire tradition has never been treated
with such consummate skill as by Théophile Gautier in his
exquisite prose poem *La Morte Amoureuse*, which first appeared
in the *Chronique de Paris* on 23rd and 26th June, 1836, when the
young author was not quite twenty-five. Although the theme
is not original yet perhaps nowhere beside has it been so
ingeniously moulded with such delicacy of style, with such
rich and vivid colouring, with such emotion and such repres-
sion. The darker shadows of the tradition are suggested rather
than portrayed, yet none can deny that there is an atmosphere
of sombre mystery, even a touch of morbid horror which with
complete artistry the writer allows us to suspect rather than to
comprehend. The very vagueness of the relation adds to the
illusion. We hardly know whether Romuald is the young
country priest occupied in prayer and good works, or whether
he is the Renaissance seignior living a life of passion and hot
extravagance. As he himself cries : " Sometimes I thought
I was a priest who dreamed every night that he was a nobleman,
sometimes that I was a nobleman who dreamed that he was a

priest. I could no longer distinguish dreams from real life ; I did not know where reality began and illusion ended. The dissolute, supercilious young lord jeered at the priest, and the priest abhorred the dissipations of the young lord." But were he humble priest, or were he profligate patrician, one emotion remained eternally the same, his love for Clarimonde. At length the Abbé Serapion dissolves the glamour. Sternly he bids young Romuald accompany him to the deserted cemetery where Clarimonde lies buried; he exhumes the body, and as he sprinkles it with holy water it crumbles into dust. Then also has the lord Romuald gone for ever. There only remains the poor priest of God broken and alone, who grows old in an obscure parish in the depths of a wood, and who well-nigh half a century after scarcely dares to stir the ashes of that memory.

There are in English not a few stories which deal with the vampire tradition, and many of these are well imagined and cleverly contrived ; the morbid horror of the thing has often been conveyed with considerable power, but yet it will, I think, be universally allowed that no author has written pages comparable to this story of Gautier. It is hardly to be disputed that the best of the English vampire stories is Sheridan Le Fanu's *Carmilla*, which the authorities upon the bibliography of this author[64] have not traced further back than its appearance in the collection entitled *In A Glass Darkly*, 1872,[65] *Carmilla* which is a story of some length, containing sixteen chapters, is exceedingly well told and it certainly exhibits that note of haunting dread which is peculiar to Le Fanu's work. The castle in Styria and the family who inhabit it are excellently done, nor will the arrival of Carmilla and the mysterious coach wherein sat " a hideous black woman, with a sort of coloured turban on her head, who was gazing all the time from the carriage window, nodding and grinning derisively towards the ladies, with gleaming eyes and large white eyeballs, and her teeth set as if in fury," easily be forgotten.

It must suffice to mention very briefly but a few short stories in English where the vampire element is present. E. F. Benson has evoked real horror in his *The Room in the Tower* and the horrible creature tangled in her rotting shroud all foul with mould and damp who returns from her accursed grave is loathly to the last degree.

The Flowering of the Strange Orchid, by H. G. Wells, introduces a botanical vampire. An orchid collector is found dead in a jungle in the Andaman Islands, with a strange bulb lying near him. This is brought to England and carefully tended by a botanist until it comes to flower. But when at last the blossoms burst open great tendrils suddenly reach out to grasp the man sucking his blood with hideous gusts. The unfortunate wretch has to be violently torn away from the plant which drips with blood scarce in time to save his life.

This idea closely resembles Fred M. White's story, *The Purple Terror*, which appeared in the *Strand Magazine*, September, 1899, Vol. xviii, No. 105. Here Lieutenant Will Scarlett, an American officer and a number of his men have to make their way across a certain tract of Cuban Territory. Spending the night in a country posada they are attracted by a pretty dancing girl who is wearing twined round her shoulders a garland of purple orchids larger than any known variety. The blossoms which a blood-red centre exhale a strange exotic perfume. Scarlett is fired with the enthusiasm of giving a new orchid to the horticultural world, and on the following morning a native, named Tito, undertakes to guide him to the spot. He learns that the natives call them "the devil's poppies" and that the flowers grow in the high trees where their blossoms cling to long green tendrils. As night falls the little company arrives at a plateau ringed by tall trees whose branches are crowned with great wreaths of the purple flower nestling amid coils of long green ropery. To their alarm they note that the ground is covered with bleaching bones, the skeletons of men, animals, and birds alike. Yet perforce they must camp there rather than risk the miasma of the lower valley. Scarlett keeps watch. In the darkness there is a rustling sound and suddenly a long green tendril furnished at the end with a sucker armed with sharp spines like teeth descends and snatches one of the men from the ground. As it is about to withdraw Scarlett with inconceivable swiftness slashes it through with his knife. But the man's clothing has even in that moment been cut through by the razor spines and his body is marked by a number of punctures where his blood is oozing in great drops. Immediately half-a-dozen and more lithe living cords with fanged mouths fall groping for their prey. The men are hurriedly awakened and with difficulty they extricate themselves by sending their whingers ripping and tearing in every direction. It appears that the vampire poppies at night send down these tendrils to gather moisture. Anything which the fearful suckers can catch they drain dry, be it man or beast or bird. Lieutenant Scarlett and his men have been deliberately led into this trap by Tito, who is madly jealous of their compliments to Zara, the dancing-girl. They hold him prisoner and threaten him with condign punishment at headquarters.

Algernon Blackwood brings together two types of vampires in his story *The Transfer*. One is a human being, the psychic sponge, who absorbs and seems to live upon the vitality of others. He is thus described by the governess : " I watched his hard, bleak face ; I noticed how thin he was, and the curious oily brightness of his steady eyes. And everything he said or did announced what I may dare to call the *suction* of his presence." There is also a yet more horrible monster, if one may term it so, the Forbidden Corner, an arid barren spot in the midst of the rose garden, naked and bald amid luxuriant growth. A child who knows its evil secret says : " It's bad. It's hungry. It's dying because it can't get the food it wants. But I know what would make it feel right." When the human vampire ventures near this spot it exerts its secret strength and draws him to itself. He falls into the middle of the patch and it drinks his energy. He lives on, but he seems to be nothing more than a physical husk or shell without vitality. As for the Forbidden Corner " it lay untouched, full of great, luscious, driving weeds and creepers, very strong, full fed and bursting thick with life."

Sir Arthur Conan Doyle in his little story, *The Parasite*, has depicted a human vampire or psychic sponge in the person of Miss Penelosa, who is described as being a small frail creature, " with a pale peaky face, an insignificant presence and retiring manner." Nevertheless she is able to obsess Professor Gilroy who says : " She has a parasite soul, yes, she is a parasite ; a monster parasite. She creeps into my form as the hermit crab creeps into the whelk's shell." To his horror he realizes that under her influence his will becomes weaker and weaker and he is bound to seek her presence. He resists for a while, but the force becomes so overmastering that he is compelled to yield, loathing himself as he does so. When he visits her, with a terrific effort he breaks the spell and denounces her unhallowed fascination in burning words. However, his victory is short indeed. She persecutes him most bitterly, and when he unburdens his troubles to his college professor the only result is a prescription of chloral and bromide, which promptly goes into the gutter. With devilish craft the vampire destroys his reputation as a scholar, and brings about ill-natured gossip and comment. She is able to confuse his brain during his lectures, so that he talks unintelligible nonsense and his classes become the laughing-stock of the university, until at length the authorities are obliged to suspend him from his position. Almost in despair he cries : " And the most dreadful part of it all is my loneliness. Here I sit in a common-place English bow-window looking out upon a common-place English street, with its garish buses and its lounging policemen, and behind me there hangs a shadow which is out of all keeping with the age and place. In the home of knowledge I am weighed down and tortured by a power of which science knows nothing. No magistrate would listen to me. No paper would discuss my case. No doctor would believe my symptoms. My own most intimate friends would only look upon it as a sign of brain derangement. I am out of all touch with my kind."

The unfortunate victim is driven even deeper still by this unhallowed influence, which causes him to rob a bank, violently assault a friend, and finally to come within an ace of mutilating the features of his betrothed. At length the persecution ceases with the sudden death of the vampire, Miss Penelosa.

The True Story of a Vampire is a pathetic little story, very exquisitely told, in *Studies of Death*, by Stanislaus Eric, Count Stenbock, who wrote some verses of extraordinary charm in *Love, Sleep, and Dreams ; Myrtle, Rue, and Cypress ; The Shadow of Death ;* and who at least once in *The Other Side* told a macabre legend with most powerful and haunting effect. A mysterious Count Vardaleh visits the remote styrian castle of old Baron Wronski, and before long attains an occult influence over the boy heir, Gabriel. The lad wastes away, and Count Vardaleh is heard to murmur : " My darling, I fain would spare thee ; but thy life is my life, and I must live, I who would rather die. Will God not have *any* mercy on me ? Oh, oh ! life ; oh, the torture of life ! . . . O Gabriel, my beloved ! My life, yes, *life*—oh, my life ? I am sure this is but a little I demand of thee. Surely the superabundance of life can spare a little to one who is already dead." As the boy lies wan and ill, the Count enters the room and presses a long feverish kiss upon his lips. Vardaleh rushes forth, and can never be traced again. Gabriel has expired in the agony of that embrace.

In a novel, *The Vampire*, by Reginald Hodder, a woman who is the leader of an occult society is forced to exercise her powers as a vampire to prevent the ebbing of her vitality. Here her ravages are pyschic rather than physical, albeit in fact the two so closely commingled that they are not to be separated. A curious feature in the tale is that this woman is represented as putting forth her energies through the medium of a metallic talisman, and various struggles to gain possession of the object form the theme of the story. It falls into the hands of persons who would employ it for evil purposes, when it constitutes a very formidable menace, but at the last after a number of extraordinary happenings it is happily recovered.

The traditional, but yet more horrible vampire is presented to us by F. Marion Crawford in *For the Blood Is the Life*. Here a young man, who has been loved by a girl whose affection he was unable to return, is after her death vampirised by her, and when his friends suspect the truth they determine to rescue him. They find him upon her grave, a thin stream of blood trickling from his throat. "And the flickering light of the lantern played upon another face that looked up from the feast,—upon two deep, dead eyes that saw in spite of death— upon parted lips redder than life itself—upon gleaming teeth on which glistened a rosy drop." The situation is effectively dealt with according to the good old tradition. A hawthorn stake is driven through the heart of the vampire who emits a quantity of blood and with a despairing shriek dies the last death.

Almost equally vivid in its details must be accounted the tale, *Four Wooden Stakes*, by Victor Roman. The ghastly events in the lonely old house with its little grey crypt, some ten miles from the small town of Charing, a place of not more than fifteen hundred souls, are most vividly described. There lived the Holroyds, the grandfather, the father, and three brothers. Whilst in South America the grandfather " was attacked while asleep by one of those huge bats. Next morning he was so weak he couldn't walk. That awful thing had sucked his life blood away. He arrived here, but was sickly until his death, a few weeks later." So says Remson Holroyd, who is left the sole survivor of the family, and who has summoned his old college friend to help him solve the secret of the hideous doom which is taking toll one by one. The grandfather was not buried in the usual way ; but, as his will directed, his remains were interred in the vault built near the house. Remson Holroyd continues : "Then my dad began failing and just pined away until he died. What puzzled the doctors was the fact that right up until the end he consumed enough food to sustain three men, yet he was so weak he lacked the strength to drag his legs over the floor. He was buried, or rather interred with grand-dad. The same symptoms were in evidence in the cases of George and Fred. They are both lying in the vault. And now, Jack, I'm going, too, for of late my appetite has increased to alarming proportions, yet I am as weak as a kitten." The next morning the visitor finds himself so weak that he is hardly able to rise and he feels a slight pain in the neck. "I rushed to examine it in the mirror. Two tiny dots rimmed with blood—my blood—and on my neck ! No longer did I chuckle at Remson's fears, for *it*, the thing, had attacked me as I slept." The host himself is in a state of utter exhaustion. That night watch is kept by the friend, and as from his concealment he is gazing into Remson's room he notices "a faint reddish glow outside one of the windows. It apparently emanated from nowhere. Hundreds of little specks danced and whirled in the spot of light, and as I watched them fascinated, they seemed to take on the form of a human face. The features were masculine, as was also the arrangement of the hair. Then the mysterious glow disappeared." After a few moments there appears a vague form of which the watcher is able to distinguish the head, and to his horror he sees that the features are the same as those of a portrait of the grandfather which is hanging in the picture gallery of the house. "But oh, the difference in expression ! The lips were drawn back in a snarl, disclosing two sets of pearly white teeth, the canines over developed and remarkably sharp. The eyes, an emerald green in colour, stared in a look of consuming hate." The horror is revealed. The house is infested by a vampire. In the morning the two friends visit the vault.   " As if by mutual understanding, we both turned toward the coffin on our left.   It belonged to the grandfather.   We unplaced the lid, and there lay the old Holroyd.   He appeared to be sleeping ; his face was full of colour, and he had none of the stiffness of death.   The hair was matted, the moustache untrimmed, and on the beard were matted stains of a dull brownish hue.   But it was his eyes that attracted me.   They were greenish, and they glowed with an expression of fiendish malevolence such as I had never seen before.   The look of baffled rage on the face might well have adorned the features of the devil in hell."   They drive a stake through the living corpse, which shrieks and writhes, whilst the gushing blood drenches coffins and floor spurting out in great jets over the very walls.   The head is severed from the body, and " as the final stroke of the knife cut the connexion a scream issued from the mouth ; and the whole corpse fell away into dust, leaving nothing but a wooden stake lying in a bed of bones."   The remaining three bodies are treated in the same way, and thus the thrall of the curse is lifted from the old house, ten miles from the little town of Charing.

Although the genius of Charles Baudelaire, when his art required it, shrank from no extremity of physical horror, yet in his exquisite poem *Le Vampire* he has rather portrayed the darkness and desolation of the soul :

Toi qui, comme un coup de couteau,
Dans mon coeur plaintif est entrée ;
Toi qui, forte comme un troupeau
De démons, vins, folle et parée.

De mon esprit humilié
Faire ton lit et ton domaine ;
—Infâme a qui je suis lié
Comme le forçat a la chaîne,

Comme au jeu le joueur têtu,
Comme à la bouteille l'ivrogne,
Comme aux vermines la charogne,
—Maudite, maudite sois-tu !

J'ai prié le glaive rapide
De conquerir ma liberté
Et j'ai dit au poison perfide
De secourir ma lâcheté.

Helas ! le poison et le glaive
M'ont pris en dédain et m'ont dit :
Tu n'es pas digne qu'on t'enlève
A ton esclavage maudit.

Imbécile !—de son empire
Si nos efforts te délivraient,
Tes baisers ressusciteraient
Le cadavre de ton vampire !

In England there is a poem—truly of a very different kind—
which appears in the life of the famous scientist, James Clerk
Maxwell, by Lewis Campbell and William Garnett, verses
written by Maxwell in 1845 when he was fourteen years of age.
The verses should not perhaps, because of the youth of the
author, be criticized too sharply, and although they show
Wardour Street fustian and gimcrack, since the piece is
of no great length it may pardonably be quoted here. It is
not entirely without a certain feeling after the right atmosphere,
and much will be forgiven on account of the precocity. It is
grandiosely entitled *The Vampyre :* " Compylt into Meeter by
James Clerk Maxwell."

Thair is a knichte rydis through the wood,
  And a douchty knichte is hee.
And sure hee is on a message sent,
  He rydis sae hastilie.
He passit the aik, and hee passit the birk,
  And hee passit monie a tre,
Bot plesant to him was the saugh sae slim,
  For beneath it hee did see
The boniest ladye that ever hee saw,
  Scho was sae schyn and fair.
And thair scho sat, beneath the saugh,
  Kaiming hir gowden hair.
And then the knichte—" Oh ladye brichte,
  What chance has broucht you here ?
But sae the word, and ye schall gang
  Back to your kindred dear,"
Then up and spok the ladye fair—
  " I have nae friends or kin,
Bot in a little boat I live,
  Amidst the waves' loud din."
Then answered thus the douchty knichte—
  " I'll follow you through all,
For gin ye bee in a littel boat,
  The world to it seemis small."

They goed through the wood, and through the wood,
  To the end of the wood they came :
And when they came to the end of the wood
  They saw the salt sea faem.
And when they saw the wee, wee boat,
  That daunced on the top of the wave,
And first got in the ladye fair,
  And then the knichte sae brave.
They got into the wee, wee boat
  And rowed wi' a' their micht ;
When the knichte sae brave, he turnit about,
  And lookit at the ladye bricht ;
He lookit at her bonnie cheik,
  And hee lookit at hir twa bricht eyne,
Bot hir rosie cheik growe ghaistly pale,
  And schoe seymit as scho deid had been.
The fause, fause knichte growe pale with frichte.
  And his hair rose up on end,
For gane-by days cam to his mynde,
  And his former love he kenned.
Then spake the ladye—" Thou, fause knichte,
  Hast done to me much ill,
For didst forsake me long ago,
  Bot I am constant still :
For though I ligg in the woods sae cald,
  At rest I canna bee
Until I sucks the gude lyfe blude
  Of the man that gart me dee."
Hee saw hir lipps were wet wi' blude,
  And hee saw hir lufelesse eyne,
And loud hee cry'd, " get frae my syde,
  Thou vampyr corps encleane ! "
But no, hee is in hir magic boat,
  And on the wyde, wyde sea ;
And the vampyr suckis his gude lyfe blude,
  Sho suckis him till hee dee.
So now beware, whoe'er you are,
  That walkis in this lone wood :
Beware of that deceitfull spright,
  The ghaist that suckis the blude.

The Vampire Bride, a ballad by the Hon. Henry Liddell, has considerable merit. It may be found in *The Wizard of the North, The Vampire Bride, and other Poems*, Blackwood, Edinburgh, and Cadell, London, 1833. These stanzas are founded upon the old tale of the knight who having placed a ring —some say his wedding-ring—around the finger of the statue of Venus whilst he is a quoiting, when he would reclaim it finds that the finger is crooked so that the jewel may not be withdrawn, whilst that night a phantom claims him as her spouse. With difficulty is he freed from the thrall of the succubus.

In 1845 there was published at the Columbian Press Weston-super-mare, a little book entitled *The Last of the Vampires*, by Smyth Upton. The chief, some critics might say the only, merit of this tale is its excessive rarity. The narrative is somewhat curiously divided into Epochs, the first of which takes place in 1769, the second in 1777, the third and last in 1780. Chapter I opens in an English village named Frampton, but in Chapter II " we find ourselves upon the borders of Bohemia " in the Castle Von Oberfels. Four chapters of no great length and somewhat disconnected in their sequence comprise the First Epoch. A little later we meet with the mysterious Lord de Montfort, and apparently he has just committed a murder, since he is one of the two men who stand in a dreary outhouse adjoining Montfort Abbey. " Red blood, yet warm, stains their murderous hands, and is seen also in pools upon the floor ; the same marks are observable, also, on their clothes." " The scene is a fearful one ; it is one of those of which the mere recital makes the blood run cold," and the writer wisely does not attempt the task. In the penultimate chapter of this extraordinary production we are introduced to " a certain young German, the Baron Von Oberfels," who weds Mary Learmont, the elder daughter of " Sir James Learmont, who being a Baronet, was, moreover, a Knight of the Bath and M.P." Unfortunately the Baron " was one of that horrible class, the Vampires ! He had sold his soul to the evil one, for the enjoyment of perpetual youth ; being bound, besides, to what are understood to be the penalties of that wretched and accursed race. Every tenth year a female was sacrificed to his infernal master. Mary Learmont was to be the next victim ; may she escape the threatened doom." But apparently, so far as I can gather, she is not so lucky for we are vaguely told : " The Baron and his bride departed on his wedding tour. Her father and mother never hear of her more." A page or two later there is " a midnight wedding " at the Castle Von Oberfels. Of the bride we are told nothing save that she had a " fair presence." " The Baron Von Oberfels was there, once more arrayed in the garments of a bridegroom." The ceremony proceeds. The grand organ peals; the heavenly voices of white-robed choristers added greatly to the beauty of the scene. " But hark! another noise is heard; sulphureous smoke half fills the sacred building; the floor opens for an instant; and mocking shrieks are audible as the spirit of the Last of the Vampires descended into perdition."

I am bound to acknowledge that after a somewhat careful reading of this curious and most disjointed little piece of seventy-six pages the only impression with which I am met is that Mr. Smyth Upton knew nothing whatsoever of what the word vampire connotes. The idea of the victims who are sacrificed for the sake of eternal youth is, of course fairly common and was very effectively utilized by G. W. M. Reynolds in his romance *The Necromancer*, which ran in *Reynolds's Miscellany* from Saturday, 27th December, 1851, to Saturday, 31st July, 1852.[66] Incidentally it may be remarked as a somewhat curious fact that this prolific novelist never availed himself of the vampire tradition in his melodramatic chapters.

The Vampyre. " By the Wife of a Medical Man," 1858, is a violent teetotal tract, of twenty-seven short chapters presented in the guise of fiction. The villain of the piece is " The Vampyre Inn," and the dipsomaniac hero—if it be allowable to use the term in such a context—is given to ravings such as these : " They fly—they bite—they suck my blood—I die. That hideous ' Vampyre ! ' Its eyes pierce me thro'—they are red—they are bloodshot. Tear it from my pillow. I dare not lie down. It bites—I die ! Give me brandy—brandy—more brandy."

A Vampire of Souls, by H. M. P., published in 1904, is a book of little value. The hero, George Ventnor, when aged twenty, is killed in a railway accident, and the narrative consists of his after experiences which are singularly material and crude. There is, perhaps, a good touch here and there, but the thing certainly does not deserve to be rescued from oblivion.

It will have been noticed that beyond the titles these two last works have really little or nothing to do with vampires at all, but we may now consider a romance which may at least be ranked as a very serious rival to—in my opinion it is far ghostlier than—its famous successor *Dracula*. *Varney the Vampire, or, The Feast of Blood*, is undoubtedly the best novel of Thomas Preskett Prest, a prolific writer of the fourth and fifth decades of the nineteenth century. It is true that his productions published by the well-known Edward Lloyd, of 231, Shoreditch,[67] may be classed as simple " shockers," but none the less he has considerable power in this kind, and he had at any rate the craft of telling his story with skill and address. There is a certain quality in his work, which appeared during the years from 1839 to the earlier fifties, that is entirely lacking in the productions of his fellows. To him have been ascribed, doubtless with some exaggeration, well nigh two hundred titles, but the following list comprises, I believe, his principal romances : *Ela, the Outcast, or, the Gipsy of Rosemary Dell ; Angelina, or, the Mystery of S. Mark's Abbey*, " a Tale of Other Days " ; *The Death Grasp, or, A Father's Curse ; Ernnestine De Lacy, or, The Robbers' Foundling ; Gallant Tom, or, The Perils of a Sailor Ashore and Afloat*, " an original nautical romance of deep and pathetic interest " ; *Sweeney Todd, the Demon Barber of Fleet Street* (the most famous of Prest's novels) ; *Newgate* (which has some capital episodes) ; *Emily Fitzormond ; Mary Clifford ; The Maniac Father, or, The Victim of Seduction ; Gertrude of the Rock ; Rosalie, or, The Vagrant's Daughter ; The Miller's Maid ; Jane Brightwell ; Blanche, or, The Mystery of the Doomed House ; The Blighted Heart, or, The Priory Ruins ; Sawney Bean, the Man-eater of Midlothian ; The Skeleton Clutch, or, The Goblet of Gore ; The Black Monk, or, The Secret of the Grey Turret*[68] *; The Miller and His Men, or, The Secret Robbers of Bohemia*. To Prest also has been attributed, but I conceive without foundation, *Susan Hoply*, an audacious piracy upon the famous novel by Mrs. Crowe, *Susan Hopley*.

Varney the Vampire, or, The Feast of Blood, was first published in 1847. It contains no less than CCXX chapters and runs to 868 pages. The many incidents succeed each other with such breathless rapidity that it were well-nigh impossible to attempt any conspectus of the whole romance. The very length would make this analysis a work of extreme difficulty, and incidentally we may note the amazing copiousness of Prest which must ever remain a matter for wonderment. Such a romance, for example, as *Newgate* runs to no less than one hundred and forty-nine chapters comprising 772 pages. *The Maniac Father* has fifty-four chapters, each of considerable

PLATE VIII

VARNEY THE VAMPIRE [see p. 331

length, which total 604 pages, and I have not selected these on account of their exceptional volume.

Varney the Vampire was among the most popular of Prest's productions, and on account of its " unprecedented success " it was reprinted in 1853 in penny parts.   To-day the book is unprocurable and considerable sums have been for many years in vain offered to secure a copy.   Indeed, it may be noted that all Prest's work is excessively scarce.

It is hardly an exaggeration to affirm that of recent years there have been few books which have been more popular than Bram Stoker's *Dracula, A tale,* and certainly there is no sensational romance which in modern days has achieved so universal a reputation.   Since it was first published in 1897, that is to say one and twenty years ago, it has run into a great number of editions, and the name has veritably become a household word.   It will prove interesting to inquire into the immediate causes which have brought this book such wide and enduring fame.   It has already been remarked that it is well-nigh impossible for a story which deals with the supernatural or the horrible to be sustained to any great length.   Elements which at first are almost unendurable will lose their effect if they are continued, for the reader's mind insensibly becomes inured to fresh emotions of awe and horror, and *Dracula* is by no means briefly told.   In the ordinary reprints (Tenth Edition, 1913) it extends to more than four hundred pages, nor does it escape the penalty of its prolixity.   The first part, " Jonathan Harker's Journal," which consists of four chapters is most admirably done, and could the whole story have been sustained at so high a level we should have had a complete masterpiece. But that were scarcely possible.   The description of the journey through Transylvania is interesting to a degree, and even has passages which attain to something like charm. " All day long we seemed to dawdle through a country which was full of beauty of every kind.   Sometimes we saw little towns or castles on the top of steep hills such as we see in old missals ; sometimes we ran by rivers and streams which seemed from the wide stony margin on each side of them to be subject to great floods.   It takes a lot of water, and running strong, to sweep the outside edge of a river clear."   Very effective is the arrival of the English traveller at the " vast ruined castle, from whose tall black windows came no ray of light, and whose broken battlements showed a jagged line against the moonlit sky." Very adroitly are the various incidents managed in their quick succession, those mysterious happenings which at last convince the matter-of-fact commonplace young solicitor of Exeter that he is a helpless prisoner in the power of a relent-less and fearful being. The continual contrasts between business conversations, the most ordinary events of the dull listless days, and all the while the mantling of dark shadows in the background and the onrushing of some monstrous doom are in these opening chapters most excellently managed.

So tense a strain could not be preserved, and consequently when we are abruptly transported to Whitby and the rather tedious courtships of Lucy Westenra, who is a lay figure at best, we feel that a good deal of the interest has already begun to evaporate. I would hasten to add that before long it is again picked up, but it is never sustained in the same degree ; and good sound sensational fare as we have set before us, fare which I have myself more than once thoroughly enjoyed, yet it is difficult not to feel that one's palate has been a little spoiled by the nonpareil of an antipast. This is not to say that the various complications are not sufficiently thrilling, but because of their very bounty now and again they most palpably fail of effect, and it can hardly escape notice that the author begins to avail himself of those more extravagant details of vampirism which frankly have no place outside the stories told round a winter's hearth. It would have been better had he confined himself to those particulars which are known and accepted, which indeed have been officially certified and definitely proved. But to have limited himself thus would have meant the shortening of his narrative, and here we return to the point which was made above.

If we review *Dracula* from a purely literary point of approach it must be acknowledged that there is much careless writing and many pages could have been compressed and something revised with considerable profit. It is hardly possible to feel any great interest in the characters, they are labels rather than individuals. As I have said, there are passages of graphic beauty, passages of graphic horror, but these again almost entirely occur within the first sixty pages. There are some capital incidents, for example the method by which Lord

Godalming and his friend obtain admittance to No. 347 Piccadilly. Nor does this by any means stand alone.

However, when we have—quite fairly, I hope—thus criticized *Dracula*, the fact remains that it is a book of unwonted interest and fascination. Accordingly we are bound to acknowledge that the reason for the immense popularity of this romance,— the reason why, in spite of obvious faults it is read and re-read—lies in the choice of subject and for this the author deserves all praise.

It might not have seemed that *Dracula* would have been a very promising subject for the stage, but nevertheless it was dramatized by Hamilton Deans and produced at the Wimbledon Theatre on 9th March, 1925. This version was performed in London at the Little Theatre, 14th February, 1927. On the preceding Thursday the *Daily Mirror* published a photograph of the late Mr. Bram Stoker accompanied by the following paragraphs. "Herewith, one of the very few photographs of the late Bram Stoker, who, besides being Sir Henry Irving's manager for years, was an industrious novelist. As I have already said, a dramatic verson of his most famous book, ' Dracula,' is to be done at the Little on Monday, and the scene of the Grand Guignol plays is appropriate, for the new piece, I hear, is so full of gruesome thrills that, in the provinces women having been carried fainting from the auditorium. Truly we take our pleasures sadly.

" The dramatic adaptation is by Hamilton Deans, whose grandfather, Colonel Deans, and the Rev. Abraham Stoker, Bram's father, lived on adjoining estates in County Dublin. Young Bram and Hamilton Deane's mother, then a young girl, were great friends. Stoker had the book 'Dracula ' in his mind, and the young people used to discuss its possibilities. Strange that it should be young Hamilton Deane who has dramatized the book and brought the play to London."

At the Little Theatre the cast of *Dracula* was as follows : Count Dracula, Raymond Huntley ; Abraham van Helsing, Hamilton Deane ; Dr. Seward, Stuart Lomath ; Jonathan Harker, Bernard Guest ; Quincey P. Morris, Frieda Hearn ; Lord Godalming, Peter Jackson ; R. M. Renfield, Bernard Jukes ; The Warden, Jack Howarth ; The Parlourmaid, Hilda Macleod ; The Housemaid, Betty Murgatroyd ; Mina Harker, Dora Mary Patrick.

By no stretch could it be called a good play, whilst the presentation, at the best, can hardly be described as more than reasonably adequate. In one or two instances the effects, upon which so much depends and which obviously demanded the most scrupulous care, were so clumsily contrived as to excite an involuntary smile. " It was only a step from the devilish to the ridiculous on Monday night," said the *Era*, 16th February, 1927. Very remarkable was a lady, dressed in the uniform of a hospital nurse who sat in the vestibule of the theatre, and it was bruited that her services were required by members of the audience who were overcome owing to the horrors of the drama. I can only say that I find this canard impossible to believe, *quodcumque ostendis mihi sic, incredulus odi*. As an advertisement, and it can surely have been nothing else, the attendance of a nurse was in deplorable taste. I am informed that after the first few weeks a kind of epilogue was spoken when all the characters were assembled upon the stage, and it was explained that the audience must not be distressed at what they had seen, that it was comically intended for their entertainment. So gross a lapse of good manners, not to speak of the artistic indecorum, is hardly credible.[69]

Confessedly the play was extremely weak, and yet such is the fascination of this subject that it had an exceptional success, and triumphantly made its way from theatre to theatre. On 25th July, 1927, *Dracula* was transferred to the Duke of York's ; on the 29th August, following to the Prince of Wales; on 10th October to the Garrick; and all the while it was given to thronging houses. It has also toured, and at the present moment is still touring the provincial theatres with the most marked success, the drama being given with more spirit and vigour than originally was the case at the Little, and Wilfrid Fletcher in particular playing the lunatic Renfield with a real touch of wistful pathos and uncanny horror. This is is extremely instructive, and it is curious that the vogue of the " vampire play " in London should be repeated almost exactly after the interval of a century. On 5th November, 1927, a new version of *Dracula* by Charles Morrel was presented at the Court Theatre, Warrington.

In America the dramatization of *Dracula* was produced at the Shubert, New Haven, 19th September, 1927. This was given at the Fulton, New York, upon the following 5th October.

Jonathan Harker was acted by Terence Neil ; Abraham Van
Helsing by Edward Van Sloan ; Renfield by Bernard Jukes ;
and Count Dracula by Bela Lugosi.

As I have before remarked, the striking fact that an indifferent play should prove so successful can, I think, only be
attributed to the fascination of the theme. Consciously or
unconsciously it is realized that the vampire tradition contains
far more truth than the ordinary individual cares to appreciate
and acknowledge. "La fable du vampire est peut-être la plus
universelle de nos superstitions. . . . Elle a partout
l'autorité de la tradition : elle ne manque ni de celle de la
philosophie ni de celle de la médicine. La théologie même en
a parlé."

NOTES TO CHAPTER V

[1] *Ghost Stories of an Antiquary* (Second Impression), London, 1905
pp. 149-179.

[2] *Der Naturforscher.* Achtundvierzigstes Stück, Leipzig, Sonnabend,
den 25 des Mays, 1748.

[3] *Werke*, Göschen, 1857, XI, 260.

[4] Cf. also *Schach Lolo* : *Werke*, Hempel, XII, 39.
> Nicht Menschen mehr, Vampyre nur erblickt,
> Die an ihm saugen und an ihm liegen.

[5] The following but poorly expresses the original :
> From my grave to wander I am forc'd,
> Still to seek The Good's long-sever'd link,
> Still to love the bridegroom I have lost,
> And the life-blood of his heart to drink ;
> When his race is run,
> I must hasten on,
> And the young must 'neath my vengance sink.

[6] In Schmidt, *Charakteristiken*, Berlin, 1886, pp. 246-247.

[7] In his *Historic Survey of German Poetry*, London, 1830, in a note upon his
translation *Ellenore* (p. 51) Taylor says : " No German poem has been
so repeatedly translated into English as Ellenore : Eight different versions
are lying on my table, and I have read others. It becomes not me to appreciate them ; suffice it to observe that this was the earliest of them all, having
been communicated to my friends in the year 1790, and mentioned in the
preface to Dr. Aikin's poems which appeared in 1791. It was first printed
in the second number of the Monthly Magazine for 1796. The German title
is Lenore, which is the vernacular form of Eleonora, a name here represented
by Ellenore." Taylor compares *Lenore* with " an obscure English ballad
called the Suffolk miracle," and he reprints (p. 52) this ample poem in full ;
*The Suffolk Miracle : Or a relation of a young man, who, a month after his
death, appeared to his sweetheart, and carried her on horseback behind him for
forty miles in two hours and was never seen after but in his grave.*

[8] Lockhart, *Memoirs*, vol. I, p. 204.

[9] Captain Basil Hall's *Schloss Hainfeld : or, a Winter in Lower Styria,*
Edinburgh, 1836, p. 332.

[10] The whole stanza is repeated thrice, xxxix ; xlviii ; and liv, with extraordinary effect :

> Tramp, tramp, across the land they speede ;
> Splash, splash, across the sea ;
> Hurrah ! the dead can ride apace ;
> Dost feare to ride with mee ?

In a note Taylor says : " By shifting the scene to England, and making William, a soldier of Richard Lionheart, it became necessary that the ghost of Ellenore, whom Death, in the form of her lover, conveys to William's grave, should cross the sea. Hence the splash ! splash ! of the xxxix and other stanzas, of which there is no trace in the original ; of the tramp ! tramp ! there is. I could not prevail upon myself to efface these words, which have been gotten by heart, and which are quoted even in Don Juan." The Don Juan reference is Canto X, lxxi :

> On with the horses ! Off to Canterbury !
> Tramp, tramp o'er pebble, and splash : splash ! through puddle.

[11] Introduction to The Chase and William and Helen, Edinburgh, 1807, p. iv.

[12] Scott, Imitations, p. 39.

[13] So Captain Basil Hall, Schloss Hainfeld, p. 332.

[14] The publisher was Miller.

[15] Eleonora. Novella Morale scritta sulla traccia d'un Poemetto Inglese tradotto dal Tedesco. Trattenimento Italico di Mrs. Taylor, In Londra, 1798.

[16] Christabel, I, 79-103.

[17] Coleridge, p. 224.

[18] Medwin, Life of Shelley, Vol. I, p. 62.

[19] Dowden, Life of Shelley, Vol. II, p. 123.

[20] Charles Middleton, Shelley and His Writings, 1858, vol. I, p. 47.

[21] Beitrage, p. 61.

[22] St. Irvyne ; or, The Rosicrucian, " By a Gentleman of the University of Oxford," was published by J. J. Stockdale, 1811.

[23] Newark, 1807.

[24] See my Introduction to Zofloya, or The Moor, Fortune Press, 1928.

[25] Byron, English Bards and Scotch Reviewers, 259-276.

[26] British Review, 1818, vol. XI. p. 37.

[27] Horrid Mysteries, of which there is a reprint in two volumes with Introduction by myself, 1927, was first published in 1796 as " From the German of the Marquis of Grosse by P. Will." The Midnight Groan, or The Spectre of the Chapel, 1808, is anonymous. The Abbot of Montserrat, 2 vols., 1826, is by William Child Green. The Demon of Venice (a redaction of Zofloya), 1810 ; The Convent Spectre, 1808, and The Hag of the Mountains (1798 ?) were all published without the authors' names.

[28] Thalaba was commenced on 12th July, 1799, and finished at Cintra in July, 1800. It was published in the following year.

[29] I have used " The Poetical Works of Robert Southey Collected by Himself," ten volumes, 1837-38. Thalaba occupies vol. IV.

[30] Vol. IV, p. 305 of this edition of Southey.

[31] Vol. XI, no. 63.

[32] Dr. Stefan Hock has not traced the German original. The French version is known to me : Fantasmagoriana, ou Recueil d'Histoires d'apparitions de spectres, revenans, fantômes, etc. Traduit de l'allemand par un Amateur [Eyriès]. Paris, F. F. Schoell, 2 vols, 12 mo, 1812. I also have in my collection Tales of Terror, or More Ghosts ; Forming a Complete Phantasmagoria, 1802. This bears as a motto upon the title page :

> Twelve o'Clock's the Time of Night
> That the Graves, all gaping wide,
> Quick send forth the airy Sprite
> In the Church-way Path to glide.

The book is embellished with a frontispiece representing a most entirely typical white-robed spectre.

³³ Byron signs the dedication of *The Giaour* to Samuel Rogers, May, 1813, In 1815 it had reached a fourteenth edition.

³⁴ *Jean Sbogar* and *Thérèse Aubert* are two well-known works by Nodier.

³⁵ Paris, 1824.

³⁶ Philippe, who was a universal favourite, died 16th October, 1824. " Sa mort fit presque autant de bruit que sa vie," says Dumas, who gives a vivid picture of the unhappy scandals and delays which, owing to the ill-advised conduct of certain Jansenistic fanatics, profaned the funeral on the 18th October, following. The famous actor was interred at Père-Lachaise, the obsequies being attended by more than three thousand people. Amélie Delaunay when quite young married an actor of medium attainments Allan-Dorval. She was soon left a widow, and after a hard struggle obtained recognition of her genius. Dumas who admired her immensely speaks of her as " l'Ève qui devait donner le jour à tout un monde dramatique."

³⁷ " Quant à Philippe, qui l'écraisait, à cette époque, de la dignité de son pas et de la majesté de son geste, c'était la représentation du mélodrame pur sang Pixérécourt et Caignez. . . Nul ne portait comme Philippe la botte jaune, la tunique chamois bordée de noir, la toque à plume et l'épée à poignée en croix." Dumas, *Mes Memoires*, Troisième Série, lxxvii.

³⁸ I quote from the article as reprinted in the *Mélanges*, I, 417.

³⁹ *Histoire des Vampires et des spectres Malfaisans*, Paris, 1820.

⁴⁰ *Le Comte de Monte-Cristo*, Chapter xxxv. I quote from the English translation issued by Collins' Clear Type Press, vol. I, pp. 466-68.

⁴¹ *La Tradition et l'Exotisme dans l'œuvre de Charles Nodier*, (1780-1844). 1923, p. 124.

⁴² *Oeuvres complètes de Eugène Scribe*, Paris, Dentu, 1876. 2me Serie, VI, pp. 41-84.

⁴³ Folie vaudeville en un acte. Paris, Barba, 1820.

⁴⁴ Paris, Martinet, 1820.

⁴⁵ Börne, *Schilderungen aus Paris* (1822 and 1823).

⁴⁶ " Polichinel ist die beste Seele von der Welt."

⁴⁷ 1794-1844.

⁴⁸ Thomas Potter Cooke was born April, 1786, and died April, 1864. His historic début seems to have been made at the Royalty in January, 1804, but his first marked success was in the rôle of Lord Ruthven, which won him great applause. The best known character of this famous actor was William in Douglas Jerrold's *Black-ey'd Susan, or, All in the Downs*, produced at the Surrey Theatre, 8th June, 1829, when it ran for nearly a year. It was frequently revived and never failed of an enthusiastic reception.

⁴⁹ 2 vols., London, 1871.

⁵⁰ This was first produced on 13th April, 1819, as an after-piece to *Jane Shore* in which Mrs. W. West had appeared for the first time in the title-rôle. In *Abudah*, H. Kemble acted Abudah ; Bengough, the genius Barhaddan ; Harley, Fadlahdallah ; Miss Cooke, Selima ; and Mrs. Bland, Zemroude. Genest says that the little fairy tale was given thirteen times.

⁵¹ *The Tales of the Genii : or, The Delightful Lessons of Horam the Son of Asmar. Translated from the Persian by Sir Charles Morell.* This book was written by a young clergyman, the Rev. James Ridley, son of Dr. Gloster Ridley, Chaplain to the East India Company. " Horam " and " Sir Charles Morell " are mere fictions. James Ridley died in 1765 immediately after the completion of the first edition of his *Tales*, which proving very popular have been often reprinted.

⁵² The play is preserved in MS. Lansdowne 807, British Museum, a volume said to contain the few remains of John Warburton's collection which escaped the kitchen fire at the hands of his cook. Sir George Buc in his note written at the end of the piece refers to " this second Maidens tragedy " apparently in allusion to the famous drama by Beaumont and Fletcher, and although not very apposite the name has continued. A scholarly and well-edited reprint of *The Second Maiden's Tragedy* has long been a desideratum. The issue which was prepared for the Malone Society in 1910 by Mr. W. W. Greg is eminently unreadable, nor has the petty recension of the text any real value

being the mere tricks in hand of an arid and sterile pedantry. Such spade work might be used by a scholar as the basis for his edition.

[53] On the last page, folio 56b, the authorship has been assigned to Thomas Goff. This name, however, was erased and that of George Chapman substituted. This again was deleted and the words "By Will Shakspear" inscribed. It is probable that the earliest attribution was made some fifty years or more before the two later, which may belong to the eighteenth century.

[54] Founded by Charles III in 1738 and built by Angelo Carasale.

[55] Some authorities say 29th March.

[56] Rev. Robert Walsh, LL.D., author of "A Residence in Constantinople," and other similar works. (Planché.)

[57] Dion Boucicault (or Bourcicault), playwright and actor, was born at Dublin, 20th December, 1822, and after a most distinguished career, died 18th September, 1890.

[58] *Journal of a London Playgoer from 1851 to 1866*, London, 1891, pp. 45-64.

[59] It may be remarked that the drawing which illustrates the last scene of the play in the Dicks' Edition is inconsistent, as it shows the characters in costumes of *circa* 1750.

[60] The first edition was of the same year. In 1822 this author published a second tragedy, *Montezuma*. Hugo John Belfour was born in 1802, he was ordained in 1826, and died young in the following year.

[61] Ein Kulturbild aus der Gegenwart.

[62] Sozialer Roman. Als Manuskript Gedruckt. Oberhausen und Leipzig, 1883.

[63] Novelle aus der Gegenwart. In *Das neue Blatt*. "Ein illustriertes Familien-Journal," IV (1873), p. 209-408.

[64] Mr. S. M. Ellis, who contributed a bibliography of Le Fanu to the *Irish Book Lover* in 1916. Dr. M. R. James in his Epilogue to the reprint *Madam Crowl's Ghost and Other Tales of Mystery*, London, 1923.

[65] Three volumes, Bentley; also in one volume. A modern re-issue in two parts by Newnes. Also reprinted in one volume, Eveleigh Nash and and Grayson, London, 1923.

[66] Vol. VII, p. 181; vol. IX, p. 212.

[67] And afterwards of 12, Salisbury Square, Fleet Street.

[68] Occasionally attributed to G. W. M. Reynolds, who, however, more than once denied the authorship.

[69] This Epilogue was generally delivered in the provinces and so banal an anti-climax completely ruined the play.

BIBLIOGRAPHY

Abhandlung des Dasenns der Gespenster Nebst einem Anhange vom Vampyrismus. Augsburg, 1768

Actenmässige und umständliche Relation von denen Vampyren. Leipzig, 1732

ALLACCI, Leone (LEO ALLATIUS). *De Graecorum hodie quorundam opinationibus*, Cologne, 1645

ANDREE, Richard. *Ethnographische Parallelen und Vergleiche.* 2 vols., Stuttgart, 1878-89

ARNASON, J. *Icelandic Legends :* translated by G. Powell and E. Magnusson, London, 1864-66

BARTELS, M. and PLOSS, H. H. *Das Weib.* Berlin, 1913

BASIN, Bernardus. *De artibus magicis.* 1482; also Paris, 1506

BASTIAN, Adolf. *Der Mensch in der Geschichte,* II Band : *Psychologie und Mythologie.* Leipzig, 1860

BELL, H. J. *Obeah. Witchcraft in the West Indies.* London, 1893.

BEUCHAT, H. *Manuel d' archéologie americaine (Amérique Pré-historique ; Civilisations disparues).* Paris, 1912

BEAUMONT, John. *An Historical, Physiological, and Theological Treatise of Spirits, Apparitions, Witchcrafts, and other Magical Practices.* London, 1705

BENT, J. T. *The Cyclades.* London, 1885

BERNONI, Giuseppe Don. *Leggende popolari Veneziane.* Venezia, Antonelli, 1814

BOUREULLE, De. " La démonologie de Dom Calmet "—in the *Bulletin de la Société Philomatique Vosgienne,* 1887. Saint-Dié. Impr. Humbert.

BREENE, R. S. *An Irish Vampire*—in *The Occult Review,* October, 1925, pp. 242-5

BROWNE, W. A. F. " Necrophilism "—in *Journal of Mental Science,* January, 1875, pp. 551-560

CALMET, Augustin Dom (O.S.B.) *Traité sur les Apparitons des Esprits, et sur les Vampires, ou les Revenans de Hongrie, de Moravie, etc. Nouvelle édition, revue, corrigée, & augmentée par l' Auteur.* 2 vols. Paris, 1751. (The first edition is Paris, 1746 ; and there was an edition Einsiedeln, Dans la princière abbaie par Jean Everhard Kälin, 2 vols., 1749)

CASTREN, M. A. *Vorlesungen über die finnische Mythologie :* deutsch von A. Schiefner. St. Petersburg, 1853

CEYNOWA, Flor. *De terrae Pucensis incolarum superstitione in re medica.* Berlin, 1851

Christliche Betrachtungen über die wunderbarliche Begebenheit mit den Blutsaugenden Todten in Servien. Leipzig, 1732

CODRINGTON, R. H. (D.D.). *The Melanesians : studies in their Anthropology and Folk Lore.* Oxford. Clarendon Press, 1891

COLLIN DE PLANCY, J. A. S. *Dictionnaire Infernal.* Editio princeps. 2 vols. Paris, 1818. (I have used the sixth, and last, edition, 1 vol., 4to, 1863. The six editions differ widely from one another. This famous work is valuable, but uncritical and even erroneous)

Histoire des Vampires. Paris, 1820
   (This work, which has been erroneously attributed to Dr Polidori, is now considered almost certainly to be by Collin de Plancy)

CROWE, Catherine. *Light and Darkness.* 3 vols. London, 1850.

CUISIN, J. P. R. *Les ombres sanglantes, galerie funèbre de prodiges, événements merveilleux, apparitions nocturnes, songes épouvantables, délits mysterieux,*

342 BIBLIOGRAPHY

phenomènes terribles, vengeances atroces, et combinaisons du crime, forfaits historiques, cadavres mobiles, têtes de la terreur. 2 vols. 12mo. Paris, 1820
Spectriana, on recueil d'histories et d'aventures surprenantes, merveilleuses et remarquables, de spectres, revenans, esprits, fantômes, diables, et démons. Manuscrit trouvé dans les catacombes. Paris, Lécrivain, 1817
Curieuse Relation von denen sich in Servien erzeigend habenden Blutsaugern. Leipzig, 1732
CURTIN, J. *Tales of the Fairies and of the Ghost World.* London, 1895
DAVANZATI, Gioseppe. *Dissertazione sopra i Vampiri di Gioseppe Davanzati, Patrizio Fiorentino, e Tranese, Cavaliere Gerosolimitano, Arcivescovo di Trani e Patriarca d'Alessandria. Seconda edizione. Napoli. MDCC. LXXXIX. Presso Filippo Raimondi. Con licenza de' Superiori.* 8vo. pp. xxx, 230
DAVIES, T. Witton. *Magic, Divination, and Demonology among the Hebrews and their Neighbours.* London and Leipzig, s.d. (1898)
DAWKINS, R. M. *Modern Greek in Asia Minor ;* with a chapter on folk-tales by W. R. Halliday. London, 1916
DE GUAITA, Stanislas. *Essais de sciences maudites.* I. Paris, Carré 1886; Carré, 1890 ; Chamuel, 1895 ; II, Paris Chamuel, 1891 ; III, Paris, Chamuel, 1897,
DEMELIUS, Christoph Friedrichs. *Philosophischer Versuch, ob nicht die merkwurdige Begebenheit der Blutsauger oder Vampyren aus den principiis naturae hergeleitet werden konne.* Vienna, 1732
DIETERICH, Albrech. *Nekyia.* Leipzig, 1893
Dissertatio physica de cadaueribus sanguisugis, sub praesidio Jon. Christ. Stockii. Jena, 1732
DOZON, A. *Contes albanais.* Paris, 1881
EAVES, A. Osborne. *Modern Vampirism.* Talisman Publishing Company, Harrogate, England. 1904
ENNEMOSER, Joseph. *The History of Magic :* translated from the German by William Howitt. 2 vols. London, Bohn, 1854
FAURIEL. *Chansons populaires de la Grèce Moderne.* Paris, 1824–5
FRITSCH, John Christian. *Eines Weimarischen muthmassliche Gedancken von den Vampyren oder Blutsaugenden Todten,* Leipzig, 1732
GARMANNUS, Christ. Frider. *De Miraculis mortuorum.* Lipsiae, 1670
GILES, H. A. *Strange Stories from a Chinese Studio,* London, 1909
GIRALDO (O.P.) le R. P. Mathias de. *Histoire curieuse et pittoresque des sorciers devins, magiciens, astrologues, voyants, revenants, âmes en peine, vampires, spectres, esprits, malins, sorts jetés, excorcismes, etc., depuis l'antiquité jusqu'à nos jours. Revue et augmentée par Fornari.* Paris, Renault, 8vo, 1846. There were other editions, 1849 and 1854, of this popular work. Fra Giraldo is described as " dominicain, ancien exorciste de l' Inquisition," but his actual existence is something more than suspect. Fornari writes himself " Professeur de Philosophie hermétique à Milan," and this is ornamental.
Globus :Illustrierte Zeitschrift für Länder-und Volkerkunde
GORRES, Johann Joseph. *Die Christliche Mystik.* 4 vols. 1836–42. French translation: *La Mystique Divine, Naturelle, et Diabolique* . . . 5 vols. Paris, 1861
GRANT, James. *The Mysteries of all Nations: Rise and Progress of Superstition.* Leith, Edinburgh, and London. n.d. 2nd ed. (Preface signed, January, 1880)
GROOT, J. J. M. De. *The Religious System of China.* Leyden, 1892–1910
The Religion of the Chinese. New York, 1910
GRUNDTVIG, N. F. S. *Danske Kœmpeviser.* No. 90. Copenhagen, 1847
HAHN, J. G. von. *Albanesische Studien.* Jena, 1854
Griechische und Albanesische Märchen. Leipzig, 1864
HANUSH, S. *Slavische mythologie.*
HARE, Augustus. *Story of my Life,* 6 vols. 1896–1900
HARENBERG, John Christian. *Vernünfftige und christliche Gedanken über die Vampyrs oder Blutsaugenden Todten.* Wolfenbüttel, 1732

HAUTTECOEUR, Henry. *Le Folklore de l'Ile de Kythnos.* Bruxelles, 1898

HAUXTHAUSEN, Baron August von. *Transcaucasia : Sketches of the Nations and Races between the Black Sea and the Caspian.* London, 1854

HEINECCIUS, J. M. *De absolutione mortuorum excommunicatorum, seu tympanicorum in ecclesia Graeca.* Helmstad, 1709

HELLWALD, F. von. *Die Welt der Slaven.* Berlin, 1890

HELM, K. *Altgermanische Religioneschichte.* Heidelberg, 1913

HERTZ, Wilhelm. *Der Werwolf.* Stuttgart, 1862

HOCK, S. *Die Vampyrsagen und ihre Verwertung in der deutschen Litteratur.* Berlin, 1900

HORST, Georg Conrad. *Zauber-bibliothek ; oder von Zauberei, Theurgie, und Mantik, Zauberern, Hexen, und Hexenprocessen, Dämonen, Gespenstern, und Geistererschein ungen.* 6 vols., Mainz, 1821

Histoire prodigieuse d'un gentilhomme auquel le Diable s'est apparu et avec lequel il a conversé sous le corps d'une femme morte, aduenue à Paris le premier de janvier mil six cens treize. Paris, 8vo, 1613. Reprinted by Lenglett-Dufresny, *Recueil de dissertations.* Tome I, Part 2 (pp. 69–71

HOSE, C. and MEDOUGALL, W. *The Pagan Tribes of Borneo.* London, 1912

HOVORKA, O. von, and KRONFIELD, A. *Vergleichende Volksmedizin.* 2 vols. Berlin, 1908–9

HUDSON, Thomson Jay. *The Law of Psychic Phenomena.* Putnam, 1905. (c. xxi : " Suspended Animation ")

HUNT, R. *Popular Romances of the West of England.* London, 1865

Ion Greanga. Edited by Tudor Pamfile (Roumanian periodical of peasant art and literature)

IVES, George. *A History of Penal Methods.* London, 1914

JOYCE, Thomas Athol. *Mexican Archæology : an introduction to the Archæology of the Mexican and Mayan Civilizations of pre-Spanish America.* London, 1914

KARL, O. F. (Karl Otto). *Danziger Sagen gesammelt von O. F. Karl.* Danzig, 1843

KEANE, A. H. *Man, Past and Present.* London, 1920

KORNMANN. *De miraculis mortuorum.* 1610

KRAUSS, F. S. " Vampyre im südslavischen Volksglauben "—in *Globus,* lxi (1892)

LAISTNER, Ludwig. *Das Räthsel der Sphynx : Grundzüge einer Mythengeschichte.* Berlin, 1889

LANCELIER, Charles. *Historie mystique de Shatan.* Daragon, Paris, 1905. (3me partie : Le Vampire)

LAWSON, John Cuthbert. *Modern Greek Folk Lore and Ancient Greek Religion.* Cambridge, 1910

LEAKE, W. M. *Travels in Northern Greece,* 4 vols. London, 1835

LEE, Frederick George. *The Vampyre.* In *Reynold's Miscellany.* Vol. I, No. 28. (New Series.) Saturday, 20th January, 1849 (pp. 444-445)

LIEBRECHT, F. *Zur Volkskunde.* Heilbronn, 1879

LUCAS, Paul. *Voyage du Sieur Paul Lucas au Levant.* 2 vols. A La Haye. 1705

Lycanthropist (The). In *Reynolds' Miscellany,* Vol. V, No. 125. (New Series.) Saturday, 30th November, 1850 (pp. 293-295)

MACCULLOCH, J. A. "Vampire"—article in *Encyclopædia of Religion and Ethics,* edited by James Hastings. Vol. XII, pp. 589-591. Edinburgh, 1921

MACHAL, J. *Slavic Mythology,* Boston, 1918

MALLEUS MALEFICARUM—v. Sprenger and Kramer

MANNHARDT, W. Über Vampyrismus—in *Zeitschrift für deutsche Mythologie und Sittenkunde.* Vol. iv, pp. 259–82. Göttingen, 1858

MAP, Walter. *De Nugis Curialium.* Edited by M. R. James. (*Anecdota Oxoniensia : Mediæval and Modern Series,* Part XIV) Oxford, 1914

De Nugis Curalium (Courtiers' Trifles). Englished by Frederick Tupper and Marbury Bladen Ogle. London, 1924

MAYO, Herbert. *On the Truths contained in Popular Superstitions.* Second Edition. London, 1851. (These papers were first published in *Blackwoods' Edinburgh Magazine,* 1847–8)

MIGNE, M. L'abbé. *Encyclopédie Théologique*, Tome Quarante—Neuvième : Dictionnaire des Sciences Occultes. Paris, 1860. *Vampires*, 783–798. See also : *Paul, Arnold*, 263 ; *Plogojouits, Pierre*, 323–324 ; *Polyinte*, 325–326. And in Tome Quarante-Huitcime, *Harppe*, 803 ; *Katha hanes*, 918–919

MORE, Henry. *An Antidote against Atheism ; or An Appeal to the Natural Faculties of the Mind of Man, whether there be not a God*. 1653. Second Edition with Appendix, 1655

MORETON, Andrew. *The Secrets of the Invisible World Disclosed ; or, an Universal History of Apparitions Sacred and Prophane*. The third edition, London, 1738

MURGOCI, Agnes. "The Vampire in Roumania ".—in *Folk-Lore*, vol. xxxvii, No. 4, 31 December, 1926 : pp. 320–49

NEWTON. *Travels and Discoveries in the Levant*. 2 vols., London, 1866

NINO, de A. *Usi e Costumi Abruzzesi*. G. Barbera, Florence, 1891

NODIER, Charles. *Infernaliana*. Paris, Sansom et Nadau, 12mo, 1882

Occult Review (The)

Ocean of Story (The)—v. Somadeva

OTESCU, I. *Credintele Ţâranului Român despre Cer şi Stele*. (Roumanian Academy phamphlet)

Ottonis Graben zum Stein unverlornes Licht und Recht derer Todten unter den Lebendigen. Wittenberg, 1732

P[ABAN], Madame Gabrielle de. *Histoire des Fantômes et des Démons qui se sont montrés parmi les hommes, ou choix d'anecdotes et de contes, de faits merveilleux, de traits bizarres, d'aventures extraordinaires sur les revenans, les fantômes, les lutins, les démons, les spectres, les vampires et les apparitions diverses, etc.* Paris, 12mo, 1819. (Quérard tells us that Collin de Plancy who was a cousin of the writer, collaborated in this work)

Démoniana, ou Nouveau choix d'anecdotes surprenantes, de nouvelles prodigieuses, d'aventures bizarres, sur les revenans, les spectres, les fantômes, les démons, les loups garous, les visions, etc. ; ouvrage propre a rassurer les imaginations timorees contre les frayeurs superstitieuses. Paris, 18mo, 1820. (Graesse mistakenly attributes this work to Collin de Plancy : *Bibliotheca Magica*, p. 88)

PASHLEY, ROBERT. *Travels in Crete*. 2 vols. Cambridge and London, 1837.

PETRONIUS. *Satiræ*, tertium edidit Franciscus Buecheler. Berolini, 1895

PHILOSTRATUS. *The Life of Apollonius of Tyana*, translated by F. C. Conybeare, 2 vols. (Loeb Classical Library), London, 1926

PHLEGON TRALLIANUS—apud *Fragmenta Historicorum Graecorum*, ed. Carolus Mullerus, vol. III, pp. 602–24, Paris, Didot, 1849

PLUMMER, Charles. *Uitae Sanctorum Hiberniae*. 2 vols. Oxford, 1900

POHLIUS, M. John Christopher. *Dissertatio de hominibus post mortem sanguisugis*. Leipzig, 1742

POLITES, N. P. Παραδόσεις τοῦ ἑλληνικοῦ λαοῦ. Athens, 2 vols., 1904

PUTONEUS. *Besondere Nachrichten von denen Vampyrs*. Leipzig, 1732

RALSTON, W. R. S. *Russian Folk Tales*. London, 1873

RANFT, Michael. *De Masticatione Mortuorum in Tumulis Liber*. Leipzig, 1728

Tractat von dem Kauen und Schamtzen der Todten in Gräbern. Leipzig, 1734

RATTRAY, R. Sutherland. *Ashanti Proverbs : translated from the original*. (The Primitive Ethics of a Savage People.) Clarendon Press, Oxford, 1916

Réalité de la magie et des Apparitions, ou Contre-poison du Dictionnaire Infernal. Paris, 1819

Revue d'Assyriologie, 1909, 61

RICAUT, Paul. *The Present State of the Greek and Armenian Churches, Anno Christi*, 1678. London, 1679

RICHARD, S. J., François. *Relation de ce qui s'est passé de plus remarquable a Sant-Erini Isle de l' Archipel, depuis l'établissement des Peres de la compagnie de Jesus en icelle*. Paris, MDCLVII.

ROBERT, Cyprien. *Les Slaves de Turquie*, 2 vols. Paris, 1844

RODD, Sir Rennell. *The Customs and Lore of Modern Greece*. London, 1892

ROHR, M. Philip. *De Masticatione Mortuorum* (Dissertatio Historico-Philosophica). Leipzig, 1679

ROUGHEAD, William. *Burke and Hare* (Notable British Trials). Glasgow, Hodge, 1919

RZAZEYNSCI, S. J. Gabriel. *Historia naturalis curiosa regni Poloniae.* Sandomiriae, 1721

ST. CLAIR, S. G. B. and BROPHY, Charles A. *Twelve Years' Study of the Eastern Question in Bulgaria :* being a revised Edition of *A Residence in Bulgaria* (1869). London, 1877

SCHMIDT, Bernhard. *Griechische Märchen, Sagen, und Volkslieder.* Leipzig, 1877

SCHOTT, Arthur and Albert. *Walachische Mährchen.* Stuttgart and Tübingen 1845

Schreiben eines guten Freundes an einen anderen guten Freund, die Vampyren betreffend. Frankfort, 1732

SIMON, jun., Friedrich Alexander. *Der Vampirismus im neunzehnten Jahrhundert.* Hamburg, 1831. (A medical pamphlet dealing with the abuse of excessive letting of blood by physicians)

SIMON, Paul Max. *Crimes et délits dans la folie.* 1886

SIMROCK, C. J. *Handbuch der deutschen Mythologien.* Bonn, 1874

SINISTRARI, O. F. M., Ludovico Maria. *Demoniality.* Translated from the Latin by the Rev. Montague Summers with an Introduction and Notes. The Fortune Press, London, 1927

SKEAT, W. W. *Malay Magic, being an Introduction to the Folklore and Popular Religion of the Malay Peninsula.* London. 1900

SOMADERA. The Ocean of Story, translated by C. H. Tawney ; edited with Intruduction by N. M. Penzer, 10 vols. London, Sawyer, 1924

SOMMIÈRES, M. Le Colonel L. C. Vialla de. *Voyage Historique et Politique au Montenegro.* 2 vols., Paris, 1820

SPENCE, Lewis. *An Encyclopedia of Occultism.* London, Routledge, 1920
The Gods of Mexico. London, Unwin, 1923
The Myths of Mexico and Peru. London, Harrap, 1913

SPRENGER (O.P.), James and KRAMER (Institor), Heinrich. *Malleus Maleficarum :* translated from the Latin by the Rev. Montague Summers, with an Introduction and Notes. John Rodker, London, 1928

STEPHEN, H. J. *Commentaries on the Laws of England.* London, 1868

STOCK, John Christian. *Dissertatio de Cadaueribus Sanguisugis.* Jena, 1732

STOLL, Otto. *Suggestion und Hypnotismus in der Völkerpsychologie.* Leipzig, 1894

STRACK, Hermann, L. *The Jew and Human Sacrifice.* Translated from the 8th Edition by Henry Blanchamp. First published in England, May, 1909

SWETTENHAM, Frank A. *Malay Sketches.* London, 1895

TEBB, W. and VOLLUM, M.D. (Colonel). *Premature Burial and How It May Be Prevented.* 2nd edition by W. R. Hadwen, M.D., London, 1905

TERTULLIAN. *De Anima*—apud Migne, *Patres Latini*, II, 687–798

THOMPSON, R. Campbell. *The Devils and Evil Spirits of Babylonia.* 2 vols. London, 1903–1904
Semitic Magic : its Origins and Development. London, 1908

THURSTON (S. J.), H. *Broucolaccas : A Study in Mediaeval Ghost Lore.* In *The Month.* November, 1897. Vol. XC. (pp. 502-520)

TOURNEFORT, M. Pitton de. *Relation d'un Voyage du Levant*, 2 vols. Paris, 1717

TOZER, Rev. Henry Fanshawe. *Researches in the Highlands of Turkey . . . with Notes on the Ballads, Tales, and Classical Superstitions of the Modern Greeks.* 2 vols., London, 1869

Travels of Three English Gentlemen from Venice to Hamburgh being the grand Tour of Germany in the Year (1734). Harleian Miscellany, vol. IV sqq., 1745

Uisus et repertus über die so genannten Vampyren. Nuremberg, 1732

VALVASOR, Iohannes Weichardus. *Gloria Carniolae Explicata.* 4to. 1689

VILLEMARQUÉ, T. Hersart de la. *Barzaz-Breiz :* Chants populaires de la Bretagne, 4th edition, 2 vols. Paris, 1846

VOIGTS, Gottlieb Heinrich. *Kurtzes Bedencken von den Relationen wegen der Vampyren.* Leipzig, 1732

WACHSMUTH, C. *Das alte Griechenland im neuem.* Bonn, 1864

WILLELMI PARUI DE NEWBURGH. *Historia Rerum Anglicarum :* recensuit Hans Claude Hamilton. 2 vols. Londini, 1856

WILLOUGHBY-MEADE, G. *Chinese Ghouls and Goblins.* London, 1928

WINSTEDT, R. O. *Shaman, Saiva, and Sufi : a Study of Malay Magic.* London, 1928

WRIGHT, Dudley. *Vampires and Vampirism.* 1914. Second Edition, enlarged, 1924

WRIGHT, Thomas. *Essays on Subjects connected with the Literature, Popular Superstitions, and History of England in the Middle Ages.* 2 vols. London, 1846

W.S.G.E. *Curieuse und sehr wunderbarliche Relation von denen sich neuer Dinge in Servien erzeigenden Blutsaugern oder Vampyrs, aus authentischen Nachrichten mitgetheilet und mit historischen und philosophischen Reflexionen begleitet.* Leipzig, 1732

ZEILER, Martin. *Trauergeschicten.* 3 vols., 1625

ZOPFT, John Heinrich. *Dissertatio de Uampiris Seruiensibus.* Halle, 1733

POETRY; FICTION; DRAMA

ARNOLD, Theodor Ferdinand Kajetan. *Der Vampir.* Schneeburg, 1801

BENSON, E. F. *The Face,* and *No Bird Sings.* Both in *Spook Stories,* 1928 *The Room in the Tower*—in *The Room in the Tower and other Stories,* 1912 *Mrs. Amworth*—in *Visible and Invisible,* 1923

BÉRARD, Cyprien. *Lord Ruthven ou les Vampires.* Roman de G. B. Publié par l'auteur de Jean Sbogar et de Thérèse Aubut. Paris, 1820. (February, 1820. Second Edition with Notes on Vampirism, July, 1820)

BLACKWOOD, Algernon. *The Transfer*—in *Pan's Garden,*1912. *The Strange Adventures of a Private Secretary in New York*—in *The Empty House,* 1906 *Blutsauger (Die)* Roman. Quedlinburg und Leipzig, 1821

BOUCICAULT, Dion. *The Phantom :* a Drama in Two Acts. New York. Samuel French, 1856. No. CLXV French's Standard Drama. Also Dick's Standard Plays, No. 697

BRADDON, Miss [Mary Elizabeth]. *Good Lady Ducayne*—in *The Strand Magazine.* February, 1896, vol. XI, pp. 185–199

BRAZIER, GABRIEL, et ARMAND. *Les Trois Vampires, ou le clair de la lune.* Folie vaudeville en un acte. Paris, Barba, 1820 (Produced at the Variétés)

BURTON, Sir Richard. *Vikram and the Vampire or Tales of Hindu Devilry* (Adapted by Richard F. Burton, F.R.G.S. etc.). London, 1870 [1869]

BYRON, Lord. *The Giaour.* "A Fragment of a Turkish Tale." London, Murray, 1813. "A New Edition, with Some Additions," (71 lines at the beginning of the poem, the amended dedication and the advertisement). London, Murray, 1813

Cadet Buteux Vampire ; ou Relation véridique du prologue et des trois actes de cet épouvantable mélodrama écrite sous la dictée di ce passeux du Gros-Caillou par son sécretaire Désaugeirs. Paris, 1820 (A parody on Nodier)

COSMAR and KRAUSE. *Der Vampyr :* Trauerspiel in 5 Abteilungen ; nach einen Spindlerschen Erzählung bearbeitet. Berlin, 1828

CRAWFORD, F. Marion. *For the Blood is the Life*—in *Uncanny Tales,* 1911

DAHN, F. *Der Vampyr.* (Werke, vol. XVII, 1898, p. 233)

Der Vampyr, oder die blutige Hochzeit mit der schönin Kroatin : eine sonderbare Gerchichte von böhmischen Wissenpater. Erfurt. 1812

Der Vampyr, oder die todten Brant : Romantisches Schauspiel in drei Acten. Brunswick, 1822

DORSET, St. John [Rev. Hugo John Belfour]. *The Vampire : a Tragedy in Five Acts.* First [Second] Edition. London, MDCCCXXI. C. and J. Ollier.

DOYLE, Sir A. Conan. *The Parasite.* 1891

DUMAS (Père), Alexandre. *Le Vampire :* Drama fantastique en 5 actes et, 10 tableaux par Alexandre Dumas et Auguste Maquet, répresenté le 20 décembre, 1851 sur le théâtre de l'Amtigu-Comique. *Thêtâre Complet de Alexandre Dumas.* Onzième Série. Paris, Michel Lévy, 1865

DUNN, Gertrude. *The Mark of the Bat.* London, 1928

ELLMENREICH, Friederike. *Der Vampyr.* Mainz, 1827 (A translation from Scribe)

FABER, H. *Le Vampire,* nouvelle traduite de l'anglais de Lord Byron. Paris 1819

FAIRFIELD, Henry W. A. *Only by Mortal Hands* (as told to Harold Standish Corbin). " Ghost Stories," vol. III, No. 4. October, 1927. Construction Publishing Company. Washington and South Aves.

FÉVAL, Paul H. C. *La Ville Vampire.* Paris, Dentu, 1875. (This is ingenuously stated to be a romance by Mrs. Radcliffe, who recounted it to the writer's aunt from whom he heard the tale)

FOSSE, Pierre de la. *Le Vampire ;* Mélodrama en 3 actes. Paroles de M. Pierre de la Fosse de la rue des Morts. (Pseudonym). 1820

GAUTIER, Théophile. *La Morte Amoreuse.* Originally appeared in the *Chronique de Paris,* 23rd and 26th June, 1836

The Beautiful Vampire. London, 1927. (A translation of *La Morte Amoreuse,* by Paul Hookham. There is also a translation by G. Burnham Ives as *The Dead Leman,* Putnam, New York and London, 1903. Other English versions have been published)

GOETHE, Johann Wolfgang von. *Die Braut von Corinth*

HAUSHOFER, Max. *Die Verbannten.* Leipzig, 1890

HEIGEL, C. M. *Der Vampyr :* Romantische Oper in drei Aufzügen. Nach Byrons Dichtung von C. M. Heigel ; Musik von P. V. Lindpaintner, 1829 (Produced at Stuttgart, 21 September, 1828)

HEROLD, A. Ferdinand. *Les Contes du Vampire.* Paris, Mercure de France, 1891. Second edition, 1902. (Indian tales)

HERON, E. and H. *The Story of Baelbrow* in *Ghost Stories,* London, Pearson, 1916. (Reprinted from *Pearson's Magazine,* April, 1898)

HILDEBRANDS, Theodor. *Der Vampyr oder die Totenbraut :* ein Roman nach neugriechischen Volkssagen. Leipzig, 1828

H.M.P. *A Vampire of Souls.* 1904 (A semi-apocalyptic novel)

HODDER, Reginald. *The Vampire.* London, 1913

HUGO, Victor. *Han d'Islande.* 4 vols., Paris, Persan, 1823

JAMES, M. R. *Count Magnus* in *Ghost Stories of an Antiquary.* London. Arnold, 1905. *An Episode of Cathedral History*—in *A thin Ghost and Others.* London, Arnold, 1919.

KEATS, John. *Lamia.* Published July, 1820

KÉRATY, M. de. *Le Dernier du Beaumanoir.* (1850 ?). [Founded on the following incident : Peu d'années avant le révolution de 1789 un prêtre fut convaincu d'avoir assouri sa passion brutale sur le cadavre encore chaud d'une femme auprés de laquelle il avait été placé pour reciter des prières]

KING, Frank. *The Ghoul.* London, 1928 (This is a mystery novel. The Ghoul is a nickname given to a master-criminal)

LE FANU, Sheridan. *Carmilla—In a Glass Darkly.* 3 vols., London, Bentley, 1872. Also in one volume, 1872. Reprinted in two parts by Newnes. Reprinted Eveleigh Nash, 1923

LIDDELL, Hon. Henry. " The Vampire Bride "—in *The Wizard of the North ; The Vampire Bride, and other Poems.* Blackwood, Edinburgh ; and Cadell, London, MDCCCXXXIII

MENGALS, Martin Joseph. *Le Vampire :* Comic Opera in one Act. 1826. (Produced 1st March, 1826)

MÉRIMÉE, Prosper. *La Guzla, ou, Choix de Poésies Illyriques,* 1827

NERUDA, Jan. *The Vampire,* pp. 847-849 of *Great Short Stories of the World.* London, New Impression. November, 1927

NODIER, Charles. *Le Vampire* (A melodrama in a Prologue and three Acts. Music by Alexandre Piccini. Produced at the Porte-Saint-Martin, Paris, 13th June, 1820). Paris, 1820

PALMA, Silvestro di. *I Vampiri*. (1800)

PLANCHÉ, James Robinson. *The Vampire. or the Bride of the Isles.* Produced at the English Opera House, 9th August, 1820. 8vo. 1820. Also Dicks' Standard Plays, No. 875

POLIDORI. *The Vampyre.* Originally published in the *New Monthly Magazine*, April, 1819. First separate edition, London, Sherwood, 1819

PREST, Thomas Preskett. *Varney the Vampire, or The Feast of Blood.* 1847. Reprinted in Penny Numbers, 1853

PRZYBYSZEWSKI. *De profundis.* Leipzig and Berlin, 1895

RACHILDE. *La Tour d'Amour.* Paris, 1891 (Necrophilia)

ROMAN, Victor. " Four Wooden Stakes "—in *Not at Night*, London, 1925

ROTTA. *Il Vampiro* : Ballet with music by Paolo Giorza. Milan. 1861 (Produced at Milan in 1861)

SCHUBIN, Ossip. *Vollmondzauber.* Stuttgart, 1899

SCOTT, G. A. Dawson. *The Vampire : a Book of Cornish and other Stories.* London, 1925. (The only Vampire in this book seems to be a metaphor)

SCRIBE, Eugène. *Le Vampire :* Comédie-Vaudeville en un acte de Scribe et Mélesville. Théâtre du Vaudeville. 15 June, 1820. Oeuvres complètes de Eugène Scribe. Comédies. Vaudevilles. 2me Série, VI. (Paris, Dentu, 1876)

Second Maiden's Tragedy (The). Licensed 31st October, 1611. MS. Lansdowne 807. British Museum. (This drama has been several times printed. It was first given to the press in Baldwin's *The Old English Drama*, Vol. I, 1825. Among the later reprints is that of the Malone Society, 1909, Edited by W. W. Greg. A scholarly recension of this play is a desideratum)

SELTZAM, Dr. *Die Vampyre der Residenz :* Wahre Skandalgeschichten und sensationelle Enthüllungen von Dr. Seltzam (pseudonym ?). 2 Parts. Berlin, 1900. (A pornographic piece of no value)

SOUTHEY, Robert. *Thalaba the Destroyer.* 1801 (Finished July, 1800)

SPINDLER. *Der Vampyr und seine Braut : Nachtstück aus der neuesten zeit—* in *Zwillinge. Zwei Erzählungen, nebst einem Anhange von Originalbriefen.* Hanover, 1826

STENBOCK, Eric Stanislaus, Count. *The True Story of a Vampire.* In *Studies of Death.* London, Nutt, 1894.

STOKER, Bram. *Dracula. A tale.* pp. ix, 390. London, Constable, 1897. Tenth edition, Rider, 1913

Dracula's Guest and other Weird Stories. London, Routledge, 1914

STUCKEN, Edouard. *Die Vampyrkatze*—in *Balladen*, Berlin, 1899

TAGLIONI, Paul. *Morgano :* Comédie-ballet in four acts and seven tableaux ; with music by J. Hatch. 1857. (Produced at Berlin, 25th May, 1857)

TOLSTOI, Alexei. *Oupir* (a short story)

TURGENIEV, I. S. *Apparitions.* tr. by P. Merimée. In *Nouvelles Muscovites.* 2e ed. Paris, 1868

UPTON, Smyth. *The Last of the Vampires.* Columbian Press, Weston-Super-Mare, 1845

VACANO, E. *Schwarze Melancholie* (A Short Story). 1865

Vampyre (The). By the Wife of a Medical Man. 1858. (A frantic teetotal tract, presented as fiction)

VAUDÈRE, J. de la. *Le mystère de Karme.* Paris, 1901

WACHENHUSEN, Hans and May Karl. *In den Schluchten des Balkan.* Stuttgart and Leipzig. *n.d.*

WAKEFIELD, H. R. *The Seventeenth Hole at Duncaster*—in *They Return at Evening*, 1928

WELLS, H. G. *The Flowering of the Strange Orchid*—in *The Stolen Bacillus*, 1895

WOHLBRÜCK, Wilhelm August. *Der Vampyr :* an opera. Music by Marschner. 1828. (Produced 28th March, 1828)

X.L. *Aut Diabolus aur Nihil :* "The Kiss of Judas." London, Methuen, 1894

INDEX

354 INDEX

A CATALOG OF SELECTED
DOVER BOOKS
IN ALL FIELDS OF INTEREST

A CATALOG OF SELECTED DOVER
BOOKS IN ALL FIELDS OF INTEREST

CONCERNING THE SPIRITUAL IN ART, Wassily Kandinsky. Pioneering work by father of abstract art. Thoughts on color theory, nature of art. Analysis of earlier masters. 12 illustrations. 80pp. of text. 5⅜ x 8½. 23411-8

ANIMALS: 1,419 Copyright-Free Illustrations of Mammals, Birds, Fish, Insects, etc., Jim Harter (ed.). Clear wood engravings present, in extremely lifelike poses, over 1,000 species of animals. One of the most extensive pictorial sourcebooks of its kind. Captions. Index. 284pp. 9 x 12. 23766-4

CELTIC ART: The Methods of Construction, George Bain. Simple geometric techniques for making Celtic interlacements, spirals, Kells-type initials, animals, humans, etc. Over 500 illustrations. 160pp. 9 x 12. (Available in U.S. only.) 22923-8

AN ATLAS OF ANATOMY FOR ARTISTS, Fritz Schider. Most thorough reference work on art anatomy in the world. Hundreds of illustrations, including selections from works by Vesalius, Leonardo, Goya, Ingres, Michelangelo, others. 593 illustrations. 192pp. 7⅛ x 10¼. 20241-0

CELTIC HAND STROKE-BY-STROKE (Irish Half-Uncial from "The Book of Kells"): An Arthur Baker Calligraphy Manual, Arthur Baker. Complete guide to creating each letter of the alphabet in distinctive Celtic manner. Covers hand position, strokes, pens, inks, paper, more. Illustrated. 48pp. 8¼ x 11. 24336-2

EASY ORIGAMI, John Montroll. Charming collection of 32 projects (hat, cup, pelican, piano, swan, many more) specially designed for the novice origami hobbyist. Clearly illustrated easy-to-follow instructions insure that even beginning papercrafters will achieve successful results. 48pp. 8¼ x 11. 27298-2

THE COMPLETE BOOK OF BIRDHOUSE CONSTRUCTION FOR WOODWORKERS, Scott D. Campbell. Detailed instructions, illustrations, tables. Also data on bird habitat and instinct patterns. Bibliography. 3 tables. 63 illustrations in 15 figures. 48pp. 5¼ x 8½. 24407-5

BLOOMINGDALE'S ILLUSTRATED 1886 CATALOG: Fashions, Dry Goods and Housewares, Bloomingdale Brothers. Famed merchants' extremely rare catalog depicting about 1,700 products: clothing, housewares, firearms, dry goods, jewelry, more. Invaluable for dating, identifying vintage items. Also, copyright-free graphics for artists, designers. Co-published with Henry Ford Museum & Greenfield Village. 160pp. 8¼ x 11. 25780-0

HISTORIC COSTUME IN PICTURES, Braun & Schneider. Over 1,450 costumed figures in clearly detailed engravings–from dawn of civilization to end of 19th century. Captions. Many folk costumes. 256pp. 8⅜ x 11¾. 23150-X

STICKLEY CRAFTSMAN FURNITURE CATALOGS, Gustav Stickley and L. & J. G. Stickley. Beautiful, functional furniture in two authentic catalogs from 1910. 594 illustrations, including 277 photos, show settles, rockers, armchairs, reclining chairs, bookcases, desks, tables. 183pp. 6½ x 9¼. 23838-5

AMERICAN LOCOMOTIVES IN HISTORIC PHOTOGRAPHS: 1858 to 1949, Ron Ziel (ed.). A rare collection of 126 meticulously detailed official photographs, called "builder portraits," of American locomotives that majestically chronicle the rise of steam locomotive power in America. Introduction. Detailed captions. xi+129pp. 9 x 12. 27393-8

AMERICA'S LIGHTHOUSES: An Illustrated History, Francis Ross Holland, Jr. Delightfully written, profusely illustrated fact-filled survey of over 200 American lighthouses since 1716. History, anecdotes, technological advances, more. 240pp. 8 x 10¾. 25576-X

TOWARDS A NEW ARCHITECTURE, Le Corbusier. Pioneering manifesto by founder of "International School." Technical and aesthetic theories, views of industry, economics, relation of form to function, "mass-production split" and much more. Profusely illustrated. 320pp. 6⅛ x 9¼. (Available in U.S. only.) 25023-7

HOW THE OTHER HALF LIVES, Jacob Riis. Famous journalistic record, exposing poverty and degradation of New York slums around 1900, by major social reformer. 100 striking and influential photographs. 233pp. 10 x 7⅞. 22012-5

FRUIT KEY AND TWIG KEY TO TREES AND SHRUBS, William M. Harlow. One of the handiest and most widely used identification aids. Fruit key covers 120 deciduous and evergreen species; twig key 160 deciduous species. Easily used. Over 300 photographs. 126pp. 5⅜ x 8½. 20511-8

COMMON BIRD SONGS, Dr. Donald J. Borror. Songs of 60 most common U.S. birds: robins, sparrows, cardinals, bluejays, finches, more—arranged in order of increasing complexity. Up to 9 variations of songs of each species.
Cassette and manual 99911-4

ORCHIDS AS HOUSE PLANTS, Rebecca Tyson Northen. Grow cattleyas and many other kinds of orchids—in a window, in a case, or under artificial light. 63 illustrations. 148pp. 5⅜ x 8½. 23261-1

MONSTER MAZES, Dave Phillips. Masterful mazes at four levels of difficulty. Avoid deadly perils and evil creatures to find magical treasures. Solutions for all 32 exciting illustrated puzzles. 48pp. 8¼ x 11. 26005-4

MOZART'S DON GIOVANNI (DOVER OPERA LIBRETTO SERIES), Wolfgang Amadeus Mozart. Introduced and translated by Ellen H. Bleiler. Standard Italian libretto, with complete English translation. Convenient and thoroughly portable—an ideal companion for reading along with a recording or the performance itself. Introduction. List of characters. Plot summary. 121pp. 5¼ x 8½. 24944-1

TECHNICAL MANUAL AND DICTIONARY OF CLASSICAL BALLET, Gail Grant. Defines, explains, comments on steps, movements, poses and concepts. 15-page pictorial section. Basic book for student, viewer. 127pp. 5⅜ x 8½. 21843-0

THE CLARINET AND CLARINET PLAYING, David Pino. Lively, comprehensive work features suggestions about technique, musicianship, and musical interpretation, as well as guidelines for teaching, making your own reeds, and preparing for public performance. Includes an intriguing look at clarinet history. "A godsend," *The Clarinet,* Journal of the International Clarinet Society. Appendixes. 7 illus. 320pp. 5⅜ x 8½. 40270-3

HOLLYWOOD GLAMOR PORTRAITS, John Kobal (ed.). 145 photos from 1926-49. Harlow, Gable, Bogart, Bacall; 94 stars in all. Full background on photographers, technical aspects. 160pp. 8⅜ x 11¼. 23352-9

THE ANNOTATED CASEY AT THE BAT: A Collection of Ballads about the Mighty Casey/Third, Revised Edition, Martin Gardner (ed.). Amusing sequels and parodies of one of America's best-loved poems: Casey's Revenge, Why Casey Whiffed, Casey's Sister at the Bat, others. 256pp. 5⅜ x 8½. 28598-7

THE RAVEN AND OTHER FAVORITE POEMS, Edgar Allan Poe. Over 40 of the author's most memorable poems: "The Bells," "Ulalume," "Israfel," "To Helen," "The Conqueror Worm," "Eldorado," "Annabel Lee," many more. Alphabetic lists of titles and first lines. 64pp. 5$\frac{3}{16}$ x 8¼. 26685-0

PERSONAL MEMOIRS OF U. S. GRANT, Ulysses Simpson Grant. Intelligent, deeply moving firsthand account of Civil War campaigns, considered by many the finest military memoirs ever written. Includes letters, historic photographs, maps and more. 528pp. 6⅛ x 9¼. 28587-1

ANCIENT EGYPTIAN MATERIALS AND INDUSTRIES, A. Lucas and J. Harris. Fascinating, comprehensive, thoroughly documented text describes this ancient civilization's vast resources and the processes that incorporated them in daily life, including the use of animal products, building materials, cosmetics, perfumes and incense, fibers, glazed ware, glass and its manufacture, materials used in the mummification process, and much more. 544pp. 6⅛ x 9¼. (Available in U.S. only.) 40446-3

RUSSIAN STORIES/RUSSKIE RASSKAZY: A Dual-Language Book, edited by Gleb Struve. Twelve tales by such masters as Chekhov, Tolstoy, Dostoevsky, Pushkin, others. Excellent word-for-word English translations on facing pages, plus teaching and study aids, Russian/English vocabulary, biographical/critical introductions, more. 416pp. 5⅜ x 8½. 26244-8

PHILADELPHIA THEN AND NOW: 60 Sites Photographed in the Past and Present, Kenneth Finkel and Susan Oyama. Rare photographs of City Hall, Logan Square, Independence Hall, Betsy Ross House, other landmarks juxtaposed with contemporary views. Captures changing face of historic city. Introduction. Captions. 128pp. 8¼ x 11. 25790-8

AIA ARCHITECTURAL GUIDE TO NASSAU AND SUFFOLK COUNTIES, LONG ISLAND, The American Institute of Architects, Long Island Chapter, and the Society for the Preservation of Long Island Antiquities. Comprehensive, well-researched and generously illustrated volume brings to life over three centuries of Long Island's great architectural heritage. More than 240 photographs with authoritative, extensively detailed captions. 176pp. 8¼ x 11. 26946-9

NORTH AMERICAN INDIAN LIFE: Customs and Traditions of 23 Tribes, Elsie Clews Parsons (ed.). 27 fictionalized essays by noted anthropologists examine religion, customs, government, additional facets of life among the Winnebago, Crow, Zuni, Eskimo, other tribes. 480pp. 6⅛ x 9¼. 27377-6

FRANK LLOYD WRIGHT'S DANA HOUSE, Donald Hoffmann. Pictorial essay of residential masterpiece with over 160 interior and exterior photos, plans, elevations, sketches and studies. 128pp. 9¹/₄ x 10¾. 29120-0

THE MALE AND FEMALE FIGURE IN MOTION: 60 Classic Photographic Sequences, Eadweard Muybridge. 60 true-action photographs of men and women walking, running, climbing, bending, turning, etc., reproduced from rare 19th-century masterpiece. vi + 121pp. 9 x 12. 24745-7

1001 QUESTIONS ANSWERED ABOUT THE SEASHORE, N. J. Berrill and Jacquelyn Berrill. Queries answered about dolphins, sea snails, sponges, starfish, fishes, shore birds, many others. Covers appearance, breeding, growth, feeding, much more. 305pp. 5¼ x 8¼. 23366-9

ATTRACTING BIRDS TO YOUR YARD, William J. Weber. Easy-to-follow guide offers advice on how to attract the greatest diversity of birds: birdhouses, feeders, water and waterers, much more. 96pp. 5³/₁₆ x 8¼. 28927-3

MEDICINAL AND OTHER USES OF NORTH AMERICAN PLANTS: A Historical Survey with Special Reference to the Eastern Indian Tribes, Charlotte Erichsen-Brown. Chronological historical citations document 500 years of usage of plants, trees, shrubs native to eastern Canada, northeastern U.S. Also complete identifying information. 343 illustrations. 544pp. 6½ x 9¼. 25951-X

STORYBOOK MAZES, Dave Phillips. 23 stories and mazes on two-page spreads: Wizard of Oz, Treasure Island, Robin Hood, etc. Solutions. 64pp. 8¼ x 11. 23628-5

AMERICAN NEGRO SONGS: 230 Folk Songs and Spirituals, Religious and Secular, John W. Work. This authoritative study traces the African influences of songs sung and played by black Americans at work, in church, and as entertainment. The author discusses the lyric significance of such songs as "Swing Low, Sweet Chariot," "John Henry," and others and offers the words and music for 230 songs. Bibliography. Index of Song Titles. 272pp. 6½ x 9¼. 40271-1

MOVIE-STAR PORTRAITS OF THE FORTIES, John Kobal (ed.). 163 glamor, studio photos of 106 stars of the 1940s: Rita Hayworth, Ava Gardner, Marlon Brando, Clark Gable, many more. 176pp. 8⅜ x 11¼. 23546-7

BENCHLEY LOST AND FOUND, Robert Benchley. Finest humor from early 30s, about pet peeves, child psychologists, post office and others. Mostly unavailable elsewhere. 73 illustrations by Peter Arno and others. 183pp. 5⅜ x 8½. 22410-4

YEKL and THE IMPORTED BRIDEGROOM AND OTHER STORIES OF YIDDISH NEW YORK, Abraham Cahan. Film Hester Street based on *Yekl* (1896). Novel, other stories among first about Jewish immigrants on N.Y.'s East Side. 240pp. 5⅜ x 8½. 22427-9

SELECTED POEMS, Walt Whitman. Generous sampling from *Leaves of Grass.* Twenty-four poems include "I Hear America Singing," "Song of the Open Road," "I Sing the Body Electric," "When Lilacs Last in the Dooryard Bloom'd," "O Captain! My Captain!"—all reprinted from an authoritative edition. Lists of titles and first lines. 128pp. 5³/₁₆ x 8¼. 26878-0

THE BEST TALES OF HOFFMANN, E. T. A. Hoffmann. 10 of Hoffmann's most important stories: "Nutcracker and the King of Mice," "The Golden Flowerpot," etc. 458pp. 5⅜ x 8½. 21793-0

FROM FETISH TO GOD IN ANCIENT EGYPT, E. A. Wallis Budge. Rich detailed survey of Egyptian conception of "God" and gods, magic, cult of animals, Osiris, more. Also, superb English translations of hymns and legends. 240 illustrations. 545pp. 5⅜ x 8½. 25803-3

FRENCH STORIES/CONTES FRANÇAIS: A Dual-Language Book, Wallace Fowlie. Ten stories by French masters, Voltaire to Camus: "Micromegas" by Voltaire; "The Atheist's Mass" by Balzac; "Minuet" by de Maupassant; "The Guest" by Camus, six more. Excellent English translations on facing pages. Also French-English vocabulary list, exercises, more. 352pp. 5⅜ x 8½. 26443-2

CHICAGO AT THE TURN OF THE CENTURY IN PHOTOGRAPHS: 122 Historic Views from the Collections of the Chicago Historical Society, Larry A. Viskochil. Rare large-format prints offer detailed views of City Hall, State Street, the Loop, Hull House, Union Station, many other landmarks, circa 1904-1913. Introduction. Captions. Maps. 144pp. 9⅜ x 12¼. 24656-6

OLD BROOKLYN IN EARLY PHOTOGRAPHS, 1865-1929, William Lee Younger. Luna Park, Gravesend race track, construction of Grand Army Plaza, moving of Hotel Brighton, etc. 157 previously unpublished photographs. 165pp. 8⅞ x 11¾. 23587-4

THE MYTHS OF THE NORTH AMERICAN INDIANS, Lewis Spence. Rich anthology of the myths and legends of the Algonquins, Iroquois, Pawnees and Sioux, prefaced by an extensive historical and ethnological commentary. 36 illustrations. 480pp. 5⅜ x 8½. 25967-6

AN ENCYCLOPEDIA OF BATTLES: Accounts of Over 1,560 Battles from 1479 B.C. to the Present, David Eggenberger. Essential details of every major battle in recorded history from the first battle of Megiddo in 1479 B.C. to Grenada in 1984. List of Battle Maps. New Appendix covering the years 1967-1984. Index. 99 illustrations. 544pp. 6½ x 9¼. 24913-1

SAILING ALONE AROUND THE WORLD, Captain Joshua Slocum. First man to sail around the world, alone, in small boat. One of great feats of seamanship told in delightful manner. 67 illustrations. 294pp. 5⅜ x 8½. 20326-3

ANARCHISM AND OTHER ESSAYS, Emma Goldman. Powerful, penetrating, prophetic essays on direct action, role of minorities, prison reform, puritan hypocrisy, violence, etc. 271pp. 5⅜ x 8½. 22484-8

MYTHS OF THE HINDUS AND BUDDHISTS, Ananda K. Coomaraswamy and Sister Nivedita. Great stories of the epics; deeds of Krishna, Shiva, taken from puranas, Vedas, folk tales; etc. 32 illustrations. 400pp. 5⅜ x 8½. 21759-0

THE TRAUMA OF BIRTH, Otto Rank. Rank's controversial thesis that anxiety neurosis is caused by profound psychological trauma which occurs at birth. 256pp. 5⅜ x 8½. 27974-X

A THEOLOGICO-POLITICAL TREATISE, Benedict Spinoza. Also contains unfinished Political Treatise. Great classic on religious liberty, theory of government on common consent. R. Elwes translation. Total of 421pp. 5⅜ x 8½. 20249-6

MY BONDAGE AND MY FREEDOM, Frederick Douglass. Born a slave, Douglass became outspoken force in antislavery movement. The best of Douglass' autobiographies. Graphic description of slave life. 464pp. 5⅜ x 8½. 22457-0

FOLLOWING THE EQUATOR: A Journey Around the World, Mark Twain. Fascinating humorous account of 1897 voyage to Hawaii, Australia, India, New Zealand, etc. Ironic, bemused reports on peoples, customs, climate, flora and fauna, politics, much more. 197 illustrations. 720pp. 5⅜ x 8½. 26113-1

THE PEOPLE CALLED SHAKERS, Edward D. Andrews. Definitive study of Shakers: origins, beliefs, practices, dances, social organization, furniture and crafts, etc. 33 illustrations. 351pp. 5⅜ x 8½. 21081-2

THE MYTHS OF GREECE AND ROME, H. A. Guerber. A classic of mythology, generously illustrated, long prized for its simple, graphic, accurate retelling of the principal myths of Greece and Rome, and for its commentary on their origins and significance. With 64 illustrations by Michelangelo, Raphael, Titian, Rubens, Canova, Bernini and others. 480pp. 5⅜ x 8½. 27584-1

PSYCHOLOGY OF MUSIC, Carl E. Seashore. Classic work discusses music as a medium from psychological viewpoint. Clear treatment of physical acoustics, auditory apparatus, sound perception, development of musical skills, nature of musical feeling, host of other topics. 88 figures. 408pp. 5⅜ x 8½. 21851-1

THE PHILOSOPHY OF HISTORY, Georg W. Hegel. Great classic of Western thought develops concept that history is not chance but rational process, the evolution of freedom. 457pp. 5⅜ x 8½. 20112-0

THE BOOK OF TEA, Kakuzo Okakura. Minor classic of the Orient: entertaining, charming explanation, interpretation of traditional Japanese culture in terms of tea ceremony. 94pp. 5⅜ x 8½. 20070-1

LIFE IN ANCIENT EGYPT, Adolf Erman. Fullest, most thorough, detailed older account with much not in more recent books, domestic life, religion, magic, medicine, commerce, much more. Many illustrations reproduce tomb paintings, carvings, hieroglyphs, etc. 597pp. 5⅜ x 8½. 22632-8

SUNDIALS, Their Theory and Construction, Albert Waugh. Far and away the best, most thorough coverage of ideas, mathematics concerned, types, construction, adjusting anywhere. Simple, nontechnical treatment allows even children to build several of these dials. Over 100 illustrations. 230pp. 5⅜ x 8½. 22947-5

THEORETICAL HYDRODYNAMICS, L. M. Milne-Thomson. Classic exposition of the mathematical theory of fluid motion, applicable to both hydrodynamics and aerodynamics. Over 600 exercises. 768pp. 6⅛ x 9¼. 68970-0

SONGS OF EXPERIENCE: Facsimile Reproduction with 26 Plates in Full Color, William Blake. 26 full-color plates from a rare 1826 edition. Includes "The Tyger," "London," "Holy Thursday," and other poems. Printed text of poems. 48pp. 5¼ x 7. 24636-1

OLD-TIME VIGNETTES IN FULL COLOR, Carol Belanger Grafton (ed.). Over 390 charming, often sentimental illustrations, selected from archives of Victorian graphics—pretty women posing, children playing, food, flowers, kittens and puppies, smiling cherubs, birds and butterflies, much more. All copyright-free. 48pp. 9¼ x 12¼. 27269-9

PERSPECTIVE FOR ARTISTS, Rex Vicat Cole. Depth, perspective of sky and sea, shadows, much more, not usually covered. 391 diagrams, 81 reproductions of drawings and paintings. 279pp. 5⅜ x 8½. 22487-2

DRAWING THE LIVING FIGURE, Joseph Sheppard. Innovative approach to artistic anatomy focuses on specifics of surface anatomy, rather than muscles and bones. Over 170 drawings of live models in front, back and side views, and in widely varying poses. Accompanying diagrams. 177 illustrations. Introduction. Index. 144pp. 8⅜ x11¼. 26723-7

GOTHIC AND OLD ENGLISH ALPHABETS: 100 Complete Fonts, Dan X. Solo. Add power, elegance to posters, signs, other graphics with 100 stunning copyright-free alphabets: Blackstone, Dolbey, Germania, 97 more–including many lower-case, numerals, punctuation marks. 104pp. 8⅛ x 11. 24695-7

HOW TO DO BEADWORK, Mary White. Fundamental book on craft from simple projects to five-bead chains and woven works. 106 illustrations. 142pp. 5⅜ x 8. 20697-1

THE BOOK OF WOOD CARVING, Charles Marshall Sayers. Finest book for beginners discusses fundamentals and offers 34 designs. "Absolutely first rate . . . well thought out and well executed."–E. J. Tangerman. 118pp. 7¾ x 10⅝. 23654-4

ILLUSTRATED CATALOG OF CIVIL WAR MILITARY GOODS: Union Army Weapons, Insignia, Uniform Accessories, and Other Equipment, Schuyler, Hartley, and Graham. Rare, profusely illustrated 1846 catalog includes Union Army uniform and dress regulations, arms and ammunition, coats, insignia, flags, swords, rifles, etc. 226 illustrations. 160pp. 9 x 12. 24939-5

WOMEN'S FASHIONS OF THE EARLY 1900s: An Unabridged Republication of "New York Fashions, 1909," National Cloak & Suit Co. Rare catalog of mail-order fashions documents women's and children's clothing styles shortly after the turn of the century. Captions offer full descriptions, prices. Invaluable resource for fashion, costume historians. Approximately 725 illustrations. 128pp. 8⅜ x 11¼. 27276-1

THE 1912 AND 1915 GUSTAV STICKLEY FURNITURE CATALOGS, Gustav Stickley. With over 200 detailed illustrations and descriptions, these two catalogs are essential reading and reference materials and identification guides for Stickley furniture. Captions cite materials, dimensions and prices. 112pp. 6½ x 9¼. 26676-1

EARLY AMERICAN LOCOMOTIVES, John H. White, Jr. Finest locomotive engravings from early 19th century: historical (1804–74), main-line (after 1870), special, foreign, etc. 147 plates. 142pp. 11⅜ x 8¼. 22772-3

THE TALL SHIPS OF TODAY IN PHOTOGRAPHS, Frank O. Braynard. Lavishly illustrated tribute to nearly 100 majestic contemporary sailing vessels: Amerigo Vespucci, Clearwater, Constitution, Eagle, Mayflower, Sea Cloud, Victory, many more. Authoritative captions provide statistics, background on each ship. 190 black-and-white photographs and illustrations. Introduction. 128pp. 8⅞ x 11¾. 27163-3

LITTLE BOOK OF EARLY AMERICAN CRAFTS AND TRADES, Peter Stockham (ed.). 1807 children's book explains crafts and trades: baker, hatter, cooper, potter, and many others. 23 copperplate illustrations. 140pp. 4⁵/₈ x 6.   23336-7

VICTORIAN FASHIONS AND COSTUMES FROM HARPER'S BAZAR, 1867–1898, Stella Blum (ed.). Day costumes, evening wear, sports clothes, shoes, hats, other accessories in over 1,000 detailed engravings. 320pp. 9⅜ x 12¼. 22990-4

GUSTAV STICKLEY, THE CRAFTSMAN, Mary Ann Smith. Superb study surveys broad scope of Stickley's achievement, especially in architecture. Design philosophy, rise and fall of the Craftsman empire, descriptions and floor plans for many Craftsman houses, more. 86 black-and-white halftones. 31 line illustrations. Introduction 208pp. 6½ x 9¼.   27210-9

THE LONG ISLAND RAIL ROAD IN EARLY PHOTOGRAPHS, Ron Ziel. Over 220 rare photos, informative text document origin (1844) and development of rail service on Long Island. Vintage views of early trains, locomotives, stations, passengers, crews, much more. Captions. 8⅞ x 11¾.   26301-0

VOYAGE OF THE LIBERDADE, Joshua Slocum. Great 19th-century mariner's thrilling, first-hand account of the wreck of his ship off South America, the 35-foot boat he built from the wreckage, and its remarkable voyage home. 128pp. 5⅜ x 8½.
          40022-0

TEN BOOKS ON ARCHITECTURE, Vitruvius. The most important book ever written on architecture. Early Roman aesthetics, technology, classical orders, site selection, all other aspects. Morgan translation. 331pp. 5⅜ x 8½.   20645-9

THE HUMAN FIGURE IN MOTION, Eadweard Muybridge. More than 4,500 stopped-action photos, in action series, showing undraped men, women, children jumping, lying down, throwing, sitting, wrestling, carrying, etc. 390pp. 7⅞ x 10⅝.
          20204-6 Clothbd.

TREES OF THE EASTERN AND CENTRAL UNITED STATES AND CANADA, William M. Harlow. Best one-volume guide to 140 trees. Full descriptions, woodlore, range, etc. Over 600 illustrations. Handy size. 288pp. 4½ x 6⅜.   20395-6

SONGS OF WESTERN BIRDS, Dr. Donald J. Borror. Complete song and call repertoire of 60 western species, including flycatchers, juncoes, cactus wrens, many more–includes fully illustrated booklet.   Cassette and manual 99913-0

GROWING AND USING HERBS AND SPICES, Milo Miloradovich. Versatile handbook provides all the information needed for cultivation and use of all the herbs and spices available in North America. 4 illustrations. Index. Glossary. 236pp. 5⅜ x 8½.
          25058-X

BIG BOOK OF MAZES AND LABYRINTHS, Walter Shepherd. 50 mazes and labyrinths in all–classical, solid, ripple, and more–in one great volume. Perfect inexpensive puzzler for clever youngsters. Full solutions. 112pp. 8⅛ x 11.   22951-3

PIANO TUNING, J. Cree Fischer. Clearest, best book for beginner, amateur. Simple repairs, raising dropped notes, tuning by easy method of flattened fifths. No previous skills needed. 4 illustrations. 201pp. 5$\frac{3}{8}$ x 8$\frac{1}{2}$. 23267-0

HINTS TO SINGERS, Lillian Nordica. Selecting the right teacher, developing confidence, overcoming stage fright, and many other important skills receive thoughtful discussion in this indispensible guide, written by a world-famous diva of four decades' experience. 96pp. 5$\frac{3}{8}$ x 8$\frac{1}{2}$. 40094-8

THE COMPLETE NONSENSE OF EDWARD LEAR, Edward Lear. All nonsense limericks, zany alphabets, Owl and Pussycat, songs, nonsense botany, etc., illustrated by Lear. Total of 320pp. 5$\frac{3}{8}$ x 8$\frac{1}{2}$. (Available in U.S. only.) 20167-8

VICTORIAN PARLOUR POETRY: An Annotated Anthology, Michael R. Turner. 117 gems by Longfellow, Tennyson, Browning, many lesser-known poets. "The Village Blacksmith," "Curfew Must Not Ring Tonight," "Only a Baby Small," dozens more, often difficult to find elsewhere. Index of poets, titles, first lines. xxiii + 325pp. 5$\frac{3}{8}$ x 8$\frac{1}{4}$. 27044-0

DUBLINERS, James Joyce. Fifteen stories offer vivid, tightly focused observations of the lives of Dublin's poorer classes. At least one, "The Dead," is considered a masterpiece. Reprinted complete and unabridged from standard edition. 160pp. 5$\frac{3}{16}$ x 8$\frac{1}{4}$. 26870-5

GREAT WEIRD TALES: 14 Stories by Lovecraft, Blackwood, Machen and Others, S. T. Joshi (ed.). 14 spellbinding tales, including "The Sin Eater," by Fiona McLeod, "The Eye Above the Mantel," by Frank Belknap Long, as well as renowned works by R. H. Barlow, Lord Dunsany, Arthur Machen, W. C. Morrow and eight other masters of the genre. 256pp. 5$\frac{3}{8}$ x 8$\frac{1}{2}$. (Available in U.S. only.) 40436-6

THE BOOK OF THE SACRED MAGIC OF ABRAMELIN THE MAGE, translated by S. MacGregor Mathers. Medieval manuscript of ceremonial magic. Basic document in Aleister Crowley, Golden Dawn groups. 268pp. 5$\frac{3}{8}$ x 8$\frac{1}{2}$. 23211-5

NEW RUSSIAN-ENGLISH AND ENGLISH-RUSSIAN DICTIONARY, M. A. O'Brien. This is a remarkably handy Russian dictionary, containing a surprising amount of information, including over 70,000 entries. 366pp. 4$\frac{1}{2}$ x 6$\frac{1}{8}$. 20208-9

HISTORIC HOMES OF THE AMERICAN PRESIDENTS, Second, Revised Edition, Irvin Haas. A traveler's guide to American Presidential homes, most open to the public, depicting and describing homes occupied by every American President from George Washington to George Bush. With visiting hours, admission charges, travel routes. 175 photographs. Index. 160pp. 8$\frac{1}{4}$ x 11. 26751-2

NEW YORK IN THE FORTIES, Andreas Feininger. 162 brilliant photographs by the well-known photographer, formerly with *Life* magazine. Commuters, shoppers, Times Square at night, much else from city at its peak. Captions by John von Hartz. 181pp. 9$\frac{1}{4}$ x 10$\frac{3}{4}$. 23585-8

INDIAN SIGN LANGUAGE, William Tomkins. Over 525 signs developed by Sioux and other tribes. Written instructions and diagrams. Also 290 pictographs. 111pp. 6$\frac{1}{8}$ x 9$\frac{1}{4}$. 22029-X

ANATOMY: A Complete Guide for Artists, Joseph Sheppard. A master of figure drawing shows artists how to render human anatomy convincingly. Over 460 illustrations. 224pp. 8⅜ x 11¼. 27279-6

MEDIEVAL CALLIGRAPHY: Its History and Technique, Marc Drogin. Spirited history, comprehensive instruction manual covers 13 styles (ca. 4th century through 15th). Excellent photographs; directions for duplicating medieval techniques with modern tools. 224pp. 8⅜ x 11¼. 26142-5

DRIED FLOWERS: How to Prepare Them, Sarah Whitlock and Martha Rankin. Complete instructions on how to use silica gel, meal and borax, perlite aggregate, sand and borax, glycerine and water to create attractive permanent flower arrangements. 12 illustrations. 32pp. 5⅜ x 8½. 21802-3

EASY-TO-MAKE BIRD FEEDERS FOR WOODWORKERS, Scott D. Campbell. Detailed, simple-to-use guide for designing, constructing, caring for and using feeders. Text, illustrations for 12 classic and contemporary designs. 96pp. 5⅜ x 8½.
25847-5

SCOTTISH WONDER TALES FROM MYTH AND LEGEND, Donald A. Mackenzie. 16 lively tales tell of giants rumbling down mountainsides, of a magic wand that turns stone pillars into warriors, of gods and goddesses, evil hags, powerful forces and more. 240pp. 5⅜ x 8½. 29677-6

THE HISTORY OF UNDERCLOTHES, C. Willett Cunnington and Phyllis Cunnington. Fascinating, well-documented survey covering six centuries of English undergarments, enhanced with over 100 illustrations: 12th-century laced-up bodice, footed long drawers (1795), 19th-century bustles, l9th-century corsets for men, Victorian "bust improvers," much more. 272pp. 5⅜ x 8¼. 27124-2

ARTS AND CRAFTS FURNITURE: The Complete Brooks Catalog of 1912, Brooks Manufacturing Co. Photos and detailed descriptions of more than 150 now very collectible furniture designs from the Arts and Crafts movement depict davenports, settees, buffets, desks, tables, chairs, bedsteads, dressers and more, all built of solid, quarter-sawed oak. Invaluable for students and enthusiasts of antiques, Americana and the decorative arts. 80pp. 6½ x 9¼. 27471-3

WILBUR AND ORVILLE: A Biography of the Wright Brothers, Fred Howard. Definitive, crisply written study tells the full story of the brothers' lives and work. A vividly written biography, unparalleled in scope and color, that also captures the spirit of an extraordinary era. 560pp. 6⅛ x 9¼. 40297-5

THE ARTS OF THE SAILOR: Knotting, Splicing and Ropework, Hervey Garrett Smith. Indispensable shipboard reference covers tools, basic knots and useful hitches; handsewing and canvas work, more. Over 100 illustrations. Delightful reading for sea lovers. 256pp. 5⅜ x 8½. 26440-8

FRANK LLOYD WRIGHT'S FALLINGWATER: The House and Its History, Second, Revised Edition, Donald Hoffmann. A total revision—both in text and illustrations—of the standard document on Fallingwater, the boldest, most personal architectural statement of Wright's mature years, updated with valuable new material from the recently opened Frank Lloyd Wright Archives. "Fascinating"—*The New York Times*. 116 illustrations. 128pp. 9¼ x 10¾. 27430-6

PHOTOGRAPHIC SKETCHBOOK OF THE CIVIL WAR, Alexander Gardner. 100 photos taken on field during the Civil War. Famous shots of Manassas Harper's Ferry, Lincoln, Richmond, slave pens, etc. 244pp. 10⅝ x 8¼. 22731-6

FIVE ACRES AND INDEPENDENCE, Maurice G. Kains. Great back-to-the-land classic explains basics of self-sufficient farming. The one book to get. 95 illustrations. 397pp. 5⅜ x 8½. 20974-1

SONGS OF EASTERN BIRDS, Dr. Donald J. Borror. Songs and calls of 60 species most common to eastern U.S.: warblers, woodpeckers, flycatchers, thrushes, larks, many more in high-quality recording. Cassette and manual 99912-2

A MODERN HERBAL, Margaret Grieve. Much the fullest, most exact, most useful compilation of herbal material. Gigantic alphabetical encyclopedia, from aconite to zedoary, gives botanical information, medical properties, folklore, economic uses, much else. Indispensable to serious reader. 161 illustrations. 888pp. 6½ x 9¼. 2-vol. set. (Available in U.S. only.) Vol. I: 22798-7
Vol. II: 22799-5

HIDDEN TREASURE MAZE BOOK, Dave Phillips. Solve 34 challenging mazes accompanied by heroic tales of adventure. Evil dragons, people-eating plants, blood-thirsty giants, many more dangerous adversaries lurk at every twist and turn. 34 mazes, stories, solutions. 48pp. 8¼ x 11. 24566-7

LETTERS OF W. A. MOZART, Wolfgang A. Mozart. Remarkable letters show bawdy wit, humor, imagination, musical insights, contemporary musical world; includes some letters from Leopold Mozart. 276pp. 5⅜ x 8½. 22859-2

BASIC PRINCIPLES OF CLASSICAL BALLET, Agrippina Vaganova. Great Russian theoretician, teacher explains methods for teaching classical ballet. 118 illus-trations. 175pp. 5⅜ x 8½. 22036-2

THE JUMPING FROG, Mark Twain. Revenge edition. The original story of The Celebrated Jumping Frog of Calaveras County, a hapless French translation, and Twain's hilarious "retranslation" from the French. 12 illustrations. 66pp. 5⅜ x 8½. 22686-7

BEST REMEMBERED POEMS, Martin Gardner (ed.). The 126 poems in this superb collection of 19th- and 20th-century British and American verse range from Shelley's "To a Skylark" to the impassioned "Renascence" of Edna St. Vincent Millay and to Edward Lear's whimsical "The Owl and the Pussycat." 224pp. 5⅜ x 8½. 27165-X

COMPLETE SONNETS, William Shakespeare. Over 150 exquisite poems deal with love, friendship, the tyranny of time, beauty's evanescence, death and other themes in language of remarkable power, precision and beauty. Glossary of archaic terms. 80pp. 5³⁄₁₆ x 8¼. 26686-9

THE BATTLES THAT CHANGED HISTORY, Fletcher Pratt. Eminent historian profiles 16 crucial conflicts, ancient to modern, that changed the course of civiliza-tion. 352pp. 5⅜ x 8½. 41129-X

THE WIT AND HUMOR OF OSCAR WILDE, Alvin Redman (ed.). More than 1,000 ripostes, paradoxes, wisecracks: Work is the curse of the drinking classes; I can resist everything except temptation; etc. 258pp. 5⅜ x 8½. 20602-5

SHAKESPEARE LEXICON AND QUOTATION DICTIONARY, Alexander Schmidt. Full definitions, locations, shades of meaning in every word in plays and poems. More than 50,000 exact quotations. 1,485pp. 6½ x 9¼. 2-vol. set.
Vol. 1: 22726-X
Vol. 2: 22727-8

SELECTED POEMS, Emily Dickinson. Over 100 best-known, best-loved poems by one of America's foremost poets, reprinted from authoritative early editions. No comparable edition at this price. Index of first lines. 64pp. 5$\frac{3}{16}$ x 8¼. 26466-1

THE INSIDIOUS DR. FU-MANCHU, Sax Rohmer. The first of the popular mystery series introduces a pair of English detectives to their archnemesis, the diabolical Dr. Fu-Manchu. Flavorful atmosphere, fast-paced action, and colorful characters enliven this classic of the genre. 208pp. 5$\frac{3}{16}$ x 8¼. 29898-1

THE MALLEUS MALEFICARUM OF KRAMER AND SPRENGER, translated by Montague Summers. Full text of most important witchhunter's "bible," used by both Catholics and Protestants. 278pp. 6⅝ x 10. 22802-9

SPANISH STORIES/CUENTOS ESPAÑOLES: A Dual-Language Book, Angel Flores (ed.). Unique format offers 13 great stories in Spanish by Cervantes, Borges, others. Faithful English translations on facing pages. 352pp. 5⅜ x 8½. 25399-6

GARDEN CITY, LONG ISLAND, IN EARLY PHOTOGRAPHS, 1869–1919, Mildred H. Smith. Handsome treasury of 118 vintage pictures, accompanied by carefully researched captions, document the Garden City Hotel fire (1899), the Vanderbilt Cup Race (1908), the first airmail flight departing from the Nassau Boulevard Aerodrome (1911), and much more. 96pp. 8⅞ x 11¾. 40669-5

OLD QUEENS, N.Y., IN EARLY PHOTOGRAPHS, Vincent F. Seyfried and William Asadorian. Over 160 rare photographs of Maspeth, Jamaica, Jackson Heights, and other areas. Vintage views of DeWitt Clinton mansion, 1939 World's Fair and more. Captions. 192pp. 8⅞ x 11. 26358-4

CAPTURED BY THE INDIANS: 15 Firsthand Accounts, 1750-1870, Frederick Drimmer. Astounding true historical accounts of grisly torture, bloody conflicts, relentless pursuits, miraculous escapes and more, by people who lived to tell the tale. 384pp. 5⅜ x 8½. 24901-8

THE WORLD'S GREAT SPEECHES (Fourth Enlarged Edition), Lewis Copeland, Lawrence W. Lamm, and Stephen J. McKenna. Nearly 300 speeches provide public speakers with a wealth of updated quotes and inspiration–from Pericles' funeral oration and William Jennings Bryan's "Cross of Gold Speech" to Malcolm X's powerful words on the Black Revolution and Earl of Spenser's tribute to his sister, Diana, Princess of Wales. 944pp. 5⅜ x 8⅜. 40903-1

THE BOOK OF THE SWORD, Sir Richard F. Burton. Great Victorian scholar/adventurer's eloquent, erudite history of the "queen of weapons"–from prehistory to early Roman Empire. Evolution and development of early swords, variations (sabre, broadsword, cutlass, scimitar, etc.), much more. 336pp. 6⅛ x 9¼.
25434-8

AUTOBIOGRAPHY: The Story of My Experiments with Truth, Mohandas K. Gandhi. Boyhood, legal studies, purification, the growth of the Satyagraha (nonviolent protest) movement. Critical, inspiring work of the man responsible for the freedom of India. 480pp. 5⅜ x 8½. (Available in U.S. only.) 24593-4

CELTIC MYTHS AND LEGENDS, T. W. Rolleston. Masterful retelling of Irish and Welsh stories and tales. Cuchulain, King Arthur, Deirdre, the Grail, many more. First paperback edition. 58 full-page illustrations. 512pp. 5⅜ x 8½. 26507-2

THE PRINCIPLES OF PSYCHOLOGY, William James. Famous long course complete, unabridged. Stream of thought, time perception, memory, experimental methods; great work decades ahead of its time. 94 figures. 1,391pp. 5⅜ x 8½. 2-vol. set.
Vol. I: 20381-6 Vol. II: 20382-4

THE WORLD AS WILL AND REPRESENTATION, Arthur Schopenhauer. Definitive English translation of Schopenhauer's life work, correcting more than 1,000 errors, omissions in earlier translations. Translated by E. F. J. Payne. Total of 1,269pp. 5⅜ x 8½. 2-vol. set. Vol. 1: 21761-2 Vol. 2: 21762-0

MAGIC AND MYSTERY IN TIBET, Madame Alexandra David-Neel. Experiences among lamas, magicians, sages, sorcerers, Bonpa wizards. A true psychic discovery. 32 illustrations. 321pp. 5⅜ x 8½. (Available in U.S. only.) 22682-4

THE EGYPTIAN BOOK OF THE DEAD, E. A. Wallis Budge. Complete reproduction of Ani's papyrus, finest ever found. Full hieroglyphic text, interlinear transliteration, word-for-word translation, smooth translation. 533pp. 6½ x 9¼. 21866-X

MATHEMATICS FOR THE NONMATHEMATICIAN, Morris Kline. Detailed, college-level treatment of mathematics in cultural and historical context, with numerous exercises. Recommended Reading Lists. Tables. Numerous figures. 641pp. 5⅜ x 8½.
24823-2

PROBABILISTIC METHODS IN THE THEORY OF STRUCTURES, Isaac Elishakoff. Well-written introduction covers the elements of the theory of probability from two or more random variables, the reliability of such multivariable structures, the theory of random function, Monte Carlo methods of treating problems incapable of exact solution, and more. Examples. 502pp. 5⅜ x 8½. 40691-1

THE RIME OF THE ANCIENT MARINER, Gustave Doré, S. T. Coleridge. Doré's finest work; 34 plates capture moods, subtleties of poem. Flawless full-size reproductions printed on facing pages with authoritative text of poem. "Beautiful. Simply beautiful."–*Publisher's Weekly.* 77pp. 9¼ x 12. 22305-1

NORTH AMERICAN INDIAN DESIGNS FOR ARTISTS AND CRAFTSPEOPLE, Eva Wilson. Over 360 authentic copyright-free designs adapted from Navajo blankets, Hopi pottery, Sioux buffalo hides, more. Geometrics, symbolic figures, plant and animal motifs, etc. 128pp. 8⅜ x 11. (Not for sale in the United Kingdom.) 25341-4

SCULPTURE: Principles and Practice, Louis Slobodkin. Step-by-step approach to clay, plaster, metals, stone; classical and modern. 253 drawings, photos. 255pp. 8⅛ x 11.
22960-2

THE INFLUENCE OF SEA POWER UPON HISTORY, 1660–1783, A. T. Mahan. Influential classic of naval history and tactics still used as text in war colleges. First paperback edition. 4 maps. 24 battle plans. 640pp. 5⅜ x 8½. 25509-3

CATALOG OF DOVER BOOKS

THE STORY OF THE TITANIC AS TOLD BY ITS SURVIVORS, Jack Winocour (ed.). What it was really like. Panic, despair, shocking inefficiency, and a little heroism. More thrilling than any fictional account. 26 illustrations. 320pp. 5⅜ x 8½.
20610-6

FAIRY AND FOLK TALES OF THE IRISH PEASANTRY, William Butler Yeats (ed.). Treasury of 64 tales from the twilight world of Celtic myth and legend: "The Soul Cages," "The Kildare Pooka," "King O'Toole and his Goose," many more. Introduction and Notes by W. B. Yeats. 352pp. 5⅜ x 8½.
26941-8

BUDDHIST MAHAYANA TEXTS, E. B. Cowell and others (eds.). Superb, accurate translations of basic documents in Mahayana Buddhism, highly important in history of religions. The Buddha-karita of Asvaghosha, Larger Sukhavativyuha, more. 448pp. 5⅜ x 8½.
25552-2

ONE TWO THREE . . . INFINITY: Facts and Speculations of Science, George Gamow. Great physicist's fascinating, readable overview of contemporary science: number theory, relativity, fourth dimension, entropy, genes, atomic structure, much more. 128 illustrations. Index. 352pp. 5⅜ x 8½.
25664-2

EXPERIMENTATION AND MEASUREMENT, W. J. Youden. Introductory manual explains laws of measurement in simple terms and offers tips for achieving accuracy and minimizing errors. Mathematics of measurement, use of instruments, experimenting with machines. 1994 edition. Foreword. Preface. Introduction. Epilogue. Selected Readings. Glossary. Index. Tables and figures. 128pp. 5⅜ x 8½.   40451-X

DALÍ ON MODERN ART: The Cuckolds of Antiquated Modern Art, Salvador Dalí. Influential painter skewers modern art and its practitioners. Outrageous evaluations of Picasso, Cézanne, Turner, more. 15 renderings of paintings discussed. 44 calligraphic decorations by Dalí. 96pp. 5⅜ x 8½. (Available in U.S. only.)   29220-7

ANTIQUE PLAYING CARDS: A Pictorial History, Henry René D'Allemagne. Over 900 elaborate, decorative images from rare playing cards (14th–20th centuries): Bacchus, death, dancing dogs, hunting scenes, royal coats of arms, players cheating, much more. 96pp. 9¼ x 12¼.   29265-7

MAKING FURNITURE MASTERPIECES: 30 Projects with Measured Drawings, Franklin H. Gottshall. Step-by-step instructions, illustrations for constructing handsome, useful pieces, among them a Sheraton desk, Chippendale chair, Spanish desk, Queen Anne table and a William and Mary dressing mirror. 224pp. 8⅛ x 11¼.
29338-6

THE FOSSIL BOOK: A Record of Prehistoric Life, Patricia V. Rich et al. Profusely illustrated definitive guide covers everything from single-celled organisms and dinosaurs to birds and mammals and the interplay between climate and man. Over 1,500 illustrations. 760pp. 7½ x 10⅛.   29371-8